NIGHT AND DAY
NIGHT

NIGHT AND DAY
NIGHT

Abdulhamid Sulaymon o'g'li
Cho'lpon

Translated and with an Introduction by
Christopher Fort

Boston
2019

Library of Congress Cataloging-in-Publication Data

Names: Cho'lpon, 1893–1938, author. | Fort, Christopher, 1988-translator.
Title: Night and Day/Abdulhamid Sulaymon o'g'li Cho'lpon; translated by
    Christopher Fort.
Other titles: Kecha va kunduz. English
Description: Boston : Academic Studies Press, 2019. | Series: Central
    Asian literatures in translation
Identifiers: LCCN 2019009577 (print) | LCCN 2019013341 (ebook) |
    ISBN 9781644690482 (ebook) | ISBN 9781644690468 (hardcover) |
    ISBN 9781644690475 (pbk.)
Subjects: LCSH: Asia, Central--Fiction. | Imperialism--Fiction. | Marriage--
    Fiction. | Man-woman relationships--Fiction.
Classification: LCC PL56.9.C47 (ebook) | LCC PL56.9.C47 K4313 2019
    (print) | DDC 894/.325--dc23
LC record available at https://lccn.loc.gov/2019009577

ISBN 978-1-64469-046-8 (hardback)
ISBN 978-1-64469-047-5 (paperback)
ISBN 978-1-64469-048-2 (ebook)

Book design by Phi Business Solutions.

Cover design by Ivan Grave.
On the cover: *Nostalgia*, by Grigory Ulko (1987). Reproduced by permission.

Published by Academic Studies Press.
1577 Beacon Street
Brookline, MA 02446, USA

press@academicstudiespress.com
www.academicstudiespress.com

Table of Contents

Translation and Transliteration   vii

Acknowledgements   xi

An Introduction to Cho'lpon and his *Night and Day*   1

Night and Day: Night, First Book   45

Glossary   273

Translation and Transliteration

Transliterating from Uzbek, a language that contains much borrowing from other tongues, into English, a language that similarly assimilates foreign words without difficulty, is no easy task—the results are inevitably imperfect. The system I have chosen attempts to create a consistent representation of the many unique cultural concepts that appear in the novel, while also maintaining accessibility for readers not familiar with Central Asia.

For words that have already been borrowed by English through other contexts—namely, Arabic, Persian, and South Asian languages—I maintain the commonly accepted English standard. For example, I write *imam* instead of *imom*, *pilaf* instead of *palov* or *osh*, and *tandoor* instead of *tandir*. Likewise, names that are known to English speakers through Arabic, Persian, and Turkish contexts, such as Nizami Ganjavi, receive the commonly accepted transliterations minus any diacritics. The larger Central Asian city names also receive their commonly accepted English transliterations. For the names of historical persons and places that are not well known, I often provide internationally accepted transliterations in the footnotes, while using their Uzbek transliteration in the text itself. For concepts specific to the sedentary Central Asian peoples, I transliterate names and those words that I gloss via the Uzbek Latin alphabet established in 1992 with some modifications.

I translate from the original 1936 edition of the text, which was printed in the short-lived 1930s Uzbek Latin alphabet, and from transliterated reproductions of that text. When Cho'lpon's novel was first republished in 1988 and in subsequent editions, the editors transliterated the original into the Uzbek Cyrillic alphabet, which was introduced in the 1940s. That transliteration erases some of the vowel harmony that the 1930s Uzbek literary language still possessed. The 1992 Latin alphabet obscures nothing when transliterating from

Uzbek Cyrillic because each letter possesses a one-to-one transliteration equivalent. The 1992 alphabet in which transliterations appear presents only a few difficulties for the English reader: "o'" is read as an ordinary English "o"; "o" is read as an open, almost full "a" sound; "x" is read as a devoiced "h" sound (often transliterated from other languages as "kh"); "q" is a devoiced guttural velar; and "g'" is the voiced pair of "q." Instead of using a different translation system for the several Russian names that appear here, I have decided to transliterate them through the Uzbek alphabet, the only caveats being that "ы" becomes "y," and the soft sign ("ъ") becomes an apostrophe. I use common English equivalents for Russian names, such as Alexander for Aleksandr, only for the tsars and other figures well known in English.

I have modified the 1992 alphabet somewhat to ensure that transliterations in the text will not look unfamiliar to Middle Eastern specialists. The 1992 alphabet prescribes a forward apostrophe to indicate a glottal stop (the Arabic phoneme ʿayn). To distinguish them from the glottal stop, the Uzbek phonemes o' and g' are rendered with a backward apostrophe as o' and g'. That backward apostrophe, however, looks similar to the turned comma ʿ, which Middle Eastern specialists generally use to transliterate ʿayn. To avoid that confusion and maintain consistency with the rest of this translation series, this text uses the forward apostrophe for the Uzbek phonemes o' and g' and the turned comma for the glottal stop or ʿayn.

When citing Russian and Uzbek sources in the footnotes of the text, I use the Library of Congress transliteration system and the 1992 Uzbek Latin alphabet respectively. I do this to ease the burden for those who might look for these sources in a US library.

The glossary that follows the text of the novel provides definitions of lacunae found in the text. In the glossary I explain the terminology relating to rank and cultural customs of sedentary Central Asians that is important to understanding the social and cultural context of Cho'lpon's time. The first appearance of a glossed word in the text, with the exception of Sufi and Fitna, which are used as monikers, is marked in italics to indicate that the reader refer to the glossary. All subsequent uses of glossed words are unitalicized.

Regarding translation, I have tried to retain a feel of the original within the English text. Sometimes this means translating Uzbek-language idioms, of which Cho'lpon uses many, literally—rather than searching for rough equivalents in English. Where idioms or cultural realia require further explanation than given in the text, I indicate their meaning in the footnotes and glossary supplied at the end of the text. Likewise, I tried to maintain some of the syntax and word order that the author employs. That being said, clarity and rhythm often required that I break up Cho'lpon's frequent long sentences into smaller units.

Additionally, punctuation posed something of a challenge. Cho'lpon makes ample use of ellipses in the original text in ways that would confuse a contemporary English-language reader. He uses ellipses 1) to indicate a speaker is trailing off; 2) to indicate that something has been left unsaid by either the narrator or the characters (this is often sexual innuendo or the act of sex itself); 3) to indicate an impending contradiction, often at the end of chapters or sections, creating suspense; 4) to simulate stream of consciousness when the narrator enters the minds of characters; and 5) to denote the narrator's incomplete sentences, which are often used when describing the layout of a new space or room. I have retained ellipses in the first case and rarely in the cases of numbers two and four.

Acknowledgements

I would like to thank Xotam Mirzaxo'jaev, Cho'lpon's nephew, and his family for kindly providing the rights to publish this translation. Unfortunately, Mr. Mirzaxo'jaev passed before this translation could be printed. I would also like to thank Dr. Naim Karimov for aiding me in deciding the textological questions that arose from the many different editions of Cho'lpon's novel. Iskandar Madgaziev of the Andijan Region Literary Museum kindly helped me locate a copy of the 1936 edition of the text and shared with me a number of notes and documents on the novel's various republications. Nabi and Zahiriddin Jaloliddin were of great assistance in liasoning with contacts in Andijan. Adeeb Khalid, Zulxumor Mirzaeva, Iqbol Mirzo, Isajon Sulton, Xosiyat Rustamova, Dildora Isoqova, Yulduz O'rmonova, Sohiba Solieva, and Mohlaroy Ahmedova deserve special thanks for providing consultation over some of the more difficult passages of the text. I would also like to thank the Embassy of the Republic of Uzbekistan to the United Kingdom of Great Britain and Northern Ireland for their generous support that made this publication a success. My wife, Elena Fort, has demonstrated infinite patience with this project, and through the reading of many drafts, I hope she has come to love the novel as much as I do. If not, I hope she at least still loves me. Finally, Dr. Oleh Kotsyuba and Dr. Rebecca Gould have been a tremendous help. This project would not have been a success without their insight, drive, and scholastic acumen.

Figure 1. Abdulhamid Sulaymon o'g'li Cho'lpon. Photograph taken in 1925.

An Introduction to Cho'lpon and his *Night and Day*

Abdulhamid Sulaymon o'g'li Cho'lpon (1897–1938) is best known as the most outstanding Uzbek poet of the twentieth century. When he emerged on the literary scene in the years following the Russian February Revolution of 1917, he became a leading voice for the new Turkic lyric that came to dominate Uzbek poetry in the 1920s. He developed a reputation for an elegiac style punctuated with colorful imagery and an innovative use of traditional symbols and metaphors. In the late 1920s, as Bolshevik-trained Uzbek intellectuals took over the literary sphere in Uzbekistan, Cho'lpon's poetic fame transformed into notoriety. He became a political pariah, the subject of constant attacks in the press. In 1934, attempting to reconcile with Soviet power, he submitted the present novel, the first book of a planned dilogy *Night and Day*, to a Soviet literary contest. Three years later, Cho'lpon was arrested by the NKVD (the People's Commissariat for Internal Affairs—Stalin's secret police) as part of Stalin's Great Terror (1936–1938). The work translated here, *Night*, was pulled from the shelves and banned; the sequel, if it existed, was likely destroyed by the NKVD. *Night* circulated in Uzbekistan in secret, influencing new generations of Uzbek litterateurs. Only with glasnost was the novel republished. It now stands as an exceptional piece of Uzbek prose. In the minds of Uzbek readers, *Night* tends to be overshadowed in the canon by the first Uzbek novel, Abdulla Qodiriy's *Bygone Days* (*O'tkan kunlar*, 1922), but Cho'lpon's chef d'oeuvre is arguably the superior work.

In post-Soviet Uzbekistan, Cho'lpon is perhaps equally well-known as a so-called "national caretaker" (*millatparvar*). In the second decade of the twentieth century, Cho'lpon and like-minded reformers, often called *jadids*, embraced a reformist discourse that involved, among other dimensions, an interest in European technology and the idea of the nation alongside traditional Islamic critiques of societal decline. The jadids implored their fellow urban Turkestanis to awaken themselves to the dangers of Russian colonialism and restore the lost glory of their people. Despite what modern Uzbek critics and Cold War-era Western researchers assert, these reformers' main rhetorical and political opponent was not Russian imperialists but the religious elite, the 'ulama, whom the jadids felt impeded their nation's progress towards modernity. For jadids, the Russian conquest of Turkestan was a result but not the cause of the decline of Islamic civilization.[1] At the end of the present volume as Cho'lpon's character Razzoq-sufi, so named for his duty to perform the call to prayer,[2] loses his grip on reality, the voices around him poignantly ask, "who is crazy? The Russians or us?" These rhetorical questions direct the reader to first seek fault for the novel's tragedies in Turkestani backwardness. Naturally, educated reformers like Cho'lpon presented themselves as the people best suited to lead Central Asia in the twentieth century, a strategy which brought them into direct competition with the 'ulama for the ears of ordinary people. Russian colonial administrators, for their part, bridled jadid ambitions, consistently siding with the 'ulama in all disputes to maintain their rule over Central Asian society.

The Russian revolutions of 1917, February and October, profoundly transformed the jadids and Cho'lpon. Whereas the Russian imperial state supported the traditional religious class, Lenin and the Bolsheviks found temporary allies in jadids. The Bolsheviks never trusted their native partners completely, knowing they were not Marxists. Nevertheless, the communists temporarily granted jadids the state tools to enact a jadid vision of modernity. As their power grew, jadid ideas and philosophies transformed dramatically. The Turkestani Muslim nation they intended to revive before the revolution became a specifically Turkic nation.[3] Before 1917, jadids wrote in both the local Turkic tongue and in Persian, often mixing the two languages. Soon after October, under the influence of Ottoman modernizers and Turkic reformists of the Russian Empire, jadids began to see Turkic culture as more suited to modernity than Persian. Cho'lpon, one of the more active proponents of this view, introduced new Turkic meters and Turkified the lexicon of local poetry. By 1924, when Stalin ordered the national delimitation of Central Asia, splitting the

---

1 Adeeb Khalid, *The Politics of Muslim Cultural Reform: Jadidism in Central Asia* (Berkeley: University of California Press, 1998), 191.

2 Razzoq-sufi is indeed a Sufi *murid* (see the glossary for more on Sufism and *murids*), but his sobriquet refers to his duties as a muezzin, the person who performs the call to prayer. In Central Asia, the sobriquet Sufi referred to a muezzin.

3 Adeeb Khalid, *Making Uzbekistan: Nation, Empire, and Revolution in the Early USSR* (Ithaca: Cornell University Press, 2015), 15.

territory into the contemporary five republics (Kazakhstan, Kyrgystan, Tajik-istan, Turkmenistan, and Uzbekistan), jadids had come to a consensus on the Turkic nature of their nation, calling the culture Uzbek, a name with Turkic origins, and the territory—Uzbekistan.

After the revolution, women's liberation became another critical part of the jadid program and one of Cho'lpon's main concerns. Jadids, like modernizing intellectuals in many other neighboring Muslim societies such as Turkey and Iran, were influenced by European concepts of sexual morality and domesticity and began to agitate for their society to adopt them. They championed monog-amous marriages based on romantic love and in turn attacked polygamy, pedo-philia, homoeroticism, prostitution, and adultery. While the jadids may have exaggerated the prevalence of these phenomena in their society, they were no doubt as in evidence here as in any other society. The jadid solution was to open women up to the world, to release them from the confines of their "four walls" (a common metaphor for women's internment in the home), and put them on more, though not completely, equal footing with men. Cho'lpon's 1920s elegies and later his prose in the novel therefore often take readers inside local women's sequestered lives, invading, with the reader, the intimacy of their homosociality in order to eliminate it. As a narrator, he mourns women's innocence and failure to recognize their own imprisonment.

As several scholars have noted, the jadid vision for women's liberation was far more limited than that of the Bolsheviks.[4] In their literary portrayals, Cho'lpon and his fellow reformers rarely acknowledged women's agency.[5] Cho'lpon's narrator often bewails Uzbek women's captivity but simultane-ously relies on it for protection of the "innocent" femininity he feels is crucial to the preservation of Uzbek cultural heritage. Like many other reformers in the Islamic world at this time, Cho'lpon saw women as mothers of the nation whom it was men's duty to protect, thus his advocacy of women's liberation was often at odds with his advocacy of the nation. At yet another level, Cho'lpon entraps his female characters: he fetishizes women's misunderstanding of their environment, transforming their ignorance into an aesthetic.

---

4 Marianne Kamp, *The New Woman in Uzbekistan* (Seattle: University of Washington Press, 2006), 32–52; Khalid, *Making Uzbekistan: Nation, Empire, and Revolution in the Early USSR*, 197–208.

5 Shawn Lyons, "Otabek's Return: Ignoring the Lessons of Jadid Reformism in Modern Uzbekistan," *Journal of Central Eurasian Studies* 5, no. 1 (2000): 2–13; Shawn Lyons, "Resist-ing Colonialism in the Uzbek Historical Novel Kecha va Kunduz (Night and Day), 1936)," *Inner Asia* 3 (2001): 175–192.

Cho'lpon's novel, as I will show in the analysis to follow, is full of the ignorance and indecisiveness that characterizes his poetry, setting it apart from many of the prevailing literary trends in the Soviet Union. Writing his novel in the early 1930s before Socialist Realism, the official literary method of the Soviet Union, had been canonized and defined, Cho'lpon proceeded along a different path. His characters do not come to the class consciousness that would be demanded by Stalinist critics in the late 1930s; rather they are "unconscious" in their indecisiveness, ignorance, and constant doubt. They misunderstand, misrecognize, and commit mistakes, always receiving epiphanies that are endlessly redacted. His characters are, in a word, incomplete beings, always deferring final judgment to another time, matching, perhaps only by a convenient coincidence, the incomplete form of the dilogy *Night and Day* (*Kecha va kunduz*). I use these characters and the structure of the novel to argue that Cho'lpon was himself undecided in his relationship to the Soviet Union, incomplete, like his novel, in his convictions, and thus always available for reinterpretation by future readers.

By bringing out the ambiguity in Cho'lpon's text and his biography, I intend to challenge the uncritical reception of jadids in post-Soviet Uzbekistan. Since Uzbekistan gained its independence in 1991, its intellectuals have done little in the way of rethinking the legacy of jadids and the larger Soviet system itself. Instead, they have largely inverted the Soviet historical narrative. Whereas the Soviet narrative held that the October Revolution freed Uzbeks from tsarist colonial oppression, gave birth to Uzbekistan, and guided its national culture to modernity, the post-Soviet narrative explicitly asserts Uzbeks' transhistorical victimization under Russian imperial and Soviet rule. According to this account, the Russian Empire and the Soviets alike stalled Uzbek development and repressed Uzbek native culture in favor of Russian culture. Cho'lpon plays a major role in both narratives: he was reviled in the Soviet Union from the late 1920s up to glasnost as an enemy of the people, but now he is unequivocally celebrated as a national hero. Both narratives lack nuance and rely more on teleology than facts. They each attribute complete conviction to their actors, effacing the ambiguity intrinsic to any indeterminate future. An examination of ignorance in Cho'lpon's characters helps us grasp the author's own inconclusive musings on the Soviet state, which consequently permits a more dynamic and exciting engagement with Uzbek literature and history.

Here I offer a biographical sketch of Cho'lpon's life and times, the history of the novel, and an analysis of its contents. Cho'lpon left no diary or other material giving an account of his life, and thus any biography of him is nothing more than a sketch that relies on the self-censored testimonies of relatives and memoirs of friends. I fill in the gaps in the biographical record by introducing the reader to the historical context of Cho'lpon's life and his poetic oeuvre. For these same reasons, we know little about the process of writing the novel. Cho'lpon left no authorial explanations about his intentions with the work and the sequel that he is rumored to have written. I therefore make abundant use of historical and literary context to form an argument about the author's goals with *Night and Day*.

CHO'LPON'S LIFE AND TIMES

Abdulhamid Sulaymon o'g'li, better known by his penname Cho'lpon, was born in 1897 in Andijan, a city in the Ferghana valley of modern-day Uzbekistan. The Russian Empire had annexed the city with its conquest of the Kokand Khanate in 1876, incorporating it into the colonial administrative unit of Turkestan. Cho'lpon's life spanned Russian colonialism, the Bolshevik Revolution, and the Stalinist purges. His views and literary oeuvre were inevitably affected by his confrontation with both the racial and religious hierarchy of empire and revolutionary calls for radical equality.

As in other European colonies with majority-Muslim populations, Russian colonial administrators in nineteenth-century Turkestan ruled from a distance. In the latter half of the nineteenth century, most Europeans believed that Islam was in its death throes as a religion. Muslims would soon see the superiority of Christian peoples and abandon their faith. Imperial rulers needed only to not provoke their colonized subjects, lest a sudden burst of fanatic revolt breathe new life into the dying creed. Therefore, Russians minimized the so-called "civilizing mission" that justified their colonial conquest in the first place. They banned Christian proselytization, left Islamic law intact, and isolated themselves in Russian quarters of major cities such as Samarqand and the Russian regional capital, Tashkent.[6]

Annexation into the Russian Empire greatly increased the fortunes of Cho'lpon's merchant father, Sulaymon *mullah* Muhammad Yunus o'g'li. While the Romanov Empire left many aspects of Central Asian life untouched, commerce changed dramatically. With new trade routes and modes of transportation, Sulaymon expanded his textile trade routes as far north as Orenburg.[7]

---

6 Daniel Brower, *Turkestan and the Fate of the Russian Empire* (New York: Routledge, 2003), 35; Paul Stronski, *Tashkent: Forging a Soviet City* (Pittsburgh: University of Pittsburgh Press, 2010), 20.

7 Naim Karimov, *Abdulhamid Sulaymon o'g'li Cho'lpon* (Toshkent: Fan, 1991), 9.

Russia's imperial presence changed Sulaymon's social and cultural outlook as well. Sulaymon was well versed in Islamicate high culture. He participated in poetry gatherings with learned men, *mullahs* and *eshons*, and even compiled his own *divan* (poetry collection), under the penname *Rasvo*, meaning "base" or "foul," a sign of humility before God. In educating his eldest child, Cho'lpon, he proceeded in the fashion traditional for precolonial Central Asia and much of the premodern Islamic world. His father sent him to a *madrasa*, a secondary school where select students train to become Islamic learned men. There, Cho'lpon learned Arabic and Persian, and was initiated into the world of Islamicate high culture.[8] However, Sulaymon soon reconsidered his son's future prospects and enrolled Cho'lpon in a Russian school. Colonial administrators, beginning in the mid-1880s, established so-called "Russo-native" schools, which taught Russian and local native languages to Central Asians. The goal of these schools was to create a class of native intermediaries to administer colonial rule in Turkestan.[9] In this school, Cho'lpon learned the basics of the Russian language, arithmetic, geography. He also received some of the native instruction typical of the *maktab*, a primary school in Central Asia, and the *madrasa*.

Cho'lpon's education at a Russian school was rare for his time. Most Turkestani parents did not trust the Russian schools, and enrollment was always low. Russian imperial administrators could often resort to drastic measures. Notably, they sometimes forcibly enrolled children from poorer members of the community in order to fill classrooms.[10]

In the late 1890s, yet another type of school, associated with a movement of progressive Muslim reformers, was introduced in Central Asia.[11] Jadids, named for the pedagogical method they advocated in these new schools, *usul-i jadid* (new method), promoted a novel means of learning the Arabic alphabet in which the local tongue, called Turki or Chagatai, was written. While traditional maktabs taught the alphabet via the syllabic method whereby students memorized syllabic combinations of letters, jadid new-method schools trained students with a phonetic method, teaching them the sounds that each of the letters represented. As a result, jadid-school students could read new, unfamiliar texts, not just a prescribed corpus of memorized texts.

Jadids may have received their name for this pedagogical method, but their interests expanded far beyond the classroom. The classroom was simply

---

8 Karimov, *Abdulhamid Sulaymon*, 10.

9 Brower, *Turkestan and the Fate of the Russian Empire*, 69.

10 Richard A. Pierce, *Russian Central Asia, 1867–1917: A Study in Colonial Rule* (Berkeley: University of California Press, 1960), 216.

11 Khalid, *The Politics of Muslim Cultural Reform: Jadidism in Central Asia*, 164–167.

a natural starting point because of the relative freedom the Russian colonial state allowed for religious minorities to regulate their own educational and religious affairs. The jadids' interest in pedagogy was logically connected to their other ideas for reform. They believed that a new kind of literacy would lead to a social and political awakening. Through newspapers and theater— the production and consumption of which jadids' functional literacy made possible—they proceeded to "awaken" their fellow Turkestanis to their ignorance by articulating a new interpretation of Islam compatible with European ideas of industry, economic growth, democratization, sexual morality, and women's rights. Driving this was an ardent belief in their Turkestani Muslim nation and a desire to return it to the glory that it supposedly possessed in a previous age, which both jadids and their intellectual rivals located in the fifteenth-century rule of Tamerlane and his descendants. To "restore" their nation, they promoted a cultural revival of the arts and new forms of political engagement with the Russian imperial state. One of their chief achievements was the creation of a public sphere; newspapers and theater created new forums to challenge traditional authorities.[12] That vibrant culture of public debate continued into the 1920s until it was severely circumscribed by the arrival of Stalinism.

Cho'lpon did not study at a jadid school, but in the mid-1910s, he began his literary career by publishing in jadid journals and joining discussion and poetry circles with these men. In 1914, he produced his first prose stories, "A Victim of Ignorance" (Qurboni jaholat) and "Doctor Muhammadiyor" (Do'xtur Muhammadiyor), both of which, like many jadid stories and articles of the time, employ characters without much depth to demonstrate the potential catastrophes of ignorance and the benefits of secular education in medicine, the natural sciences, and the humanities.[13] These stories are largely didactic and lack aesthetic ornamentation. Towards the February Revolution, he met and became close friends with Abdurauf Fitrat (1887–1938), the most prominent jadid of the 1920s, who remained a mentor to Cho'lpon throughout his life.[14] Fitrat pushed the younger man to engage more in poetry and reportedly suggested to him the pen name Cho'lpon—meaning "morning star" or "Venus"— because as a poet he stood out among his peers.[15]

---

12 Ibid., 114.

13 Abdulhamid Cho'lpon, *Asarlar*, vol. 2 (Toshkent: Xazina, 1998), 461.

14 Naim Karimov, *Cho'lpon: Ma'rifiy roman* (Toshkent: Sharq, 2003), 63.

15 Naim Karimov, *XX asr adabiyoti manzaralari* (Toshkent: O'zbekiston, 2008), 207. In another work, Karimov alternatively suggests that Munavvar Qori, another jadid leader, gave Cho'lpon the name. See Karimov, *Cho'lpon: Ma'rifiy roman*, 63–64.

When the February Revolution came, Cho'lpon and his fellow jadids were quick to embrace it. Muslims reformers saw in the revolution a chance to increase Turkestan's autonomy within a new federation containing the territories of the former Russian Empire that would devolve power to the regions and champion democracy. Post-Soviet Uzbek historiography emphasizes that Cho'lpon and other jadids' eventual goal was independence, not simply autonomy, but this interpretation ignores jadids' precarious position in their own society. Jadids did not advocate independence because if Turkestan separated from the Russian state, they feared they would be left to the mercy of the 'ulama, who enjoyed more popularity among the masses than jadids.[16] Because of jadids' socially marginal position and their understanding of history as expressed in their literature, Cho'lpon and his compatriots' literary works at this time portray the February Revolution as something of a *deus ex machina*: it appeared as a sudden and unprecipitated solution to their problems. In a country moving to the left, suddenly the jadids were on the right side of history.

Cho'lpon's first published poem celebrated the February Revolution and socialist movements for these very reasons, seeing revolution as salvation from without. Published in 1918 but written in April of 1917, this excerpt from "Red Banner" (Qizil bayroq) demonstrates the poet's interest in the democratic and anti-imperial politics promised by socialism.[17] It is important to remember that the poem by no means signals support for the Bolsheviks, who were one among many socialist parties at the time. I have translated the below excerpt in a fashion that somewhat captures the caesura-inflected style of the original. The original contains fifteen syllables per line and is read with slight pauses every four syllables (4–4–4–3). The rhyme scheme, which I have not captured here, is abab.

> Red banner!
> There, look how it waves in the wind,
> As if the *qibla* [direction that a Muslim should face when praying] wind
> is greeting it!
> It is not glad to see the poor in this state,
> For the poor man has the right because it is his.
> Has the red blood of the poor not flown like rivers

---

16 Khalid, *Making Uzbekistan: Nation, Empire, and Revolution in the Early USSR*, 17.

17 Abdulhamid Sulaymon o'g'li Cho'lpon, *Asarlar: To'rt jildlik*, vol. 1 (Toshkent: Akademnashr, 2016), 331.

To take the banner from the darkness into the light?
Are there no workers left in Siberian exile
To take the banner to the oppressed and weak people?

You, bourgeoisie, conceited upper classes, don't approach the red banner!
Were you not its bloodsucking enemy?
Now the black will not approach those white rays of light,
Now those black forces' time has passed!

The red banner, in scarlet red blood, that blood—the blood of workers,
Those oppressive executioners, those haughty classes, have spilt that blood,
The oppressed love more than anything that call to unite and awaken,
While those murderers, those upper classes, plug their ears!

Oh, seize the flag, wave it high over the oppressed,
The oppressed who have given their blood and lives.
From the workers, soldiers, and the downtrodden there will be greetings,
From the evil merchants, the bourgeoisie—only pain, sorrow, and grief.
From the angels—justice and satisfaction.
And from my pen, my paper, and myself—love![18]

As is typical of jadid literature at this time, Cho'lpon underplays Central Asian agency in the toppling of the Russian Empire by showing the February Revolution here as an event to which Central Asians have contributed little. As the first stanza indicates, Cho'lpon describes the revolution, the red banner of socialism, as the active observer of a passive Muslim East. The banner is blown in the direction of the *qibla*, the direction of Mecca, suggesting that the socialists of Petrograd must take their revolution to the Muslim world. The conclusion of the second stanza highlights the passivity of Central Asians in the revolution by calling on the workers imprisoned and in exile in Siberia, outside Central Asia, to bring the banner to the "oppressed and weak people," by which Cho'lpon means his own community. The reference to the blood and lives given by the oppressed to the red banner in the final stanza, in keeping with the view of Central Asians as passive, indicates that the revolution is not so much the product of their sacrifices as it is a cosmic gift given in redemption of their suffering.

---

18 Cho'lpon, 1:17.

Throughout the poem, Cho'lpon adapts Chagatai poetic language to the politicized times by recasting traditional images used in mystical poetry into new roles. Blood, often used as a metaphor in Sufi poetry for mystical experience, is literalized here as "red blood" and becomes a call to political action, identified with the revolutionary cause.

Cho'lpon's poetic persona of the 1920s was rooted in the complex intersections of ethnicity, class, and revolution in 1917 Central Asia. After the February Revolution, Russians and native Muslims, both 'ulama and jadids, jockeyed for power in Tashkent until October 27, 1917, when the Tashkent soviet, a committee of socialist railroad workers and soldiers allied with the Bolsheviks, took power in the city by force and declared itself sovereign over all of Turkestan. The soviet and its supporters were entirely European and therefore hardly representative of majority-Muslim Turkestan.[19] While the 'ulama tried to negotiate with the soviet, which denied all Muslim claims to authority because there were no Muslim proletarians, many jadids left for the Ferghana valley city of Kokand where on November 27, 1917, they established the short-lived Kokand Autonomy. Cho'lpon, like other reformist Muslim poets, wrote several poems celebrating the formation of the Autonomy as a rebirth of his Turkic nation. In less than three months, once the Tashkent soviet could afford the expedition, it destroyed the Autonomy, killing thousands in the process.

After this juncture in 1917, Cho'lpon's poetic output increased greatly. He spent much less time on marches and odes. Instead, contemplative and elegiac lyric made up the bulk of his poetic oeuvre in the 1920s. Perhaps his most famous work of this period is his 1921 lament "To a Devastated Land" (Buzilgan o'lkaga), an elegy for the destruction of Turkestan caused by the outbreak of war between the Red Army and Basmachi, the Central Asian fighters opposed to Soviet power.[20] The following is a prose translation of an excerpt from the poem, which, like the previous poem, is written in a syllabic meter that alternates the number of syllables in each stanza. In the first part of the excerpt below there are fifteen syllables per line read this time with a caesura after the first eight syllables (8–7 and sometimes 8–4–3). The second part of the excerpt contains twelve and eleven syllables, read 4–4–4 and 4–4–3 respectively. The

---

19 Khalid, *Making Uzbekistan: Nation, Empire, and Revolution in the Early USSR*, 71.

20 Historians of the Cold War era and modern Central Asia have looked to the Basmachi as a national or religious movement against the Bolsheviks, but recent accounts offer a more informed picture. See ibid., 86–89; Kirill Nourzhanov, "Reassessing the Basmachi: Warlords without Ideology?" *Journal of South Asian and Middle Eastern Studies* 31, no. 3 (Spring 2008): 41–67.

final two lines repeat the fifteen syllable structure of the first two lines. The rhyme scheme is aabbccdd.

> Hey, mighty country whose mountains greet the sky,
> Why has a dark cloud descended on your head?
>
> ....
>
> They have trod over your breast for many years,
> You curse and moan, but they crush you nonetheless,
> These haughty men with no rights to your free soil,
> Why do you let them trample you without a murmur as if a slave?
> Why do you not command them to leave?
> Why does your freedom-loving heart not unleash your voice?
> Why do the whips laugh as they meet your body?
> Why do hopes die in your springs?
> Why is your lot in life only blood?
> Why are you so despondent?
> Why do you no longer have that smoldering fire in your eyes?
> Why are the wolves running through your nights so sated?
> Why do those flying bullets not raise your ire?
> Why is there such destruction across your plains?
> Why do you not rain storms of vengeance?
> Why has God forsaken you, sapped you of His strength?
>
> Come, I will read you a little story,
> I'll whisper a tale of years past in your ear,
> Come, I'll wipe the tears from your eyes,
> Come, let me look on your wounded body until I can't look anymore.
> Why is that poison arrow in your breast?
> That poison arrow of an overthrown kingdom.
> Why do you not desire vengeance?
> Why do you not want the death of those enemies?
>
> Hey, free land that has never known slavery,
> Why is that shadowy cloud lodged in your throat?[21]

---

21 Cho'lpon, *Asarlar: To'rt jildlik*, 1:88–89.

Nearly all readers, particularly Stalinist critics, saw through the thinly veiled metaphors here; Cho'lpon condemns the civil war and the Bolsheviks in particular. Indeed, the denunciations of Cho'lpon's anti-Soviet views that began in 1926 referenced this poem specifically.[22] The poem's narrative pessimism, consonant with its elegiac form (the poem is a *marsiya*—the Persian genre name for a lament or elegy), is present throughout Cho'lpon's oeuvre of the 1920s. Cho'lpon also exhibits here a fascination with nature that never left him throughout his career. He exercises personification and chremamorphism, the identification of people with animals and natural objects, extensively. Here the land becomes a woman whose breast has been trampled by invaders and conquerors. Cho'lpon's lyric persona calls out to the effeminized land, just as he calls out to oppressed women in many other poems, desperately and unsuccessfully imploring them to rebel against its tormentors.

As the 1920s proceeded, Cho'lpon, justifying Fitrat's confidence in him, became the most prominent poet among his Turkestani peers, not only because of his exquisite elegies, but also because of his formal innovation. He mastered a new form of versification, which was introduced to the Central Asian Turkic language around the time of the revolution, called *barmoq* (finger) meter. In previous centuries, Turkic-language poets wrote their works in ʿaruz meters, which were borrowed from Arabic verse via Persian. ʿAruz meters rely on the interchange between long and short vowels typical in both Arabic and Persian. When the meters were adapted to Chagatai in the fifteenth century, poets mapped the Persian vowel system onto the Turkic language because Central Asian Turkic did not have vowels of variable length. In the 1920s, Fitrat and others insisted on the adoption of barmoq, which had first been pioneered by Turkish poets in the Ottoman Empire, because it was, according to them, better suited to Turkic languages.[23] Barmoq is a syllabic meter that requires an equal number of syllables in each line as we have seen in Cho'lpon's poems above. Alongside barmoq meter, Cho'lpon and Fitrat also transformed the vocabulary of local poetry. Before the 1920s, Turkic-language poets wrote with copious amounts of Arabic and Persian words in a pedantic, often esoteric style. Cho'lpon pioneered a new

---

22 Edward Allworth, "Bilim Ochag'i 'The Source of Knowledge': A Nationalistic Periodical from the Turkistan Autonomous Soviet Socialist Republic," *Central Asiatic Journal* 10, no. 1 (March 1965): 61–70; Ingeborg Baldauf, "A Late Piece of Nazira or a Symbol Making Its Way through Early Uzbek Poetry," in *Cultural Change and Continuity in Central Asia*, ed. Shirin Akiner (London, New York: Kegan Paul International, 1991), 29–44.

23 Abdurauf Fitrat, "Aruz Haqida," in *Tanlangan Asarlar*, vol. 5 (Toshkent: Ma'naviyat, 2010), 228.

Turkic vocabulary for poetry, writing in a language more understandable to the rural masses who were not literate in Persian. Fitrat and Cho'lpon's interest in all things Turkic was not unique: the early 1920s saw an increased fascination with specifically Turkic culture, and jadids and other Central Asian intellectuals hailed the embrace of Turkic roots as a superior path to modernity.[24]

Despite these innovations, Cho'lpon was formally more conservative than many of his contemporaries. While he pioneered a new lexicon and meter, he retained much of the traditional imagery and themes of Chagatai poetry. Natural imagery, chremamorphism, themes of longing and loss are quite typical of Islamicate poetry, and Cho'lpon, like many in the canon before him, inno-vated by endowing this common material with new meaning, not by doing away with it altogether.[25] In the latter half of the 1920s, Uzbek poets such as Oltoy and Shokir Sulaymon would take up the futurist poetics of Russian poets Mayakovsky and Kruchyonykh, experimenting with sound, speech registers, and graphic representation, but Cho'lpon never expressed interest in this kind of writing. His modernism, if we might call it that, was a homegrown one based on jadids' new political consciousness and engagement with European thought about the nation.[26] Cho'lpon's art, as the coming pages show, emerges from a mix of traditional Islamicate poetics, new Turkic forms and vocabulary, an interest in the psychologism of proletarian prose, and an aestheticization of his political and historical philosophies.[27]

---

24 Khalid, *Making Uzbekistan: Nation, Empire, and Revolution in the Early USSR*, 15.

25 For more on the conservative nature of early twentieth-century Uzbek poetics, see Inge-borg Baldauf, "Educating the Poets and Fostering Uzbek Poetry of the 1910s to Early 1930s," *Cahiers d'Asie Centrale* 24 (2015): 183–211.

26 Devin Deweese offers a compelling critique of the fetishization of modernity in jadidism. I agree with him that the reform jadids proposed emerged from a tradition of Islamic reform that existed long before the twentieth century. See Devin Deweese, "It Was a Dark and Stag-nant Night ('til the Jadids Brought the Light): Clichés, Biases, and False Dichotomies in the Intellectual History of Central Asia," *Journal of the Economic History of the Orient* 59 (2016): 37–92.

27 Post-Soviet Uzbek and American scholars have often connected Cho'lpon's lyric with that of the Russian symbolists, but there's little evidence of this other than the poets' common preference for the elegy and use of symbols. Cho'lpon's symbols, however, emerge from the language and tradition of Islamicate poetry, not the self-consciously Orientalizing language of the Russian symbolists. By the time Cho'lpon made it to Moscow in 1925, symbolism had long since been out of vogue and its major pro-Soviet figures, Alexander Blok and Valery Bryusov, had already died. For scholars making this connection, see Lyons, "Resisting Coloni-alism in the Uzbek Historical Novel Kecha va Kunduz (Night and Day), 1936)," 176; Normat Yo'ldoshev, "Cho'lponning ramziy lirikasiga doir chizgilar," *O'zbek tili va adabiyoti* 1–2 (1994): 45–48; Dilmurod Quronov, *Cho'lpon hayoti va ijodiy merosi* (Toshkent: O'qituvchi, 1997), 29.

After the liquidation of the Kokand Autonomy, Cho'lpon began a bohemian life, moving from job to job and wife to wife. In 1918, he went to Russia as part of a travelling Uzbek theater troupe. There he made a lifelong friend, Mannon Uyg'ur, a theater director, and in Orenburg, he married a Tatar woman, Mohiro'ya, about whom little is known.[28] In 1921, he accepted Fitrat's invitation to work at *Axbori Buxoro*, the main newspaper of the People's Soviet Republic of Bukhara, which was created in 1920 in place of the Bukharan Emirate, a protectorate of the Russian Empire within Turkestan.[29] There he fell ill and was diagnosed with diabetes, from which he would have multiple stints in hospitals for the rest of his life.[30] In 1923, pursued by Soviet critics and secret police, Fitrat left for Moscow, while Cho'lpon returned to his hometown of Andijon, taking up the position of deputy editor of the local newspaper *The Emancipated* (*Darxon*).[31] In Andijon he married a woman named Soliha (whom he divorced in 1931).[32] A quarrel with his father in the same year, likely over Cho'lpon's reformist views, led him to abandon his home and move to Tashkent.[33] In 1924 Cho'lpon was among twenty-three other Uzbek dramatists, directors, and actors selected to study in Moscow at the Uzbek Drama Studio, which had been established in 1921.[34] Cho'lpon's prior experience in theater made him ideal for this spot. While in Moscow, he became thoroughly acquainted with Russian literature and theater and may have even met with some of the Silver Age greats such as Mayakovsky and Yesenin.[35]

Drama became a large part of Cho'lpon's oeuvre thanks to his time at the Uzbek Drama Studio. He had dabbled in theater before, but many of his major dramas came after his study of Gogol (he translated *The Government Inspector* [1836]), the Italian playwright Gozzi, and other dramatists while in Moscow.[36] During that time, he became fascinated with the poetry and drama

---

28 Quronov, *Cho'lpon hayoti va ijodiy merosi*, 12.

29 Karimov, *Abdulhamid Sulaymon o'g'li Cho'lpon*, 16.

30 Quronov, *Cho'lpon hayoti va ijodiy merosi*, 18.

31 Karimov, *Abdulhamid Sulaymon o'g'li Cho'lpon*, 16.

32 Ibid., 20–21.

33 Ibid., 18.

34 Ibid., 22; Khalid, *Making Uzbekistan: Nation, Empire, and Revolution in the Early USSR*, 186; Karimov, *Cho'lpon: Ma'rifiy roman*, 275. Dilmurod Quronov asserts that Cho'lpon only left Uzbekistan for the drama studio in 1925. Quronov, *Cho'lpon hayoti va ijodiy merosi*, 22.

35 Naim Karimov notes that other Uzbek litterateurs in Moscow met with these Russian poets, so it is not out of the question that Cho'lpon did as well. Karimov, *Cho'lpon: Ma'rifiy roman*, 287–288.

36 Quronov, *Cho'lpon hayoti va ijodiy merosi*, 23.

of Rabindranath Tagore, the Bengali writer who in the 1920s was becoming well known among modernists throughout the world.[37] In 1926, Cho'lpon reworked and published *Bright Moon* (*Yorqinoy*), a play he had written in 1920. Its mystical quality is close to that found in Tagore. He produced several other dramas after this point, but only two other plays, *A Modern Woman* (*Zamona xotini*) and *The Assault* (*Hujum*), survive.[38]

As Cho'lpon left for Moscow in 1924, Stalin initiated the national delimitation of Central Asia, a move that has commonly and mistakenly been interpreted as a surreptitious Bolshevik imperial strategy to "divide and conquer." The 1924 delimitation created the Kazakh, Uzbek, and Turkmen Socialist Soviet Republics (SSR) (Kyrgyzstan and Tajikistan were autonomous republics within Kazakhstan and Uzbekistan until 1936 and 1929 respectively) from the Turkestan, Bukharan, and Khivan SSRs.[39] Stalin made the decision based on his and Lenin's attempt to combat Russian imperialist tendencies and defang bourgeois nationalism, which, according to Marxist theory, threatened the development of class consciousness by encouraging a false national consciousness. However, much of the implementation of Stalin's decision—the negotiation of borders, the naming of communities, and the creation of common languages—was done by native elites like jadids. The Bukharan SSR, the government of which was composed largely of jadids and their allies, may have had more autonomy vis-à-vis Moscow than its Uzbek successor, but Uzbekistan, a homeland for Uzbeks, was the achievement of a jadid goal.[40]

In 1927, Cho'lpon returned to Uzbekistan to make use of his drama schooling by staging plays around the country. But a rude surprise awaited him. Around the middle of the decade, the Bolshevik Party felt that its hold on power in Central Asia was strong enough to take ideological control of the region. Beginning in the latter half of the 1920s, jadids and other old-generation national elites were expelled from the party in favor of a new generation of Uzbek intellectuals trained by the Komsomol (the Communist Youth League)

37 Karimov, *Cho'lpon: Ma'rifiy roman*, 235.

38 Ibid., 313. Naim Karimov suggests that all but "Hujum" have been lost, but "Zamona xotini" was found and reprinted in 1992. See Abdulhamid Cho'lpon, "Zamona xotini," *Sharq yulduzi* 10 (1992): 6–58.

39 For more on the national delimitation, see Arne Haugen, *The Establishment of National Republics in Soviet Central Asia* (New York: Palgrave Macmillan, 2003); Francine Hirsch, *Empire of Nations: Ethnographic Knowledge and the Making of the Soviet Union* (Ithaca: Cornell University Press, 2005), 145–186; Khalid, *Making Uzbekistan: Nation, Empire, and Revolution in the Early USSR*, 257–315.

40 Khalid, *Making Uzbekistan: Nation, Empire, and Revolution in the Early USSR*, 273–274.

and other party-associated organizations.[41] Both Cho'lpon and Fitrat quickly became symbols of the old generation and were therefore attacked frequently in the press. Poets of the new generation who fancied themselves dedicated socialists attacked Cho'lpon for his poetry's supposed decadence, pessimism, and anti-party views. Though they condemned jadids, we should not forget that many members of this new generation were students of jadids. They too believed in the need to spread education among Uzbeks, liberate women, modernize everyday life, and restore the Uzbek nation to its former glory, but they also saw themselves as superior to their predecessors in political will. They would achieve modernity for Uzbekistan where jadids like Cho'lpon had failed because of conservatism, timidity, and complacency. As a result of the attacks, several old-generation thinkers were arrested and exiled to Siberia. Cho'lpon escaped a probable arrest by again heading to Moscow in 1932.

During his second extended stay in the Soviet capital, Cho'lpon, like other persecuted writers across the Soviet Union, avoided controversy by reducing his publishing activity. He had never been a prolific poet: he published only three collections by 1932, *Springs* (*Buloqlar* [1922]), *Awakening* (*Uyg'onish* [1923]), and *Secrets of Dawn* (*Tong sirlari* [1926]). But around 1927, he largely stopped publishing original works and turned to translation. His friends and contacts in Uzbekistan's Communist Party found him a job as a translator in Moscow.[42] There he translated Shakespeare's *Hamlet*, the first half of Maksim Gorky's *Mother* (1907), and various works of Turgenev, Chekhov, and Leonid Andreev into Uzbek. He also met and married a Russian woman, Ekaterina Ivanovna (her surname is unknown).[43]

A lull in secret police activity allowed Cho'lpon to return to Uzbekistan in 1934. The latter half of the 1920s until 1932 was a period of denunciations, violence, and a strong push to construct socialism. Scholars have referred to these years, specifically 1928 to 1932, as the "Cultural Revolution."[44] The time is best known for Stalin's annulment of Lenin's NEP (New Economic Policy), the beginning of collectivization, the inauguration of the first five-year plan, and massive

---

41 Ibid., 316–341.

42 Karimov, *Abdulhamid Sulaymon o'g'li Cho'lpon*, 27.

43 Quronov, *Cho'lpon hayoti va ijodiy merosi*, 25.

44 Sheila Fitzpatrick, ed., *Cultural Revolution in Russia: 1928–1931* (Bloomington: Indiana University Press, 1978); Sheila Fitzpatrick, *The Cultural Front: Power and Culture in Revolutionary Russia* (Ithaca, London: University of Cornell Press, 1992), 1–15; Regine Robin, *Socialist Realism: An Impossible Aesthetic*, ed. Catherine Porter (Stanford: Stanford University Press, 1992), 5.

purges of the established intelligentsia in favor of inexperienced, politically engaged youth. The period that followed has been dubbed the "Great Retreat," though recent research notes that Stalinism was not a total betrayal of revolutionary ideals; indeed, it achieved many of the economic goals of the Bolsheviks such as forced industrialization and collectivization.[45] Nevertheless, when the first push to collectivize failed, along with other violent modernist projects, Stalin decided to make peace with the old intelligentsia and—to an extent—with traditional culture.[46] These conciliations permitted Cho'lpon's return.

Once back in Uzbekistan, Cho'lpon too decided to compromise with the Soviet state. He continued translating, rendering into Uzbek the second part of *Mother*, Gorky's *Egor Bulychov* (1932), Alexander Pushkin's *Dubrovsky* (1833) and *Boris Godunov* (1825), and the Iranian-Tajik communist Abulqosim Lohuti's *Journey to Europe* (1934).[47] He well understood why his poetry was criticized and attempted to rewrite his poetic biography. Because critics had lambasted him for the pessimism of his verse, his collection *Soz* (Lyre [1935]) emphasized his new optimistic persona and his enthusiasm for Soviet rule with poems such as "The New Me" (Yangi men) and "May First" (1 May), which celebrated international workers' day. A 1934 poem, "Ten Years without Lenin" (O'n yil Leninsiz), panegyrizes Lenin on the tenth anniversary of his death.[48] In 1934, he also submitted the first book of his dilogy of novels *Night and Day* to an Uzbek literary contest designed to encourage the writing of socialist prose.[49]

Determining Cho'lpon and other Uzbek litterateurs' position on Stalin and Soviet politics at this time is fraught with complications because Soviet rule had rather ambiguous effects on the region. The Soviet system allowed jadids to pursue the creation of a nation-state, mass native-language education, women's liberation through unveiling, and campaigns against Islamic clergy, the enemies

---

45 The "great retreat" was coined by Nicholas Timasheff. See *The Great Retreat: The Growth and Retreat of Communism in Russia* (New York: E. P. Dutton & Co, 1946). The term has been criticized recently by a new generation of scholars who have focused on the period as a consolidation of socialist gains. Timasheff's "great retreat" assumed that the Stalinist Soviet Union, by returning to bourgeois cultural values, would also soon become a market economy, which clearly did not happen. See Stephen Kotkin, *Magnetic Mountain: Stalinism as Civilization* (Berkeley: University of California Press, 1995), 357; Terry Martin, *The Affirmative Action Empire: Nations and Nationalism in the Soviet Union, 1923–1939* (Ithaca: Cornell University Press, 2001), 414–415.

46 See Fitzpatrick, *The Cultural Front: Power and Culture in Revolutionary Russia*, 8–9; Robin, *Socialist Realism: An Impossible Aesthetic*, 4–8.

47 Karimov, *Abdulhamid Sulaymon o'g'li Cho'lpon*, 29.

48 Abdulhamid Cho'lpon, "O'n yil Leninsiz," *O'zbekiston sovet adabiyoti* 6 (1934): 61.

49 O'zbekiston respublikasi Markaziy davlat arxivi (O'zRMDA) f. 2356 o. 1 d. 9 l. 1–2.

of jadids.[50] As for collectivization, it, oddly enough, did not produce the same disastrous results that it did in Ukraine and Kazakhstan. While rural Ukrainians and Kazakhs suffered and died of famine, Uzbeks were saved by the early fruit harvests in their warmer climate. New research suggests that many Uzbek farmers enthusiastically participated in dekulakization because they truly bore grudges against the richer peasants who cheated them and acted as usurers, as seen in Cho'lpon's novel.[51]

On the other hand, the new generation's attacks on their jadid predecessors demonstrated that Stalin had no tolerance for pluralism and democratic debate. How to implement the party line was a matter of negotiation, but the content of the party line was Stalin's and Stalin's alone. Many were dissatisfied with the failure of the Soviet Union to create an Uzbek proletariat; they harangued Moscow for turning Central Asia into a cotton plantation. Among themselves, they accused the Bolsheviks of imperialism and chauvinism.[52] Throughout the late 1920s, the repeated failures to Uzbekify the party apparatus in Uzbekistan raised the ire of anti-colonial Uzbek thinkers. By the early 1930s, such efforts came to a complete halt. Native rule subordinate to Moscow continued, but only Uzbeks competent in Russian could climb the ranks.[53] As for Cho'lpon, he must have been particularly incensed that his art and elegies had been the subject of frequent denunciations. Memoirists tell us that Cho'lpon, indeed, hated Stalin and wrote his fair share of poems mocking the mustachioed menace.[54] The brief thaw in 1934 nevertheless offered some hope to the alienated, a chance for the Soviet Union to achieve the utopian ideals it had long promised, and therefore, we should read Cho'lpon and others' moods at this time as extremely disappointed but also hopeful for change. After all, they had no idea what was coming.

What was coming was a new set of purges, commonly known as Stalin's Great Terror, and Cho'lpon did not escape this time. Critics began denouncing him in the local press again in 1936. In 1937, he was called to 25 Stalin Street, the inauspiciously named location of the Uzbek Soviet Writers' Union, to answer for his lack of productivity and other errors, but this meeting was

50 See Khalid, *Making Uzbekistan: Nation, Empire, and Revolution in the Early USSR.*

51 Marianne Kamp and Russell Zanca, "Recollections of Collectivization in Uzbekistan: Stalinism and Local Activism," *Central Asian Survey* 36, no. 1 (2017): 55–72.

52 Khalid, *Making Uzbekistan: Nation, Empire, and Revolution in the Early USSR*, 339.

53 William Fierman, *Language Planning and National Development: The Uzbek Experience* (Berlin: De Gruyter, 1991), 165–192.

54 Mutavakkil Burhonov, "Nurli siymolar," in *Fitna san'ati*, vol. 2 (Toshkent: Fan, 1993), 196–208.

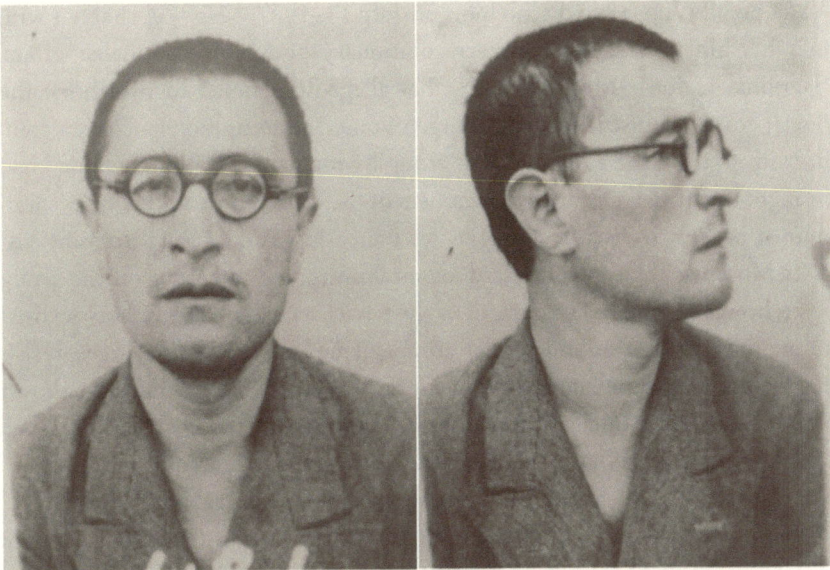

Figure 2. Cho'lpon's mugshot in his NKVD file. Courtesy of Hamid Ismailov.

only a prelude to his NKVD arrest. Cho'lpon now likely knew that his days were numbered because he decided to treat the terrifying situation with levity:

Ziyo Said [a playwright]:	You had a word with [Mannon] Uyg'ur.
Cho'lpon:	Then we talked about Arabic words, but that's a lie, I am not an Arab, I am not a nationalist. I hate Arabic, to hell with Arabic words. (laughter)[55]

Critics commonly leveled the accusation of "nationalism" against Cho'lpon and others, suggesting through the facile charge that jadids were hateful chauvinists opposed to Soviet internationalism. Soviet critics considered the jadid desire in the 1920s to purify the Uzbek language by ridding it of non-Turkic vocabulary as a particular manifestation of this "nationalism," hence Cho'lpon's mention of "Arabic words." Cho'lpon first denies the charge, only to embrace it jokingly.

---

55 The transcript of Cho'lpon's speech before the Writers' Union can be found in Republic of Uzbekistan Central State Archive. O'zRMDA f. 2356 o. 1 d. 29. Reprinted in Abdulhamid Cho'lpon, "Nutq," in *Fitnai san'at*, ed. Mahmud Yahyo and Erkin Siddiq, 2 vols., (Toshkent: Fan, 1993), 2:187–195.

The NKVD arrested Cho'lpon on July 13, 1937.[56] He was charged with membership in a secret counterrevolutionary bourgeois nationalist group, "National Union" (Milliy ittihod), that allegedly planned to overthrow the Soviet government and install a bourgeois one. The accusation had only a grain of truth to it: in the early 1920s, a group by the name "National Union" had brought together high-ranking members of the Turkestan and Bukharan communist parties to discuss strategies for increasing Turkestan's autonomy vis-à-vis Moscow. The capabilities, ideological unity, and intentions of the group were, however, greatly exaggerated by the Soviet secret police.[57] Others accused of membership in this and similar groups denied the NKVD's charges, resisting for months while being beaten and tortured. Cho'lpon acquiesced almost immediately.[58] It is unclear why he readily admitted to false charges, but Uzbek historians speculate that he knew there was no longer any point in resisting.[59] On October 4, 1938, an NKVD firing squad executed him.[60]

His works, along with those of others who were executed alongside him like Fitrat, were banned in the Soviet Union from 1938 until Stalin's death, though they circulated among Uzbek intellectuals and students in secret. After Khrushchev's famous "cult of personality" speech at the twentieth party congress in 1956, both Cho'lpon and Fitrat were rehabilitated; however, publication of their works continued to be proscribed.[61] Only during Gorbachev's glasnost', which began in 1987, did Cho'lpon's works start to reappear in print. As the Soviet Union was falling apart, Uzbek intellectuals recovered Cho'lpon's legacy. In the short period of glasnost' before independence, they cautiously set him within the Soviet canon, arguing that he had been an unjustly persecuted and misunderstood pro-Soviet writer. Then, as the Soviet Union collapsed and the narrative of Uzbekistan's historical victimhood took over, they transformed him into an anti-Soviet national visionary, a people's poet, and a martyr for the cause of independence.

---

56 Karimov, *Abdulhamid Sulaymon o'g'li Cho'lpon*, 32.

57 Khalid, *Making Uzbekistan: Nation, Empire, and Revolution in the Early USSR*, 143–147.

58 Naim Karimov, "Cho'lpon uchun kishan," in *Adabiyot va tarixiy jarayon* (Toshkent: Mumtoz so'z, 2013), 355–363.

59 Ibid., 362.

60 Karimov, *Abdulhamid Sulaymon o'g'li Cho'lpon*, 33.

61 An anthology of Uzbek poets, *Tirik satrlar* (Living Lines), containing a set of Cho'lpon's poems was published in 1968, but as soon as Uzbek critics discovered Cho'lpon's presence in it, they denounced it and the publisher discontinued the print run. See Ozod Sharafiddinov, "'Tirik satr'larning qiyin qismati," in *Sardaftar sahifalari* (Toshkent: Yozuvchi nashriyoti, 1994), 48–58.

HISTORY OF THE NOVEL AND ITS PUBLICATION

It is unclear when exactly Cho'lpon began writing his *Night and Day*, but scholars speculate that he started around 1932 during his time in Moscow.[62] As mentioned above, he submitted the first part of *Night and Day* to a contest for Uzbek
socialist prose works towards the end of 1934. The judge, who wrote the report on the novel (Oydin, a major Soviet Uzbek poetess),[63] noted that it lacked
the proper ideological qualities necessary to be awarded a prize and expressed
doubt that the proposed sequel, the content of which she seems to have known
somewhat, would fix the political mistakes.[64] Nevertheless, the judges collec-
tively recommended the novel for publication.[65] The first chapter of the novel
was published in the journal *Soviet Literature* (*Sovet adabiyoti*) in the third issue
of 1935, the second chapter was published in the tenth issue of *Rose Garden*
(*Guliston*) in the same year, and the entire novel was published in October 1936
as a book. It received a short laudatory review in *Young Leninist* (*Yosh Leninchi*)
in February of the following year, while all the other major critics held their
tongues.[66] Few dared to associate themselves with Cho'lpon publicly because
of his reputation in the press. Only in August of 1937, three critics coauthored
a scathing review after Cho'lpon's arrest, targeting the writer for "replacing class
struggle with pornography [parnografiya]," and "showing jadids as revolutionaries for the people" rather than as "allies of the Russian bourgeoisie and imperial officers."[67] The book was banned along with the author's name.

Glasnost allowed its republication. In 1988, the novel was republished
serially in *Star of the East* (*Sharq yulduzi*), the largest literary journal in the

---

62 Karimov, *Cho'lpon: Ma'rifiy roman*, 408.

63 While female Russian poets such as Anna Axmatova and Marina Tsvetaeva objected to the
    gendered designation of themselves as poetesses, this was never the case with female Uzbek
    poets, who self-identified with the gendered *shoira* (poetess).

64 O'zRMDA f. 2356 o. 1 d. 9 l. 15–17.

65 Ibid. l. 1.

66 Xotam Qirg'iz, "'Kecha va kunduz' haqida," *Yosh Leninchi*, February 12, 1937. Shawn Lyons
    claims the novel received another review in 1936 that also praised the novel for revealing
    the "historical truth" of jadids' collusion with the Russian imperial government. He quotes
    from a 1994 collection of articles which I have been unable to locate. See Lyons, "Resisting
    Colonialism in the Uzbek Historical Novel Kecha va Kunduz (Night and Day), 1936)," 190,
    192; Salohiddin Mamajonov, "Cho'lponning nasriy va dramatik ijodi," in *Cho'lponning badiiy
    olami*, ed. Naim Karimov (Toshkent: Fan, 1994), 80.

67 A. Sharifiy, O. Sharafiddinov, and F. Sultonov, "'Kecha va kunduz' haqida," *Qizil O'zbekiston*,
    August 6, 1937.

Uzbek language.[68] *Star of the East* (*Zvezda vostoka*), the journal's Russian-language counterpart, released a Russian translation the following year.[69] Despite the freedom permitted by glasnost, the editors of the 1988 serial publication felt obligated to censor certain parts of the novel. Because Cho'lpon had been accused of anti-Russian nationalism, the editors removed references to Russians that could be perceived as chauvinistic, despite the fact that Cho'lpon probably did not identify with the characters who utter them. They also added an epigraph from Gorky to increase the novel's Soviet credentials. As far as I can tell, there was little threat in 1988 that representatives from Moscow would be concerned with the anti-Russian sentiments of a writer repressed fifty years earlier. The editors had more to fear from Uzbek critics, some of whom likely participated in Cho'lpon's repression and built their careers on it. Since Uzbekistan gained independence in 1991, Uzbek publishers began printing the novel as a reproduction of the 1936 edition transliterated into the Cyrillic orthography.[70] Uzbek and Russian scholars produced another translation of the novel into Russian based on the uncensored manuscript in 1991, and Stéphane Dudoignon translated the novel from Uzbek into French in 2009.[71] This translation of the novel follows the version of the text published in 1936 and post-1991 republications (some of these offer explanatory and textological notes), while the footnotes indicate where the text of the 1988 serial publication differs.

The sequel to the novel has served as the source of much controversy among Uzbek literary scholars. In all extant editions, the present novel is clearly labeled "Book one: Night," indicating that Cho'lpon intended a sequel *Day*

---

68 Abdulhamid Cho'lpon, "Kecha va kunduz: Roman," *Sharq yulduzi* 2 (1988): 64–148; Abdulhamid Cho'lpon, "Kecha va kunduz: Roman," *Sharq yulduzi* 3 (1988): 79–142.

69 Abdulkhamid Chulpan, "Noch' i den': Roman," trans. Abdulkhamid Ismoili, *Zvezda vostoka* 9 (1989): 8–57; Abdulkhamid Chulpan, "Noch' i den': Roman, okonchanie," trans. Abdulkhamid Ismoili, *Zvezda vostoka* 10 (1989): 6–72.

70 There are two extant copies of the 1936 edition. One is held in the personal archive of Ozod Sharafiddinov (1929–2005), the Uzbek scholar who led the charge to republish Cho'lpon in the 1960s and later under glasnost in the 1980s. This is the text from which reproductions of the novel have been printed. The other is held in the literary museum in the author's home town of Andijan. I have access to the latter copy, which, other than lacking pages 37 and 38, should be identical to the copy in the Ozod Sharafiddinov archive.

71 See Chulpan, *I prozvuchi eshche, moi saz: Roman, drama, stikhi*, ed. A. Sharafutdinov, trans. I. Shipovskii (Tashkent: Izdatel'stvo literatury i iskusstva imeni Gafura Guliama, 1991); 'Abd al-Hamid Sulayman Tchulpan, *Nuit*, trans. Stéphane Dudoignon (Saint-Pourçain-sur-Sioule: Bleu autour, 2009). Dudoignon was unaware that the novel was published during glasnost. Stéphane Dudoignon, "Postface," in *Nuit: Roman traduit de l'ouzbek par Stéphane A. Dudoignon* (Saint-Pourçain-sur-Sioule: Bleu autour, 2009), 424–425.

to complete the suggestion of the dilogy title, *Night and Day*. Naim Karimov, the foremost expert on Uzbek jadids, suggests that the projected sequel was merely a myth made to appease Cho'lpon's Soviet critics and that *Night* should be considered a novel complete in and of itself.[72] Dilmurod Quronov, a specialist on Cho'lpon's prose, has argued the opposite. He contends that Cho'lpon not only planned a second novel but most likely wrote it before his arrest. In a 1937 article, Cho'lpon mentions his "novels" in the plural, and an unidentified incomplete work was discovered among his belongings upon his arrest.[73] If the NKVD possessed a copy, the opening of their archives to a select few senior Uzbek scholars in the 1990s would have turned up the sequel. Because there has been no mention of scholars finding such a text, it is likely that the NKVD destroyed it as they often destroyed confiscated texts in the event that those texts could not lead to additional arrests.

READING AND INTERPRETING THE NOVEL

Most scholars have interpreted the novel as an attack on the Soviet Union and its socialist ideology, reading Cho'lpon as an unambiguously anti-Soviet author, but there are ample reasons to doubt this easy conclusion.[74] Cho'lpon's *Night and Day* is certainly unique for its time. Its language, plot, and interests are, as earlier noted, little like the canonized works of Socialist Realism, the demands of which would become increasingly stringent by the time of the

---

72 Karimov, *Abdulhamid Sulaymon o'g'li Cho'lpon*, 77.

73 Dilmurod Quronov, *Cho'lpon nasri poetikasi* (Toshkent: Sharq, 2004), 271–272.

74 Halim Kara, "Resisting Narratives: Reading Abdulhamid Suleymon Cholpan from a Post-Colonial Perspective" (PhD diss., Indiana University, 2000), 185–186; Quronov, *Cho'lpon nasri poetikasi*, 277; Matyoqub Qo'shjonov, "'Kecha va kunduz' romanida obrazlar tizmasi," *O'zbek tili va adabiyoti* 3–4 (1992): 8–13; Dudoignon, "Postface." Many of these works read Cho'lpon's novel as an anti-Soviet allegory, an approach I find particularly unproductive because it permits the critic to impose his/her own teleology onto the text and forgets the uncertain time in which the text was written.

Shawn Lyons's work is unique in this regard. He argues that the discourse of anti-colonialism found in Cho'lpon's work is a double-edged sword, which inevitably finds the author, despite his intent, supporting colonialism as much as he resists it. I agree with some of his argument, but I would suggest that Lyons's equation of Russian colonialism and Soviet imperialism is problematic. Lyons's piece is unfortunately undermined by some critical misreadings of the text. He mistakes *noyib to'ra*, the Russian official, for a native official and suggests that Zunnun, *noyib to'ra*'s cook, is married to the woman who is, in fact, *noyib to'ra*'s wife. See Lyons, "Resisting Colonialism in the Uzbek Historical Novel Kecha va Kunduz (Night and Day), 1936)."

Great Terror. However, scholarly accounts of the construction of the novel within the framework of Cho'lpon's oeuvre and the literary and historical context of the time are almost nonexistent. All appearances suggest that Cho'lpon intended to reconcile with and show support for the Soviet government with this novel and its potential sequel, but much of his drama and prose from the late 1920s on pose more questions than they resolve. In his writing, he constantly reworks and revises assumptions, never ending on a sure conclusion that would clearly support or reject socialism. His prose emphasizes mistakes and misunderstandings, highlighting the characters' ignorance of their surroundings. In showing his ideological loyalty, Cho'lpon borrows from the texts and techniques of socialist writers, but he mainly makes use of those practices that enhance the indecisiveness of his characters. Although his goal was to support socialist ideology and to write an ideologically correct novel, Cho'lpon's commitment, first and foremost, was to an aesthetic of the indecisive, an aesthetic which emerged from his background in Muslim reform. The resoluteness required by late 1930s Socialist Realism was ultimately inimical to his method.

Scholars and contemporaneous observers have argued that Cho'lpon wished for his novel to scandalize and offend the Soviet establishment because its plot is nothing like the model Socialist Realist plot that lionizes a socialist hero and his victory over class enemies. The first recorded use of the term Socialist Realism was in 1932 in a speech given by the literary critic Ivan Gronsky, but its interpretation only solidified later in the decade, a few years after the writing of Cho'lpon's novel.[75] According to the Socialist Realist "master plot" outlined by Katerina Clark (2000), Socialist Realist novels realize the Marxist-Leninist theory of history allegorically. Marxism-Leninism held a dialectic unique from other Marxisms: the proletarian masses would, through education, rise from an original state of "spontaneity" to "class consciousness." This dialectic was realized in literature through "spontaneous," impetuous, decisive protagonists who hone and focus that energy with the help of a Bolshevik teacher into "consciously" directed action in concert with others.[76] Canonical novels containing this plot include *How the Steel Was Tempered* (1934) by Nikolay Ostrovsky and *Chapaev* (1925) by Dmitry Furmanov.

Cho'lpon's novel, however, begins with ignorance—his characters rarely understand themselves, others, and their surroundings—and does not advance

---

75 Katerina Clark, *The Soviet Novel: History as Ritual* (Bloomington: Indiana University Press, 2000), 27.

76 Clark, 15–24.

much beyond that. The novel follows the paths of three characters that inter-
sect at various points over the course of several years, ending in 1916, a year
prior to the Russian Revolution. *Night and Day* opens with the girl Zebi, who
has recently reached marriageable age. The beauty of her voice catches the ear
of Miryoqub, the retainer of the Russian-affiliated colonial official Akbarali
mingboshi. Although Akbarali already has three wives, Miryoqub encourages
his master's interest in Zebi and arranges a fourth marriage. During that time,
Miryoqub meets a Russian prostitute, Maria, with whom he falls in love and
agrees to leave Central Asia. As the new couple leaves for Moscow, Miryoqub
becomes acquainted with a jadid, Sharafuddin Xo'jaev, and nominally becomes
a jadid. After Miryoqub's departure, the action returns to Central Asia, where
Zebi's new co-wives intrigue against her and her husband. Mingboshi's second
wife plans to poison her, but Zebi unwittingly gives the poison to Akbarali. Zebi
is taken to court, convicted of murder, and sentenced to exile in Siberia. The
incomplete paths of Miryoqub and Zebi imply a sequel that details their participation in revolution and return to Central Asia, but the near absence of revolution and socialist ideas in the first book has been used by both Stalinist and
contemporary critics to argue for Cho'lpon's anti-Soviet intentions.

That inference, however, forgets the political fluidity of the period from
1932 and 1934 when Cho'lpon was writing. After the failure of collectivization
and the Cultural Revolution, Stalin permitted the reconciliation of many persecuted writers to the Soviet literary establishment. Cho'lpon, as we know, took
full advantage of this. When Socialist Realism was first coined in 1932, its contents, form, and overall meaning were largely undetermined.[77] Stalinist critics
attacked Cho'lpon for his failure to match an ideal form of Socialist Realism,
but that ideal only congealed during and after Stalin's Great Terror. Before that
time, demonstrating ideological loyalty in literature could take multiple forms.

Nevertheless, as critics have correctly pointed out, Cho'lpon's poetry-in-
prose style in the novel certainly suggests that ideology was not his priority.[78] In
Night and Day, Cho'lpon's prose mimics the style of his own poetry. His novel
is full of original and striking metaphors that bring Central Asian daily life into
the very narration of the text. Of the star overlooking his heroine Zebi's night-
time journey, he remarks: "the brightest star—so bright that it looked as if it
were face to face with its onlookers—trembled as it burned like the eyes of a
young girl cutting an onion." In this example, Cho'lpon interweaves the scenery

---

77   See Robin, *Socialist Realism: An Impossible Aesthetic*, 37–74.
78   Khalid, *Making Uzbekistan: Nation, Empire, and Revolution in the Early USSR*, 382.

of the novel with the coming-of-age experiences of his female characters: in Cho'lpon's time, parents prepared their daughters for a life of domesticity by exposing them at an early age to the demands of Uzbek cuisine, of which the onion is a major component. Metaphors connecting nature and Central Asian culture are a ubiquitous feature of Cho'lpon's prose. We see it even in the first lines of the novel. When Zebi enjoys a brief moment of liberty, the narrator compares it to the blossoming and expansion implied by the Uzbek word for summer: *yoz*. This word is homonymous with the verb *yozmoq*, meaning to expand. Cho'lpon extends the metaphor by equating the impositions of her misogynist father with the contraction implied by winter. "If the cold old man hadn't returned, the two young girls' pent up tension from the long winter would have *expanded* [*yozilgan*] with the warmth of spring and produced even more mischief" (italics are mine—C. F.). Cho'lpon often associates Zebi's father with winter, describing him as "cold" and his visage as a "brow from which snow falls" (a figure of speech for "glowering"). The effect of the description identifies Razzoq-sufi with a winter that limits his daughter's freedom. This is hardly the straightforward prose style one would expect of an ideological novel.

Yet Cho'lpon attempted to reconcile his poetry-in-prose to Socialist Realism not long before his death. In a 1937 article, he locates the same approach to nature in the writings of Maksim Gorky, the father of Socialist Realism. "Gorky is a poet," Cho'lpon writes, "His writings demonstrate that he is more than a prose writer; each sentence evinces a poet with a tender heart, a lover of beauty, and a writer enamored of nature. I myself love beautiful similes and images of nature and try to include them in every work of prose I undertake."[79] In the 1930s, Cho'lpon translated Gorky's *Mother*, which had been declared the earliest Socialist Realist novel, into Uzbek and used his knowledge of Gorky's style to justify his own. Indeed, Cho'lpon is correct regarding the elder writer's style, though Gorky's romantic moments were increasingly underemphasized in socialist criticism as the 1930s advanced.

Cho'lpon's oeuvre has more in common with Soviet ideology than previous scholars of his work have acknowledged. Throughout his literary career after the revolution, Cho'lpon was deeply concerned with the question of Central Asian women's liberation. Like many other jadids and contemporaneous Muslim reformers elsewhere, he believed that his society had unfairly limited women by confining them to the home, forbidding them to appear in public without the full-body covering known as the *paranji*, and restricting their

---

79 Abdulhamid Cho'lpon, "Ustodning xislatlari," *Qizil O'zbekiston*, June 18, 1937.

educational opportunities.[80] In their project to advance women in society, the jadids found a powerful ally in the Bolsheviks. Progressive Russians had long been concerned with what they called the "woman question" and in the 1920s advocated for the full equality of women with men. The Bolsheviks, particularly those among the younger generation, were far more radical than Central Asian reformers, calling for the end of the family in order to create radical equality among the sexes.[81] In 1927, jadid-influenced women, supported by the Bolsheviks, launched "the assault" (*hujum*)—a campaign for women to remove their paranjis. The "assault" met with a considerable backlash from patriarchal Uzbek men, who used violence to keep women in their place.[82] Cho'lpon, for his part, supported the *hujum* through his dramatic work in the late 1920s, translating from Russian and authoring a few songs for the musical drama *The Assault* (*Hujum* [1927]) by Vasilii Ian (1874–1954).

Cho'lpon's drama *A Modern Woman* (*Zamona xotini* [1928]), unpublished in his lifetime, is initially aligned with Soviet ideology in its support for women's liberation, but because of the ambiguity characteristic of Cho'lpon's art, the play questions the end result of those politics. Ultimately, it demonstrates contradictions within Cho'lpon's own self: in his lyric he bemoaned the ignorance and docility of Turkestani women, but here he exhibits ambivalence toward his heroine who overcomes that passivity. The play's final act shows the principal female character and the eponymous modern woman, Rahima xola, in the role of a successful head of a village *ispolkom* (executive committee). She scolds and

---

80 For a comparison of early twentieth-century Central Asian gender politics with contemporaneous Muslim societies, see Kamp, *The New Woman in Uzbekistan*. For a look at the relationship between gender and politics during Iran's constitutional revolution, see Afsaneh Najmabadi, *Women with Mustaches and Men without Beards: Gender and Sexual Anxieties of Iranian Modernity* (Berkeley: University of California Press, 2005). For gender politics in modern Turkey, see Deniz Kandiyoti, "Slave Girls, Temptresses, and Comrades: Images of Women in the Turkish Novel," *Feminist Issues* 8, no. 1 (1988): 35–50; Deniz Kandiyoti, "Gendering the Modern: On Missing Dimensions in the Study of Turkish Modernity," in *Rethinking Modernity and National Identity in Turkey*, ed. Sibel Bozdogan and Resat Kasaba (Seattle: University of Washington Press, 1997), 113–132.

81 For more on the ambitious program of sexual liberation of some on the Russian left, see Wendy Z. Goldman, *Women, The State and Revolution: Soviet Family Policy and Social Life, 1917,1936* (Cambridge: Cambridge University Press, 1993); I. S. Kon, *Seksual'naia kul'tura v Rossii: Klubnichka na berezke* (Moscow: O.G.I., 1997); Dan Healey, *Homosexual Desire in Revolutionary Russia: The Regulation of Sexual and Gender Dissent* (Chicago: University of Chicago Press, 2001).

82 For more on the *hujum* and the reaction to it, see Marianne Kamp, *The New Woman in Uzbekistan* (Seattle: University of Washington Press, 2006).

punishes corrupt officials, religious authorities, and village misogynists, but the play ultimately concludes on a tragic note. To reach her position Rahima xola has to sacrifice part of herself, namely her femininity. Cho'lpon emphasizes throughout that the modern woman is actually very masculine. Rahima xola is described in the character descriptions as *erkaknusxa* (literally: man-copy) and in becoming the head of the ispolkom, she takes on what is traditionally a man's role. In fact, she ousts her husband, Rustam, from that position after he beats and almost kills her with a knife laden with symbolism. The knife is suggestive of a phallic object not just in a Freudian sense, but also in Uzbek culture in which a knife appearing in a dream or in an act of fortune-telling portends the birth of a son. When she becomes head of the ispolkom herself, she in turn beats "backward" interlocutors with an equally phallic whip. In the play's conclusion, she announces her decision to marry the emasculated and sexless Jo'ra, an old man who has never married.

In a short soliloquy, Rahima xola regrets that her husband abandoned her and that Jo'ra cannot replace him. At that moment, Rustam bursts in and again confronts her with a knife. The stage directions suggest that her femininity returns in this final scene. According to those directions, her cries and wails are to "fully express her womanhood."[83] The police interrupt their encounter and arrest Rustam, but as they drag him away, the couple's son, Adhamjon, chases after Rustam, calling "father, father" and ignoring his mother's cries. The tragedy on which Cho'lpon ends his otherwise empowering play demonstrates the author's uncertainty about both the Soviet and his own program for the future Uzbek woman. Rahima xola, the author hints, may be a liberated woman, but she cannot be a father to her son. His verse frequently lamented the passivity of women, but Cho'lpon here discloses his discomfort with the solution his earlier critique implied. A powerful female protagonist cannot maintain the femininity that Cho'lpon in his verse hails as authentically Uzbek and worthy of saving.

Through this conclusion, the play suggests that women should not have to defend themselves at all and that Central Asian men have forgotten their roles as protectors and heroes. Rahima xola's husband Rustam's name is no accident, for it alludes to the hero of Ferdowsi's *Shahname* (The Persian Book of Kings). Cho'lpon's Rustam, however, is a degenerated hero who has lost touch with his roots. Instead of using his strength to protect his wife and fellow villagers, he consorts with prostitutes, drinks, and beats his wife. Cho'lpon thus leaves his Rahima xola in an unresolvable situation: her husband refuses to act responsibly, and the

---

83 Abdulhamid Sulaymon o'g'li Cho'lpon, "Zamona xotini," in *Asarlar: To'rt jildlik*, vol. 3 (Toshkent: Akademnashr, 2016), 246.

author condemns her to tragedy for taking action herself. Despite the novelty of this figure in Cho'lpon's oeuvre—powerful heroines like Rahima xola were popular in the dramaturgy of the *hujum* and Cho'lpon's drama is something of a parody—Cho'lpon grants her a tragic fate all the same. In denying her a happy end, Cho'lpon expresses his ambivalence to the problem of women's emancipation.

Cho'lpon's unabating interest in ambiguity and the unresolvable is the product of his aestheticization of jadid political rhetoric and philosophy of history as expressed in jadid literature. Like other Islamic reformers of previous generations, many jadids saw history as a cyclical series of declines and ascents away from and towards civilizational peaks.[84] In jadid literary works, the main agent in this history is God, not Muslims, and only His actions can renew Muslim society. The reformers' role was to attune their ignorant brethren to the will of God so as to return the community to His favor. Jadid works across genres therefore depict the time of decline and ignorance in which they felt their society existed and then conclude, before the revolution, with a catastrophe, often sent by God, which warns readers and spectators of the follies of their ignorance, or, after the revolution, with salvation in the form of a *deus ex machina*, often the revolution itself. Though jadids certainly exercised agency in their society, much of their literature does not reflect that fact and instead, suggests that salvation comes from without. The depiction of ignorance naturally suggested certain rhetorical modes—elegy and lament of lost glory, exhortation and admonition to regain that glory, or satire of the time of ignorance—all of which became the favorite rhetorical modes of jadids. In the early 1920s, several jadids came to the realization that their art, as expressed in the above rhetorical modes, emerges precisely from the depiction of decline. They therefore endeavored to indefinitely defer the moment of consciousness in order to fully exploit the aesthetic possibilities of ignorance. Ironically, the jadid aesthetic came to work at cross purposes with jadid politics: while their politics called for an end to the age of ignorance, the jadid aesthetic demanded its continuation. This aestheticization of ignorance explains Cho'lpon's ambivalence to the events he depicts in the novel. On one level, he detests the ignorance of his countrymen and desires that they awaken, but on another, he is fascinated by the opportunities for creativity that ignorance permits.

Cho'lpon's 1920 poem "Someone's dream" (Xayoli) beautifully demonstrates how the author reconfigures ignorance from the object of political condemnation into an engine productive of artistic material. Cho'lpon in this poem

---

84   For more on Islamic reform and the Islamic understanding of history, see Samira Haj, *Reconfiguring Islamic Tradition: Reform, Rationality, and Modernity* (Stanford: Stanford University Press, 2009).

suggests that there is a creative energy in sleep, in unconsciousness—jadids often implored their brethren to "awaken" from their "ignorant slumber"— which is maintained by its unfinalizability or unrealized potential. To wake up from such a sleep is to lose something of the possibilities engendered by that sleep's dream. This poem has a syllabic meter of eleven syllables per line and is read with a caesura every four syllables (4–4–3). The rhyme scheme, which I have captured here, is abcb.

> I hid the spark of love inside my heart,
> Tucked it away in the depths of my dream.
> Concealed in my bosom, the wound from that spark
> Burns and burns, tearing each stitch at the seam.
>
> I hear: "take your desire" from
> The morning [*azonlar*] with its dev'lish voice;
> But I ignore it and continue my tales,
> Thanking the angel that granted me choice.
>
> That devil, toying with its hair,
> Responds in anger: "Your stories are all in vain!"
> Its words arrive at my ear changed:
> "I flow," it says, "like blood from red and golden veins."
>
> "Now flow with me," it says, "you lord of tales,
> Await in me all your desires and your throne;
> In that golden and bloodred water,
> Your soul, once clothed in black, will take on new tones."
>
> Leave me, oh devil, torture me with nightmares no more.
> My shield is broken, my sword in two snapped.
> Do you see me? I'm crushed, and I lie now,
> Under a mountain of misfortune, trapped.
>
> Oh angel, at my last breath, still I am enthralled,
> Come, look at me, and let the heavens fall.[85]

---

85 Cho'lpon, *Asarlar: To'rt jildlik*, 2016, 1:49.

The artistry of this poem is closely related to its lack of a conclusive awakening. A devil, tempts the speaker to awaken from his sleep—I have rendered *azonlar*, the calls to prayer, as "morning" to show how the poet continues his metaphor of dream—and achieve the "desire" of his dream in reality. That devil identifies the lyric persona as an artist—"lord of tales." In declaring that the persona's "stories are all in vain," the devilish voice invites the artist to stop toying with the artifice of dream; however, the speaker refuses because he finds art, the ability to weave his tales, within dream. Cho'lpon then ends the poem not with the happiness and prosperity—that is, awakening—that the devil offers but with a crushing death. Rather than exiting the state of ignorance for which sleep and dream were so often metaphors in the literature of his jadid predecessors, Cho'lpon chooses to remain within that state, even as it leads to a tragic end. By rejecting an exit from dream because of the artistic play it permits, Cho'lpon suggests that art emerges from the indefinite deferral of awakening.

This aesthetic of ignorance on display in "Someone's dream" is Cho'lpon's main structural device in *Night and Day*. Drawing on this aesthetic and the author's experience as a dramatist, the novel is filled with dramatic irony: the characters are ignorant of their political, social, and familial environments. They know far less about their predicaments than we as readers do. The plot develops through self-discoveries, but these are always preludes to further epiphanies, and thus character development is a never-ending process. Ultimately, every discovery or recognition is a misrecognition that postpones enlightenment to another time.

The inability to understand one's self and others plays a large role in the novel's character interactions. Cho'lpon, perhaps because of his education in Russian literature during his two periods in Moscow, frequently employs one of Tolstoy's favorite techniques—that of non-verbal communication. Often his characters communicate not so much through words, but through glances, gestures, body movements, and facial expressions. For Tolstoy, a longtime lover of Rousseau, this bodily communication is closer to nature and thus conveys more than do words, which are abstracted from nature and therefore false. For Cho'lpon, on the other hand, non-verbal communication often indicates that something remains indeterminate and unable to be articulated. For example, after their trip to the village, Zebi's friend Saltanat realizes how her actions have unwittingly begun the process of Zebi's betrothal to Akbarali. She decides not to tell Zebi to avoid upsetting her, but after imagining Zebi's life with Akbarali, she involuntarily screams and embraces her friend. Even when Zebi later discovers Akbarali's plans, she never quite understands Saltanat's embrace:

Suddenly she remembered Saltanat's behavior in the cart: Saltanat had cried out "mingboshi!" She had become pale and lost consciousness. When she opened her eyes and stared at everyone, she then looked directly at Zebi and threw herself into her arms. Then two days ago Saltanat's mother came and conducted a conversation in whispers with her mother. Since then, her mother had looked like she was constantly mourning.

Oh, if only Saltanat were with her now! She could have shared these things with her, and Saltanat would have comforted her, right? Did Saltanat already know? Wouldn't she have said something in the cart if she knew? They talked the whole way, and she didn't say anything about this. Or could she have been hiding it? If she was hiding it, was she really Zebi's friend? What kind of friend is that?

As seen in this passage, bodily communication inadequately replaces speech. Saltanat says only one word, mingboshi, and expresses her thoughts largely through looks and embraces. Saltanat's embrace, meant to relay her remorse and misery at not sharing her secret with her friend, fails to achieve its goal. At the time of the embrace, Zebi is dumbfounded, and later she understands only betrayal in that hug and not Saltanat's perhaps misguided, but well-meaning intentions. Saltanat, to Zebi's chagrin, does not speak to her.

The characters' ignorance of their surroundings and themselves is further reflected in the way Cho'lpon describes actions. A surprising number of the main characters' movements are depicted as involuntary. Cho'lpon, for example, describes Zebi's unwitting attraction to the young O'lmasjon with the following: "at that moment, her voice became alien to her. The voice producing those words sounded to her ear as if it came from the far side of the creek." Like many of Cho'lpon's characters, Zebi cannot account for her own actions. Zebi often feels as if another entity has control over her, such that she acts contrary to her will.

Cho'lpon's narrator openly sympathizes with his characters, but also criticizes and mourns their lack of self-consciousness. He inserts himself into the story to mourn Zebi's situation and the societal imprisonment of women:

Why don't the poor women who grow up inside four walls, who don't see anything other than the sharp looks of those permitted inside, sense the tragedy of their sheltered lives? If they are so used to seeking little joys inside their four walls, can these poor things ever believe that the shameful joys which wander in from outside are part of something greater?

The narrator's interruption here is little different than the work his lyric persona performs in his poetry. We have already seen how Cho'lpon's lyric persona bewails his war-torn homeland in his 1921 poem "To a Devastated Land" by likening it to a silent, slavish woman, and here we see the same rhetorical strategy.

Ignorance becomes a structuring device not just through Cho'lpon's prose style and narration, but also through plot structure. Misjudgment, miscommunication, and misrecognition provide most of the turns in the narrative. Akbarali's youngest wife, Sultonxon, invites Zebi to her house without grasping the consequences—that Akbarali will fall in love with Zebi and that Sultonxon will lose her status as favorite wife. Zebi's father warns her not to sing during her trip to the village, but losing herself in the moment she releases her voice, which leads to her eventual marriage to Akbarali. One of Akbarali's elder wives, Poshshaxon, mistakenly murders him when she intends to poison Zebi, which leads to the novel's climactic trial. Miryoqub and Maria constantly misunderstand one another, unable to speak the same language. Each mistake draws the characters out of their usual environment and transforms them. Sultonxon, a naïve young girl, realizes the pain of her elder co-wives. Zebi, a poor girl at the beginning of the novel, is forced into a life of luxury with a man who revolts her. Miryoqub and Maria wind up married after a disastrous misunderstanding, which should have separated them forever: Miryoqub gives Maria a check, signifying, to him, his loyalty but, to her, that he sees her only as a prostitute. That such mistakes, even at the novel's conclusion, continue to dictate the action, undermines the sense of closure that the epiphanies experienced by characters in the course of the novel may suggest.

Because incomplete epiphanies play a role throughout the novel, we should regard Miryoqub's conversion to jadidism, the conversion which both Soviet and post-Soviet authors have cited as evidence of Cho'lpon's anti-Soviet stance, as an unfinished transformation and not necessarily a product of Cho'lpon's antagonism towards the Soviet Union. Miryoqub is, at times, as Soviet critics accused, a scheming capitalist, a sexual profligate, and very nearly a jadid, but Cho'lpon's narrative emphasizes the ephemeralness of these identities and denies them authorial approval. Miryoqub undergoes a number of epiphanies based on the contradictory advice he receives from various interlocutors and as a result of his own self-questioning. In several episodes that take place only in his mind, his self is split in two, and one half of Miryoqub submits the other to an eerily prescient interrogation à la the NKVD. Cho'lpon no doubt knew about the many secret police arrests and questionings of the late 1920s and early 1930s, but the interrogation in the novel has literary precedent, as discussed below. Interrogator-Miryoqub attacks his other self for his sexual licentiousness and callousness toward women, but in those interrogations, the Miryoqubs' capitalistic inclinations always win out. The defendant Miryoqub justifies his every transgressive sexual act by arguing for his lack of choice in the matter or by suggesting it as merely a way towards greater wealth, which appeases the money-grubbing interrogator. Miryoqub assuages his conscience of his guilt in several matters by persuading his greedy interrogator, but the reader senses that Miryoqub is letting himself off easy with unconvincing arguments. Miryoqub, Cho'lpon therefore hints, will have further epiphanies still.

Those familiar with jadid literature once again doubt the conclusiveness of Miryoqub's epiphany when he meets the jadid Sharafuddin Xo'jaev and seemingly becomes a jadid. His conversion to jadidism is noticeably undermined by the parodic nature of the text in this episode. Because Miryoqub and Maria cannot communicate with one another—neither know the other's language— Cho'lpon formats the pair's meeting with the jadid Xo'jaev in a train headed to Moscow as a series of hypothetical diary entries, the collection of which he calls a *sarguzashtnoma* (travelogue). The travelogue genre went by many names in Turkic and Persian Central Asian letters. Zokirjon Xolmuhammad o'g'li Furqat (1859–1909), a generation previous to the jadids, is the only writer to use the term sarguzashtnoma, but whatever its name, the travelogue genre in jadid letters had a few fixed attributes which proved ripe for Cho'lpon's parody.[86] Jadid travelogues are monologic texts: they beat their readers over the head with an uncompromising view of progress and ruthlessly criticize Central Asian society by comparison with others. Cho'lpon's sarguzashtnoma parodies these previous travelogues by way of its dialogism. The jadid Xo'jaev, more pamphlet than person, speaks like the narrator of these travelogues: he praises the benefits of education through European examples and berates the backwardness of his countrymen. But his speech passes through the prism of Miryoqub's hypothetical diary in which Miryoqub questions and misunderstands him. At the end of their encounter, Miryoqub notes that he does not entirely trust jadids:

> Now I will never say that the path of our fathers is the only one. But I can't
> say that the jadids are right either. Though I do understand what the jadids

---

86 Jadid authors employed a variety of terms to designate their travelogues. Mahmudho'ja Behbudiy called his *sayohat xotiralari* (travel reminiscences) and Fitrat—*bayonoti sayyohi hindi* (notes of an Indian traveler). Fitrat's text is a fictional travelogue of an Indian traveler who visits Bukhara.

have to say more easily and quickly than what others say. Is it just that they talk well?

Cho'lpon's sarguzashtnoma furthers his parody of this genre of Muslim reform through yet another level of dialogism. Xo'jaev's diatribes are read opposite Maria's hypothetical diary, which often directly contradicts the jadid's rhetoric. Xo'jaev implores Miryoqub to idolize Maria as a culturally superior individual because of her Russian background. She, Xo'jaev argues, will teach Miryoqub and his children to be cultured and educated individuals. But Maria's hypothetical diary entries show us her utter ambivalence to culture and education. At times, she desires a more enlightened Miryoqub, and at others, she envies his new relationship with Xo'jaev:

> I've been reading my fortune and "unhappiness" keeps coming up. Not promising. He's going to take my Jakob [Maria's name for Miryoqub— C. F.] away! Is there anything worse than this culture? That cultured *sart* does nothing but talk from morning to evening.

As is common in Cho'lpon's treatment of women, here Maria exhibits a fickleness that undermines readers' impression of her character, but this time it also undermines Xo'jaev's confidence in Maria's cultural superiority. Central Asian jadids often condemned Muslim women as ignorant for their engagement with superstitions and magic. Ironically, the Russian woman Maria's fortune-telling with her cards is just the kind of "backward" behavior that a jadid like Xo'jaev would have condemned in Muslim women. Likewise, Xo'jaev rants about the vices of Tashkent, among them prostitution, as instruments that deprive Muslims of their agency, and yet he praises Maria, who, unbeknownst to him, is a former prostitute. Cho'lpon's support of his jadid character and Miryoqub's conversion to jadidism is hardly without irony and ambiguity.

Not only does Cho'lpon parody and ironize jadid rhetoric in the novel, but he also plainly paints Xo'jaev and the novel's other Muslim reformer character, the inspector of village credit unions, Hasanov, negatively, imbuing them with the fictitious anti-Soviet qualities for which jadids were condemned in the late 1920s and 1930s. In the train, Xo'jaev repeatedly attacks Russians as the absolute enemies of Muslims, a chauvinistic view more consistent with the negative Soviet portrait of jadids than actual jadid thought. Cho'lpon's Xo'jaev says of Russians:

> We hate those people. They are our enemies! They are our enemies in every sense! It's not so often that we find a friend from among them. But those that we do find are good. Very good friends. But when we embrace them, we're always ready to escape their clutches!

Jadids indeed disliked the illiberalism of the Russian Empire and naturally blamed colonialism for many of the ills, such as alcohol and prostitution, that they believed had poisoned Turkestani youth. However, their presentations of Europeans, Russian or otherwise, as Adeeb Khalid notes, were "uniformly positive."[87] Attacks on Russians like Xo'jaev's above are characteristic largely of the jadids of the Soviet imagination. Hasanov similarly embodies an anachronistic Soviet impression of jadids. He belittles Akbarali mingboshi for his blind adherence to the tsarist state, hinting that the mingboshi's loyalties should lie instead with Turkestanis' coethnic and coreligionist Ottoman Turks. In reality, jadids had sympathies for the Ottomans, but the majority of them remained steadfastly faithful to the Romanov Empire. They felt their show of allegiance would raise the status of their community in the empire, which would then permit more Turkestani participation in Russian political life.[88] To show them as supporters of the Ottoman Turks again discloses an anachronistic Soviet view. By giving his jadid characters such ahistorical negative characteristics, Cho'lpon's novel clearly suggests that we should doubt Miryoqub's acceptance of jadid ideas.

Even as the capitalist and temporarily jadid Miryoqub angered Stalinist critics in 1937, we should note that Cho'lpon's psychological prose was entirely consonant with the prose of the Russian Association of Proletarian Writers (RAPP), the dominant literary organization in the Soviet Union until the inauguration of Socialist Realism in 1932. RAPP, contrary to the demands of later Socialist Realism, prized deeply psychological writing. In his 1928 monograph, Vladimir Yermilov, a leading RAPP critic, entreated proletarian writers to "illuminate and electrify the vast and humid cellar of the subconscious."[89] Doubt, indecisiveness, and fickle minds were the stock-in-trade of proletarian writers. In introducing a character like Miryoqub, Cho'lpon was no different than many other Soviet writers who wrote for RAPP.

---

87   Khalid, *The Politics of Muslim Cultural Reform: Jadidism in Central Asia*, 138.

88   Ibid., 235–243.

89   Quoted in Evgeny Dobrenko, "Literary Criticism and the Transformation of the Literary Field during the Cultural Revolution, 1928–1932," in *A History of Russian Literary Theory and Criticism* (Pittsburgh: University of Pittsburgh Press, 2014), 51.

In fact, Cho'lpon almost certainly borrowed from a proletarian text popular in early 1930s Uzbekistan in crafting his Miryoqub. In 1932, the head of the Uzbek Writers' Union, Rahmat Majidiy held up Russian and Ukrainian writing as models for Uzbek prose writers and singled out for praise *The Valley* (1929), the novel of Ukrainian VUSPP (the Ukrainian division of RAPP) writer Ivan Le.[90] Written thanks to Le's time in Uzbekistan, *The Valley* follows the Uzbek socialist Saidali as he constructs an irrigation system in the Ferghana valley.[91] Saidali falls in love with a married Russian woman and finds himself in an internal dialogue in which two parts of his self pit his socialist pedigree against his lustful urges. Le's psychological doubling of his Saidali should be familiar to any reader of Cho'lpon's novel. As Le writes:

Two Saidalis began to heatedly and passionately argue:

"I've taken this woman from another man for myself, a woman who doesn't concern herself with the tasks of the party and the people, a woman who decorates herself, a petty bourgeois who walks around wagging her tail. The shame of class inequality, of not having paid my party dues for two months, of not being on the party list for two months. I've surrendered my ideology and my purity." This new Saidali, who looked soft and inexperienced, began to contemplate things he had never thought about before.

But the broad-shouldered, strong Saidali's body put a stop to any excessive softening of his character. It wasn't a second person, but just a dark cloud that had lowered over the corporeal Saidali.

"I haven't lost my cold nature, my dedication without my party membership. I still go to meetings every day, I still give reports. My briefcase

---

90 Nina Nad'iarnykh, *Ivan Le: Krytyko-Biografichnyi Narys* (Kyiv: Radians'kyi pys'mennyk, 1967), 79. Just two years later, Majidiy would harshly criticize Le for a positive jadid character in the novel. See Rahmat Majidiy, "Doklad R. Majidiy o literature uzbekskoi SSR," in *Pervyi vessoiuznyi s'ezd sovetskikh pisatelei, 1934: Stenograficheskii otchet* (Moskva: Sovetskii pisatel', 1990), 127–128.

Cho'lpon could have encountered Le's novel while in Uzbekistan from 1930 to 1932 or during his second stint in Moscow from 1932 to 1934. An E. G. Grigor'ev translated the novel into Russian in 1930. See Ivan Le, *Roman mezhgor'ia*, ed. A. Chernenko, trans. E. G. Grigor'ev (Khar'kov: Proletar, 1930). Le brought the novel to Uzbekistan in 1928 or 1929 where he found a translator for it. The translation into Uzbek was published in 1933. See Ivan Le, *Tog' oraliqlari*, trans. Abdulla Qahhor (Toshkent-Samarqand: O'zdavnashr, 1932). Thus, for Majidiy to have known about it in 1932, Russian-language copies or translation drafts must have been available in Uzbekistan.

91 Ivan Le, "Hamza," *Sharq yulduzi* 11 (1959): 98–101.

hasn't left my arm. The time for relaxing has passed. We will let them bring the masses to work, awaken them on their own initiative. After all, they aren't made of stone."[92] [...]

"The two of us. ..." Lyuba searched for the right words. "You're an Uzbek, and I'm ... ," and she was silent. She realized that she had already said too much. Crushed by this mad white woman, he was licking his wounds.

Anger and hopelessness sparked in his eyes. It was as if something that had been cohesively joined had suddenly split. He himself had been shattered and broken; deprived of hope, he searched for shelter. Saidali began to lose himself from the pain.

"Uzbek! Asian! A black! You just needed some kind of prostitute to fill your need for 'culture'? You know, you Europeans ..."—he couldn't finish his sentence. A nearly forgotten sound was barely audible in his ears: "cut her throat." And he started searching his belt for his knife.[93]

Saidali's love, he believes, is a betrayal of his ideological credo. It takes him away from his party duties and makes him question his values. He contemplates whether he will remake himself or remake her. Notably, Saidali accuses Lyuba of essentializing and exoticizing him; she, he alleges, makes him into a "prostitute" for her "cultural tourism." Cho'lpon imbues his Miryoqub with this same conflict, only he inverts Le's formulation. Miryoqub's doubling leads to an interrogation of himself by himself and eventually a discussion about raising his "cultural level," which will supposedly transform his Asiatic, lustful nature and unite him with a Russian woman, herself a prostitute.

> "Oh, Miryoqub! Sly Miryoqub! Tricky Miryoqub! Miryoqub, you fox! You devil, Miryoqub! Miryoqub, you are a slave, you are depraved and shameful! Have you ever bowed your proud head in your life, have you ever abandoned your dog [meaning his sexual lust] for even a second? Is that it? If you're a dog, then don't hurry, you'll still have time to jump on your bitch. You'll have time. You have the money! That money can buy you whatever you want. You have enough to have an unending chain of pleasures to satisfy your canine urges!"

---

92 Le, *Tog' oraliqlari*, 31. I translate from the Uzbek translation of the novel because I cannot locate the original 1929 Ukrainian novel or the 1930 Russian translation. Le republished the novel in 1957 but with substantial changes due to criticism. See Konstantin Trofimov, "Moi Drug Ivan Le," *Raduga* 12 (1987): 151–156.

93 Le, *Tog' oraliqlari*, 50.

"The seventh [girl] is yours! Yours! That tender creature has nothing but you now! That woman is yours now! You can't have her like a prostitute anymore! You can't hurt her! You can't destroy her hopes! She looks at you as a man now; you're no longer a client; you've managed to get rid of that impression. Do you hear her voice? This is not the voice of a depraved woman waiting for her next buyer. That's the sad song of a woman who curses her fate. The song is not one of lust! It is the innocent song of a woman waiting for her bridegroom! It is the song of a young creature who has finally been linked with her love! The grateful melody of a mother bird who has returned to her nest! Miryoqub! Miryoqub! Miryoqub!"

Miryoqub was now two: one is fleeing, the other pursuing; this escape and pursuit between his two selves had him panting by the time he reached *noyib to'ra*'s home and rang the bell. [...]

[Maryam thought,] "a cultured Jakob [Maryam's name for Miryoqub] is naturally better than a wild Asian Jakob who doesn't know Russian. He pulled me out of that swamp; now if he becomes a cultured person because of me, all the better!"

This intriguing play with doubles, psychological battles, mental interrogations, and questions of cultural belonging were not unique at the time, though Cho'lpon was the first to bring these ideas into the Uzbek canon. Despite the lack of socialist content in the novel, Cho'lpon wrote very much in line with the psychological prose put forward by contemporaneous proletarian novels.

Unfortunately, the absence of the second novel will always give rise to debate, but there is enough evidence in and around the present novel to suggest that Cho'lpon intended to make Miryoqub a socialist in the sequel, especially given the historical transformation of jadids themselves. Throughout the novel, it is suggested that only socialists have a program to destroy empire, while jadids are interested in its preservation for the purposes of developing the nation through capital accumulation. Historically this is true: jadids wanted Turkestani autonomy within a federated system like that proposed by the provincial government after the February Revolution. They had little interest in overturning economic relations and undoing the state. Only with the October Revolution did jadids become radicalized, seeing the Soviet state as a means to overcome all the ills of empire and colonialism (to questions of class they were largely indifferent). The early 1920s saw Central Asia become a hub for

anti-colonial discourse. Jadids and socialists exchanged ideas and strategies with visitors from the colonized and dominated world such as India,
Afghanistan, and Iran.[94] By the 1930s, when Cho'lpon wrote, former jadids
like himself were now familiar with Marxist teachings and knew, to an extent,
how to discuss them. Cho'lpon therefore anachronistically instils in his
Miryoqub both anti-colonial and anti-capitalistic tendencies alongside their
opposites. We see the potential for a socialist Miryoqub, when, despite all his
fears about the loss of his land and capital, he spontaneously vows to destroy
empire.

> "Very well, master. Tomorrow afternoon everything will be as you ask.
> We'll destroy the empire the day after tomorrow."
>
> "What do you mean?"
>
> "I meant we'll do away with lust ... sweet dreams, master! Goodbye,
> ladies!"

Miryoqub suddenly speaks of undoing empire because he, through his internal self-interrogations, has identified empire with lust. Through further such
interrogations, he later identifies lust with his capitalistic greed. After all, he for-
gives himself his promiscuity by justifying his multiple sexual partners as necessary for business transactions. As he undergoes his conversion to jadidism,
he attempts to do away with his lust and commit himself to one woman, Maria.
Given the transformation of many jadids into socialists and the focus of Uzbek
socialists in the 1920s on the matter of women's liberation, one might assume
then that Miryoqub's battle against lust will lead back through his chain of logic
such that he begins to attack capitalism and empire.

A prosopographical point adds credence to the argument that Miryoqub
would become a socialist in the sequel. Several prominent jadids married Russian
women before becoming socialists. Hamza, the penname of Hamza Hakimzoda
Niyoziy (1889–1929), became one of the most revered Uzbek socialists in the
late 1920s. After he was murdered in the Uzbekistani enclave of Shohimardon
in 1929, enterprising Uzbek socialists ignored his jadid background and canonized him as the first Uzbek Socialist Realist writer. Before 1912, he achieved
notoriety in his Central Asian community by marrying a Russian woman.[95] After
the revolution, Botu (the penname of Mahmud Hodiev (1904–1938) became
one of Fitrat's favorite pupils and a superior Uzbek poet. In 1923, he moved

---

94 Khalid, *Making Uzbekistan: Nation, Empire, and Revolution in the Early USSR*, 105.

95 David C. Montgomery, "'Shohimardon': Forging a Link in the Chain of Soviet Uzbek Literary Orthodoxy," *Central Asian Survey* 3, no. 1 (1984): 88.

to Moscow where he married a Russian woman, Valentina Petrovna Vasil'eva, and became a fervent socialist.[96] In Moscow, he began to condemn his former teacher and Cho'lpon, accusing them in the press of anti-Soviet positions.[97] In having Miryoqub marry Maria, Cho'lpon may have been following several prominent historical examples of jadids becoming socialists.

In fact, through Miryoqub's marriage to Maria, Cho'lpon may have intended the novel as something of an apology for himself. If Miryoqub is set on his way to becoming a socialist by marrying a Russian woman, then Cho'lpon was as well. While in Moscow in 1932, Cho'lpon married a Russian woman, a marriage which some Uzbek scholars have read rather cynically as Cho'lpon's way to deflect accusations of bourgeois nationalism.[98] Regardless of intent, this move coincides with his conversion to socialism in several respects. Cho'lpon married a Russian woman in the 1930s just as he began to produce new poetry in which he declared his optimism and pro-Soviet views. Cho'lpon may well have intended to explain his own slow conversion to socialism through the confused, ignorant Miryoqub, who, though at first duped by jadids, eventually becomes a socialist.

The second novel, should it ever be found, probably reads much like *A Modern Woman*: that is, nominally in support of socialism but creating more questions than answers by way of its inconclusiveness. A few of Cho'lpon's works in the 1920s include the deus ex machina endings sometimes employed by jadids, but it is difficult to believe that he could stretch such a minimalistic conclusion with a style so antithetical to his writing across the space of an entire novel. Cho'lpon's 1928 short story "The Baker Girl" (Novvoy qiz) includes just such a deus ex machina, and here the exception truly proves the rule of Cho'lpon's aesthetic. The story revolves around a young woman who was abused and raped by a man, O'lmasboy, before the revolution. As in *Night*, the narrator laments the girl's powerlessness and inability to rebel. Likewise, chremamorphism abounds as the narrator likens the girl to a sea and her rapist to an insurmountable mountain. Long, run-on sentences, again coincident with the prose of *Night*, describe her suffering in detail. The final chapter breaks with this style completely. The events take place after the revolution and are narrated in short, staccato sentences. At the conclusion, the girl appears in a Soviet court intent on bringing prerevolutionary criminals to justice. She takes the stand to face her rapist, but thanks to the Soviet Revolution she is no longer a victim: she is suddenly omnipotent. Instead of testifying and reliving the powerlessness

---

96 Salohiddin Mamajonov, "Alangali yillarning otashin shoiri," in *Yoz kuni* (Toshkent: G'afur G'ulom nomidagi Adabiyot va san'at nashriyoti, 1980), 5–6.

97 Khalid, *Making Uzbekistan: Nation, Empire, and Revolution in the Early USSR*, 333.

98 Karimov, *Abdulhamid Sulaymon o'g'li Cho'lpon*, 32.

of the past, she releases a powerful scream that knocks O'lmasboy off his feet. Returning to the story's central metaphor, Cho'lpon emphasizes the seemingly impossible and thus miraculous nature of the act: "the sea, formerly silent and obedient like a slave, spoke [...] the mountain crumbled."[99] Such an ending might fit a short story but could not suit an entire novel.

Day most likely reads like *Night*, full of misunderstandings and a lack of self-knowledge, the only difference being that the action takes place after the revolution. It is also possible, though less likely given Cho'lpon's other works in the 1920s and 1930s, that *Day* could simply have been an artistic failure much like the second volume of Gogol's *Dead Souls* (1842). Unable to write the story of the righteous in a way that, in his own assessment, matched his brilliant satire of the wicked, Gogol burned the manuscript of his sequel. Accustomed as he was to the rhetoric of elegy and satire, Cho'lpon may have found it impossible to describe a new, post-ignorance era.

While the question of what Cho'lpon wrote in his sequel will likely remain the subject of speculation, the present novel may well suit Cho'lpon's aesthetic best in its incomplete form. Working through the literature of his jadid predecessors, Cho'lpon early in his career came to the conclusion that his and their art emerged from the perpetuation of the very state of ignorance that jadids maligned. Realizing this aesthetic plan in *Night* and in his other works such as *A Modern Woman*, Cho'lpon celebrates the ignorance of his characters by reveling in the misunderstandings that result from it. Many of his characters, particularly the men, undergo epiphanies, but these epiphanies are ultimately fleeting and inconclusive, undermined by the irony and parody that the author employs. Though by the 1930s Cho'lpon most certainly intended to demonstrate in his work that he now supported Soviet ideology, we only see that support through his use of irony. He ironizes his presentation of jadids in the novel and parodies their literature, which necessitates doubt in Miryoqub's conversion to jadidism. Ultimately, *Night* concludes in the same way as Cho'lpon's "Someone's Dream," in which he first articulated his aesthetic. Just as the lyric persona remains in dream (i.e. ignorance) and is crushed by a tragic death, Zebi is crushed by the weight of the Russian state for a crime of which she had no knowledge. She does not awaken to a bright future, and even by the end of the trial in which she is convicted of murder, she does not fully understand what has happened to her. Whatever

---

99 Abdulhamid Sulaymon o'g'li Cho'lpon, "Novvoy qiz," in *Asarlar: to'rt jildlik*, vol. 2 (Toshkent: Akademnashr, 2016), 352.

the second novel *Day* might have contained, *Night* fully accords with the prolongation of ignorance that is Cho'lpon's aesthetic.

I hope that with this translation, new minds will begin to grapple with Central Asian literature and provide innovative responses to Cho'lpon, his novel, and the literature and politics of both his time and ours. This novel raises many questions, only a few of which I have been able to answer here, but I am confident that with *Night* translated into English, students of the region and of literature will give the novel still more thorough treatments than mine.

Christopher Fort

SUGGESTIONS FOR FURTHER READING

Allworth, Edward. *The Preoccupations of Abdalrauf Fitrat, Bukharan Nonconformist: An Analysis and List of His Writings*. Berlin: Das Arabische Buch, 2000.

———. *Evading Reality: The Devices of Abdalrauf Fitrat, Modern Central Asian Reformist*. Leiden: Brill, 2002.

Brower, Daniel. *Turkestan and the Fate of the Russian Empire*. New York: Routledge, 2003.

Deweese, Devin. "It was a Dark and Stagnant Night ('til the Jadids Brought the Light): Clichés, Biases, and False Dichotomies in the Intellectual History of Central Asia." *Journal of the Economic and Social History of the Orient* 59, no. 1–2 (2016): 37–92.

Frank, Allen J. *Bukhara and the Muslims of Russia: Sufism, Education, and the Paradox of Islamic Prestige*. Leiden: Brill, 2012.

Hayit, Baymirza. "Two Outstanding Figures in Modern Uzbek Literature: Qadiri and Cholpan." *Journal of the Royal Asiatic Society* 52, no. 1 (1965): 49–52.

Ismailov, Hamid. *The Devil's Dance*. Translated by Donald Rayfield. Sheffield: Tilted Axis Press, 2018.

Kamp, Marianne. *The New Woman in Uzbekistan*. Seattle: University of Washington Press, 2006.

Khalid, Adeeb. *The Politics of Muslim Cultural Reform: Jadidism in Central Asia*. Berkeley: University of California Press, 1998.

———. *Islam after Communism: Religion and Politics in Central Asia*. Berkeley: University of California Press, 2014.

———. *Making Uzbekistan: Nation, Empire, and Revolution in the Early USSR*. Ithaca: Cornell University Press, 2015.

Northrop, Douglas. *Veiled Empire: Gender and Power in Stalinist Central Asia*. Ithaca: Cornell University Press, 2003.

Sartori, Paolo. *Visions of Justice: Sharīʿa and Cultural Change in Russian Central Asia*. Leiden: Brill, 2016.

Sahadeo, Jeff. *Russian Colonial Society in Tashkent, 1865–1923*. Bloomington: Indiana University Press, 2007.

Night and Day: Night First Book[1]

> When spring comes, the work begins.[2]
>
> —Folk saying

1

Every year the coming of spring joy tickles hearts. Warm blood rushes to nature's trembling bodies once again.

The ever-so-green *sochpopuks* of the willows begin to quiver like a young woman's intricate braids. Under the ice the somber cheeks of the murky running waters begin to smile; the water, though tired and limping, like a freed slave, begins to gnaw its way forward towards the satisfaction of liberty. Birds begin to appear one by one at the ends of branches. The first bird of spring brings the pleasure of the season's first well-fried corn. Planted last year, the cobs have just recently poked their heads out from that kohl root that will be applied above the eyes. Oh, how that green of spring, which not long ago emerged from wintry ice that melts in warm hands, so loves to lie on the courtyard platform of the eyes.[3]

---

1 The 1988 serial publication of the novel contains as its first epigraph the following citation, perhaps more a paraphrase, taken from Gorky's 1931 article "For Labor."

> Knowledge is obtained by comparison, our youth has no perspective on what it sees; young people do not know the past and for that reason they do not understand the present.

The text printed in Cho'lpon's lifetime did not contain this epigraph, and neither do versions of the text printed after 1988.

2 The folk saying "*hamal keldi, amal keldi*" indicates that spring has come, *Hamal* being the first month of the year (March 22 to April 21) according to the solar Hijri calendar.

3 Traditional sedentary Central Asian homes, which are often walled-in compounds with an enclosed building serving as one of the four walls, contain platforms, *supa*, in the courtyard on which residents sleep or relax in the summer. The use of the courtyard platform here con-

Oh, how the cool wind that playfully toys with those bare women[4]—with their hair and their curls, with the ends of their headscarves—never touches the flower-embroidered skullcaps of men. Spring frolics in the revelation of its beauty.

Why is life so beautiful and sweet in spring?

....

Zebi's soul had felt compressed all winter, as if rusting, but it began to expand with spring's warmth. She had just begun thirsting to ride out into the fields and meadows in a horse-drawn cart, even one covered in straw. The chain of matchmakers that poured into her house uninterruptedly all winter had stopped momentarily for the last one to two weeks, and now the creak of a door, the slow steps of a woman, and the rustle of a *paranji* no longer terrified her young heart.

Ever since she had seen a few farms and some wide courtyards, though her family lived in the city, her heart had started to long for the fields and meadows, for faraway places.

Her father hadn't yet returned from the morning prayer, her mother was busy milking the cow, and she was sweeping their small courtyard. The sudden opening of the outside door set her heart aflutter. In one hand she held her broom, the other hand was on her knee, she stared intently at the open door. It couldn't have been her father since not much time had passed since he had left for the prayer, having closed the big door on a heavy chain while coughing and clearing his throat as usual. This man, who couldn't tell *haram* from *halal*, had the habit of sitting for a long time at prayer, staying to put out the candles in the mosque long after others had left.

Through the door hurried in a young girl Zebi's age. This girl, still not yet a woman, wore a paranji that older women had wrapped over her to protect her from wandering eyes. The long hems of the paranji enclosed her girlish arms like a well-kept secret.

The tightly covered girl, entering the female side of the house almost jumping, threw off her paranji, and, full of youthful energy, ran up to Zebi and embraced her. The two of them looked at each other rejoicing. Zebi laid her

---

tinues the metaphor equating natural and cultural life by suggesting that the *supa* is the plane created by the kohl line which women drew to connect their eyebrows, a traditional sign of beauty.

4 Here the author uses "bare" to mean uncovered women. In a homosocial setting, women were not required to cover themselves, whereas they would be if men outside the family were present.

broom on the ground without returning it to its place. Their cheeks bright, hearts bursting, they took one another by the hand and headed towards the porch to sit together in Zebi's father's place.

Saltanat still hadn't explained why she had arrived at Zebi's home panting and exhausted so early. They were engrossed in each other, in sharing *mahram* secrets, in advising one another how best to sew designs and stuff skull caps with paper. Saltanat suddenly opened up regarding her arrival:

"I didn't rush here so early without a reason. ..."

"I sensed it. ... My heart fluttered."

"Why, friend?"

"Those terrible matchmakers, you know. ... They came without end all winter."

"I am sick of them too, they're exhausting. That's why I came to invite you to the village."

"Oh, what a wonderful idea! The water in the canals has already peeped out from under the ice."

Zebi's face was filled with all the signs of her winter fatigue. Her tired eyes, which stared so intently at the stitches in the blankets underneath her, were cloudy like glass under warm breath. Saltanat's face, on the other hand, like a shining star, was full of contentment and happiness, far from any worry, and reflected the waves of joy escaping from the deepest corners of her heart. She couldn't sense the heavy despair in Zebi's words. Although her eyes were on Zebi, her thoughts were in another place altogether.

"Do you know Enaxon? My friend in Yoyilmasoy?"

Zebi lifted her head and looked at her friend. That look showed that she couldn't remember Enaxon. Saltanat added, "Last fall, do you remember, she came to us with her sister-in-law? At that time, I invited several guests, but you didn't come, your father didn't reply to my invitation. ..."

Zebi shook her head.

"Yes, yes ... I know, I know. I didn't see her myself, but I heard."

"When she came that fall, her sister-in-law invited me to visit her in return. I've been planning to go as soon as spring came. She just recently reminded me. I'm going there with some other girls soon. I'll take you with me."

"When?"

Saltanat understood a good deal from Zebi's short question. That question alone showed that, if she could, Zebi would that very day take her paranji (without putting it on!) and rush as far away from her home as possible. Realizing this, Saltanat said, "I want to take you with me, dear friend!"

And the two young girls once again embraced each other in their boundless happiness.

....

A mother's heart is usually tender. Zebi's mother, as soon as she heard Saltanat's invitation, gave her consent.

"Very well, go be free and frolic. Winter has made your hearts tense. ... Young things. But ..."

Zebi knew her mother's answer well ahead of time. Qurvonbibi was a mother who wanted nothing but her daughter's happiness. She wished and truly desired everything good and beneficial in the world for her only daughter. "But ..."

The poor girls didn't have a chance to bring to crest again their waves of joy when Zebi's mother added that "but" to her words of agreement.

They all fell silent. Each of them saw a singular impediment before their eyes: Zebi—her father, Qurvonbibi—her husband, and Saltanat from beneath her eyelids saw the old man as cold as snow.

Only a mother can clear such cloudy weather.

"When your father comes from his morning prayers," she said looking at Saltanat, "let me try to reason with him. He won't refuse me." Then she looked at Zebi: "You, dear, prepare the house, see your friend in, and set the table. I'll speak with your father over tea and tell him what you told me."

The girls remained silent because both knew Razzoq-sufi's character well. To get him to accept even the most agreeable of things one had either to be his master or be wealthy. The man had never listened to a single word of advice from his equals. For Razzoq to accept advice from women, or, to be precise, one little suggestion from his wife, he would have had to be remade from head to toe.

For that reason, Zebi's eyes grew wide with worry as she stood silently in the house. She began to cry.

After she prepared the table for breakfast, she stuffed tea leaves into the pot by the hearth.

"No word of father?" she asked her mother. Qurvonbibi, after looking first at the door to the street, at the sun rising up between the trees next to the door, and then at her daughter by the hearth, answered.

"I don't know. Could prayers have gone late? Put the tea down quickly, finish sweeping the spots you missed, and come here."

Though she had no desire to take up the broom again, she dreaded that her friend might think that she wasn't an obedient daughter. She silently took the broom in one hand, put her other hand on her knee, and started to sweep the ground. Having waited for Zebi to start the tea, Saltanat got up from her place behind the table in the house and went out to check on her friend. Zebi ran up to meet her and apologized.

"Friend," she said, "Father is still at prayers. That's his way. He should come any minute. Don't be upset."

The sincerity with which Zebi uttered her request could only be expressed between young girls in a close friendship. One had to see Zebi's face as she said that "don't be upset" with the broom in one hand and the other hand on her knee, never lifting the broom from the ground and only holding her head up to know that her whole being was submitted to Saltanat's will. Her soul, her aspirations, her love, her joy. All of these flew towards Saltanat; they were shot at her, they wrapped her up, moved her, embraced her! Zebi's face, clear as the moon and bright as the sun, openly revealed the truth of her being.

Saltanat didn't see her friend's sincerity with her eyes, but understood it through her heart. She understood so well that she didn't bother to answer Zebi, but suddenly grabbed the broom in her friend's hands. She knew that if she could take the broom and sweep some for her friend, then that would be a sufficient response to Zebi's sincerity. Zebi released the broom, but quickly said, "Voy, what are you doing! Put it down, I'll do it myself!" and seized the broom. Saltanat didn't give it back; Saltanat ran, she chased; lost in themselves, instead of sweeping the courtyard the two friends turned Zebi's home on its head, their noise and shouting disturbing their whole world as they chased one another.

Razzoq-sufi, who preferred the quiet of a graveyard, the silence of a mosque, whose very soul was coarse and frowning, returned to this chaos!

A voice emerged from the doorway: "What is this hell?!" he bellowed like lightning striking a tree, petrifying the two young girls in their places. Qurvon-bibi, ever faithful to her husband, had already shouted, "enough already!" a few times herself. If the cold old man hadn't returned, the two young girls' pent up tension from the long winter would have expanded with the warmth of spring and produced even more mischief. In fact, the girls had completely forgotten themselves. How could their games with one another not release the coiled spring of their agitation, not break the dam holding back the flood? To stop such madness from overflowing, of course, equally mad screams and thunderously powerful force were needed.

Razzoq-sufi had such power in excess. This man, as a *jadid* denizen of the city said of him, "was one of those ancient monsters put out for display." The old woman that shot him from her womb perfectly healthy and swaddled him for the first time was named Hamroh. She had a reputation for jokes and mischief. After swaddling him, she looked at the face of her child, which hadn't yet been disfigured by manhood, and coddled him with these words: "My dear guest, who has upset you? Who has hurt you? Tell me! Unfurrow your brow! You have come into the bright world! Give thanks! Be happy! Laugh a little! Smile! Grin!"

Razzoq-sufi, who hadn't laughed then, still has not laughed. There is a big difference between laughing and crying. There is again a great distance between laughing and maintaining quiet gravity. It cannot be said that Razzoq-sufi ever laughed.

He "laughed" in situations where laughter couldn't be avoided, but his laugh was pained like that of a sick person; it was unpleasant like a cold joke, injurious like false well wishes.

One day Zebi said with a serious face: "Father has never laughed." As soon as she heard her daughter's words, Qurvonbibi scolded her. She openly scolded her daughter for speaking the truth, but how many times had Qurvonbibi repeated the same truth to herself in secret? It is easy to speak of someone else's faults with a sharp tongue, but those who can speak of their own faults with their own tongue are rare, and though Qurvonbibi had a very sharp tongue, she couldn't count herself among that rare class.

As sharp as her tongue was, Razzoq-sufi was to the same extent a reticent, tight-lipped, boring man who kept to himself. In the outside world, that is the world outside his home, his sole, ever-present task was to answer "yes, yes" to those who were more powerful than he and to shake his head "no, no" to those less powerful. While he was at home, not one word that could be called mean-ingful, healthy speech which an adult uses around children ever left his lips. He didn't think it necessary to move his tongue in the presence of womenfolk, and his muteness before his family members was a point of pride. "This tongue," he told himself, "moves only in remembrance of God. This mouth opens only for God. The mouth and tongue are the dearest and most blessed parts of a believ-er's body. Should they really be embarrassed by being used in front of such a low creature as a woman? If they were meant to be used with women, then God on high would have granted dogs speech! No, only the most necessary phrases should be used with women. Those creatures should only be spoken with con-cerning the most urgent matters and that's all!"

Every Uzbek man calls his wife—his lawful partner in life—by his daughter or his son's name. It just won't do to call his wife by name. If his wife's name was Maryam and his daughter's Xadicha, a faithful Muslim wouldn't bring shame on himself. He would call his wife Xadicha. Most mother-daughter pairs would both answer, "yes, sir!" and the true head of the family would specify: "I mean the elder, the elder!" But he would never say Maryam.

Our Razzoq-sufi, our faithful Muslim didn't observe this tradition. He always called his lawful partner in life *Fitna*. "Fitna, bring me my turban!" he would declare. "Fitna, where is your damn daughter?" "Fitna, give me some money!"

Whether she caused havoc in her husband's life on purpose or it was just her nature, Fitna wasn't an inaccurate label for Qurvonbibi, who was no stranger to guile and perfidy. Even if she wasn't all that upset by the fact that her husband didn't speak a word in front of womenfolk, she suffered from his not speaking to her, and she knew how to use all manners of tricks to coax words from him and even excite his tongue into singing. With one word, she would not just upset her husband: she would enrage him. Just look at how Razzoq-sufi wags his tongue in front of the womenfolk! Oh my!

"They say your elder master is quite upset with you," Qurvonbibi said to Razzoq-sufi one day.

Razzoq-sufi's face, normally hard and motionless like a stone, suddenly came to life with various movements and changes.

"What did you say, Fitna? Why was he upset?"

"You flirted with a boy who came to have his braid cut. ..."[5]

That was it! Razzoq-sufi, normally a master of brevity, turned into a preacher.

"Love is of two kinds, Fitna. Don't speak of what you don't understand! There is miraculous love, true love."

---

5 It was a common practice in Islamic mysticism for the mystic to transcend his earthly bonds through contemplation of earthly beauty found in young boys and, more rarely, women. Male bodies were, in fact, considered superior objects of beauty for contemplation. In prominent Sufi writings and poetry, ʿishq, the unrequited love for these young boys and the accompanying anguish, often serves as a metaphor for the Sufi's quest to overcome the distance between himself and God. ʿIshq was not simply a metaphor, and many indeed acted on their lust; however, it was considered sinful to do so, hence Qurvonbibi's teasing. Despite the seeming taboo against homoerotic love, many engaged in the practice. See Najmabadi, *Women with Mustaches and Men without Beards: Gender and Sexual Anxieties of Iranian Modernity*, 17–19.
Late nineteenth- and early twentieth-century Muslim reformers like Cho'lpon, influenced by European sexual mores, began to condemn homoeroticism as well as adultery.

Qurvonbibi, not understanding her husband, suddenly became bored.

"Really, is that the case? I didn't know. I'm the ignoramus," she said, trying to avoid a long diatribe.

After his wife had turned around and left, Razzoq-sufi quieted down. Suffice it to say, when he became angry, he would talk himself into the grave. And oh, how he would talk!

When Razzoq-sufi was at home, he was usually picking weeds by the creek, locking the door and gates, cutting firewood; or, if not, he would continuously walk inside with his hands behind his back, then outside, then into the courtyard, keeping his mouth sealed shut as if his lips had been stung by bees. In the summer, he normally slept in the afternoon; in the evenings, he lay awake, screaming "idiot!" to himself in a loud voice so that neither his family nor his neighbors could sleep. On those days when his elder master wasn't present he, according to neighbors, would sit in the cool prayer hall and sleep with great satisfaction. Sometimes the other *murids* would throw him into the mosque's pool. When he was at home, he would cool the house, like he did his lodge, lie down, and if he had fallen asleep after the early afternoon prayer, he would just barely wake up in time for dinner, usually to the sound of Qurvonbibi's screaming. The late afternoon prayer usually fell victim to his naps, for which he heard all kinds of reproaches from his wife. But his tongue wasn't up to it, and he wouldn't say a word.

In the winter, he would fall asleep in the evenings. "If I spend the scarce winter daylight sleeping, how will I spend the winter evening that is longer than the Kashgar?[6] Sleep is life's measure!" he told himself.

He shared this philosophy only with worthy and dignified people. His poor family members and womenfolk in general were deprived of this great philosophy, derived from sleep!

If he was in the city, he never spent a night in a place other than his home. At whatever celebration his elder master was, he would come home towards dawn. He rarely went outside the city. Only together with his elder master (only with that one person!) did he go to celebrations, large parties, fruit and melon festivals. While at those events, his bed at home went cold for four to five days. In Qurvonbibi's words, "he is relaxing," and in Zebi's, "he is enjoying himself." One time, after one celebration dragged out nearly a week, on the sixth day our Razzoq-sufi left for home without asking his master! That left his elder master upset with him for quite some time.

---

6 A river in the Western Chinese province of Xinjiang.

With that in mind, Qurvonbibi pressed him on another occasion.

"Why did you run away from your master after you left together with him? You've seen all the respect he is given and received from him an abundance of blessings. Do you have a store in the city that didn't open on time or a watermill that suddenly stopped?"

Razzoq-sufi was forced to open his blessed mouth and wag his prized tongue in front of the lesser sex.

"Wretched Fitna! Will you let me alone or won't you already? *Ḥubb al-waṭan min al-Īmān*, that is, 'love of home comes from faith!' If you don't know that, you're hopeless. Only gypsies have no home in this world. Are you calling me homeless?"

Razzoq became a bit heated and continued.

"Do you want to say that because this house was your father's, that it is yours? If that's what you're saying, then I'll get a passport and get on the Russians' rails and I'll go to Mecca! May you lose your house, Fitna!"

This time Qurvonbibi begged and pleaded, just barely managing to talk him out of it.

Truthfully, Razzoq-sufi's desire to go on the *hajj* was strong. Every year he brought it up. Once or twice he even got a passport. Only, for some reason, he could never separate his feet from the soil of his city.

Regarding his reproach—"love of home comes from faith"—was it true that he really couldn't leave his "home"? There's a secret to that.

He did not have a single professional skill or craft. He neither traded, nor farmed, nor wrote for a living. Nevertheless, his table was never without bread and his pot was never cold.

One year his brother came from a faraway village for three to four days. Because he too was a faithful old man, they got on well. They went to the lodge every day together.

"Razzoq, do you really plan to pass your life without taking up any kind of work?" his brother asked him as they were leaving for the lodge.

"Heeey," said Razzoq-sufi, protracting his monosyllabic objection with a self-satisfied laugh, "no one has the wealth that I do, brother! Being my elder master's beloved servant, blessings flow like water from all four sides. Do we thirst at the river? You're a strange one!"

After they had gone a little farther laughing, Razzoq-sufi said seriously:

"My wife and daughter are tricky ones, thanks be to God. My daughter sews a skullcap, and it looks as if it was made in Europe! They deal with the household's needs. As long as I can lie down and turn my prayer beads, everything is fine!"

Razzoq-sufi's brother visited again a year prior to our story in the fall. This time a serious issue was raised. One or two days after the guest arrived they started conversing:

"Razzoq, you yourself say 'home, home,' but you don't know your own home."

Razzoq-sufi fumed at "you don't know." "Why don't I know, brother?! Please tell me!"

"Don't get angry. I'll tell you. Is your home not the place where your parents passed, where your umbilical blood was spilt, where you light a candle for the spirits of your parents?"

Razzoq-sufi was silent. Tears seemed to well up in his eyes.

"Why are you silent?" his brother asked.

"What can I say to the truth? You're amusing. …"

"In that case your home is our village."

"Yes, our village. …"

The two of them were silent for a moment. Razzoq-sufi took his tooth-brush out of its case but then slowly put it back. His brother took the autumn leaf that had fallen on his knee by its stem and twirled it, saying:

"I came to take you back to our village. We once fought over the land left to us by our parents, decided to split it, and then you left for the city."

Razzoq-sufi's voice wavered as he sighed:

"Why do you bring up what's already been decided? The past is the past. … Let the land dry up and the inheritance too."

"No, Razzoq! Don't speak that way!"

His brother's words were harsh like a command. Razzoq-sufi raised his head and looked straight into his brother's face. Razzoq's brother continued:

"Nothing is more precious than land! Our deceased father, our grandparents, our ancestors—all of them received their subsistence from that parcel of land. True?"

Razzoq-sufi responded, barely audibly, "True …"

"Why do you flee from the land?"

Razzoq-sufi couldn't manage another answer to this important question other than: "Where is there land for me? You have your parcel of land and it's not enough for you."

His brother gave a brave answer; while starting his answer, his face involuntarily smiled and his toothless, bare mouth opened with joy.

"I evened out the hill on the far side of the river and opened it up for planting. Now I just need labor and capital."

"What can I do?" asked Razzoq-sufi; his voice was very low. "What am I able to do?"

His brother became serious.

"Leave the city!"

Razzoq-sufi was going to say something to his brother's demand. His brother didn't let up.

"Don't dismiss me! Listen to what I have to say!"

Razzoq-sufi was silent. His brother continued:

"Leave the city! Sell your house! You can get good money for a house in the city. We'll find a small house in the village. We'll get it for half or even a third of that money. We'll use the rest on tools. We'll find another parcel of land close to ours. You're still healthy, we can work together. Right?"

Razzoq-sufi didn't utter a word; he took his white skullcap in his hands and began to fold it.

"Well, say something!"

Razzoq-sufi said nothing and got up. Without hesitating, he took two steps towards the inside of his house. Then he turned around and spoke.

"Let me put on my turban and robe. We'll read the Friday prayer in the lodge. We're late …"

As they were leaving for the lodge, his brother raised the question again.

"Just say it. We'll leave for the village! Death is what you should be thinking of! Let's not be far from one another when it comes time to die; let's not die thirsting for one another's company."

Razzoq-sufi pointed to a colt in the street.

"What a beast, hey, isn't that a fine horse? Oh my!"

Silence set in. Then he started speaking again.

"Well, what do you say? Will you answer my question?! Even an old woman prays aloud."

"Over there is the bathhouse of Umarali, the Kokand court official. It's been here for 170 years. Not one brick has been moved. … If you go inside, you can hear bells ringing. …"

His brother, unable to get his point across, asked Qurvonbibi for advice, who, in turn, sent him to Razzoq-sufi's master.

"Where is Razzoq himself?" the *eshon* asked.

"He is at home … his teeth hurt …," his brother answered.

The eshon laughed. "His teeth hurt? Oh no! A toothache is a frightful thing. Go tell him: go to the barber in the corner of the market, have him take his pincers and yank the bothersome tooth out. That will cure him. Go. Amen, God is great!"

With that Razzoq-sufi's brother became despondent and set out for his village. He mounted his horse and, while he said his goodbyes, Razzoq remained inside reading the *Book of Wisdom*.[7] Draping a headscarf over her face, Qurvonbibi saw him to the gate. With her long sleeve, she dried her tears and saw off her guest from the village. Standing next to her mother, Zebi sang loudly with her sweet voice, "Goodbye! Send aunt Adolatxon next time. Bring a gift." After the guest was out of sight, she asked her mother: "Why did father not come to see uncle off?"

Qurvonbibi gave a short answer, "Damn your father's character, child!" She turned to go back into the house.

Qurvonbibi had worries other than her brother-in-law. The village guest's arrival had only added to her troubles. Truthfully, poor Qurvonbibi was worried about clothing and material needs, but most of all, about her daughter's dowry. Those worries sat in her mind until her patience was exhausted and she would begin bickering with her husband. Razzoq-sufi had no tolerance for her bickering. He would respond with screaming, telling her "God will deliver!"

But is Qurvonbibi not human? Patience can be exhausted.

One day she broke out, saying, "God will deliver, of course! If his servant moves and desires, He will deliver! Don't they say, after all, that God created the means to ensure that deliverance? Your eshon's wife read to us from *Sufi Olloyor's book*;[8] a profession, he says, is a religious duty!"

Razzoq-sufi didn't give an answer to his wife's jabbering. Without a word, he turned away from her. Qurvonbibi didn't relent; she raised her voice further still. Razzoq-sufi almost let out one of his laconicisms, but decided it would be better to deal with it all at once—angrily he barked at her: "Enough, you bitch!"

....

The anxiety and nervousness playing lightly in Zebi's heart gained in strength with her father's pronouncement "What is this hell?!" Under the gaze of the cold sufi, who had interrupted her frolic, she felt like a bird whose cage,

---

7 The well-known book of Ahmad Yassavi, a Sufi and poet of the twelfth century who wrote in the Turki language of Central Asia rather than in Persian, the more popular court language. He was popularized as an Uzbek poet in Cho'lpon's time.

8 A religious tome called *Firmness of the Weak* regarding morality written by Sufi Olloyor (1644–1721), a poet and scholar trained in Bukhara, who wrote in the local Turkic tongue and was considered an Uzbek poet in Cho'lpon's time.

just at the moment that it expected the door to be opened, is put under a lock as big as its head.[9]

The anxiety of both girls, particularly Zebi, hit its peak as the sufi slammed the door. Had they not become absorbed in their game and forgotten everything around them? Had the misery left over from the black winter days, the congealed torment of living inside four walls for months, the suffering endured from their fathers, the troubles brought on by the matchmakers not reached an end? Had the powerful waves of youth not washed over and purified them like a spring rain? Confronted with her friend's sweet manner, had Zebi not forgotten about her strict, stubborn, backward father? Had Saltanat, when she took the fraying broom, not forgotten her parents, her home, and the promise she made upon leaving the house to return quickly?

They say the stick shames the most those whose heads it catches unaware. These two girls, caught up in their mischievous game, were certainly unaware. They came to after the sufi's club-like blow of a voice; he stood in front of them like a big mountain, and they were struck dumb despite themselves. The mountain would have to be climbed, but it wasn't one that young girls could ascend. The two read the great burden of their fear in one another's eyes.

After Razzoq's yell, the two of them ran hurriedly into the house, took cover behind the window, and started to observe Razzoq-sufi. Though their eyes were on him, their ears were trained on Qurvonbibi. Her words would either untie the tightly secured knot in their hearts or tighten it into a noose, and the two young things would be separated from one another for months.

Before coming into the house, Razzoq-sufi stopped by the door and turned starkly pale. He handed his turban to Qurvonbibi, took his yellow robe off and threw it on the table across the room. He said in his normal voice, that is, he screamed, "Bitches!"

"If young things play, what is the problem? Are you really that bothered by them?" said Qurvonbibi.

"Don't speak, ass!"

Qurvonbibi fell silent. Razzoq-sufi looked over towards the table. The table was set for breakfast, and a dish with bread and a teacup with jam sat upon it. He sat down at the table, while Qurvonbibi brought him tea from the hearth.

---

9 The original is unclear here, a fact which the editors of a recent edition of Cho'lpon's works attribute to a technical error at the printing press, stating that part of the sentence was cut off. I have done my best to render it based on context. See Abdulhamid Sulaymon o'g'li Cho'lpon, *Asarlar: To'rt jildlik*, 2:361.

Seeing the expression on Razzoq-sufi's face, what little optimism the two girls had disappeared. Zebi couldn't hide her hopelessness.

"We should just die now and forget fun. Now father will never let me go. ..."

Saltanat too expressed her worry.

"What can we do now? If you don't go, I won't go either. ... Enaxon will be upset!"

"If we had sat quietly, do you think he would have been lenient?" asked Zebi.

Saltanat said nothing. After a moment Zebi added:

"Damn him. I have never seen him be lenient. They say demons throw big stones into rivers. They must have thrown the biggest one on my father's chest. 'This is your heart,' they must have told him, wretched things!"

That last comparison affected Saltanat; she let out a chortle. Zebi quickly covered her friend's mouth.

"Voy, be careful now! You'll only make it worse!" she said.

Saltanat controlled herself only with difficulty. The two of them unblinkingly stared at the old man and woman.

The sudden laugh of the old woman, who had for some time been sitting silently and looking at her husband, returned some hope to the girls. "Did you see?" they mimed at one another.

Truthfully, Qurvonbibi, as if she was looking for a word her husband would approve of, kept smiling bravely and calmly. She started speaking.

"I want to send Zebi somewhere. ..."

Though Razzoq-sufi didn't yell this time, he asked coarsely and angrily:

"Where? Why?"

"Xalfa eshon's young daughters at Oydin lake invited a few friends to a 'spring welcoming' party. She invited Zebi and her friend Saltanat. Saltanat has a cart ready, she came here to tell Zebi. How can we say no?"

Razzoq-sufi, who normally said no, this time didn't say no but fell into thought. The girls were elated with Qurvonbibi's efforts and became hopeful.

"Qurvonbibi did it!" said Saltanat.

"My mother is a master of words. Look how she mentioned an eshon. You need only say 'eshon,' and my father wouldn't notice if he died. God made him for the eshons."

After Saltanat heard these words of Zebi's, she suddenly believed that Razzoq-sufi had said "ok." She threw her arms around Zebi and embraced her.

"That's it, friend, that's it! We're going!" she said.

"Don't count your chickens before they're hatched! My father is not a person to so easily agree to anything. Look at how silent he is: he still hasn't said a word."

After a lengthy silence Qurvonbibi made a serious face.

"Why don't you say something? Just say ok! You're a grown man. It's shameful. Some good women and some proper girls are there. If it's them you're worried about, you know them," she said.

Razzoq-sufi for some reason said, "I know, Fitna, I know," and became silent again.

Qurvonbibi took on a serious countenance once again.

"Then say no. Let me tell Saltanat so she can leave!" She's been here since morning. Suddenly her husband's tongue twitched.

"Wait, Fitna, don't tell her no—she should go. When will she come back?"

"The day after tomorrow in the morning or evening."

"Have her do as the eshon's wife wishes."

Razzoq-sufi got up from his place and put on his shoes.

"She shouldn't be singing while there," he said, "if *nomahram* people hear her voice, I am not agreed to it."

After his few words, Razzoq-sufi, who spoke like a real person this time to Qurvonbibi's joy, returned to his usual silence. A little later he donned his turban and took his robe in his hand.

"Bring me the farm bag, Fitna! If you can't find it, bring me two bags!" he yelled.

Just as Qurvonbibi handed him the bag, she sensed that her husband had come into some money and that his pleasant mood was due to thoughts of whatever he was going to buy.

Razzoq-sufi cleared his throat and left. The two mischievous girls in the house embraced each other once again.

....

The cage's little door had opened!

The bird's wings were spread: all that remained for them to do was to take flight with a coo into the open space, into the wide blue skies. They had to move quickly, throw on that paranji for all to see (that is, to not see), and get to the cart.

How could they not be elated at the opening of that little door? How could they not feel joy? How could they not taste the sweetness of freedom? How could they not be grateful for a mother who overcame such a stubborn man with a masterful solution? How could they not embrace her, kiss her?

The two girls ran out of the house and each hung themselves on Qurvon-bibi's neck in gratitude for her benevolence. Hurrying to express their appreciation in a measure equal to the act, they poured out their limitless joy. They so hung on the old woman, so nuzzled up to her, so roughly made her a part of their game that the old woman suddenly felt weak and tumbled onto the table. They screamed with the force of a whistling tea kettle. They so played with the old woman that she gasped for air from exhaustion and could barely breathe.

"Enough, you damn girls. Enough, I said, enough. You'll be late!" she said.

As the old woman begged, the two girls reached the apogee of their excitement. One let up while the other continued on. They teased each other:

"Is that how it is? Voy, repent! Xalfa eshon's daughter invited us? Voy, repent," they said as they tickled one another.

Finally, the girls were dead tired and they ceased to torture the old woman. They each sat down with an "uh!"

When they opened the door with a bang and hurried out into the street, the cotton factory let out a thin, piercing whistle signaling that it was twelve o'clock.

2

Saltanat's family prepared for their trip late into the evening. They prepared a flatbread and samosas. As they boarded the two-wheeled horse-drawn cart near the gates to Saltanat's home, the day began to recede. The cart exited the city and as it entered the steppe, the dark curtain of evening covered the face of the earth. The land, which had only just emerged from under the snow, now slumbered under the cool spring air and its pleasant breeze. The moon hadn't yet come out; only the countless stars, which disrupted the evening's darkness, shone over the hill like lit torches. The brightest star—so bright that it looked as if it were face-to-face with its onlookers—trembled as it burned like the eyes of a young girl cutting an onion.

The girls were silent. The cart driver, probably bored, slowly began a song. His bass voice was quiet, but Saltanat was roused.

"O'lmasjon, are you there? If you're going to sing, sing right!" Another friend of Saltanat's, Qumri, supported her, addressing the cart driver:

"Yes, what a beautiful voice you have. Won't you sing a little louder? The steppe is wide. The louder, the better."

O'lmasjon laughed. He carefully turned around in the darkness. Because the girls were sitting with their veils lifted, he could see some of their faces. He stood up with a smile and looked at the girls.

"Among you is a much-famed singer. Strange that you're so obsessed with me!" he said. "You must have thought that you needed to do ablutions with sand."

All the girls looked at Zebi. From every side, their voices rang out:

"Yes, true!"

"Truly. How could we just sit here without saying anything?!"

"There's a real voice among us."

Zebi sat without a peep. She had feared that they would call on her to sing. Of course, the strength of her desire to frolic, laugh, and enjoy herself was over-powering. But she was her father's daughter: it was her responsibility to restrain all kinds of strong desires, to suffocate the passion and desire of her will. Zebi was used to it. When she heard the young man refer to her, her body shivered. The compliments of her friends only added to her worries. She didn't know what to say. She had to give a considered response; she couldn't let temptation get the better of her. But in her agitation and nervousness.

O'lmasjon stood up.

"Yes, very good, she is among you! Bring your singer here!" he said.

Zebi finally moved her tongue, "Let's just talk. It's so dark!"

"What's gotten into you?" said one of the girls.

"It's not good, in this darkness … better to talk … just sweet, sweet words …"

O'lmasjon seized at these last words.

"Instead of those sweet, sweet words, it's better to sample a sweet, sweet song, sister. When we first heard about your voice, waves of blood rushed to our hearts."

Saltanat jokingly added, "Voy, repent you! Waves of blood? It must have been torture."

O'lmasjon didn't let up.

"It is in your power to relieve these blood-filled hearts with just one exhalation of song, sisters! We came into this world to enjoy ourselves, so let's do that!"

Saltanat this time begged the silent Zebi.

"Dear friend, would you just sing a little something? All of us are thirsty for your voice. …"

Zebi gently chided her friend: "How can you ask that? You heard with your own ears what my father said! What will happen if he hears? If he finds out …"

Saltanat stopped her friend:

"I know, friend, I know! I heard your father's words with both ears. If I were forcing you in front of a crowd of people, you would have the right to be upset. But we are in the steppe; there's no trace of other people in the dark of night. Won't you just sing a couplet or two?"

"And if some nomahram hears?"

Although Zebi said these words with conspicuous determination to keep her promise to her father, all the girls exploded with laughter. Again, voices rang out.

"And is this girl nomahram?"

"Is O'lmasjon?"

"What does it matter?"

Zebi was hurt. With a quivering voice, she turned to Saltanat:

"If I'd known you were going to do this, I wouldn't have come."

The girls, surprised to see that their request had so soured Zebi, became quiet. O'lmasjon whispered under his breadth, "Oh, what a pity!" before giving the horse a few cracks of the whip to get it moving.

The horse picked up its gait and the wheels of the cart started to rumble. Everyone was silent. Only Saltanat and Zebi whispered between themselves. Saltanat managed to calm her friend. Moreover, she managed a promise from Zebi that if the other girls began singing first, then Zebi would join.

Suddenly she turned to the other girls.

"Well, girls, let's sing ourselves!"

"Yes, that's right!" echoed the O'lmasjon.

Giving the other girls no time to answer, Saltanat started.

A long, long rope …

The other girls joined in:

For the swing.
A little dress for
The bride.
Fill the sleeves
With mulberry.

After a couple of lines Zebi's beautiful, powerful voice joined in, ringing out like tea striking an immaculately clean cup. That voice, like the brightest star shimmering in the night sky, quickly separated itself from the others. Having up to now listened to their song silently while urging the horse on, O'lmasjon, enamored with Zebi's voice, let out a sigh. He let the whip hang from his fingers like an autumn leaf from a tree branch.

Saltanat's perspicacity did not fail her; now Zebi was singing the wedding song alone. O'lmasjon and the other girls became all ears. The horse, listening intently to the sweet rhythms of her beautiful voice, lowered its head and began slowly swaying as it stepped. When the song ended and the girls moved on to other songs, Zebi couldn't be stopped. But really, who would have wanted to stop her? The soft winds coming in from the wide expanse of the steppe carried the sounds of the girl's voice on their wings to far away places. Oh, in the distance the flickering lights of a village, like the stars above, burned as though intoxicated with the captivating sounds that came over the wind.

Zebi had untied the tight knot that wound her being. She had escaped Razzoq-sufi's cold countenance and his watchful eyes; she had forgotten the words he had repeated so intently; all those things that her father dubbed haram suddenly scattered; all the nonsense about nomahram was trampled under the horse's hooves; this girl, imprisoned in the four walls of Razzoq-sufi's home, who knew nothing but her captivity, transformed the pain locked in her heart into a melody that filled the empty, boundless steppe.

The cart stopped in front of a small door. O'lmasjon knocked on the door with the hilt of his knout and the tiny, weak voice of an old woman called out "Who's there?" The village was already asleep.

....

O'lmasjon answered the old woman's question with a joke:

"I've brought a cart of guests from the city! Now your house is ruined! In two days, all your food will be gone! Now hurry up, open the door! Our stomachs are growling."

The girls laughed. When the old woman heard their giggling she suddenly understood who was asking.

"Ah, Saltanat, is that you?" she asked.

With that the girls heard the rustling of the small chain as it fell and the creaking of the door. Leaving the door half open, the old woman ran into the *ichkari* for *suyunchi*.

"Well, get off, girls!" O'lmasjon yelled triumphantly.

Only his command was unnecessary. Having heard the rustling of the chain, the girls had already begun to jump off the cart. Along with the old woman, and carrying lanterns that billowed smoke more than they illuminated anything, a girl about Zebi's age emerged from the house, rubbing her eyes: "Oh dear, I fell asleep! Oh no, sleep took me!"

"Oh, my dear! Enaxon! My best of friends! Is that you?" cried Saltanat, taking her paranji in her hand and running in. They embraced one another. After greeting each of the girls, Enaxon again took Saltanat by the hand, and the two of them headed inside. The voluminous voices of the two friends' reunion drowned out all other sounds.

But outside on the cart, a catastrophe was taking place, about which the two happy friends hadn't a clue.

Saltanat's mother and grandmother, knowing that they were sending their child to a faraway place, hadn't forgotten to take a few precautionary measures.

"Can we really send such young girls so far away by themselves? Can't one of us join them?" asked Saltanat's mother of her mother-in-law.

Her mother-in-law answered decisively: "Of course, my dear! If we let them go by themselves, we can't expect them to behave!"

The conversation between her elders hurt Saltanat, who was standing in front of the tandoor oven, baking a flatbread with Zebi, perspiring large droplets of dew-like sweat. She suddenly spoke up: "Will a wolf eat us? Why mix old women with girls? A person could die from the boredom of it!"

Her grandmother ignored her cheek. "My dear, my child, finish making your bread! You'll be late. This isn't your business!" she said and continued to advise her daughter-in-law.

Their conversation resulted in both women staying home. They sent Savribibi, an old woman who had been living near them for about two or three months, in their place, to be their eyes and ears.

The girls weren't upset that this old woman had joined them. On the contrary, they were quite glad. As soon as she set foot in the cart and found her place among the girls, the old woman put her head down on Zebi's lap and fell fast asleep, not opening her eyes until they arrived at the village.

While the girls were jumping from the cart and entering the house, Zebi slowly woke the old woman. "Auntie, get up, we've arrived!"

There was no answer from Savribibi. Zebi again softly tried to wake her, but she remained silent. O'lmasjon made his way around the cart to help.

"We're here, get up, auntie!"

The old woman opened her eyes from the bass male voice, but answered sleepily, "just a moment, my dears … ok, I'm getting up …," and went back to sleep.

Flustered and tired, Zebi completely forgot that the cart driver was nomah-ram to her, and looked at him silently. The moon had risen high in the night sky. O'lmasjon laughed softly. The young girl, seeing the sweet smile of the young man under the moonlight, felt a tremble pass through her body. She blushed and looked away. Her look must have had a different effect on O'lmasjon. He reached up to help wake the old woman. His hand on top of the old woman's head felt the touch of another hand, and a new tremble, greater than before, washed over both hands. The young girl, who only today had encountered a man without others around, fell into a trance. She didn't immediately withdraw her hand, jerking it away only when she came to. But the young man's strong hands seized it tightly, lowering it below Savribibi's head. The two youths stood like that for several moments.

The happy guest and her hostess sitting in the ichkari together only after some time went out to check on the two missing guests. When they stepped out, the young pair had still not released one another's hands. As for the old woman, she was still soundly asleep, unaware that her whithered body had played host to such a vexsome meeting.

The girls gathered to wake their "most attentive"[10] guard and help her down from the cart. She slumped into Saltanat and Enaxon's arms, her eyes still showing signs of sleep, and babbled something as she entered the house. Zebi went to jump off the cart, but the young man came around and offered his hand to help her down. There was no thud of feet on the ground that had accompanied the other girls' disembarking.

They drank tea with milk and then lay out to sleep where they had eaten.

O'lmasjon drank the cream and ate the bread that had been brought for him, tied up the horse, and lay down on the cart. Sleep eluded him. Strange and sweet thoughts unlike any in his life before filled his mind. He looked up at the moon in the sky and contemplated the moon on earth[11] and laughed sweetly as he did before.

Those inside slept soundly. Only there was one girl, who, in her surprise at these new, strange, sweet feelings, had suddenly woken up. Looking longingly at the moon, she contemplated her earthly existence with a sigh and her cheeks turned red like a pomegranate.

---

10 Several versions of the text have "dog-like" here instead of "most attentive." A recent academic edition of the text convincingly contends that Cho'lpon here uses the latter. The vowel harmony of the 1930s Latin script in which the text was originally printed accounts for the difference in opinion.

11 This is a reference to Zebi. Women are typically likened to the moon in Persianate poetry.

The stray dogs of the village had taken over the streets, barking ever more fiercely from all sides; the creek at the end of the street began to roar like a hungry tiger.

3

Enaxon was the daughter of a poor family. Her father had died when she was young, so her mother turned to Enaxon's brother for help. Her brother Xolmat had been working for as long as he could remember. Even in the playfulness of youth he looked after the entire village's herd and aided his family in what ways he could. Many of the villagers still fondly remembered his time as a herder. When they met him on the street, they would say:

"You've orphaned our herd by leaving us!" They'd shake their heads and walk past.

Such jokes always put a smile on his face, raised his spirits, and healed his always busily working hands. His wife's dowry gave him a small rice field, and he spent all his energy tending to it; he started work before everyone, came home well after them, and worked harder than them. He was barely able to support his six-person family. His mother had aged and started to stoop; his son and daughter were still babies, so the housework fell to his wife and sister. The two of them did not neglect to help Xolmat with his work in the field either. They had their uses in the field. Xolmat put so much energy into his work, and because he was supporting the household by himself, the two women tried to accept his every demand gladly without offence. What kind of exacting demands could a poor man, who knows nothing but his work, have, you might ask? All his passions, needs, and thoughts, whatever they might be, must have revolved around his family.

Of course, his wife and sister were still young things; they weren't without their youthful caprices and desires. It wouldn't be right to say that their caprices were completely without merit. After all, they were young; and, like their peers, they had dreams and aspirations. Their hearts wished for much. Who says that a prisoner in a dungeon can't dream? Is it bad if the beggar dreams of being a king? Sometimes when these powerful day-dreams surfaced from either his wife or sister, the experienced old woman would sense it and do what she could to prevent any consequences. If there was some matter that Xolmat wouldn't take well, she never let him know and took care of it herself; when necessary, she talked softly, and when necessary she made threats, putting water on the fires of passions that appeared in the girls' hearts. She never permitted sparks to become wildfires, extinguishing them when she could. If their desires were appropriate, she tried to satisfy them as best she could. Taking them in her hands, she saved Xolmat from excess worries.

Saltanat and her friends' arrival on the cart was precisely one of those desires. The friendship and closeness between Saltanat and Enaxon's families had been passed down from their fathers and grandfathers. Members of their families had for some time regularly gathered once or twice a year. The previous autumn, after the harvest, Enaxon and her sister-in-law had come and stayed with Saltanat for a week. It was then that Enaxon invited her friend and a few of her peers to come to her village when spring first bloomed. Once spring came and nature had received new life, Enaxon sent for them again. The old woman found her daughter's desire appropriate, of course. Her daughter-in-law joined Enaxon in her excitement, so there was no reason for the old woman to refuse them.

"What a grand idea!" the old woman said as she began planning. "We'll need to make this happen ourselves so that Xolmat doesn't concern himself in the least. If possible, we won't tell him. He'll find out when the guests arrive."

Enaxon looked at her sister-in-law. Even though the latter understood Enaxon's inquiring glance—"Well, speak, what do you think?"—she didn't dare speak first in front of her mother-in-law and stayed silent. Enaxon was forced to speak up herself.

"Agreed. You know best, Mother. But we can't feed them just dry bread. You know best yourself."

Having heard this, the daughter-in-law interjected her small contribution.

"Of course, particularly guests who have come from so far."

"Right, I know best!" said the old woman. She spoke quickly, cutting off her daughter-in-law. "In autumn, you two spent a week there. As tough as it was for them in their poverty, they sent you back sated. The two of you praised them for weeks. ..."

"So true!" said Enaxon. "Saltanat's father is just a milk salesman; he has no land, no shop. He has many mouths to feed ... with all that, what didn't they do for us?"

The daughter-in-law, despite her previous reluctance, spoke next.

"Yes, as you say," she suddenly confirmed.

With that, everyone became quiet. The old woman looked for something to say but sank into thought. She slowly sat down on the second rung of the ladder that lay against the roof of the cattle shed. The girls squatted down on the ground. The old woman started to run her fingers over the wood of the ladder, while Enaxon squeezed the chewing resin she took from her mouth into a ball. The daughter-in-law drew figures on the ground with a twig. All three were absorbed in themselves. The old woman, thinking about the same things she had thought about all day, kept her eyes firmly fixed on the girls; the girls themselves alternated looking at one another, at their mother, and at the ground. The old woman broke the silence.

"Damn this poverty, damn it!" she said and sighed. "There's just no way …"

After another silence, she raised her voice:

"Would they really come just to drink our wheat porridge? They'd stay for three or four days. Can we really not do something suitable?" she asked.

The two girls became as though they had just woken up.

"Of course, of course!" they said together.

Right at that moment Xolmat appeared by the threshing floor. They didn't have time to turn back and look at him when he said:

"Mother, are you here?" The old woman cut off her daughters and stood up from her place.

"Don't hurry this matter, we'll think on it and something will turn up," she said and ran to Xolmat's side.

Later that night as they prepared to sleep, the old woman called her two daughters to her side and spoke her mind.

"After much thinking, this is what we can do. I've set aside a few things from the savings that we have been collecting in the event of my death. Now, Enaxon, you take a few things from your dowry; daughter-in-law, you add something of your own. Tomorrow we'll send someone down to the bazaar, let him sell what he can, and bring back what he gets.

After the old woman had sorted through her "death fund," that was it.

"Agreed, Mother!" said Enaxon, "Everything I own is yours, you decide what we should sell. If you insist, I will choose. …"

"I will bring my things to you tomorrow," said the daughter-in-law.

The old woman went to lie down. The two youths stayed behind and advised one another what to pick out from their things. Because neither had much of anything of value, their conversation dragged on for some time.

When morning came the old woman had a miraculous bundle in her hands. Their boy put the bundle in his saddle bag, hopped on his dirty jade, and turned towards the town.

That same day a second invitation was delivered to Saltanat, and the saddlebag returned filled to the brim.

Though Enaxon prepared a meal as best she could, called together all the neighbor girls, and gathered some broken-string *dutars*, she couldn't help but feel embarrassed. She wanted to bury all her dear guests in whatever hospitality and festivity she could muster. Her poverty limited her, but she still had to pamper them. She kept thinking of her powerlessness and fell into hopelessness and despair. When she could take the pain and anger in her heart no more, she tried talking with her mother.

"It would be better if I died!" she said. "I can never treat my guests as they deserve!"

The old woman, who usually spoke softly, suddenly raised her voice in anger.

"If what we have won't work, then go to the bazaar and sell yourself! Then you'll meet them just as you want. ..." she said.

"It's impossible to share my suffering with you," said Enaxon. She backed away from her mother as tears came to her eyes.

She sat down by the little canal running through their courtyard with that suffering in her heart. When she told her sister-in-law, she agreed with her immediately.

"Such nice girls! Whatever you do for them is never enough! Just look at Zebi! Zebi! When we went to them in the fall, we didn't see her, right?"

"Her damn father, that cold Razzoq-sufi, never responded to Saltanat's invitation. ... What a beautiful voice that girl has! When she sings, your ear becomes intoxicated. A person could die from happiness, having heard her voice. ... Her very breath is sweet! Enamoring!"

"Here's what I'll say. We made soup, pumpkin samosas, pilaf. ... It will have to do. Our poverty won't allow anymore. ..."

Here Enaxon released a deep sigh. Then she continued.

"If we could just make the meat samosas, dumplings, steamed lamb stew that they only have at the richest of parties. ..."

She suddenly became agitated and hopped up.

"Pumpkin samosas! Pumpkin samosas! Damn poverty to hell! They say that the poor are God's most beloved servants; can that really be true?"

Submerged in thought, a pleasant smile began to appear on the face of Enaxon's sister-in-law as she threw straw into the flowing water. She stood up, and her sweet smile stretched nearly to her ears as she moved towards Enaxon.

"Don't be sad, dear sister," she said, "I've found a way. We can treat our guests to an enchanting evening just as the wealthy do!"

"How?" asked Enaxon, staring dumbfounded into the eyes of her sister-in-law as she took both her hands.

"We may not have money, but we have friends and acquaintances who do. We'll tell them, have them arrange things. ..."

Enaxon's face suddenly brightened up. A smile ran wide across her lips. She understood exactly what her sister-in-law meant.

"You'll tell the *mingboshi*'s daughter? You mean let her invite us over?"

"Either her or, if she won't, would his youngest wife Sultonxon?"

"Would she really?"

The two girls stopped on this point and began to discuss. Then:

"Leave it to me. Don't worry about it. I'll take care of the guests myself. Agreed?" her sister-in-law said. They began walking toward the house again.

"Good advice! Sister-in-law, my friend, do this for me!" said Enaxon as she hugged her tightly.

Her sister-in-law stopped suddenly.

"We didn't invite anyone from his house already, did we?" she asked.

Enaxon stopped as well.

"No!" she answered. "You mean who from there knows about our get-together? We thought no one from there would be interested. What should we do now?"

"Let's invite both his daughter and his youngest wife tonight. If they don't come at first, we'll send for them again, and they'll come for sure on the second invitation. What am I saying?! Zebi's voice and her songs will lure everyone from their house here. Don't worry at all. I'll buzz over there myself. If they hear one or two of those songs tonight, then they'll surely invite us there tomorrow."

Both of them, their faces shining like stars as they headed inside, perked up their ears as they heard Zebi's melodious voice singing "My Black Hair."

....

Their efforts met with resounding success, as if a drop of water had morphed into a sea. Into the warm and inviting embrace of this poor, penniless family came all the girls of the village. The old women of neighboring households also came. That night, life even came into the sleepy old woman who was chaperoning Zebi and the other city girls. The girls, seeing her vibrancy, couldn't control their laughter and sincerely rejoiced. Zebi was joined by not one, but two dutar players, a few dancers, and two singers. No one had any leftover attention to pay to the dinner given by Enaxon because they were all engrossed in the pleasure of song. It must have been for this reason that not one of the girls seated on the porch, who filled the air with their voices as they traded gossip, saw how the mingboshi's women curled their lips as if to say, "Is this really hospitality?" The hosts put away the food and the party started. Everyone forgot themselves as they returned to their childhoods.

Others joined the three sweet-voiced girls, raising their melodies to the sky. Young men from the village, who had little trouble climbing over the short, crumbling walls of the courtyard, began to gather and listen. Squatting on either side of the porch, where the rays of the dim lamp light barely reached, they took in the pleasant sounds of the singers. Among them were Xolmat and the cart driver, O'lmasjon. Both of them stood against the trunk of the mulberry tree. Though Xolmat looked on intrigued, he had no interest in the singers themselves. O'lmasjon strained to pick out Zebi's voice from the others. As soon as he heard it, he couldn't conceal the joy that made his heart jump from the depths of his chest.

"Didn't I tell you what a voice Zebi has, eh Xolmat?" he said, after which his face immediately turned red and he looked at the ground.

"You certainly did!" said Xolmat. Then he asked, "you said her name was Zebi?"

"Yes, Zebixon!"

There was just a hint of boasting, of pride in his voice, as if by adding that "xon" to her name he had said "my Zebi." That hint must have been clear to Xolmat, who looked at him disapprovingly.

"You've really fallen for her, eh?" he said.

Xolmat's words embarrassed O'lmasjon, and he started to argue.

"Nooo, I was just saying that her voice is wonderful—her voice!" he said. But he recognized that his heart would call his tongue a liar. He knew already that Xolmat wouldn't believe him. To not dwell on the topic anymore, he turned the conversation elsewhere. "What would you say about her voice; it's really marvelous, right?" he asked Xolmat.

"Yes, quite good. She's a friend of Saltanat, you said?"

"Her best friend."

"Whose daughter is she?"

"A man named Razzoq-sufi. …"

"Razzoq-sufi?"

"Yes, Razzoq-sufi. What a gift from God she is, but He gave her to the wrong person. To some poor, bitter old man!"

"And she has many suitors?"

"Their threshold has nearly eroded away from the feet of so many match-makers, they say. … Only God knows who will have the fortune of receiving her!"

"Pray to God because you know they say, 'He who has no hope is lost.'"

Having said that, Xolmat turned to the boy and gave him a devilish look.

Just then, the girls stopped their song, and a dissonant chorus of female voices let out a cry of applause: "Superb, well done!"

The men were forced to contain their excitement. Only a few of the older woman knew of their presence. When the dancing ended, some of the girls got up from their places and moved about, others left for the hearth to drink tea, and still others traded places with those sitting closer to the front. Then the men started to move about as they were forced to back up out of sight. One of the guests, Qumri, stepped away from the party for a moment, heading in the direction of the mulberry tree. Upon seeing the two men there, looking at one another and laughing quietly, she turned white and let out a muffled, "Voy, the shame!" She ran back to Saltanat's side and whispered to her, "Boys from the village have surrounded us. When I went over to the mulberry tree, two of them stared at me, eyes bulging. … One of them is our cart driver. …"

At that moment, having heard the two girls whispering, Zebi fell into a panic, stretched out her neck and listened closely. She only managed to make out Qumri's last words: "One of them is our cart driver. …" Her heart fluttered, and suddenly she turned around and looked. In the dim illumination of the lamp she saw the old women fussing about. Nothing else was visible. Her heart nevertheless found no quiet. Her lips started to quiver. She shot up from her spot at once; the girls made way for her and she walked past. Before she could step off the porch everyone's eyes were on her. When she made her way to the ground, all the girls returned to their conversations. In the courtyard, the old woman that had stood guard last night met her and kissed her on the forehead.

"God save you from the evil eye, my child!" she said. Kissing her above both eyes again, she turned and headed towards the ichkari.

"Yes, auntie. What are you going to do in the house?" asked Zebi.

"I'm going to sleep, my child, I'm an old thing, can I really stay up halfway through the night? You all are young, enjoy yourselves. Let me relax. …"

The old woman's character made an impression on everyone, particularly on Zebi for whom this terse, sleepy woman seemed much more pleasant than those other old gossips.

Having calmed herself a bit, Zebi entered the darkness. She too was going to the mulberry tree next to the raised platform in the courtyard. The cart driver, standing in the blackness, recognized the girl coming towards him from the light and suddenly cried, "There, she's coming!"

This cry of his was involuntary. Xolmat, who had already come to understand the matter, managed to distance himself from the boy. He gave him a meaningful glance, laughed, and slapped him on the shoulder: "I told you, 'He who has no hope is lost,' brother. … Ok, let's go," he said and disappeared into the thick darkness.

The boy couldn't see whether Xolmat was there or not. In his confusion, he didn't even remember to say those words of gratefulness that usually come naturally. He again involuntarily leaned up against the mulberry tree's stout trunk, his heart barely contained in his chest.

Zebi heard the boy's words—"There, she's coming." If she had been in her right mind, she would have reacted just like Qumri and turned back. It was as if she didn't know herself and couldn't think. Another controlled her legs, moving them step by step. Her limbs had been charmed by the curse of some malevolent force, and they moved where that force dragged her. For the first time in her life the young girl felt as if her heart had become a stranger to itself, as if possessed by another's.

Zebi ran her eyes over her surroundings, slowed her pace, and stopped at the large mulberry's right side. The boy was on the left side.

The two of them kept silent for some time. Neither knew how to begin nor what to say. Finally, the boy managed to find words.

"Tomorrow morning … should I ready the cart?"

"Why?"

"We're not leaving?"

Zebi couldn't muster an answer. Not a word to answer this question came even close to her mind, which continued to become hazier and hazier. Just to exchange her words with his, she responded, "What's the rush?" Her words tapered off as they exited her mouth. At that moment, her voice became alien to her. The voice producing those words sounded to her ear as if it came from the far side of the creek.

The boy came to. He chuckled and then bravely extended his hand towards the right side of the mulberry. But across the long distance that separated the two of them no second hand greeted his. Zebi, in fact, didn't even detect that someone had reached out towards her. When the boy felt no objection but also no answer from Zebi, he withdrew his hand and this time bent his neck forward, looking for the girl with both eyes. With a giddy voice, he asked, "We'll enjoy ourselves for another day or two? We'll let the horse rest?"

When there was no answer from Zebi, he added, "Ok, fine, whenever you say, 'Hitch up,' I'll be ready."

Zebi leaned against the mulberry, forgetting where she was standing. Unable to reply, she lost herself in difficult thoughts. She began to think about the dark days awaiting her in the near future, about a happiness whose true colors and appearance were not yet known. Was all of her happiness not tied to Razzoq-sufi's wrathful self? Could that cold old man really hold the power to make this joyous songbird happy or unhappy? Could his pithy "yes" or "no" serve towards the unending joy of the poor girl or her suffocating death? The unfortunate girl expected not one blessing from her father whose brow and cheeks had never been lifted by a smile in his life. As she thought about her father, she began to look at herself as a person condemned to death and at her father as the executioner. And she shuddered! Her travel to the village, the unexpected meeting with the cart driver, the vexing thoughts and feelings from that meeting all forced the poor girl to think over these black thoughts. Such black thoughts were nothing new to her, of course. Since she had reached womanhood and the matchmakers had begun crowding their house, the miserable girl hadn't had a day without them. Were the last two days during which she gave herself over to song and dance not an escape from such concerns?

As she drowned in the black thoughts combined with the sweet fantasies, which standing next to that troublesome boy had wrought, a voice sounded out from the porch.

"Hey, why has everything become so quiet? Where is Zebi? Saltanat, my dear, won't you find your friend?"

Another voice sounded in agreement: "Right, everyone has frozen stiff! Hey, girls, what has happened with you?"

Suddenly a few voices began to call: "Zebi, Zebi!"

The girls got up from their spots and began to walk around.

Those cries would have woken anyone from a heavy sleep. Zebi startled awake from her intoxication and gave a hurried answer, "here I am. ... I'm coming. ... I'm coming. ..." Only this time her voice sounded like that of an invalid, dying from an incurable sickness.

The cart driver understood immediately and quickly said, "Go, have your fun! Don't be afraid, don't be upset!" Then he took his place under the mulberry again.

A pair of girls ran over to Zebi and accompanied her back. One of them was the mingboshi's youngest wife Sultonxon.

This time they started dancing. Almost all the young girls joined in. Qumri turned out to be a much better dancer than the other city girls. Of the village girls, only two or three knew what they were doing. They even involved the old women. Enaxon's mother, a short and hunched woman, danced, making everyone laugh. They couldn't convince Enaxon to join. She excused herself, noting that she was there to serve her guests. The mingboshi's daughter took her turn, but his youngest wife would have none of it, and no one could force her. Zebi sat with the dutar players and the singers, singing along with their cheerful melodies. When the dancing ended and the hosts had laid out pilaf for everyone, the moon was already high in the night sky. After the pilaf, one of the more proper village girls stood up and announced, "Tomorrow we await guests."

After that, the mingboshi's youngest wife Sultonxon consulted with her eldest co-wife's daughter, got up, and turned to Enaxon: "In that case, your guests will come to us the day after tomorrow, alright? Now, let us depart!"

She and her co-wife's daughter got off the porch, and the other girls began to get up as well. The fateful night ended, and the guests went their separate ways.

4

Having been friendly and chatty with her co-wife's daughter on the way back, Sultonxon, upon learning that the mingboshi hadn't yet returned from the city, went into her house and made up her bed. Without getting undressed, she laid her head on a pillow and fell asleep.

When in the morning she opened her eyes from a restful sleep, one of her neighbors, Umrinisabibi, was sitting at her bedside. This middle-aged woman often came to visit, helping the mingboshi's wives manage their household affairs in exchange for a little money, which she put away for her youngest daughter's dowry. She had married off her eldest daughter just two years prior.

Sultonxon just barely opened her eyes and said, "It's good that you've come, Umrinisabibi. I was going to send for you myself. Tomorrow, Enaxon's guests from the city will come to us. You have to see to it that they are fed well and enjoy themselves. We should start making bread today."

"I came to talk with you about just that," said Umrinisabibi.

"Good. After breakfast let's start the dough. You'll have to go to a few places and then ask around for some dutars."

Umrinisabibi moved closer to Sultoxon and said, "I came with advice of another kind. …"

These words, said in a near whisper, and the darting of Umrinisabibi's eyes around the room, made the young wife's heart skip a beat. She turned toward her neighbor.

"Why are you whispering? What do you mean? Come closer! Hurry up, for the love of God!"

Umrinisabibi now leaned in towards the young wife's ear.

"I heard that you invited those city girls here yesterday. My daughter Bahri was there last night. …"

Having said that, she was silent for a moment. The young wife's small, black, playful eyes opened wide and fixed themselves upon her neighbor's mouth. Umrinisabibi again worriedly looked around.

"Can a person really take an axe to the branch on which she's sitting like that?" she said. "I couldn't sleep last night and left the house this morning thinking about you."

Sultonxon became pale and then a redness ran across her cheeks as if both had been slapped. Her mouth fell open and her chest heaved slightly as if a needed treatment eluded her now sickly body.

"Get to the point. What are you trying to say?" she said, gasping. Umrinisabibi stretched out her neck to her as far as she could to look at the open door. Then she again bent down to the ear of the young wife.

"It's been only five months since you've been married. Do you really want a rival? You must have known what a hound your husband is!"

"Voy, dammit all! Have I lost my mind?!" she screamed and buried her face in the pillow, beating her clenched left hand against her face.

"My dear, you acted like a complete child. You didn't think. Word of this singer girl's voice has already made the rounds. She's on everyone's lips. Could a rabid womanizer like your husband hear that nightingale-like voice and not immediately call for a matchmaker?"

The young wife suddenly got up from the ground and threw herself on Umrinisabibi's shoulders.

"What have I done, auntie? I lost my senses, my senses! What do we do now? Tell me, what can I do?"

Umrinisabibi stroked her young friend's head.

"Don't worry," she said. "What's done is done. Somehow we'll repair that branch!"

"But how?"

"Don't rush, let's think. We'll figure it out."

The two of them were silent, lost in thought. Umrinisabibi began to fiddle with the ends of her white gauze kerchief, while the young wife took the gold ring from her finger and played with it. Suddenly she brought the gold ring up to her eye, turned it here and there, and after giving it a good look, she reached over to Umrinisabibi and put it on her little finger. Thinking and thinking, Umrinisabibi, without even remotely sensing its value, stared intently at this gold ring that had made its way from a stranger's hand to her own. When she came to, realizing what an expensive little thing this was and what she had just won for her daughter Bahri, her cheeks turned crimson from joy. She quickly took the ring from her finger and wrapped it securely in her kerchief.

"Now, speak, auntie!"

"I'm surprised at what I'm about to say. You've invited guests. Now, somehow, you'll have to take back your invitation. You'll have to keep this a secret from your co-wives. It's good that your co-wife's daughter didn't do the inviting. Had she, that would have been irreparable."

"Damn me, Zebi's voice was such ecstasy that I couldn't think of anything! I asked my co-wife's daughter: 'should you invite them or should I?' Look at me! Thank God, she was so conscientious. She told me, 'I can't have guests without my mother's permission. You invite them.'"

"Well, if you think about it, she too acted foolishly. But now her foolishness is your gain."

Umrinisabibi was silent for a moment and then again bent down.

"Now you somehow pretend that you have fallen ill, I'll go and tell Enaxon. I'll tell her that if you get better, I'll let her know myself. That should do it. Tomorrow or the next day the guests will leave anyways. Zebi is the daughter of that strict Razzoq-sufi. They say he only let her out for one or two days, no more. ..."

The young wife had still not come to and once again threw herself on Umrinisabibi's neck.

"But how can that be? It will look bad. Word will spread through the whole village ... Will my co-wives really not say a word? If we could just find some other way. ..."

The young wife looked deeply into Umrinisabibi's eyes again.

"If we said that my mother is ill, that would be fine by me!"

"Ok, we'll make your mother the ill one. She'll send for you urgently, you'll ask forgiveness of your guests, and leave for her. Then you'll stay with her until the city girls leave."

"How will we do it?"

"That's easy enough. I'll put on my paranji and head over to your mother's. I'll explain everything to her and return right away. A person will come not long after me for you, and you'll leave with him. Later tonight I'll go and tell Enaxon."

The young wife was finally satisfied with this plan and kissed Umrinisabibi above her eyes.

"I'll never forget this favor of yours, auntie," she said. "I'll prepare your daughter's wedding and, if God wills it, give her away myself! Go now! Here, there's bread in the bowl and raisins on the plate, take these and go. Be quick, dear auntie!"

Umrinisabibi jumped up, took the food in her kerchief, and exited the house. As she left through the courtyard, the young wife saw her off from the threshold.

One of her co-wives outside probably asked Umrinisabibi what she was doing in the house and for that reason she set one foot back in the courtyard and cried out, "Sultonxon has invited guests for tomorrow, I'm leaving to see to it!"

Sultonxon quite liked that loud and harsh voice.

....

The mingboshi's middle wife, Poshshaxon, was overjoyed to hear that the singer girl would soon be their guest. But her husband had already left for the city. She knew well that if he were home it wouldn't be difficult for him, having heard that city girl's voice, to add himself a new wife. Her husband's womanizing was well known not just to her, but also the whole country. She didn't hesitate to ally with her former enemy, her elder co-wife Xadichaxon, to somehow give Zebi to her husband. It must have been for that reason that she had breakfast in Xadichaxon's home, and pretending to tell Xadichaxon the most mahram of secrets, she tried to win the older woman to her side.

"No word from our husband so far?" she asked, smiling.

"Yes, our husband spent the night in the city. Do you think he had a look at another girl or two?"

"Will his eyes ever be sated? Their glance always seems to fall on still others."

"Do you really think our will has anything to do with it? God made him that way."

"God must so like these men. ..."

"And what about us? Are there any among us that don't like them? Take some bread! Here's some jam."

"We have bread and jam every day. Let's talk of other worries."

"But not everyone has bread and jam. Only those that have it have it. We should be grateful. ..."

"A thousand times thanks be to God, of course. ... You know yourself, you've experienced it ... something that scrapes at the heart. ..."

"My heart, dear, has been so scraped that there's nothing left. The flame in my heart is nothing but a dried-up wick. Now, as God wills it, you'll live through what I have. Truth be told, my dear, I wouldn't wish my suffering on another. Take some bread."

Poshshaxon felt the bitter, sharp feelings behind her co-wife's words as spears that pierced right through her breast. When she first became a co-wife to this poor woman, Xadichaxon clawed at her heart and burned her with the fires of envy and hatred. At that time, Poshshaxon had ignored it: she laughed, smiled, frolicked, and turned up her nose, looking at the sky as she took each step. Xadichaxon suffered, languished, tormented herself, and spent days in bitter tears. But mingboshi didn't even give Poshshaxon a chance to bear him a child before another co-wife and rival was added. All her former pride disappeared, her airs and graces were trampled, her joy extinguished, her face withered, her lips turned the color of fall leaves, her hopes smashed, her legs moved as if dragged. Since Sultonxon had joined their household, her lips didn't exit from between the closed vice of her teeth, her eyes teared up at the slightest thing, and in her chest, lay one of those stones that demons toss about. Sure, her stomach was full, she was clothed, had no lack of fine things, and no need to work. But at her side another star burned and twinkled, blinding others, so what benefit did material comforts present?

After Xadichaxon's laconic yet veritable words the two sat in silence, chewing on dry bread, while Poshshaxon thought these things over. It was, of course, not easy to admit in front of her old enemy that she had been right all along. With the youngest co-wife now shining on mingboshi's silver belt like a flawless ornament, Poshshaxon knew she had to recognize her now harmless rival's innocence, comfort her broken heart, and with that, win Xadichaxon to her side. Now was the time for the two, who had been made equal before the third, to take their revenge. She put her empty teacup down on the table.

"You are right," said Poshshaxon. "As sad as they are, your words are true. I can't say anything to you about this, particularly because when I came you already had a child. ... I know."

She took the cup of tea that her co-wife had just offered to her and continued.

"Thinking of it now, neither you nor I are guilty. Which of us married this man because we wanted to? Our parents married both of us off without our consent. Who looked at the tears in our eyes?"

Here Xadichaxon objected.

"No, don't say that. I wanted to marry him. At that time, our husband was young, he wasn't much of an official, just an *ellikboshi*. His first wife didn't give him a child and after just two or three years of marriage, she died. When we first got married, he would say, 'You are the sight that opened my eyes.' I had no reason to complain. I wasn't upset with my fate. Fazilat was born not long after our wedding. Usually a child connects parents. ... After her birth, I was very happy. It was right around that time that my mother died. My father left for the hajj and stayed there. But I endured these misfortunes without suffering. If you had to ask why, I guess I would say that my heart was satisfied. ..."

A tear came to Xadichaxon's eye; she wiped it with the long sleeve of her flower-patterned shirt. Then she looked over with teary eyes at Fazilat, who was sleeping on the courtyard platform outside under the already high sun. She poured out the last two drops of tea, drank them in one gulp, and, after putting the cup and teapot away, she continued.

"After your husband became an official he went bad. His office ran him ragged. He abandoned his village and moved here. He bought this enormous property, built these big houses. His heart went into trade, streets and roads. ... He didn't have time for his child, his wife either. The sycophants and spongers flocked to him. Those looking to find him a wife or give advice multiplied. One of them soon put on a wedding and you joined me. ..."

Poshshaxon couldn't take it any longer.

"If only I had wanted to come! They tied my legs and dragged me like a slave. I came regretting my birth and that I hadn't died of illness in childhood."

"I know, my dear, I know. ... Parents arrange the marriages of most women. However it happened, you became my co-wife. ..."

"It would have been better if I had died! How many years, how many months of quiet did I have as your co-wife? You at least had five or six years. What complaints can you have? I enjoyed myself not one whole year. One night I heard the sounds of a wedding and the next morning Sultonxon entered. ... Would it not have been better if I died that morning? As soon as my father found out about mingboshi's wealth and property, he said 'I'll give her to you,' and that was it. I wonder: what need does my father have of them?"

"Damn that wealth, dammit! I envy Enaxon's sister-in-law. She has not a thing of value. They just barely get by. She has two little children like lambs. Her husband is always at her side. She doesn't suffer the pain of having a co-wife."

"Really, what can you say?"

The two were silent. Then Poshshaxon spoke up.

"I can't stand it anymore, I just can't stand it anymore! I can't stand this pain!"

She looked around and then bent over the table towards Xadichaxon.

"If I could only bring another for him and show that damned girl. I'd break that haughtiness of hers. ... I'd bring her down to earth. ... If only that, I'd set your table, wash your hands, sew your daughter's clothing; I'd be at your service! Believe me or don't!"

"You're suffering such that I can't but believe you. ..."

To a woman in whose heart the passion and energy demanded by spousal rivalry had long since died, the well-wishes of her former rival sounded comforting. If another girl were added on top of Sultonxon, she would be the fourth and that familiar pain would at least subside by a quarter. Having happened upon this conclusion, Xadichaxon couldn't say no to her former enemy's hand now extended in friendship. She only awaited a clearer and more concrete statement of her future alliance with Poshshaxon. Her co-wife didn't keep her waiting.

"A clap, they say, takes two hands! If the two of us work together, we'll show Sultonxon. Then our pain will decrease—yours by two notches, mine by one. The two of us can finally live amicably, like sisters. We'll split whatever wealth is left from our husband between ourselves; we'll divide it up fairly. Our youth has already gone to the winds. So best to take of the wealth. It will be useful in our age."

These were the words Xadichaxon was waiting for. Actually, were they not the very words that she had in mind herself? When she had been alone all those years, were these not the very thoughts and desires she had? Today the two co-wives' hearts beat as one! The two had finally understood one another, finally helped one another! What is better than this, really? What one person can't do alone, two people can. And what two people can't, three people can. Now the whole point was that three people, two co-wives and a daughter, would act in unison.

"That scoundrel can't possibly say no to another marriage, if we find the right girl! Let's think on it." said Xadichaxon.

Her co-wife suddenly stood up, walked over to her, and, like the closest of friends, put her hand on her shoulder and kissed her cheeks. These kisses were not those of a deceiver or hypocrite. On the contrary, they were sincere. At that moment, Poshshaxon's body was wrapped in the fires of her spousal rivalry with Sultonxon, her eyes burned and sparked with its flames, and her cheeks were red-hot coals.

After those genuine kisses, Poshshaxon jumped up, ran towards the door, checked it, and returned.

"What is there to think about? The best of the world's girls has come to our village by herself. If we could just invite her as a guest … what more would we need?

"Who are you talking about?"

"That singer girl, Zebi, among Enaxon's city guests."

Xadichaxon looked at her co-wife approvingly.

"You've found her, then! You are a tricky one! I've heard about her too. A tragedy, they say."

"If that's the case, then our job gets easier. Many have heard of her, no doubt those who would sing her praises to your husband. Do you think those that told me and Sultonxon wouldn't tell others?"

Outside, a cough resounded. Fazilat, who was lying on the platform, had got up and was coming in. The two women broke off their planning and began to talk about household matters.

After washing her hands and face, Fazilat entered. Before she could cross the threshold, her mother asked, "Did you wash your face?"

"Yes!" said the girl.

"There's tea in the little pot in the hearth. Bring it here."

The girl brought in the tea, but before she even sat down, she started speaking.

"I came home last night tired and went right to sleep. If I hadn't done that, I would have woken you up and told you everything I saw."

"What did you see?" asked her mother.

"Well, out with it," seconded Poshshaxon quickly.

"What can I say! You should have seen it. A singer named Zebi came; if you had heard her voice, you would have felt yourself drunk!"

The two women looked at each other, silently smiling.

"Who else did you see?"

"The girls that came with Zebi were so nice, so beautiful, so warm and joyful."

Her mother couldn't contain her laughter. She added, barely audibly, "We might move our notches further still."

"What are you whispering, Mother?" asked the daughter.

"Nothing," said her mother, "I just said something to myself. Forget it."

The middle wife understood her joke and countered with a laugh of her own.

"And how did they treat the guests?" asked her mother.

"Yes, tell us about the food," said Poshshaxon.

"What can they have at a poor person's home? Bread, raisins, dried apricots. Some carrot jam. Towards the end they served pilaf with flaxseed oil ... a little meat here and there—not much."

"You could starve with food like that!" said Poshshaxon.

"Certainly!" said the girl's mother.

"Who was looking at the food anyways?" said Fazilat. "Everyone's eyes were on the dancing, singing, and the girls, particularly Zebi. No one left until the evening was over. No one wanted to leave. We came back after midnight. When we came, you were all sleeping soundly."

"Their food was so miserable; you didn't invite them here, did you? We would see them off right."

"Truly!" added Poshshaxon.

"I didn't dare invite them without asking you. Sultonxon and I talked about it, and she invited them."

The two co-wives' eyes suddenly, like a father's eyes who has just gotten word of his son's birth, were set ablaze with bright flames. They looked at one another as if their glances could pass along congratulations.

"Sultonxon?" asked her mother.

"Yes, Sultonxon."

"How thoughtful Sultonxon is!"

"Did the invitation really need much thought?" asked the girl.

Xadichaxon slyly winked at her co-wife.

"Did you hear what she said? Tomorrow we'll have guests from the city! Sultonxon herself invited them, herself!"

Poshshaxon made no effort to hide her eternally cunning eyes, quipping, "Naturally she'd do that as the favorite wife of his excellency, mingboshi! Who will say something to her? What limits can she have?"

"Sultonxon is truly thoughtful!" repeated Xadichaxon. "So thoughtful!"

The two co-wives again looked at one another with their sly eyes and smiled like the co-conspirators they were.

The poor girl, unable to grasp what those smiles meant, was stunned, looking now at her mother and then at her aunt and back again.

The day after Enaxon's feast, she and her guests returned late from another party. They were incredibly tired because the household that had invited them was on the other side of the village. Zebi lagged behind the others to hand the gifts she had received to the cart driver, so Enaxon's mother, exploiting the moment alone with her daughter, shared her opinion of their already well-known guest.

"Your friend Zebi really is a rare one, my child. Such a kind, sincere, caring girl you don't often see among today's youth. Not one other girl has even talked with the poor cart driver, who brought you all from such distances and has waited here for so long. Saltanat, his own neighbor, hasn't even talked with him. Only Zebi has come to see him, to talk with him. ..."

The last sentence the old woman pronounced softly, almost whispering.

"You're right, Mother!" Enaxon responded. "Zebi is rare, but ..."

Having said that, Enaxon couldn't restrain herself and burst out laughing. Her mother was surprised.

"Why are you laughing? Am I wrong?"

"No," said Enaxon, laughing again, "everything you said was right. I was thinking about something else. ..."

Enaxon was the first to see Umrinisabibi, who, covering her face with a kerchief instead of a paranji, was approaching them slowly. She ran out to meet her, her cheeks still aglow from her laughter just moments ago. As a matter of fact, it was Enaxon whom Umrinisabibi needed.

She took Enaxon by the arm. "Walk this way, my dear, I have a message for you."

Enaxon invited her onto the porch for some tea and bread, but her guest refused. Only when the two of them approached the wall of the neighbor's house did Umrinisabibi stop her.

"My dear girl, how can I tell you this? I'm embarrassed to say ..."

After such an introduction Enaxon's heart felt as if something cold had touched it.

"What happened?" she asked with noticeable agitation.

"Sultonxon sent me ..."

Having said that, Umrinisabibi stopped and looked the girl in the eyes. Though the girl's face was difficult to make out in the dark, she wanted to see her reaction and choose her words accordingly. The girl, with still greater anxiety in her voice, repeated her question.

"What happened?"

"Sultonxon's mother has come down with something. ... Just now a man on a horse came for Sultonxon and took her to her mother. From early morning, I had been at mingboshi's seeing to the preparations for tonight, when she called me to her to tell me the news. 'I'm leaving now, I have no choice, go quick and give Enaxon my apologies,' she told me. I didn't even have time to put on my paranji, I came here so quickly."

"So now they won't receive my guests?"

"Without Sultonxon, who can host them? Is there anyone in that home who can entertain and serve guests like her? You know yourself, my dear."

The terrible news clearly upset Enaxon. Not knowing what to say, she sank into thought. Umrinisabibi saw the effect of her message and tried to comfort her.

"Your friends will surely come again. Sultonxon won't forget her part. She is a good girl. Let Saltanat know. She's a sensible girl, she'll understand."

"What need is there to draw this out then?" said Enaxon. "What's done is done. Why is fate so cruel to me?"

"Don't say that, my dear! You're still young, you still have time for plenty of talk, feasts, and parties. You don't think Sultonxon is upset?"

"What good is there in her being upset? What's done is done. ... Fine, let it be."

"Be well, my dear, I must go. I left the dough, the food out in my rush here. I must go and clean up. Her co-wives, you must know, aren't much good for that."

"You won't stay just a bit?"

Those words limped off Enaxon's lips.

"Be well!" said Umrinisabibi. Avoiding the porch, she hugged the wall and quickly disappeared from view.

All the plans and dreams that Enaxon had harbored from the first evening were destroyed. Now she couldn't give her friends the send-off she desired. Without saying anything to anyone, she called her sister-in-law over and told her what had happened. She joined Enaxon in her disappointment, but had no help to offer her.

The two talked for some time, contemplating all manner of solutions and whom to ask for advice, but couldn't manage a single answer. In the end, they decided that tomorrow morning they would tell Saltanat, and if she decided that they would leave, then Enaxon would have no choice but to let them go.

But they wouldn't say anything to the guests until morning. They were tired from their travel around the village, from the parties, and lay down to sleep immediately.

Enaxon's mother looked at her the next morning during breakfast and said, "My girl, are you taking your friends to Sultonxon's today?"

She couldn't have just said that! The question caught the daughter and her sister-in-law off guard because they still hadn't had time to tell anyone. They were going to tell Saltanat herself after breakfast once they had gotten up the courage. Now this simple old woman put their pain on display for everyone. The girl, trying to contain her alarm, looked at her sister-in-law. The latter immediately knew what her glance meant and answered the old woman.

"There's been something of a misunderstanding with Sultonxon. We'll take our guests wherever they want to go. If needed, we can always stay here and have a good time."

The old woman didn't stop with her unnecessary questions.

"Why was there a misunderstanding with Sultonxon?"

The two girls now had to tell the truth. The daughter-in-law looked at Enaxon and then continued.

"Sultonxon's mother fell ill with something and called her daughter to her village last night. If she's there, what can we do?"

Saltanat now opened her mouth.

"We could just ready the cart and leave now."

Two of the city girls announced their agreement. But Zebi pushed on Saltanat's shoulder and whispered into her ear, "What's the hurry? What did you forget in the city? Since we're here, shouldn't we enjoy it?"

Just then the mingboshi's daughter, Fazilat, walked in, greeting everyone. The young girls got up, greeted her, and invited her to the table. The girl, however, refused. She stopped at the edge of the porch to announce:

"I have come to invite guests. Sultonxon's mother has taken ill, and Sultonxon has left. My mother and her co-wife Poshshaxon had no choice but to invite you themselves. This evening you must come!"

She bid farewell and left.

Enaxon, who saw their unexpected guest off through the door, felt a wash of calm come over her anxious heart, and a joyous redness covered her cheeks.

5

If it weren't for the silver belt on Akbarali mingboshi's waist, the silver-hilted sword on that belt, and the gold-brocade robe on his shoulders, no one would have taken him for an official. Those who saw him in ordinary clothes would have said that he was a village merchant or a cattle-driver with connections to Semirech'e; or, if not that, then a camel herder constantly in search of grazing pastures. His cheekbones were sharp, his forehead low and covered in wrinkles. His nose was of average size, but it was crooked at the end. His eyes were slanted and had inflamed red webs of veins in the corners. The first signs of cataracts were visible in one. His chin was wide, his jaw meaty. His sparse beard thickened in the middle of his chin and extended down like a goat's. If a particularly belligerent[12] woman on the street were to seize it and pull, there would be nothing left! There wasn't much more to his mustache. Even though it was short and smooth thanks to the barber To'xtash's efforts, it somehow looked ugly, like a forest with half its trees felled. Long thin hairs on either side hung down like mouse tails. He once thought to take a razor to both sides so that Akbarali might look like a real person rather than a mustachioed clown. To'xtash, a man dedicated to his craft, gathered those wretched things, whispering to himself "art for the sake of art." Akbarali mingboshi, hearing his suggestion to do away with the mustache, immediately rejected it. What would the people think of an official without a mustache?[13] For that reason, the hairs continued to hang in their ridiculous fashion. The Russian nobles in the city, who had helped mingboshi climb to his current rank, had their fun at his expense, joking that his thin "braids" were like "two men hanged." Although this simpleton *sart* official didn't understand their insults, the nobles themselves were familiar with the famous Russian author's "seven men hanged,"[14] both in word and in deed. ...

In those moments that Akbarali mingboshi found himself alone with his conscience, Miryoqub's great services to him came to mind, and he couldn't but admit his gratefulness to his beloved servant. To be honest, it was thanks

---

12 The 2016 academic version of the text gives a dialectical word meaning "belligerent" rather than the word given by most versions of the text, "darker (in complexion)." The difference is a result of varying transliterations of the 1930s Latin script, which possessed vowel harmony.

13 In Central Asian society prior to Stalin's cultural revolution, it was unbecoming of a grown man, particularly a man accorded respect in the community, to be without a beard. Beardlessness was interpreted as a sign of immaturity and childishness. In many cases, it was seen as a disease, and the beardless man was ostracized or relegated to an abject social position. Beardlessness in men also carried a sexual connotation indicating that the beardless (*besoqol* in Turkic) was interested in homosexual relationships as the dominated party. See Najmabadi, *Women with Mustaches and Men without Beards: Gender and Sexual Anxieties of Iranian Modernity*, 17.

14 The Russian author referred to here is Leonid Andreev (1871–1919), whose 1908 short story "The Seven Who Were Hanged" follows the inner struggle of five revolutionaries and two peasants condemned to death in tsarist Russia. Cho'lpon translated several of Andreev's short stories into Uzbek while in Moscow.

to Akbarali's gift of a colt to the previous mingboshi that he received the title of ellikboshi, after which he spent the next six years galloping between the mingboshi's office and the various villages with a notebook, evicting villagers and redirecting water where needed. Over the course of those six years, he earned himself the cost of not just one colt but several, and his four or five *tanob*s of land transformed into several plots. Yet his work as ellikboshi still didn't allow him much rest. For that reason, Akbarali mingboshi couldn't forget the spring festival organized by the merchant Ostanaqul one fall because it was precisely at that festival that he met Miryoqub for the first time.

Since that time mingboshi had forgotten many things. But he always remembered how just two days after the festival, Miryoqub sent him two carts of melons, two wheelbarrows of grapes, and two *chorak*s of unwatered wheat. If his memory didn't deceive him, not a month passed after having walked out of his house one morning with his new silver belt on that he had an armed guard greet him at his gate that evening. After he was appointed mingboshi, he bought his present house in Miryoqub's village and moved there to be close to him. He forgot other things, but not this.

The elders of the village, talking among themselves, said that no previous khan had ever ruled their land so long. Mallaxon, Xudoyor, Nasriddinbek, and the like had come and gone seemingly with every movement of the spring clouds.[15] But Akbarali mingboshi had now thirteen years occupied his post, and all the while his wealth, esteem, and power grew unabatingly.

"God granted him to us, God!" said the elders. "God told him, 'Take it, my servant,' and that's all there was to it."

Some of the youth couldn't help themselves: "God gives to such unjust people! Why does he not throw us poor a little something?!"

Having heard this, the elders ran after the youth, brandishing sticks, and the youth fled.

---

15   Mallaxon, Xudoyor, and Nasriddinbek were three of the last rulers of the Kokand Khanate, a Ferghana valley state that lasted from 1709–1876. Muhammad Xudoyorxon was, for the Russians and jadids, the most notorious Khan of Kokand, reigning three separate times from 1845 to 1875 (1845–1858, 1862–1863, 1865–1875). An uprising in 1875 forced his third and final abdication. The Kokand Khanate was conquered and its territories were annexed into the Russian Empire in 1876. Xudoyorxon's younger brother Mallaxon overthrew him in 1858 and reigned until he was overthrown himself by Xudoyorxon in 1862. The Russians placed Nasreddinbek on the throne in 1875 after the uprising of that year but decided the following year to incorporate the lands of the khanate into their empire. For more on the Kokand Khanate, see Scott Levi, *The Rise and Fall of the Khoqand, 1709–1876: Central Asia in the Global Age* (Pittsburgh: University of Pittsburgh Press, 2017).

"Why are you running? God will give you yours, come and get it!"

The elders well knew that this wealth, esteem, and power weren't granted by God to a simple and coarse person that could hardly form a sentence without Miryoqub's help. The greetings and bows that Miryoqub received every time he appeared on the street were no less than those given to the mingboshi. In fact, they were probably more. Mingboshi was very rarely seen on the street, and when he was, it was at night behind several guards; during the day, he only went out in his gold-brocade robe to see the city's notables on his thoroughbred. No one strained themselves too much greeting and bowing to him because bending over once every month or, hell, once in ten days is no hard thing. But Miryoqub was always on his feet and always on the streets. Most of the time he walked, but he was always in a hurry. If you offered him an "*Assalom alaykum*!" you would only receive a "*Vaalaykum*" in return, probably because he was hurrying. If he turned his head in your direction and greeted you, it was always with a glance of his smiling eyes. Your back really would give out bowing to this "real mingboshi" whose business took him every which where at all hours of the day.

Unlike their previous efforts at nicknaming—they called a local grocer "European grocer"—the village elders weren't mistaken in awarding Miryoqub the moniker "Miryoqub the sly." They justified their choice with ease: "nothing comes out right if his hand hasn't touched it."

The mingboshi owned so much land and water that he himself couldn't keep track of his holdings. But although God had granted his favorite servant such wealth and supported him in everything, He left him in arrears regarding children. In fact, he had no children other than his eldest wife's daughter, Fazilat. To whom would he leave all that wealth? To his childless wives, to complete strangers? His constant marriages must have been his strategy to rectify the inheritance problem, but even then, he had no luck. Sequestering himself alone in his house, where not even a shadow could hear him, he would tell himself: "that damn girl better not be from another man."

Miryoqub, as mingboshi got older, sometimes asked himself: "was it not mingboshi's hopeless situation that caused his womanizing?" One day at *noyib to'ra*'s, they were sitting with the host drinking when noyib to'ra's wife unexpectedly brought their grandson in. He was golden-haired, round like a watermelon, chubby, and white like cotton. Mingboshi suddenly took the boy in his hands, and, despite the boy being an infidel and a Russian, embraced him closely and kissed him. The boy must have been frightened by the mingboshi's unpleasant face because he started sobbing uncontrollably. They took the boy out. Immediately after, mingboshi poured himself a full glass of vodka, downed it, and then another, and another. Miryoqub's nudging, gesturing, the hosts' reprimands and later threats—none of it had any effect. Once mingboshi was completely inebriated, he asked them to bring the boy in again. His mother had no desire to give her little lamb to a drunk, but mingboshi began to beg. He even started weeping. Noyib to'ra ordered that the boy be woken up and delivered, but mingboshi had already lost consciousness and collapsed on the divan by the time the boy came in.

Deprived of both child and wits but buried in land, water, money, and other riches, mingboshi was entirely in Miryoqub's hands. Mingboshi never knew the amount of the harvest that came from his lands nor how much made its way to Miryoqub's coffers. When necessary, mingboshi actually asked Miryoqub for money. If his household needed flour, rice, meat, oil, or anything else, Miryoqub took care of it. Mingboshi, who since receiving his appointment knew nothing but life's pleasures, never asked Miryoqub how he managed.

Miryoqub would hardly have earned the name "sly" if all his work had been for mingboshi alone. He received the name because there was no profitable opportunity that he didn't have his hands in. In the village there were two groceries, a butcher shop; and, in the district, two teahouses. People in the know said that four of the five ran by Miryoqub's initiative alone. In the city, a new cotton factory had recently opened shop along the main road. Its warehouses were so big that at harvest time the cotton had to be weighed on three scales. They said that Miryoqub was a shareholder in that factory. It couldn't have been a coincidence that his two-wheeled yellow phaeton and chestnut mare were usually hitched there. He was a member of one of the big banks' auditing commissions and conducted meetings once a week in that capacity. On top of that, no one ever saw him pay the smallest of taxes or buy one license.

What kind of misfortunes didn't occur with mingboshi? What kind of strange accusations written by skilled lawyers didn't bring investigators over to mingboshi? How many times did the district governor call him in? In such times mingboshi, taught well by Miryoqub, always answered "I don't know" and denied any fault in the matter. And while those official interrogations were conducted, Miryoqub always conducted a few of his own unofficial ones. After staying in the city for one or two days, he would return to the village, having cleared mingboshi of all charges. If mingboshi went to one of the Russian nobles, Miryoqub, of course, accompanied him, and no one ever asked, "Why is he here?" After all, Miryoqub wasn't an official and wasn't a secretary or interpreter for mingboshi, nor did he even know Russian. Why did he always follow mingboshi like a tail? Why?

Miryoqub spent a good part of his time at mingboshi's home, though his house was in the same village. They say that his house was guarded every night by one or two policemen, only no one had ever seen them, and even if they had seen them, they wouldn't, no, couldn't talk about it.

....

One day Miryoqub was at noyib to'ra's house. The gift he had brought this time must have finally so impressed the nobleman that the latter sat him down and talked of several things. When the noble's tongue tired and the first signs of a yawn appeared on Miryoqub's face, a person came in from outside. On his shoulders were two gold hammers; he was tall and had a greying beard and thick mustache. His smiling face was marred by one eye that was constantly squinting. He was most certainly one of those educated engineers common in Turkestan. He exchanged pleasantries with noyib to'ra, but said nothing to Miryoqub and quickly moved towards the table in front of him. The guest attempted, unsuccessfully, to move the chair with a powerful jerk of his hand. He then looked at his watch and threw himself down on the chair.

Noyib to'ra gestured at Miryoqub and turned to his guest, "Are you acquainted with our Miryoqub, my friend? He is a rare one!"

The guest lightly nodded in Miryoqub's direction. Miryoqub smiled, revealing his irritation and injured pride, while the engineer, a moment ago smiling, suddenly scowled. Noyib to'ra must have sensed this, and laughed softly and warmly, glancing at Miryoqub as a loving father looks at his favorite son. Miryoqub, like a pampered son, answered noyib to'ra with a smile. With that, the curtain descended on Miryoqub's participation in the interaction, and the two Russians talked among themselves. The engineer hummed and hummed like a nightingale!

Miryoqub knew that lawyers were a talkative bunch, but he never expected such garrulity from an engineer. Gradually, he started to catch something of their Russian conversation. When noyib to'ra noticed that Miryoqub was listening intently, he started to orate in a fine tone, perhaps to match the guest's. At that point, our Miryoqub stretched out his hand and took a large book from the table. The book was full of pictures. He began to leaf through it noiselessly.

The nobleman forgot Miryoqub as if he wasn't there at all. Only when a few slurs about sarts came from the engineer's mouth, did noyib to'ra direct at Miryoqub his fatherly glance. Even though Miryoqub's eyes were on the book, his ears, like a snake stalking its prey, were fully on the conversation. Noyib to'ra didn't notice.

In that now quite drawn-out conversation, Miryoqub's ear caught hold of something very strange, and his jet-black eyes burned with a charmed fire. His head lifted involuntarily from the book, and his cheeks flushed red. This time they must not have said anything derogatory about sarts because the nobleman didn't look Miryoqub's way. The two interlocutors must have thought that their topic had nothing to do with Miryoqub and his people because they didn't interrupt themselves, continuing as if their sart listener wasn't in the room.

After the engineer left Miryoqub stood up and requested to depart. When noyib to'ra saw him out, he remembered the engineer's uncouthness and asked Miryoqub's forgiveness repeatedly. Miryoqub only smiled, not saying a word. The nobleman took Miryoqub's smile as a sign that he was satisfied and had calmed down.

But Miryoqub could hardly calm down. Could an engineer (after all, he wasn't a nobleman like noyib to'ra), a simple engineer, touch Miryoqub to the quick? No, those insults were like those he heard every day! If he took offense to everything, would he not come down with consumption in just four days? No, no! He had forgotten the insults the moment they had been pronounced. They were gone forever like last year's snow; like after a spring rain there was no sign of them.

The engineer had said something new, something previously secret, in that conversation: the Russians were preparing to build a rail line down from this city to such-and-such a place. A company had already submitted its plans to the appropriate Petersburg chancelleries, and they had promised to approve them. The company would take out a loan from some bank, and engineers would come soon to check on the project. That engineer had been sent here for the construction.

Miryoqub knew immediately where the railroad would be laid. He had formed a plan just as soon as his ears pricked up during the conversation.

Not a week went by before Miryoqub set to work. In less than a month, Miryoqub had bought several hundred tanobs directly along the path of the future track. Almost all of the lands had no access to water, were barren and abandoned, so they cost nothing. Many of the owners had never seen such swiftness in the exchange of property, and others started saying that Miryoqub had lost his mind.

Once the company received permission to lay rail track and began the preparations, Miryoqub informed noyib to'ra of what he had done.

"You're just like an American, Miryoqub!" said the nobleman. "Don't be offended, but you shouldn't have been born a sart!"

Miryoqub not only was not offended but was actually pleased and blushed again as before.

Along the new track's path was a boundless desert. A desert, a completely arid desert. It had water, but only deep underneath the earth's surface. Farmers around it over several generations had tried to make the land arable, but their efforts had been in vain, and all hopes for the land only met with disappointment. The ruins of these fruitless attempts at working the land, however, were still visible: canals, sown areas, controlled-burn lands, land boundaries, a few dried mulberry trees.

Miryoqub with a little money and a lot of ingenuity managed to acquire this desert. When news of the track began to spread, no one called Miryoqub crazy anymore.

Before construction of the railroad had finished, Miryoqub brought water to the surface with the help of pumps. Miryoqub paid out of his own pocket and, when needed, from mingboshi's, to construct a canal through the middle of the desert. Then he began to rent out the land to landless farmers. In not much time a village appeared there, and it was named for the patron who had supplied the water—"Parpi village" (noyib to'ra's name was Fyodor, and the sarts called him "Parpi to'ra.")[16] One end of the village was chosen as a site for the train station, and next to it teahouses, stores, and other buildings started to go up. After the rail line opened, a commission chose a nearby site for a cotton factory. A group of three Bulgarians also bought land in the village for their company and put a fruit orchard and vegetable garden into operation.

However it happened, just a few years after the train began running, Miryoqub had very little land left. Everything had passed to other people. Miryoqub had no particular love for land, and its loss didn't upset him much. The land may have gone, but Miryoqub was all the wealthier for it. How much he had made only God and his favorite servant, black-eyed Miryoqub knew!

....

Darkness had already set in when the mingboshi on his dun horse, along with his Russian secretary Sokolov and the police chief Mirzabobo, approached the gates of his home. The mothers of the children playing on the street had begun to call their children—"enough already, it's late." Before mingboshi could

---

16 In both the Uzbek and Tajik languages, many dialects interchange the phonemes p and f. For this reason, Fyodor, the Russian name, has some likeness to Parpi or Farfi.

even stop his horse, the police guards outside ran over and opened the gates. The creak of one leaf of the gates merged with the piercing drone of the call to prayer. The bellowing of the cows and the light bleating of separated calves longing for their mothers mixed in with these sounds, creating a somber yet pleasant melody. Without dismounting, the mingboshi asked, "Has Miryoqub come?"

Mingboshi's Muslim secretary Hakimjon, putting his hand on his chest out of respect, answered, "Yes, he is here. He is sleeping in the front room."

The mingboshi smiled, obviously happy with himself. "That impudent scoundrel dares to sleep so early! Go, wake him up!"

The two police guards began to help mingboshi dismount. He continued laughing.

"Hey you, impious one. Sleeping during the prayer!"

Miryoqub came out from the front room, rubbing his eyes. Not stepping off the porch, he yelled, "be well, master!" Mingboshi turned and continued laughing.

"Oh, you Godforsaken! What are you sleeping at this hour for?? It's time to pray!"

"Yes, master, of course. I fell asleep waiting for you."

"When did you arrive?"

"Late afternoon. Since then I've been sitting and waiting."

"You were waiting? You fell asleep! Well, what is the matter? Tell me your news."

"Let's hear from you first. You were in the city. Whom did you see?"

"Whom did I see? I saw noyib to'ra."

"And what did he say?"

"What was there to say? Come closer!"

Miryoqub signaled to the guards as he approached mingboshi. Once they had left, mingboshi lowered his voice and began.

"The farmers of Qumariq have submitted a petition against me. 'Mingboshi's lands drink up all the water, and we receive none. It's been several years now that our crops dry up and die,' they complain. That is what I learned from noyib to'ra. ..."

As mingboshi trailed off, his brow furrowed, and Miryoqub saw his narrow eyes repeatedly blink.

"Master, remain calm, tell me what happened from start to finish. I don't think there's anything to worry about."

Mingboshi ignored his solaces and only raised his voice in anger.

"Who did this? Tell me who!"

Miryoqub never argued or raised his voice with mingboshi. As he had always done, he approached the problem indirectly.

"No matter who has done it, we will find out. Tell me exactly how noyib to'ra addressed you and what he said to you."

"I'm saying to you: tell me what bastard did this!" Mingboshi began to raise his voice again.

"It's from what noyib to'ra said that we will find out," said Miryoqub calmly. "Now tell me what he told you."

Mingboshi still hadn't calmed down, but he began to answer Miryoqub in that same tone.

"Noyib to'ra said, 'I know you well. You are a man that respects the poor. If a complaint were submitted against you, I would never be able myself to accuse you of wrongdoing. The servants to whom you entrusted your lands must be at fault. Call them together and instruct them that for every two times they water your lands, they must once water the lands of the poorer farmers. We cannot let their crops die.' So, now do you know who complained? Tell me!"

"It's not enough. What else did he tell you?"

"He said nothing else. Even if he did, do you think I'd remember it?"

"Think. I must know everything he said."

"Fine. 'In those lands, there are two landowners of strong repute: Yodgor and Umarali; they too hold much land and water, and thus the situation is bad. Were they poor, the matter would be different—I pay no heed to the poor. But do not upset our law-abiding, respected subjects.'"

"Ah, well now it's clear: Yodgor the goat and Umarali the noseless were behind it! Noyib to'ra, it seems, told you everything."

Mingboshi smiled.

"Oh-ho, sinful, huh! God gave you such a tongue! Be wary!" He lowered his voice. "If I don't teach Yodgor and Umarali a lesson, I'll never find peace. Do something, I'm telling you!"

"Of course, master! Wait for now. I have to find out more."

"What more is there to find out? Who besides them is there?"

"We must be careful, master! There will be time for lessons. Let's continue investigating, we might still find more."

Mingboshi clearly doubted him.

"What did you say? Did you say there might be more to this? What do you mean?"

"I mean caution is needed! Caution! If we find out more, we'll know better! Give me two days, and I will deliver all that I can find to you."

"Fine, do what you can! Only don't drag your feet! Ok?!" To show that he trusted Miryoqub, mingboshi gave him a slap on the back.

"Agreed, master, have patience," said Miryoqub. The two were silent. Then mingboshi yelled in the direction of the guards.

"Hey, you, out there!"

Hakimjon came running.

"Go find out if dinner is ready! I'm starving!"

Hakimjon ran inside. Mingboshi turned to Miryoqub.

"Now, tell me, what of your news?"

Miryoqub immediately answered, "Wedding."

Mingboshi was surprised at this single, unexpected word.

"Wedding?"

"Yes, a wedding."

"What wedding? Who's putting on a wedding?"

"I am. ..."

"You? For whom?"

"For you!"

"Ah, you sinful one, you! For me?"

"Yes, for you."

Mingboshi's interest was piqued.

"Enough with this mystery. Tell me what you have in mind. What have you done?"

Miryoqub sat closer and began.

"In the city, a servant of God has a daughter worthy of both worlds!"

Mingboshi laughed.

"Repent, impious! Say 'God forbid!'"

Instead of repentance, Miryoqub continued to tell of his shameful doings. Mingboshi only laughed more.

"Oh, you are depraved, depraved indeed! God has cursed you and will have you yet!" he said gleefully.

Miryoqub continued slowly.

"She is fifteen, maybe sixteen years old. Exactly in her prime."

"There are a lot of those 'prime' girls in the village."

"But she has another quality. ..."

"Yes?"

"She sings very well, like a nightingale. Like the Prophet David,[17] they say. ..."

Mingboshi laughed again.

"Repent now, impious! Say 'May God honor him and grant him peace!'"[18]

"Yes, I will pray on it later!" said Miryoqub after which he continued, "I will have her married to you."

"People are indeed talking of her voice. Have you heard it yourself?"

"No! My wife and daughter heard it and now sing praises every day. Her voice is on everyone's lips."

"I told you not to believe rumors. Those gossips also said that Shamsiddin the miller was a good singer, they lifted him to the sky with their praises. Did you ever hear him? A donkey's braying is more pleasant."

"Master! If you could just hear her. ..."

"Don't speak of what cannot be!"

"Why can't it be? The girl is here now, in our village. Tell your elder wife, let her invite her to your home. Hear her!"

"In the village? With whom?"

"At Xolmat's."

"Our Xolmat? That Xolmat? That poor farmer who starves and starves but somehow keeps on living? How can he entertain guests? He can't even feed himself!"

"Exactly. If you have your wife invite the girl, Xolmat himself and his guests will be glad."

"Well then, if that's the case, let her invite them. We'll have a listen. ..."

Mingboshi leaned towards Miryoqub's ear.

"Do you think she'll be jealous?" he asked.

"Only your youngest wife will be jealous. Your eldest wife, whatever her troubles, is smarter than that."

"Alright," said mingboshi standing up, "I'll check in on the ichkari. Dinner should have been ready by now. You sit, don't leave!"

He began slowly moving in the direction of the ichkari. Still feeling playful, "Oh-ho, impious you!"

---

17 In Islam, the Prophet David, or Dawud, is said to have been a great singer.

18 Mingboshi mistakenly prompts Miryoqub to use this phrase. It is typical to say, "peace be upon him" (*'alayhi as-salam*) after naming a prophet in Islam, but "may God honor him and grant him peace" (*salla ilahu 'alayhi wa-salam*) is reserved for Muhammad.

Once he made it to the ichkari and called his eldest wife, the guests of whom he and Miryoqub had spoken were already in Poshshaxon's home around an extravagant table. Poshshaxon, suspicious of Umrinisabibi, had already chased her off. Not knowing how to tell Zebi and the other guests of the impending misfortune that was about to befall them, Umrinisabibi paced about her house like a moth. Both mingboshi's elder wives' heads were in the clouds from elation. Sultonxon's home was empty, she had no idea what was going on at her co-wife's place. The musicians had already gathered and were readying their instruments.

At mingboshi's call two wives came running. Mingboshi silently signaled to Xadichaxon, "Come here alone!"

Poshshaxon returned to the house, but, still desiring to hear whatever her husband had to say, found a discreet place to listen.

Mingboshi spoke shortly with his wives; to speak to women on their level was an affront to his masculine honor.

"Invite those city guests, who have come to Xolmat's, over here and put together a big dinner for them," he said. "They've come all the way from the city; it wouldn't be right to just let them eat Xolmat's dry bread!"

Not giving Xadichaxon time to answer, he added, "What happened with dinner? Hurry it up! I'm starving!"

Xadichaxon laughed softly, "They're already here, that's why our dinner will be a little later. I'll bring you bread and tea."

Mingboshi was surprised to hear that the guests were already in his house.

"They're here? When did they come?"

"Around evening."

"Good, good." He paused for a moment and then repeated himself, "Good, good." Then suddenly he asked, "Is that singer girl here?"

"She is," said Xadichaxon.

"When she starts singing, let me know! Alright?" With that he turned around and left without waiting for his wife's answer.

The young girls had not seen such ceremony in all their lives and answered that abundance of food and drink with an abundance of merriment. When they, tired from singing, eating, and games, made it home, dragging their feet from exhaustion, it was already well past midnight. They told the two old women there to have their cart hitched at dawn and immediately fell asleep. They slept soundly like innocent babes swaddled in their careless youth, while the two old women, their worried voices becoming one continuous sound, whispered frenetically.

One of them was our Umrinisabibi. She told the other of all the evil plans that had been laid for the young life of our beloved Zebi.

....

Having set out on their way, Zebi, who began to sing with all her voice as soon as they exited the village, had seemingly been freed from years of sorrow and worry in just four to five days. She was unaware of the schemes in which she had become entangled. Enaxon's mother, after hearing the frightening news about Zebi from Umrinisabibi the previous night, called Saltanat to her side as the guests were leaving and told her. Saltanat, seeing her friend in her ecstatic state, decided not to speak of it. It would be better if her mother told Qurvonbibi. While the young girl was so grateful for and appreciative of the entertainment and fare provided at mingboshi's, her heart sank at the idea of her friend becoming yet another wife to that hideous old man. All the girls had heard praises of mingboshi's wealth and esteem, but they had also heard terrifying words about his unparalleled repulsiveness. None of Zebi's friends were interested in possessing the affluence that mingboshi's wives had; their eyes didn't bulge with envy at those women's fortunes. When their conversations had touched on the topic of wealth, they screamed "Wealth be damned!" with unmasked disgust.

As the other girls sang, Saltanat didn't join in, engrossed in thought. She imagined herself in place of one of mingboshi's wives. She was dressed in a silk shirt, pants from China, a velvet camisole, an expensive shawl, slippers made of American leather. Around her were a wide courtyard, tall porches, pleasant houses. She was across from a thick mirror that reflected everything beautiful in its onlookers. Golden bracelets, ruby rings, fingers red as coals with henna, eyes painted with kohl. On the table, all kinds of fruits. Ripe pears that bring satisfaction as they touch the lips. Sweet pomegranates from Quva with enormous seeds. As she reached out her hand to take the ripest of the pears, another hand seized hers. Her girlish passions were awakened, her heart started to beat with a soft and pleasant agitation: her cheeks became red like the pomegranates on the table. She had forgotten that in this fantasy she was mingboshi's wife and fully released herself into this new life. The young man across from her opened and closed his glowing and passionate eyes. And the hand that touched hers was his. Finally, our young Saltanat slowly turned towards her beloved and suddenly, losing herself, screamed out: "Mingboshi!"

The other girls, who had until now been singing blissfully, jumped in fright.

"Voy, what's happened to you, Saltanat?" asked Zebi.

The girls crowded around her. Saltanat had both hands on her breast, her face had become pale; she threw herself into Zebi's arms. She slowly opened her eyes and looked across at her friends. Exhaustion showed in her fearful glance. Then her eyes settled on Zebi, looking at her as the guilty look upon their victims.

"What happened to you, Saltanat?" again asked Zebi.

Saltanat opened her arms and again hugged Zebi. "Zebi! Dear friend, Zebi!" she said as she tightened her embrace.

The girls, not knowing what to think, stared at the two.

The cart driver, O'lmasjon, who had stopped the cart after Saltanat's sudden scream, turned around to see what was the matter. He stared at the girls bewildered. He knew that the hugging and cries of "My dear, my sweet" wouldn't end soon, so he shrugged his shoulders and urged the horse on with his whip. When he stopped to water the horse, Zebi and Saltanat had already started whispering with one another.

After entering the city, the girls got off the cart near their homes one by one until only Zebi and O'lmasjon were left. Since their moment alone under the mulberry, they still hadn't had a chance to articulate the strange feelings in their hearts. Now that they had finally found some time, they were overwhelmed by a rush of sensations that left them panting, unable to form words. They couldn't say more than two words about anything. If the two young hearts had a desire at that time, it was only that their destination be a little farther or, as the old folks say, that the road might be made a little longer. The horse, hungry now, sensed that it had returned to familiar places and that its stable was close by. Unaware of the lovers it carried, it picked up its pace and "shortened the road."

When the cart arrived at the neighborhood mosque, Razzoq-sufi along with a few other people headed out on a different cart.

"It looks like my father is going somewhere," Zebi said spontaneously, unable to hide her joy.

"It looks like a long trip. Safe travels!" said O'lmasjon and laughed softly.

At that moment, it was as if a mountain had been lifted from Zebi's heart.

6

Razzoq-sufi returned from the village a day after Saltanat's mother had told Qurvonbibi the horrible news concerning her daughter.

Before entering the house, he gave his things to his wife and asked, "Where is our daughter?"

This hurried question pierced the chest of the unfortunate mother like a barb. She turned pale.

"Why are you silent, hey, Fitna? What happened to you?" asked Razzoq-sufi. How strange that he would take notice of his wife's condition!

Qurvonbibi stammered and barely managed to string some words together: "here … here … your daughter is here. …"

There was an anxious rapidity to her words. Not waiting for her husband's reply, that same anxiety prompted another three questions.

"What is it? Why are you asking? Should I call her?"

The speed and confusion of the questions could impress even upon a man like Razzoq-sufi the undying love of a mother for her only child. Razzoq-sufi forced a smile.

"How can I not ask about my daughter? You're acting strangely. Make up my bed, I'm going to sleep some. A man goes without sleep at a wedding."

Qurvonbibi started to regain her senses.

"Who put on the wedding?"

"A wealthy man. What a meal he laid out! He invited my eshon, and we went together. We even conducted *zikr*!"

But the mother's heart didn't calm with that.

"Why did you ask about Zebi?" she continued.

This time, Razzoq-sufi became upset.

"Can't I ask about my own daughter?!" he cried.

"Yes, fine, fine. Don't yell!" she said and quickly went into the house.

Embroidering in the courtyard by the pool, Zebi didn't hear her father come in. Only his last scream reached her ears; she heard "my own daughter" particularly clearly. She became anxious and got up. While her parents were still inside, she quietly made her way to the courtyard platform and, with both eyes on the door, waited anxiously for her mother to come for her.

Razzoq-sufi, after entering the house and closing the doors, spoke again.

"When did Zebi come back?"

"The day you left."

"Do you know how many days she was gone for? I told her two days!"

"Xalfa eshon, Zebi said, didn't let them go earlier."

"Xalfa eshon! Am I in charge, or is she?"

"You yourself said, 'Fine, do what the eshon's wife says,' did you not?"

"To hell with what she says. You can't keep a child away for so long!"

The old woman didn't know what else to say. What could she say to this enraged man who yesterday entrusted his daughter to the eshon's wife and today curses her? Nevertheless, Qurvonbibi, taking the defense of her daughter upon her shoulders, was forced to come up with an answer.

"Can't she enjoy herself for three or four days after being locked up here all winter? You yourself don't come home for days at a time!"

"If she becomes like me, then let her go where she wants to!" screamed Razzoq-sufi in reply.

The old woman didn't yield, and raised her voice: "If a woman were like you, could she really go wherever she wanted? Who takes care of our family? Is there a man that heats the oven and bakes the bread? Or do you want your daughter to die of consumption from being cooped up all the time?"

These irate voices that were reaching their peak carried to Zebi in the courtyard, only increasing her unease. She could no longer stand it: she got up from the platform and sat down by the window of her father's room. Now the voices in the house chased after her ears, giving them no respite.

"Don't talk nonsense, Fitna! I've had enough! Don't make me mad!"

Qurvonbibi knew well that her husband had a temper. Once she heard this last warning, even Zebi, sitting outside, began to worry for her mother. The old woman softened her voice and, suppressing her anger as much as she could, said:

"Ok, fine, I won't scream. You too tell me calmly now: why did you ask about Zebi just as you stepped in? It sounded like you had something in mind for her. ..."

Her mother's suddenly calm voice may have soothed Zebi's worries temporarily, but now that the conversation had turned to her, her stress increased tenfold. She could no longer hear them, leading her to near hopelessness. All she could do was keep her eyes glued to the door with the hope that her torment would soon end.

"Come here!" said Razzoq-sufi.

Zebi heard these two words clearly, but after that, her parents set to whispering. Now Zebi could hear nothing. As much as she pressed her ear up against the door, the voices that came through were muffled by the wood. She heard only whispering but couldn't understand what was being said.

After Qurvonbibi sat down next to her husband, Razzoq-sufi started.

"Your damn Zebi went to the village and sang for all to hear. I heard many things from the villagers. If I killed her, that would be letting her off easy!"

The mother was going to say something, but Razzoq-sufi cut her off.

"Listen to me!"

Zebi heard her father's "if I killed her" and strained to hear his next words. But the couple began to whisper again.

"Some of those close to mingboshi sought me out and tried to talk with me about your damn daughter."

"Who did they want her for?" asked the old woman hastily.

"For who? For mingboshi!"

"Which mingboshi?"

"Akbarali mingboshi! You don't know him."

The old woman couldn't restrain herself. Her alarm almost made her yell her next words.

"If he's a mingboshi, then he already has a wife. That godforsaken bastard wants another?"

That, Zebi heard very well. She didn't notice how both her hands had already covered her chest. Her heart was beating slowly as if she were ill, her now pale body was slack like a rag. She slumped at the door weakly.

The events of the past few days came to life in her mind. The large house of mingboshi ... the extravagant gatherings ... the two co-wives who had appeared so friendly with one another ... Sultonxon's sudden disappearance. ... Then everything she had heard about mingboshi began to ring in her ears: he was an incorrigible womanizer. ... With three wives, he was only able to father one daughter. ... From the pain of childlessness, he had become the cause of all kinds of misfortune. ... Power, wealth, fine things bring him no happiness. ... He was ugly as death, repulsive. ... Those who saw him were frightened. ... And yet he had such pretty and tender wives. ... What poor things. ...

Suddenly she remembered Saltanat's behavior in the cart: Saltanat had cried out, "Mingboshi!" She had become pale and lost consciousness. When she opened her eyes and stared at everyone, she then looked directly at Zebi and threw herself into her arms. Then two days ago, Saltanat's mother had come and conducted a conversation in whispers with her mother. Since then, her mother had looked like she was constantly mourning.

Oh, if only Saltanat were with her now! She could have shared these things with her, and Saltanat would have comforted her, right? Did Saltanat already know? Wouldn't she have said something in the cart if she knew? They talked the whole way, and she didn't say anything about this. Or could she have been hiding it? If she was hiding it, was she really Zebi's friend? What kind of friend is that?

These thoughts distanced Zebi from her best friend by miles. Now she no longer trusted Saltanat's smiling face, nor Enaxon's. She was some kind of powerless creature, a slave with hands bound; there wasn't a person in the world she could trust, she was alone and estranged.

She was comforted by the thought of the one person who was willing to defend her, the person inside heatedly arguing on her behalf. Her mother, only her mother. ... But her mother was powerless before her cold-hearted father's limitless obstinacy ... just one weak soul ...

The conversation continued inside. From time to time, voices were raised and then suppressed.

"What did you say?" asked the old woman.

The tone of her voice undoubtedly betrayed her agitation: "He couldn't possibly have agreed to their offers?!" she thought.

Razzoq-sufi said nothing and only chuckled. In that chuckle was a hint of playfulness: "It was me. How could I have said nothing?" it seemed to say. He turned to his wife with another uncomforting look.

"Would I really give my daughter to that impious, immoral man?" he said.

A sense of relief washed over the old woman.

"Thank God. You said that?"

Razzoq this time mocked his ignorant wife.

"Idiot!" he said. "They only hinted at it, just barely tossing a thread out to start a deal, and I am supposed to say 'no' suddenly like a chip falling from the roof?"

"Then what did you say?"

"They well know that I don't need that man as a relative. What else is needed?"

The conversation stopped there. When the old woman exited the room, she found Zebi lying by the door like an invalid. Her young and lively eyes reflected years of labor and suffering.

....

Razzoq-sufi's words, full of false piety though they were, and Qurvonbibi's attempts to regain her trust, managed to calm Zebi a little. She sat under the green leaves of the young willows by the pool with her embroidery, and a light breeze fanned her chest, which was filled with some indeterminate anxiety. As she sang, her somber song joined the unhappy melodies of the wind and rode beyond the walls of their home. Her despondent voice often reached the ear of O'lmasjon, who had made it a habit to come by since the day of their return. Pretending he needed to adjust the saddle, he would stop his cart near the wall of her house and try with all his might to follow that pleasant and dear sound. On one occasion, he put his whip on his belt and climbed on the cart as if to break off a branch that hung over the wall. Even then he wasn't tall enough, so he climbed still higher onto the wheel. With one hand, he grabbed the top of the wall, and while stretching the other out to the willow, Zebi caught his eye: the caged bird had stopped singing and put all her love into the stitches of her embroidery. So that passersby didn't take notice, O'lmasjon tried to break off the branch of the tree, all the while keeping his eyes on Zebi. Finally, the branch gave way. Zebi lifted her head to see a man's hand hanging over the wall.

"Voy, God take me now! A man!" she cried.

Like a trapped bird, she threw down her embroidery and ran inside the house. The young man, who didn't expect anything of the like, was astonished. Just then a cry came from one of the faithful on the street.

"Hey, son, get down from there!" said a cold voice that woke him from his daze.

As soon as he had jumped down from the wheel of the cart, the person approached him.

"What a shameless child you are! You should know better, big as you are. Shamelessly looking into a home with nomahram women! If that Razzoq-sufi saw you, he would rip you to pieces!"

The young man, both his cheeks red, said with a voice barely audible, "I wanted to break off a whip for my horse. ..."

He ran his eyes over the wall again with a look of hopelessness before saddling his horse and setting off.

Saying that she could no longer stand the four walls around her, Zebi one day left to see Saltanat. Saltanat, feeling embarrassed and guilty before Zebi, accepted her friend with the utmost ceremony. In her overly courteous behavior, something affected and feigned was detectable. Still unaware of how much Saltanat knew about the events in the village, Zebi interpreted Saltanat's unprecedented kindness as something else. And was only overjoyed by it. Why was our Zebi so happy? She knew that O'lmasjon wasn't just a neighbor of Saltanat, but also a relative of Saltanat's mother and one of the favorites of their household. Like Zebi's family, Saltanat's didn't have a son, and, for that reason, this boy was always in their home and was practically one of their own. The boy had now become a young man. Now was precisely the time when relatives and neighbors began to talk of a wife for him. Did Saltanat not wish to marry her favorite relative to her best friend? Could Saltanat's mother and grandmother not be aware of their daughter's desire? They couldn't possibly dislike Zebi, could they? If they did, would they have let their daughter become so close with her? Did Zebi not receive the same affection from Saltanat's relatives that she did from her friend? Particularly on this occasion? While Saltanat was constantly revolving around Zebi, serving her in every possible way, her mother and grandmother were also busily doting on their guest. Who wouldn't want a girl like Zebi as their daughter-in-law? What home would not welcome Zebi into its embraces? After all, mingboshi wanted her in addition to his three wives!

The thought of mingboshi immediately interrupted Zebi's string of happy fantasies. They scattered like millet spilled and spread in all directions. Her face, which was earlier smiling and red with anticipation, now went pale, withered, and died like leaves touched by a hot wind.

Saltanat, who must have thought that the respect she and her relatives now showed Zebi would expiate her guilt before her friend, was in seventh heaven. Engrossed in her own thoughts, she had no idea of Zebi's torments.

Zebi's goal in coming, to return to our story, was to see the young man who had hung over her wall and broken a branch. But just try to find a merchant or a cart driver at home!

It had been four months since O'lmasjon had begun his work as a cart driver. In those four months, had he spent as many as four full days at home? He left early in the morning, returned around midnight, and that was only if he stayed within the city! If not, he might spend two to three nights away from home.

The same day that Zebi had come to Saltanat's home, O'lmasjon's mother in the neighboring home complained of her son's vagrancy.

"To hell with his career!" she said. "I don't see my poor son all day! And what does he get for all that work? What does he bring home? Not a scrap. The cart boss licks up all the cream, of course. His wretched underlings do the running, while he gets all the spoils. Is that fair?!"

Her husband became angry, "Quit your jabbering already! You should be grateful! If he were a gambler, he would let all of our things ride, not just his passengers, what would you do then? If he sold our house for drink like Ahmadali's son, what would you do? It's only been four months. His earnings haven't been much, but when he gets used to it, he'll bring home his fair share. He's still young, let him work some. Is there any rest without work?"

"He's worked for four months, but he's aged four years in that time!" His mother didn't give in: "Four years! Is it easy to bear and raise a child? You were always on the street, gossiping with your friends! 'It's only been four months.' That's easy to say! No, damn that cart. We'll find other work for him. This won't do. To hell with the boss!"

"You think other work would be easier, do you?" interjected the father again. "Is there any easy work in this world? If you have money and power,

Figure 3. Traditional Turkestani two-wheeled horse-drawn cart (*arava*).
Source: *Turkestanskii al'bom: Chast' etnograficheskaia, 1871–2.*

sure you can find more just by talking. But God Almighty doesn't give those to everyone! He gives them to whom He gives them!"

The mother didn't yield.

"You'll just sit there and say, 'God's will,' then? God's favored can just say, 'Ripen, apple, and come to my mouth,' while the rest of us have to suffer? He who looks finds! If you look, you'll find a better job for your son. Let him have some time to relax!"

"It was just yesterday that he got back from the village after spending a week with those girls. Did he not relax there?"

The way his father said, "with those girls" had the same warmth and excitement that one might expect from O'lmasjon's unmarried peers. His mother noticed.

"When you're going on fifty, better to die already then take an interest in girls! I see how you talk about them; I could wring oil from your lips! You'd like to take another one as a bride, wouldn't you?! Maybe you should think about your unmarried son first!"

The father could only laugh vociferously.

"Then you tell me what he did there in the village!"

The mother quickly gathered an answer.

"While he was enjoying himself there for five days, do you know how many things I had to sell? Material for three shirts, two belts, Saltanat's European shawl!"

"Who did you give the money to? Did your O'lmasjon eat through that much money already?"

"When did O'lmasjon eat? O'lmasjon hasn't had a bite. I gave it to the cart boss for the horse and cart. He had told O'lmasjon that unless we return the lost income from the trip to the village that he wouldn't give our son one kopeck for a whole month. The boy came home crying. Saltanat and I sold things from our dowries so that he could at least earn something. You talk and talk, but know nothing."

The father stopped his laughing and wanted to say something serious, but when Saltanat and Zebi came through the door, he lowered his head and left.

Zebi had heard some of what was said between O'lmasjon's parents through the thin walls of Saltanat's home, and only now understood just how costly their trip to the village had been for these poor families. She began to reproach her friend.

"We all went to the village together, but you and O'lmasjon's mother took all the expenses on yourselves. I could have helped. ..."

Saltanat hugged her friend.

"It was just a shawl. Did I not come away with another one from ming-boshi's? It evened out!"

"And O'lmasjon's mother?" asked Zebi. "The poor thing's house is coming undone. No, friend, I will send you something tomorrow! Tomorrow without fail!"

Saltanat didn't want to hear her friend's rebuke, so she quickly changed the subject.

"Very well, let's go! We'll console O'lmasjon's mother."

They took each other by the hand and entered O'lmasjon's home.

Upon entering, Zebi's hopes sank. O'lmasjon hadn't been home since yesterday. They waited until dark, thinking that he would come that night, but there was no word from him. Saltanat tried to convince Zebi to stay the night, but Zebi, afraid of her father, refused. Once it was dark, the family decided to send one of the old women to see Zebi home. When they started their first turn on the way back, O'lmasjon appeared around the corner. He was urging on his tired horse as it dragged its feet. Zebi unwittingly stopped and O'lmasjon likewise halted his horse suddenly. Neither dared to say anything to one another. To protect them from one another, the old woman spoke instead.

"Hey, why did you stop?" she asked Zebi. Then she turned to O'lmasjon: "O'lmasjon, why did you stop, my boy?"

O'lmasjon managed an answer: "Because I saw you, auntie! Where are you headed so late?"

"I am accompanying our guest home," she said. Then, after taking another few steps, she turned around: "Go quickly, your mother is worried!"

And she prodded Zebi forward. Zebi, scared of the old woman, didn't look back, but kept moving quickly as her heart beat uncontrollably and her knees trembled.

O'lmasjon gave his horse an angry crack of the whip. His tired body burned from this perilous encounter. Again, feeling alien to herself, Zebi couldn't restrain pearl-like tears from beading down her cheeks.

7

While the two young hearts suffered from their hopeless love as though bound by heavy chains in a dark prison. Akbarali mingboshi took in his powerful hands a new newspaper, wrinkling it. As he read it, he cursed the letters with the clumsy tongue of a frequent gambler.

The jadid newspaper, which just barely managed two editions a week, contained the following, which Hakimjon read to mingboshi:

> The absolute ruler of ... *volost'* Akbarali mingboshi closed the only jadid school in all of the district and drove off the teacher without ever paying him. Over the course of its three months of operation this school successfully taught local children, as much as its resources allowed, to determine white from black, good from evil. Mingboshi could not free up any funding for the school, busy as he was acquiring new wives. He has no qualms about adding a fourth, and perhaps even a fifth or sixth, wife to his current three.
>
> Teacher M. M.

Hakimjon, who had found the newspaper and was now sitting across from his master, already regretted his gift. He had worked as a secretary for mingboshi for several years now, and even though he had seen his master angry and steaming many times, he was surprised that this little article could have such an effect. Mingboshi had taken the first cup of tea from the secretary's hand and put it at his side without so much as sipping, forgetting about it in his rage. Hakimjon didn't dare replace the now cold tea. The tea in the pot had become cold now anyways. Hakimjon's eyes were trained on mingboshi, his red cheeks, his clenched fists. He still had the crumpled newspaper in them. Hearing his master's terrifying voice, Mirzabobo, who was leaning against a tree on the other side of the courtyard, was also caught unaware. He told the guard at the gate, "Don't let any petitioners in. The master's mood has soured." No one was to be let in except Miryoqub. Both Mirzabobo and Hakimjon strained their backs from the tension held in their motionless bodies. Mingboshi repeatedly opened the newspaper, read a few lines, and wrinkled it in his grip, continuously asking, "Where is Miryoqub?" Every time he asked, Mirzabobo would run out to the gates, look around, and return. He never gave his master an answer, only looking on in silence.

Mingboshi eventually threw down the newspaper and stood up.

"I asked: where is Miryoqub?!" he boomed.

This was the roar of a wild beast and not a man! Mirzabobo stammered, "Should I … get a horse … and ride to his house? Or … check the city?"

"Now you start thinking, you son of a bitch?!" mingboshi barked.

He then took some agitated steps towards the ichkari. They could hear his roaring voice from there, but his three wives didn't know why he was upset. They looked at one another and then with raised brows signaled to the elder wife to go check. Xadichaxon took a few steps towards the disturbance.

"What happened to you?" she asked. She started to quiver slightly.

Mingboshi answered with the rudest of single words. The other two wives slowly retreated to the back of the room and left for their houses. Xadichaxon froze in place.

"There are thirty pounds of weight on my shoulders. Do I need another ten?!" he bellowed so even those who had exited could hear.

The three wives didn't understand what that weight was. Xadichaxon thought that mingboshi must have been cursed by someone, and now she would have to dispel it. This thought must have passed through the other two's heads as well. But Xadichaxon had more conviction than her rivals and dared to offer her assistance.

"It looks like your rivals had it out for you. Do you need me to cast a spell for you?" she said.

"You women only know your superstitions and spells and healers. If your eyelid starts to twitch, you run to your healer right away," said mingboshi.

As soon as he said this, signs of renewed content ran across his gloomy face. Xadichaxon, feeling a little more confident, retorted, "you said yourself that you had 'a weight on your shoulders,' didn't you?"

Mingboshi laughed.

"If I said, 'a weight,' then ask what kind, you stupid bitch!"

Those inside the house came out and moved closer to the pair.

"Aren't the three of you enough of a burden for me?!"

"How have we burdened you?" asked Xadichaxon.

"Read the newspaper and see. Because of you three, my name has been dragged through the dirt! Are the three of you worth even one of my hairs? If he'd take you, I'd give you to that newspaper pimp myself! One wife is enough for me. If she'd just give me a child. Who am I going to leave all this wealth to? To three childless women?"

"Why are you accusing us all equally? What about Fazilat, your daughter?"

"Does your Fazilat mean anything to me? Another few years and she'll be pouring water on someone else's hands. Is a daughter really a child? Which one of you was worth anything to your parents?!"

Although she had no place to argue, Xadichaxon had something else to say, but she was interrupted by the creaking of the front gate. Before she could utter a word, Mirzabobo's stout voice called out.

"Master, Miryoqub has arrived!"

Mingboshi had already run out towards the gate.

Once he left, the three women gathered and began to discuss their husband's strange behavior. After several impractical suggestions, they decided that Xadichaxon would go to the healer tomorrow morning.

Miryoqub greeted mingboshi with the same upsetting news that he had been fuming about the past few hours.

"Master, they slandered you in the newspaper! Here, look!"

Not a *salom* or an *alaykum* was said. Before he even got off his cart, Miryoqub handed the newspaper in his hand to mingboshi, slyly smiling. To mingboshi Miryoqub's grinning face looked uglier than a dog's.

"Get down from there, damn your ugly mug! To hell with you and your newspaper!"

He took the newspaper and threw it back in Miryoqub's face.

Miryoqub only laughed, picked the newspaper up from the ground, dusted it off, folded it, and put it in his pocket. Then he took mingboshi by the arm and guided him to the platform.

"Sit down, master!" he said, sitting down across from him. "Why are you so tense? What happened? Has the world ended?"

Mingboshi well knew that there was no one who cared about him more sincerely than Miryoqub, so he was puzzled at this behavior. Without even getting down from the cart, he had handed him the newspaper and said "Master, they're slandering you!" with a smile. What was that? Was he dreaming? Or was his most reliable of fortresses crumbling? Was Miryoqub plotting against him? Could he get by without Miryoqub? Were all his wealth, esteem, and honor—all of it!—about to be carried away by the wind like the fuzz from a reed? If Miryoqub was the same as he always was, then he wouldn't have spoken of this news until mingboshi himself brought it up. Of course, there are such people that cannot keep their mouths shut. But they wouldn't have gone by the name Miryoqub and especially not Miryoqub the sly. Miryoqub's teeth were stronger than his lips! And if he could bite his lips, then he could certainly bite his tongue. But Miryoqub never did anything unintentionally!

After calming his fears with this final conclusion, mingboshi recovered and then cursed himself for throwing the newspaper back at Miryoqub. His playful nature returned, and he smiled.

"Stop your joking now," he said in an ordinary, perhaps even soft voice, "Give me some advice. They dragged my name through the mud."

Miryoqub, still smiling, spoke calmly.

"Yes, that's what we should have done earlier. The matter can't be discussed while angry and fuming. This is not a matter with some poor man where you can just call him before you and have Mirzabobo throw him in the dungeon. You can't just scratch away this kind of itch. The person that wrote this is the teacher at the school you closed: a jadid! He's already gone home to his town and had their newspaper people contact those in Tashkent. Even those more powerful than us can't deal with this by ordinary means. And those who write in the newspapers usually know the laws and stick to them. Only those close to the governor general have a say. Those jadids sure are know-it-alls."

"What's a jadid? What does that mean?"

"I told you when you closed the school."

"So I should remember it?"

"Jadid must mean 'new.' They supposedly bring new things to us. A new way of reading, new schools, new customs, new dress, everything new. …"

"Were old things bad?"

"I can't say. In a word, the goal of the jadids is to bring new things."

"Like a new mingboshi and new judges?"

"Well of course they would like a more favorable mingboshi."

"By the way, your jadids didn't write anything about Shamsiddin mingboshi and To'raqul, the district boss. Why did they write about me?"

"You haven't heard how they praised Abdusamat mingboshi?"

"Ah, you mean last year?"

"Yes, last year. Oh, how they commended him."

"I just can't understand your jadids! I've only taken four wives in all my life. And one of them had already died by the time I took the others. Abdusamat has had around ten. Four of them are still alive.[19] Why doesn't your jadid write about him?"

"He's not my jadid, master! As far as I know, jadids like those who support new things."

"Yes, you're right. Wasn't it Abdusamat who opened a new school in his village?"

"Abdusamat mingboshi keeps a teacher in his home to educate his boys. He funds a jadid school and encourages local parents to send their children. He even reads the jadid newspaper."

"That's why the jadid eye doesn't fall on his ten wives."

"Yes, jadids curse the wealthy men who don't take care of their schools as 'stupid, ignorant,' and this and that. The rich man who gives just a little bit of help is raised to the sky as better than our esteemed wealthy men in such and such a way. They would have written the same things about you if you hadn't closed the school and just said yes to a few of their demands."

Mingboshi leaned over to Miryoqub and whispered, "Noyib to'ra wouldn't allow it. What was I supposed to do?"

"Noyib to'ra is a tricky one. He could have ordered it closed himself, but he didn't. He had you do it so you would take the blame. Now the stick has come and broken over your head!"

"No, wait, I'll go to noyib to'ra and tell him to fix this. He told me to do it, after all. How can he say no?!"

"Do you think he's afraid to say no? He'll say no and give you nothing."

---

19 Islamic law, Sharia, allows a man to take up to four wives provided that he is able to support them all and care for them equally, a matter which could be determined by a Sharia court if one of the wives or her family brought suit.

"Why? I did what he asked. Why?"

"Because otherwise he would have closed the school himself. He won't give you a thing."

"And you think I'll let him say no?" Mingboshi said with a smirk.

Miryoqub answered mingboshi's smirk with a quip of his own: "What will you do? Hit him?"

"Can you hit such a man?" Mingboshi clearly hadn't thought through his suggestion.

"Then why ask?"

Mingboshi was silent. He put his hand to his temple and began to scratch.

The two were silent for some time until mingboshi spoke again.

"We have to think of something. I can't just let this go unpunished. … Shamsiddin, To'raqul, Abdusamat. They trumpet their accomplishments. … What do you think?"

"You're right, master. They've been celebrating too long!"

"If I could just have Mirzabobo bring that teacher here, shackle him up in our dungeon. Maybe then my heart would have some peace. …"

"I told you already, you won't even find his ghost around here."

"Then what can we do?"

Miryoqub didn't answer. He was weighing their options. After mingboshi repeated the question he spoke.

"What can you do, master? You'll just have to grind your teeth and endure."

Mingboshi shot up from his place.

"You think I'm so impotent to just endure it, just take their blows?!" he said, raising his voice. "Get me my passport, I'll just go to Mecca!"[20]

"Sit down, master!" said Miryoqub, having raised his voice some as well. "This isn't something to be done with bile and screaming. Let's think. We'll find something."

Miryoqub got up and went to the porch; a teapot stood there, and, after pouring cold tea into a cup, he drank it in one gulp. He returned to his place and began speaking quicker and more assuredly than usual.

"I saw the newspaper in the city and started thinking there. I haven't been able to find an answer, so I've been laughing. It's better to laugh than cry when you can't cross a wide canal, you know?"

"I know."

---

20 Here the hajj is referred to as a form of exile, as it was in the case of many powerful Muslims who were forced to relinquish their positions.

"The hero who fails overcomes grief with laughter," added Miryoqub.

Mingboshi was quiet for a moment.

"Whatever, we still have to do something." This last sentence no longer sounded like the roar of an enraged beast, but rather the complaint of a cat doused in water.

Miryoqub, still thinking, raised his head.

"We'll write a response in our newspaper. If the jadid mocked you in his newspaper, then we'll praise you and revile him in ours. The scales will tip back in our favor. Those trumpets that they're playing for Abdusamat and the others will be nothing but reeds. That will be enough!"

"Yes, great!"

"You're agreed?" Miryoqub made sure.

"Agreed!" said mingboshi. "You'll write it yourself?"

"Do you think about what you're saying, master? I can barely read the newspaper. How would I write something? We'll find a writer, a man of the pen. I'll do it when I go to the city."

"Fine," said mingboshi, "just take care of it."

Then he got up from his seat and went over to Miryoqub, leaned down, and spoke directly into his ear.

"If money is needed, don't worry. Money we have. Respect is another thing, respect!"

....

Two weeks after that conversation Miryoqub brought the government-run sart-language newspaper[21] to mingboshi and silently handed it to his master. The following letter was printed in it:

> After the delivery of warm greetings to the respected nobleman editor of the newspaper, I have the honor to announce that in the newspaper of the jadid class, a letter was printed in which undignified addresses were directed towards Akbarali mingboshi. In answer to this impertinence it is incumbent upon us to comment with regard to the truth. For nearly fourteen years, Akbarali mingboshi has served His Highness the White

---

21 This newspaper was *Turkestan viloyat gazeti*. Funded and run by the colonial Russian government, articles were authored by Russian orientalists, jadids, and the latter's political opponents, 'ulama. Jadid newspapers, on the other hand, were self-funded projects.

Tsar[22] loyally and has never in that time been deemed deserving of reprimand. The governing nobles of the city and *uezd*, the rich and the poor, the most esteemed and educated and so on have never expressed dissatisfaction with the aforementioned mingboshi. To the contrary, he has been a constant presence in their prayers and well wishes. As concerns the uncouth schoolteacher, he appeared only petty and miserable to our citizenry. He, no doubt, is impious and ignorant of his duties as a Muslim. He told the students of his school such things contrary to the teachings of Islam. For example, that the earth is round, that is to say like a watermelon, as a result of which the citizenry became upset and caused disturbances. The esteemed Akbarali mingboshi, in the interests of the protection of our land's general peace, closed said teacher's school. Rich and poor, teachers and students, *imams*, eshons, and murids are grateful for his conscientiousness and foresight and direct their prayers for His Highness the White Tsar and his representative, the governor-general because they have appointed as their servitors in our land such lovers of justice and truth, such protectors of order.

God's most humble servant *mullah* Rivojiddin, God save him from slander, had the honor to write of this righteous man.

After the letter was read to him, mingboshi was beyond glad. Now the celebration had come to his street. His trumpets would bring down the sky and drown out all others. Now all the world across its seven continents would know what an excellent official he was. The White tsar must have translators for all the seventy-two languages in the empire. After it is translated, the White tsar will hear the letter himself. Maybe he will even read it himself. Maybe he won't need a translation and read it in the original. After all, would it be unexpected for the tsar to know all the languages of the people he ruled? Mullah Rivojiddin was such an excellent writer! Just look at how he writes: clear like water, whoever reads it will understand and be enchanted! Why won't the White tsar understand? Soon a letter will come from Petersburg to Tashkent, to the viceroy: "They say I have an unsurpassed official there, follow his example, serve me like he does." And then, oh and then, you'll look and the nobles will come to him from Tashkent! The city governor and his chief of police will honor him! Then his enemies will seem no more important than a buzzing mosquito.

---

22   In colonial Central Asia, locals referred to the Russian tsar as the White tsar.

This time he held the newspaper to his breast. He wanted to leap up, his head swirling in these fantasies, and embrace Miryoqub, who was seated across from him. He wanted to share with him all his wealth, but stopped himself. However much you give such a man, it is too little.

Miryoqub had new business for his master, but mingboshi, who was swimming in joyous thoughts, couldn't have devoted anything to matters other than the newspaper.

"Master, it looks like you are satisfied, correct?" asked Miryoqub with a little pride, though his words were devoid of any greasy, sly obsequiousness.

Fully expressing his joy, mingboshi nodded in agreement.

"What can I say?"

"Well then listen further to what I have to tell you."

"What further?"

Mingboshi immediately forgot his joy as a wave of anxiety fell over him. No good message could come after this happy news. If it was something good, wouldn't Miryoqub have told him before the letter? He must have thought, "I'll calm him down first and then deliver the bad news." No, to hell with these thoughts of honor and duty! The privileges that came with his title were little when compared with its difficulties. Heavy weighs the crown!

In his question, "What further?" mingboshi hinted at all the fears that ate at him. The fox named Miryoqub sensed the anxiety in those two words. He wasted no time.

"Today you can celebrate!" he announced and then continued.

The matter concerned the petitions from those Qumariq peasants, who complained that their lands received no water. Miryoqub told of how, after their last conversation, he had gone there, found everything out, and taken the appropriate steps. The "appropriate steps," of course, included a little education of the petitioners as well.

"Good. You said Yodgor the goat and Umarali the noseless were behind it. Now you've learned that for certain. Now tell me what you did about them."

Miryoqub smiled.

"What did I do, you ask?"

"Yes, what did you do?"

Mingboshi, emphasizing these last words, leaned over to Miryoqub. Miryoqub continued, smiling.

"I told your *mirobs*, 'Give a little water now and then to the low-lying lands.'"

Mingboshi raised his voice, "that was how you taught them a lesson?"

"Would I have done that if I hadn't already taught them a lesson?" said Miryoqub, smiling again.

"Then what did you do?"

"Have a conscience, master! We can afford to give Qumariq some water after your lands have been irrigated. There's more than enough water. No one will raise a fuss. It was your mirobs who were guilty. They relied too much on your esteem and became complacent."

"Why?"

"Simply because. After they watered your lands, they didn't turn the water toward Qumariq. All that stored water filled the old canals and started to turn the unused lands into swamps. Those downstream were afraid to direct the water themselves. And your mirobs did nothing."

"If there's too much water, then fine, let them have it," said mingboshi. "I won't say anything. But those two still need to be taught a lesson. Why did they complain about me?"

"If there's a lesson to be taught, will we lock them up and beat them? Or should we just scold them in front of everyone? Or ..."

Mingboshi cut Miryoqub off.

"Well, do something!" he screamed. He lowered his voice and added, no less angrily, "At least bring them here and give them to Mirzabobo!"

"We can't just beat them for submitting one complaint. If they complain to the governor again or, if not that, if they go higher up, it will be bad. You know how lawyers are!"

Mingboshi had no response. He couldn't breathe. He couldn't fathom how these two landowners, who were his subordinates, could just be let off. He started to kick the ground with his fat legs in their huge shoes.

Miryoqub again set about calming mingboshi, going over to his side with that smile that was all too familiar and, with a voice which even the worst of enemies would trust, said, "The farmers themselves will give them their lesson!"

Seeing that he had mingboshi's interest, he shared with him what he had been up to in Qumariq. He told him that he met with three broad-shouldered young men from among the poor farmers who were suffering and told them that mingboshi had nothing to do with their dry lands, that Yodgor and Umarali were the guilty ones. When the young men asked how those two were guilty, he led them to a place called Sadaqayrag'och and showed them the vegetation there. Sadaqayrag'och truthfully was one of mingboshi's lands, but because it was well shaded, the cotton there hadn't grown much nor had it sprouted seeds. All around it were Umarali's and Yodgor's lands. Because their lands had drunk up the water directed to that small plot of mingboshi's, their crops appeared far better than his. He showed them the two landowners' crops and said, "Now look, whose land is getting the most water?" The young men clenched their fists and raised them menacingly in the direction of those lands.

Later Miryoqub invited the men to a sit-down, having told them that he had a secret to share with them. Their lips quivering and hearts fluttering in this clandestine atmosphere, Miryoqub made them promise not to share his words with anyone. He then told them of the complaint that Umarali and Yodgor had submitted against mingboshi. According to Miryoqub, they wrote that mingboshi had refused water only to them. Their lands suffered, while others' flourished. When the young men heard this, one of them shot up from his seat, raising his fists, and shouted, "I'll find them and kill them, those greedy bastards!" To win them over once and for all, Miryoqub stood up with the young man and announced, "mingboshi is not opposed to sending his extra water to your lands. He just doesn't want his water to go to those two. He told me it would be better for everyone's lands to dry up than give any more to them. It doesn't matter, though, because any water that we send down doesn't make it to your lands, those two take it all!" These last words were salt in the wounds. The three men said almost in one voice, "Have mingboshi give the water and we'll deal with them!" Miryoqub called mingboshi's mirobs before the three and ordered them to release the water.

Mingboshi listened to Miryoqub's recounting of his ruse with all the delight of a child listening to a fairy tale. He imagined the misfortunes that were about to fall on the heads of those two landowners in the coming days. He now thought that, like a child who has outgrown its clothes, Miryoqub's moniker "sly" no longer fit him. He would have to find him a new one. One thought up by villagers just wouldn't suit him. It would have to be something like Emir Navoiy or Mavlono Jomiy, or at least Shah Mashrab.[23]

Mingboshi lost himself in sweet thoughts about the intrigues planned in Qumariq and the master of intrigues, Miryoqub. As Miryoqub stared at mingboshi's face, which was intoxicated with an unprecedented pleasure, a plate full of dumplings emerged from the ichkari and was placed in the

---

23 Emir Navoiy refers to ʿAli-shir Navaʾi (1441–1501), a poet and statesmen in the state of Husayn Bayqara (1438–1509). He is best known as the first poet to successfully advance the Chagatai language, the common literary language of Central Asia until the twentieth century, as a language adequate for poetic composition. Contemporary Uzbeks, like Choʾlpon, consider him the first Uzbek poet because of his contribution to Chagatai, the cultural heritage of which, they argue, belongs exclusively to Uzbeks. He held the title of Emir, a commander,

middle of the table. Miryoqub's eyes moved over to the fat, oily, yogurt-laden dumplings, and then slowly back to mingboshi's face, which had dropped down to the food. He suddenly noticed that there was almost no difference between the two: mingboshi's slovenly, unkempt face was just as greasy as the dumplings.

Mingboshi, without a thought to washing his hands and without any offers to serve his guest, sunk both hands into the plate and began his assault. Miryoqub headed over to the canal to run some water over his hands. To have time to eat himself, he had to slow mingboshi's monstrous appetite; the shrewd servant stole his attention with a carefully crafted question.

"So, master, how about that wedding of yours?" he said, shaking the water from his hands.

Mingboshi, without lifting his head from the plate, with one dumpling in his mouth and another in his hand, hurriedly answered, "You know best! How would I know?"

Miryoqub immediately understood that mingboshi could have no thoughts other than his stomach now. When he got back to the table, the plate had already been half emptied. The two were silent. Mingboshi looked as if he had stuffed cotton into his mouth.

When just a few dumplings were left here and there, mingboshi lifted his head from the plate, though his eyes and hands still remained trained on it.

"Well, master," asked Miryoqub, "are you full?"

"Yes! You have some!" said mingboshi and pushed the remaining dumplings over to Miryoqub. Luckily, Miryoqub had already saved a few others for himself.

The plate was emptied and cleared, and in its place a large teapot was set down. Now mingboshi could talk.

"Well, speak now, impious!" he said. "What did her father say?"

"Tell me what you think of the girl first. Did you like her voice?"

"Why ask? I swear on all the saints and prophets that if that girl is mine, I will never take another wife!"

---

so mingboshi's inclusion of him here is somewhat unmerited given that he is speaking of epithets rather than titles.

Mavlono Jomiy refers to the Persian-language poet and friend of Navoiy, Nur ad-Din Abd ar-Rahman Jami (1414–1492). Mavlono, more often transliterated as mawlana, is an address of respect applied to Islamic learned men in Central Asia and the Indian subcontinent. Baba Rahim Mashrab (1657–1711) was a Central Asian poet and Sufi mystic, popular in folklore for his subversive antics. Shah is the title taken by Persian dynastic rulers, but it was used as an epithet for Mashrab posthumously.

"Don't swear on anyone just yet. When you took the last two, each time you said, 'Enough! This is the last one!' Don't make promises that you can't keep. If she's the one, deal with it then without making any promises."

"Just look at your lack of faith, impious! I am speaking sincerely. God is one and my word is one!"

"Aha! You're going there now? You've done that before!"

"What can I say? If I have her, then I'll renounce the other three. I will never look at them again. I'll give everything I have to her."

"What's happened to you, master? Have you lost your mind?"

There was visible suffering in mingboshi's eyes. The words that emerged from his mouth didn't match those that were in his heart. Miryoqub was taken aback by this state that he hadn't yet seen from his master. He just kept nodding and repeated his "aha."

Another silence took hold. Only Miryoqub's tea sipping could be heard as he became lost in thought. Mingboshi was busy needlessly swirling his tea in the cup as it cooled.

"Aha!" Miryoqub said again. "Her damn father wants nothing to do with it."

"Hmm?" said mingboshi, waking up. He put his tea down and turned his entire body toward Miryoqub.

"That damn Razzoq-sufi is too pious, master."

"What did he say?"

"Should I repeat it?"

Mingboshi suddenly lost his patience.

"What else are you going to do?! Hide it now that you've mentioned it?!"

"He mocked us: 'You think I'm going to give my daughter to a man who has never bowed his head in prayer?'"

Mingboshi for some reason guffawed.

"What a saint!" he managed. "He won't give his daughter to an impious man? A damn saint, right?!"

"He added that you're impious, you're an adulterer."

Mingboshi kept laughing.

"You made me that way, impious! Just get it done. I'll have that girl! Who will he give her to if not me?"

Miryoqub, still thinking through the matter, took his watch from his pocket.

"Aha," he again repeated, "it's almost midnight. I must go, master."

"Wait," said mingboshi, standing up. "What's your plan? Am I supposed to just give up now that her father has said no?"

Miryoqub put on his shoes and turban and then returned to mingboshi.

"Don't worry, master!" he said. In his voice sounded a seriousness and decisiveness that invited trust. "We'll convince her father. The girl will be yours. I'll take care of it."

Mingboshi slapped him on the back a couple times.

"I trust you, you, my tiger, my tiger!"

Yawning, mingboshi put on his slippers and entered the ichkari, while Miryoqub, accompanied by Mirzabobo, exited. As the village dogs barked and howled, he thought of various ways to break the will of that stubborn Razzoq-sufi.

8

The women in Razzoq-sufi's home had long forgotten the word mingboshi. Like fierce winds that accompany the coming of spring, mingboshi had come and gone, and their home had become quiet. Qurvonbibi had received new orders from her neighbors and set to work sewing mats. Zebi had set her bed next to the pool and become engrossed in her embroidery. O'lmasjon broke off a branch for his horse every time he came by. Only now the girl never ran into the house and instead only covered her face, both cheeks burning red from her illicit act, while her eyes smiled, looking out from behind the veil. ...

Summer had set in. The sun warmed its earthly tandoor. The birds that had earlier spread their wings and frolicked among the clouds now settled on the branches of trees to avoid the heat. When a rare rider and cart passed by, the dust they kicked up rose over the walls. ... People, animals, trees, and nature itself suffocated from the hot air.

Even Razzoq-sufi became docile. He hadn't even gone to his master for the last few days. He had the women cover the windows with sheets, making the house completely dark, and remove all the mats to run water over the bare floors of the rooms. He didn't leave the house from morning till evening. In front of him was cold tea, at his side—a fan, and he performed his zikr. Sometimes he read lines from Ahmad Yassaviy's *Book of Wisdom*,[24] sobbing. ... Other times, he would sing softly like a *hafiz*.

"It looks like you've quit your brotherhood!" Qurvonbibi quipped one day.

"Enough with your nonsense, Fitna!" Razzoq yelled, submitting himself back to his readings.

24　See note 7 on p. 56.

"Your eshon won't be mad? What kind of murid are you?" she started another day.

"Who would want to meet in this heat? You're a strange one," he responded. This time, he turned away and fell asleep.

When someone called for him soon after, he was in a deep sleep, and Qurvonbibi had already left to deliver a mat to her neighbor.

Zebi heard the yelling at the door, tied a scarf over her hair, and went to see who was there.

"Who are you? What do you want?" she asked from behind the door.

A simple and somewhat ugly, yet contented voice answered.

"Are you one of Razzoq-sufi's women? How are you, are you well?"

"Yes, praise God," responded Zebi.

"I came to speak with your father. ..."

"He's sleeping. Should I wake him? Is it urgent?"

"His eshon sent me. You must wake him. The eshon said he needs to see your father immediately."

"Alright, I'll wake him."

Actually, Razzoq-sufi had already awoken from the first call. He opened the sheet over the window inside and called out to Zebi in the courtyard.

"Who is it? What did he say?"

The murid outside heard Razzoq-sufi's voice and answered.

"It's me, Razzoq, me. Xudoynazar!"

Once he realized who it was, Razzoq-sufi didn't bother to ask why he had come.

"Wait, I'm coming."

He quickly went towards the pool and began his ablutions.

By the time Qurvonbibi returned from her neighbor's, her husband had already left, and Zebi had cleaned up the house. Zebi was singing a song about how a young man had climbed over the wall of a house for a red apple.

"Hey, Zebi, where is your father?"

"His eshon sent for him."

Zebi answered briskly so as not to interrupt the song, which she immediately began again. But her mother was very interested in what had happened because her father had been holed up for more than a week without leaving.

"God give long life to our eshon! What a nice thing he did! If a man lies in the house for that long, he starts to smell. ..."

"The mats really have become rank," joined Zebi.

"Take them out and lay them in the sun. Or take them to the courtyard and beat them," said Qurvonbibi, counting the smooth coins she received for the mats in her hand. "What a good thing, my dear child. If the eshon can't lift your father's lazy body, then who can?"

After a brief silence, she brought up her old grief with her husband.

"Oh God, to not see his frowning brows again. ... My heart is filled with woe. It snows from his cold brow, his appearance is that of winter, like an icy blizzard. ... If I could just have someone to talk to, to consult with. ... If only he could, like other faithful Muslims, have a profession that brought home a few coins a day. ... No, no! He goes to parties and weddings, fills his stomach, but doesn't have any other duties. He never thinks, 'I have a wife, I have a daughter, what do they eat?' He got used to that free soup at the lodge, and now he'll never agree to work, to sweat. How his brother tried: 'Come to the village, we can work together!' But no! Does he even have the constitution to work? Even if hungry, he wouldn't lift a finger to do something about it. And every year he scares us with a trip to Mecca! He has no money to his name, but every year he gets a passport. Like someone who really plans on going he spends all his money on flour and oil, bakes bread. Once the preparations are done, he forgets about the trip, and those moocher murids in the lodge eat the bread for free! My patience is at an end with it!"

Zebi, having brought the mats to the courtyard, listened to her mother's complaints, astounded at the woman's mountain-like fortitude. She decided there and then that she would endeavor to help her mother in whatever way she could so that she didn't have to bear the burden alone. Did she not know that Qurvonbibi's mats weren't the only thing providing their income, but also her own embroidered belts and caps?

"This is our fate, Mother, what else can we do?" Zebi tried to calm her mother.

The two started to beat the dust from the mats.

"Of course, my child, nothing can be done about fate. But sometimes the heart can only endure so much and needs to pour everything out. ..."

They both went silent and continued working. After a moment the old woman asked, "Why did his eshon call him? The person who came didn't say anything?"

"I don't know, it sounded urgent. He said, 'Bring him here quickly.' Father did his ablutions in a hurry and left."

"Good. There's probably a wedding somewhere. Your father probably won't even come back; they'll go to the village right away. They wouldn't have called him otherwise. ..."

"All the better if he leaves for the village!" said Zebi.

A joyful smile spread across her face at that moment.

"I'll call Saltanat over. If she comes, we'll have a great time."

"Very well. If your father doesn't come home tonight, you'll call her tomorrow."

The girl's smile, having spread out like a drop of water in the sand, suddenly disappeared. Dark clouds of worry gathered over her now serious eyes.

"We have neither flour nor rice. Are we really going to treat guests to stale bread again?" asked Zebi. And without waiting for an answer, she added, "Will there ever be salvation from poverty?"

"Don't worry, my child, we won't send your friend away hungry. We will figure something out."

Zebi looked at her mother with eyes wide open.

"Truly?"

Qurvonbibi took the coins from the knot in her handkerchief and handed them to her daughter and said with all the happiness of a hunter having hit his target, "Here, my child, the money from my mats has found a use!"

Zebi threw her arms around her mother's neck; after her mother stroked her softly a few times, she nuzzled her face into Zebi's hair. The two worn and pained hearts allowed themselves a little joy.

....

The joy in those four walls was as momentary as a passerby's glance. So quick that if you saw its appearance you might not even note its departure.

Why don't the poor women who grow up inside four walls, who don't see anything other than the sharp looks of those permitted inside, sense the tragedy of their sheltered lives? If they are so used to seeking little joys inside their four walls, can these poor things ever believe that the shameful joys which wander in from outside are part of something greater?

Zebi usually went to sleep not long after the evening prayer and woke with the morning prayer, but that night she stayed up talking with her mother to see whether her father would return. Talking about whatever came to mind, the two went through three pots of tea. When the whole country had gone to sleep, there was still no word from Razzoq-sufi, so mother and daughter decided that he must have gone somewhere with his eshon. Zebi went to her bed with the sweet dreams of her friend's visit.

She woke up much later than usual the next day because of especially satisfying dreams. When she opened her eyes, she immediately saw that the outside door was wide open. Her father had returned. She was surprised she had slept so soundly: her father usually made such a clatter when at the door. In the time between hearing someone answer his call and the door opening, the ill-tempered Razzoq-sufi often took his walking stick to the door, beating it with all his might. Zebi must have slept like a corpse to not have heard that racket. Now any attempt to invite Saltanat over had gone to the winds. Razzoq-sufi's head wouldn't rise from his pillow for another few weeks. Now the young girl, in the very bloom of her life, would spend God knows how long by the pool, needle in hand.

She got up, washed her face and hands, lit the fire in the hearth, and put the pot on. Then she closed the outside door and went inside the house. The house was dark inside since both windows were covered. She silently began to listen: she distinctly heard sobbing. She kept listening. It was her mother. Her heart skipped a beat. Then she heard her father's muttering.

"God gave women tears. So cry!"

Everything inside the house went quiet. Qurvonbibi's crying was extinguished with a final sigh, and she too became quiet.

After a long silence, Razzoq-sufi could be heard clearing his throat. He said with his usual authoritative voice, "Well, get to it, bring the tea!"

The old woman, in a downtrodden, soft voice, answered, "Should I bring it here or will you come out?"

"Who would sit in this heat!?" he screamed.

When her mother exited, Zebi hung on her neck. Qurvonbibi's eyes were red and her eyelids swollen.

"Why were you crying, Mother?" asked Zebi.

Unable to respond immediately, she paused for a moment.

"It's nothing …" she muttered.

That near-empty answer scared Zebi's already worried heart.

"What does that mean? Does a person cry for nothing?"

Qurvonbibi was silent again.

"Mother, something terrible must have happened. You're hiding something from me!" said Zebi forcefully.

For the first time in her life, the worry in her heart had come to her tongue.

The mother knew that she would have to give her daughter a satisfying answer, but she couldn't come up with the words.

"Why ask, my child? You know how your father is. He constantly upsets me for no reason."

"Well, what did he say?"

"What hasn't he said? He says he's leaving us … that he's tired of us."

Although Zebi believed her mother, and was relieved somewhat, her mother all the while thought, "How can I convince her of what I know to be a lie?"

"That's just how father is," said Zebi, "if he's in a bad mood, he always threatens to leave. He'll calm down in a few days. He's never left before."

Zebi's reasoning somehow calmed her mother. Her words and voice had the comforting simplicity and innocence of a child in them. Her daughter was still so naïve! Whatever Qurvonbibi said, Zebi would believe! But how long can a mother deceive her poor daughter like this? How long would her daughter's innocence last? Would her deception not be shattered soon enough by the truth? At that point would she find the words to lie again? Could she patch the girl's broken heart with motherly love alone? When Zebi left to sit on the platform, her worries alleviated, the mother, still standing motionless on one edge of the porch, couldn't rid her mind of these questions. Having seen her daughter's renewed insouciance, she felt a little at ease. She went to the platform and began kissing Zebi on the forehead.

When Zebi went inside to call her father, he for some reason yelled, "Go back and drink your tea!"

Neither mother nor daughter offered resistance. Zebi attributed this strange behavior to her father's bad mood. She couldn't see the agony that had returned in full force to her mother's eyes. While her mother suffered trying to keep the secret, her thoughts playfully moved from O'lmasjon to Saltanat and back. Again, that pleasant song of hers ran over the quiet waters of the pool. Becoming absorbed in her embroidery and threads, she stitched a pattern of peaks and troughs that reminded of a smiling face. Again, that cart driver looked on in secret and shared in the girl's same sad song.

One day after a cart delivered two sheep to their home, she, without another look at her mother's troubled eyes, suddenly understood the meaning of Qurvonbibi's constant tears. And it was like a stone crushed her heart.

The sheep came just after breakfast and the butcher was ready before lunch. Razzoq-sufi, rolling up his sleeves and picking his long robe up from the ground, went out to retrieve the baskets and barrels of goods outside. The ground had not yet been covered in the blood of slaughtered sheep, when voices carried over the walls from outside.

"Congratulations on the wedding, Razzoq!"

"How wonderful it will be!"

"Such wealth only God can grant his humble servants!" said the well-wishers.

Now the girl began to cry with her mother. As their wailing increased in strength, so did the congratulations from outside. The whole neighborhood wished Razzoq-sufi happiness and applauded him!

....

After more extravagant wedding gifts than an average household could hope for, Qurvonbibi's eyes ran out of tears. Zebi's eyes, however, had still not tired. Saltanat had come over twice since the announcement of the wedding. Qumri and her other friends came several times and tried to comfort Zebi. To no avail! Tears came of their own accord, pouring out of her eyes like water flowing from a canal. Her mother, who had a hundred times over dried her daughter's tears with her sleeves, had since become accustomed to those salty drops and now silently went about her business, preparing for the wedding.

Razzoq-sufi's hands had blistered from carrying the flour, rice, and sheep that were delivered every week. His stomach distended from daily pilaf. His boots glistened like a mirror from wiping his oily hands on them. The two women shed tears only behind his back. The bounty of food and gifts had, it seemed, poured out from the crack of the girl's broken heart. But the old man was constitutionally incapable of understanding hearts or heartbreak; the impending wedding only brought about hopes of imminent pilgrimage.

Qurvonbibi, who had lost her senses on the day the very first sheep was sent, had gradually come to. With time Zebi's tears also dried up. She now went about her chores like before, but lifelessly, as if a shadow. As before she never disobeyed her mother, performing every command she issued, but her utter disinterest, the wooden, puppet-like hands and fingers that washed dishes and clothes filled Qurvonbibi's eyes with tears. Zebi no longer spoke and, of course, didn't sing or even hum, increasing her mother's sorrow all the more. Her mother now thought, "Will this poor, unfortunate thing even make it to the wedding?"

After Razzoq-sufi had returned home the day his eshon called him, he told his wife matter-of-factly: "I gave your daughter away to mingboshi. Make the preparations." She had been in mourning ever since, but despite so much time passing she never asked her husband why he agreed to the marriage when earlier he had so adamantly refused. Honestly, she just could not bring herself to ask. Qurvonbibi, who had often tested her husband's wits, now fearfully avoided him just as her daughter did. But Zebi's permanent silence began to weigh on her, and one day while Zebi was away, she broached the subject.

"My head is spinning and I still don't understand."

"What are you saying, Fitna?" Razzoq-sufi retorted in his usual dry and cold manner.

Qurvonbibi sighed and then choked on air. After another sigh, she regained her composure and began again.

"How could you do it? How …"

"What is it that I've done, bitch?"

"Before … you said, 'I'll never … that damn mingboshi,' you boasted, 'my daughter will never … to that impious!' Where are your boasts now? What happened? How can such a devout murid give his daughter to an impious alcoholic like that?"

"And what if I did, bitch? It's my daughter. …"

"Your own daughter … why not find someone equal to her. I'm surprised your eshon didn't forbid it."

Qurvonbibi found a bit of confidence and raised her voice. If she was on his eshon's side, then she could shame him.

"Yes, yes, now I've figured it out! Your eshon, God keep him, knows nothing about this! Otherwise you would never have done it."

Instead of becoming angry and screaming, it was as if he was glad, and a smile ran across his face.

Qurvonbibi continued, raising her voice still further.

"Just you wait! I'll go tell your eshon myself. It may be too late for him to do anything, but I will make sure you never hear the end of it from him."

"Oh, you fool, Fitna!" said Razzoq-sufi laughing, "You really don't know! You're so stupid! You're such a woman!"

Qurvonbibi didn't retreat.

"I'm dying from grief, and all you can do is smile and say, 'The goat thinks of its life and the butcher—of meat.' You think I can't tell your eshon?!"

"Go, tell him! Tell him!" taunted Razzoq-sufi, still laughing, "show him your stupidity so he knows too, Fitna!"

"Aha! And you're so smart! Just wait! Maybe you'll start thinking once your eshon starts scolding you. You're still drunk from all the pilaf!"

Razzoq stopped laughing and became serious.

"Enough, you fool, fine!" he shouted. "You know nothing, yet you keep chattering away! If you go to him, my eshon—the very one who badgered me incessantly until I agreed to give Zebi to mingboshi—what will you say?"

Qurvonbibi involuntarily cried out, "Voy, take me now, God! Is your eshon in his right mind? Voy, what new woe is this!"

The poor woman struck her head with clenched fists.

"Yes, knock some sense into your head, Fitna!" said Razzoq-sufi again in that serious tone. "Hit it hard. If you don't get smarter, you'll at least rid me of your nonsense!"

The two were then silent. Razzoq, still serious, focused his eyes on one point, while Qurvonbibi lowered her hands and stopped. Then she spoke calmly.

"Even if he insisted, couldn't you have refused?"

Despite her protest, the tone of her voice conveyed that she recognized her defeat. Razzoq-sufi sensed it. He tried to soften his composure, as if to justify himself before his wife.

"Just speak calmly now, Fitna. It's as if you're ready to bring down the world," he said, "I argued with him for a long time. I told him I would never give my daughter to an impious person. But he was steadfast: 'a millennium of our worship is equal to one day of his service to us. How many faithful Muslims has mingboshi helped and how much suffering has he alleviated? How many thieves and brigands has he punished? How many wrongs has he righted? Piety is piety, but his service to the faithful is also piety! The latter might even be worthier of God's blessing!' What can I say to that? What can be said? I am illiterate and cannot read, I don't know black from white, while he is a mullah, a man of great learning, he understands God's will, he knows Sharia and our order's teachings. How can I refute him?"

This is how Razzoq-sufi, cursing himself and, oddly for him, commiserating with his wife, recounted what he had done. Seeing her husband like this, Qurvonbibi understood that this marriage was their family's irrevocable fate. She looked at her husband warmly and began to sympathize with him some.

She said, with a heaviness in her heart and a lump in her throat, "I wouldn't have said anything. Now look at our daughter, who has become a lifeless shadow. … I fear for her. …"

"Invite her friends, Fitna. Let them have their fun. I'll talk to mingboshi and hurry this up. Let's be done with it as fast as possible."

"Your daughter was already going to call Saltanat. Because you came home …"

"I will go to the lodge. Have her invite them. There's enough flour and rice for whatever you need. Here's money, do whatever you like. Go to the bazaar. Do whatever her heart desires!"

With those words, he took out a new ten-ruble note, wrinkled it between his fingers with a crackle and handed it to the old woman with a childish joy on his face that she had never seen before.

She looked at the note and the lifeless image on it, which immediately brought her daughter to mind. Again, she couldn't hold back the tears that came to her eyes.

9

Poshshaxon led Zebi's future co-wives and in-laws into the city to bring the fiancée to her future husband, never noticing, despite her cleverness, that an it-ty-bitty girl, equal to the great Poshshaxon in cunning, Umrinisabibi's daughter, accompanied them. As the Uzbek saying goes, "The itty-bitty one takes down the great khan." When the caravan of in-laws left for the city, Poshshaxon drove off Umrinisabibi, who had surreptitiously climbed onto the cart, telling her, "If I see you at the wedding or after, I'll have mingboshi throw you in a dungeon!" But she either didn't see or simply paid no heed to the woman's daughter in the cart. The girls that Poshshaxon assigned to take care of Zebi hovered around her like devils in angels' guises, charming her with pistachioed smiles and sweet words, keeping her warm for mingboshi, never doubting in their inevitable success. Poshshaxon, who demanded constant reports from her "eyes," also found time to attend to her future co-wife. After several heartfelt conversations, she confidently told herself, "I've done it! I've broken her, I've overcome her stubborn will!" Nothing good comes of self-deception though! Umrinisabibi's itty-bitty girl had no problem washing away with just a few words all the good will created by Poshshaxon's girls. Sultonxon, who had been tearing her hair out in anguish, had tasked Umrinisabibi to deal with the future co-wife. Now she could laugh her devilish laugh and clap until her hands tired. Who knew?

The itty-bitty one found a few minutes in the city and few in the village to say everything that she intended. She painted such a picture of mingboshi that if a demon had come to be her groom, she would have cried out, "My love!" From the young girl's sincere tongue came heartbreaking tales of "tears from Sultonxon's innocent eyes," and the one thousand and one "deceits" of "the two allies" (Xadichaxon and Poshshaxon). When Zebi, as the wedding neared, ignored Poshshaxon's girls and began to allow only her mother to see her, the two "allies" started to fret. Zebi soon isolated herself in the big house given to her on mingboshi's property and sat behind the silk curtain. The two "allies" forgot their duties, assigning the preparation of dinner to others, and gathered in Poshshaxon's home. They discussed the change in Zebi's behavior and looked for the cause; they contemplated and suggested several plans of action. But they all failed to notice the itty-bitty one's shrewdness.

Unable to think of anything to resolve the situation, they became despondent. The day of the wedding had come. Soon the groom would enter his new bride's home, while their courtyard would be full of women, children, and people from all corners of the earth. Oh, the noise and chaos, the head just spun from it! If yelling and screaming were heard from the bride's house, the noise in the courtyard would suddenly become quiet. If only they could think of something!

All the while, the noise in the courtyard continued to increase.

"Wait, what's happening?" said Poshshaxon suddenly.

Outside a choir of women's voices arose. All the women were raising a fuss and repeating something. The two "allies" ran out to the courtyard.

An itty-bitty thing had happened.

Zebi was sitting with her mother behind the silk curtain in the corner of her new house by the window. She didn't seem all that upset. She was even laughing at what the women outside were saying. Two women—who they were no one knew—were standing under the window talking, of course about mingboshi and Zebi. Zebi listened to them, her heart fluttering, while her mother tried to distract her. The two women continuously raised their voices. They were easily heard among the crowd, and Zebi had no problem ignoring her mother.

"Your daughter is of age, why not give her away to mingboshi?" asked one of the women.

The other voice answered over the din clearly, "They say there are snakes as thick as human thighs in the Buvatavakkal hills. Why not just give my daughter to them?"

Zebi involuntarily let out a worried cry and threw herself into her mother's embrace. All the women in the courtyard ran towards the sound and started chattering: "Voy, what happened? What happened? Take me now, oh woe!" The voices were coming from all sides now. They surrounded the curtain, but the voices of the two women still sounded above the rest.

Just a few moments later, the two disappeared. No one knew where they came from or who they were. Do two women really stand out in all the chaos?

Poshshaxon and Xadichaxon tried to ascertain what had happened, but they received all kinds of uncertain answers. Some said, "The bride heard someone slandering the groom." "I heard it myself," said others. The women inside blamed the ones outside and vice versa.

Zebi, her woeful eyes trained outside and her hand on her breast, lay down helplessly. She said nothing, answered none of the questions from her mother, and didn't even recognize Enaxon, who had come to her side. Her face went white like cotton and her eyelids twitched.

Poshshaxon put a lock on Umrinisabibi's door and went to consult with her "ally" again. This time the meeting was very short. Only minutes separated them from mingboshi's lifting of the curtain.

"If we don't allow your husband in today," said Poshshaxon, "then we might still have time to convince Zebi. Then we'll bring him in," she held back a chuckle, "and he'll know what to do."

"Ah," said Xadichaxon, "we'll just hope that everything is in order down there."

"Right. ... In any case, tomorrow, if God wills it ..."

"You're right, let's hold off today. Your husband can stand another day."

"Yes, of course. Let him blame himself. Sultonxon has won for now."

"Don't remind me. Umrinisabibi had a hand in this, probably."

"Of course! Tomorrow ..."

"She's probably gloating, damn woman."

The two were silent for a moment.

"Any more thoughts?" asked Poshshaxon. "So it's decided, we don't let him in today?"

"I don't see another way. But who's going to convince the stubborn man to hold off?"

"You're a strange one! Who will convince him? Your Miryoqub, of course."

"He's your Miryoqub."

"He's all of ours. ..."

"Well then, call him in."

"No, you're the eldest, you call him! I won't have any part of it!"

Xadichaxon went out to the front door to call Miryoqub. Poshshaxon ran over to Zebi's house to check on her.

....

Sultonxon had left for her mother's a few days before the wedding. As she packed, she questioned whether she needed to ask permission. Who would she have asked? Mingboshi's mother was long since dead, so the role of head matriarch fell to her elder co-wife, Xadichaxon. Could she have begged her? Or could she have gone to Poshshaxon with a courteous bow and asked her? What would they have said? Even if pleasant words, "Oh my dear, oh my sweet child" were on their tongues, on their minds would be: "Die already, oh how good your death would be! Are you hurt and now you want to run away? Run, run, and don't look back, no time to put on your shoes, get!" She had to ask mingboshi, of course. There was no way around it. He was her husband and thus her shah, all a woman's will is in her husband's hands. But mingboshi now had no eye for her. It was as if she didn't even cast a shadow. Oh, how often just a year ago he had said, "My Sultonxon." He was always at her side. But as soon as Zebi had set foot in their house, it was as if Sultonxon didn't exist. Like yesterday's dusk, she was forgotten!

Covered in her paranji, she approached Umrinisabibi's door and stopped suddenly. She looked back and headed towards Xadichaxon's house.

"I'm leaving for my mother's. I'll get some air there for three or four days."

Could Xadichaxon have just agreed? Could she, perhaps from impatience, have said nothing or even just chuckled? No! Could this snake ever miss her victim's most vulnerable spot?

"Voy, what are you doing, Sultonxon? What a wedding you'll miss."

Sultonxon muttered with difficulty, "I'll come back ... by the wedding. ..."

As soon as she reached Umrinisabibi's door she broke out sobbing.

She didn't stay long. She shared her sorrow and after she found some relief, she advised Umrinisabibi how to use the itty-bitty one, and then left for her mother's. She didn't return in time for the wedding.

The day after Zebi arrived at mingboshi's home, Umrinisabibi made it to Sultonxon around breakfast. Her lungs practically in her mouth and panting, she told of what she had managed. The itty-bitty one's great deeds, particularly the two women outside Zebi's window, raised Sultonxon from the dead. Her eyes, closed from exhaustion and sleeplessness, were suddenly opened. New rings would soon shine on the withered fingers of Umrinisabibi. The two hugged one another and fell into a mutual state of ecstasy.

"No, it's still early! Still early ..." Sultonxon protested suddenly.

"What are you saying, my dear?"

"It's still too early to prepare a funeral."

"What do we do then, my dear? They won't let me in there. My daughter made it in, but after yesterday, the two wives put a lock on her door."

"No! We'll find a way, we have to."

"Yes, my dear, of course."

"We'll find one! Find ... find ... find one. ..." Sultonxon, now thinking about something else, kept repeating these words as if in a trance. Suddenly she asked:

"Where's Enaxon? Will they let her in?"

"She's always at Zebi's side."

"Well then, speak with her. Speak with her today. Go now."

"All right, I'll go."

"Look at me!"

Sultonxon put both hands around Umrinisabibi's shoulders and brought her face in close.

"Look at me, auntie! Enaxon is Zebi's friend. Her most sincere friend. She didn't want Zebi to marry mingboshi. She still doesn't want it. Don't be afraid and speak to her. The subject will come out naturally, and from that she'll ask your advice!"

Umrinisabibi filled her large bundle with flour and rice and took off.

When she arrived at Enaxon's, the girl's whole family was sitting around a bag of corn, shucking.

"My dear Enaxon. I'm in a hurry. I just have a few words to say to you."

The two went out into the courtyard. They sat down by the canal and Umrinisabibi started.

"How is Zebi doing, my dear? Tell me just a little bit. I've been suffering, not knowing anything. I've fallen in love with that girl. She's the apple of my eye."

"Who doesn't love her? Everyone does. But love is one thing, her happiness is another. ..."

"Don't speak of it, dear. The poor thing has seen things that others haven't even dreamed of."

They paused. Umrinisabibi wetted her kerchief in the water and wiped her face.

"I can't, my dear. ... I can't just sit in one place anymore. I've asked my daughter Bahri, but she is in shock, without words. She was there last night. She even went to the city together with everyone. When I ask, it's as if she is mute or without a tongue. She only answers, 'I, I. ...' Our hearts are breaking for Zebi. I ran here, my dear, to ask you."

Our innocent Enaxon believed all these lies.

"Zebi is fine now," she said "It's just that yesterday she heard someone say something bad before the groom's entrance. ..."

Enaxon then explained in detail everything that she had heard the day before. Umrinisabibi knew what had happened, but she reacted as if she was hearing it for the first time: "Voy, God! Voy, take me now! Voy, how terrible! That really happened?"

"Now everyone is confused. They're asking what will happen tonight. If such an event already broke out before the groom came in, what will happen when he finally makes his entrance?"

"Exactly, my dear!"

"I don't want to go back. But it wouldn't be right to not be there. It's because of me that she fell into this trap. When she looks at me, my heart skips a beat from guilt."

"You're right, my dear. Everything you say is right."

"Those damn elder wives arranged all this, and now they're not even sure what will happen."

"Curse them."

"If Sultonxon were there, she would be gloating."

"Curse her."

"They say she's spending a lot on the fortune teller. Her father's rich, isn't he? And her mother has quite a large dowry."

"Curse them."

"But it's not Sultonxon's fault really."

"You're right, auntie."

"And the elder wives aren't at fault either."

"Of course, auntie."

"To be a co-wife is its own tragedy."

"Yes, of course, auntie."

Enaxon sighed and stood up.

"I'll wait a little longer and then go. I can't leave her to suffer alone. I'll force myself. I just don't know what we can do. …"

"What can we do?" said Umrinisabibi. "Whatever tears there may be, the pair is set and must be joined, my dear!"

"If it were left to me, I would never see them wed," said Enaxon and sat down again.

Umrinisabibi was waiting for her to say exactly that. She immediately went over to Enaxon's side of the little canal and sat next to her. Remembering everything she learned from her young teacher, she put both hands on Enaxon's shoulders and brought her head close to Enaxon's, looking directly in her eyes.

"Are you a true friend to Zebi? No, my dear, for God's sake tell me, are you her genuine friend?"

"Have you any doubt? I would give my life for her!"

"Well, then, listen to me and tell Zebi this: starting today, she should, even if she has to fake it, pretend to lose consciousness for a half hour, maybe an hour."

Umrinisabibi suddenly lowered her voice.

"You know, my dear, this groom is the kind that if a woman doesn't start herself, he can't do anything! He's old, there's no treatment for it. I'm surprised that he keeps taking new wives."

"It's his money that drives his sickness!" interjected Enaxon.

"You're right, my dear, it's all in his wealth!"

Umrinisabibi, now whispering, said, "You know, my dear, the White tsar is fighting with seven other kings. All of his people have been killed, they say ... there's no one left in his land. If not today, then tomorrow they'll send all the mingboshis off to war."

"What gossip from those sweet lips!"

"It's true. Hakimjon said it, I'm told. ... He's mingboshi's secretary, right? He knows languages, reads newspapers."

"Who told you this?"

"I heard it from somewhere. A place where Hakimjon goes often. You, my dear, don't say any of this to Zebi. She'll figure it out ... she's a smart girl. When mingboshi goes to war, everyone will be freed from him. The White tsar's enemy is very powerful. They say he has a bullet that can kill without making a sound. They say it descends from the heavens on wings and strikes its target. Mingboshi is just the kind of man who could die even without a bullet. If they tell him, 'You're going to war,' that's it. His heart might just explode!"

"Oh God, please let what you say come true!" said Enaxon.

Just then they heard Xolmat's voice calling Enaxon.

The two confidantes stood up and headed towards the ichkari.

From that night on, Zebi's "epilepsy" began to act up every day after evening prayers.

10

Mingboshi never expected this turn of events. Like others, he thought Zebi's sudden "epilepsy" was nothing more than girlish timidity, and it would soon disappear. He spent his afternoons in uneasiness, and come evening he would anxiously await some joyous word from the ichkari. But five evenings in a row the news was inauspicious: "The girl is having another bout." In those five days mingboshi, as he saw it, suffered the pain of five years. He put all his official duties in the hands of Hakimjon and even handed his official seal over on the third day. Miryoqub, who never sat in one place for more than a minute, didn't leave mingboshi's side for a week. He spent his time calming and reassuring mingboshi, who was beside himself, ready to do something stupid.

"You said yourself," began Miryoqub, "you needed a bird that would come at your call, that you haven't the will for those wild birds that won't be trained. That's what we have here, and you'll just have to grit your teeth and bear it, master!"

"This is where your patience has gotten me!"

"Oh-ho! It hasn't even been three days! You're that anxious? Wild birds have to be taught and deceived carefully and slowly. If you scare them, they'll up and fly away."

"Then let her fly away! I'll show her out the door."

"What are you saying, master? Look at me. What do you mean? If you tell her 'Leave!' she'll gladly go home. She'll fly like the wind. Your 'Leave!' is like opening up the cage for that bird. Who will regret it? Do you think she will?"

Mingboshi paused and then softened his voice.

"You are right. Age poisons the mind it seems."

In those five days, Miryoqub and Xadichaxon became very close and almost never left one another's sides. If Xadichaxon called on him three times a day, then he would call on her five. They whispered with one another all the time, planning something.

After five days of Zebi's "epilepsy," Miryoqub noticed that mingboshi had soured. He ordered the servants to bring out his two-wheeled yellow phaeton.

"Well, master, let's go!" he said.

Despite mingboshi's objections and excuses, Miryoqub took him by the hand, sat him down in the phaeton, and, with an armed guard behind them, set off for the city.

In the city, Miryoqub took his master to the largest and most popular tea-house.

"Have breakfast, master, drink some tea. Sit here and enjoy the view. I'll be back soon!"

He sat in the phaeton and left.

Mingboshi ate the oily bread with cream, but his head was spinning in stupefaction: why would his servant bring him to the city? He thought and thought, and finally he had it. "Some urgent matter must have come up. If not, we wouldn't have rushed here. That Miryoqub doesn't do anything without thinking it through."

He kept thinking.

"These kings fighting with one another has been a disaster. Noyib to'ra said that many have died already. My secretary Sokolov disappeared without word. It's been three months now. The country is slowly boiling like a samovar. It will boil over soon! And the results will be bad. I look at people's faces. It doesn't matter whether Russian or Muslim, they all look ready to swallow one another. Everything is getting more expensive. Won't the White tsar's coffers dry up soon? If I were him, I would just give up that territory, return to peace, and calm people down. Who puts his head on the block for somebody else's land?"

This was the first time mingboshi had thought such things. He wasn't a person used to thinking about politics, but rumors were on everyone's lips. Everyone was saying that all the nobles and all the mingboshis would be sent to war soon. All the men of the territory would be put on a train to that place called Girmani, they said. Mingboshi was not unaffected by the stories. Didn't mingboshi, like everyone else, believe that the end-times had come? "Time really must have come to an end," he would think to himself. "I would go on the hajj if the way were open." But right after that he thought, "Where was I when the way was last open?[25] God granted me my piety rather late."

He kept thinking and eventually fell asleep, leaning against a column in the teahouse. When he opened his eyes, Miryoqub was already in front of him. "Well, let's go, master!"

This time they boarded not his phaeton, but the carriage of a cabby and stopped in front of the stairs of an older one-story building in the Russian quarter of the city. Mingboshi was beside himself with joy: he knew the place.

"Well, let's go, master!"

"Couldn't you have told me in the village? You didn't say anything until we got right up to the stairs."

"Would I have sent you somewhere bad, master?" asked Miryoqub and laughed.

Mingboshi laughed too and repeated his old adage, "Oh-ho, impious!"

The building was one of the city's many well-known places of ill repute. People stopped here solely for debauchery. For that reason, behind the front gates were several small rooms. In the dark, windowless rooms were a bed, three chairs, a table for food, and a bookstand. A person, devoid of lust, who entered these rooms, which looked pleasant only during the moments of highest passion, felt oppressed by an unknown fear. While waiting for the girls' entrance, even people like our mingboshi, who was no stranger to the place and could hardly boast of fastidiousness, would look at their dirty surroundings with a sudden desire to leave as quickly as possible.

---

25 The most popular hajj routes in the Russian Empire from Turkestan passed through Istanbul, therefore, when World War I broke out in 1914, hajj traffic diminished considerably. See Eileen Kane, *Russian Hajj: Empire and the Pilgrimage to Mecca* (Ithaca: Cornell University Press, 2015), 157.

When mingboshi entered the room this time, he couldn't believe his eyes. The room was impeccably clean, the walls lined with pictures of flowers and naked beauties, the pendulum of the clock on the wall swung playfully with a tick-tock, and even though it was still noon, lights under pink shades were glowing. In fact, there were two rooms, one behind the other, with the door open between them. The first room was bigger than the second. It had a big table covered by a white tablecloth; on top were all kinds of foods, sweets, and drinks. At the center were fake flowers. A beautiful rug adorned the floor. The chairs were new and clean. On one side of the room, there was a large wardrobe with mirrors, and behind it was a bed with snow-white sheets and two downy pillows. In front of the bed lay a mat. In the other room were a shelf and another bed with white sheets and downy pillows. Another rug was in front of that bed. And nothing more. The lights in each room gave off different colors, but nevertheless had the effect of tickling a person's desires with their mystery and peculiarity. The smooth, white bodies of the naked women on the walls seemed alive, as if beckoning. Their playful eyes, their lifted eyebrows: messengers of passion and desire! Their breasts small and firm like apples.

Mingboshi's involuntarily smile made no secret of the joy that he felt immediately upon entering the room. He slapped Miryoqub on the shoulder.

"Well done, impious! You really took care of everything!"

"Take off your belt, master," said Miryoqub, "These two rooms are yours. Don't worry about a thing. Eat, drink, enjoy yourself. The foul old man's capricious daughter will eventually tire from her antics. Whenever that is, she'll be yours! Don't think about her; there are girls far more striking here."

It must have been from his pure ecstasy that mingboshi at that moment opened up to Miryoqub.

"Do you know, Miryoqub? If I had just tried to take her …"

Miryoqub opened his eyes wide and sat down by mingboshi.

"What are you saying, master? What is this? A new word to add to the old?"

"I'm surprised too. I just tell myself if I could only hear her sing. My love[26] is for her song and voice, there's no lustful dog in me."

"Aha! No dog! In you? Oh, God Almighty."

"I swear it."

Miryoqub jumped up.

---

26 Mingboshi here uses the word 'ishq, which is used in Sufi texts to describe a spiritual love that is not to be acted on.

"All right then!" he said. "Leave your dog here and when you're done, you'll come back a man. Then the girl will be yours. Good, master! Here you can be as much of a dog as you like."

Mingboshi then for some reason began to think about ridding himself of his animalness and becoming a man, so if he didn't hear Miryoqub's last words, we can't blame him. The disgusting creature had long forgotten that he belonged to the human race.

"I'm going to go walk around, master."

"Where are you going?"

"Don't ask, master. Look to your own enjoyment. You have to bury that dog here! If you need something, you already know, the button is here, just push it. A person will come in from over there, tell him what you want quickly; they have everything."

He started towards the door, but turned back once he reached it.

"Master," he said, leaning towards mingboshi, "Pour them all a glass. Then pick one and call her to you. The rest will leave. That's how it's done here!"

"And if I'm not satisfied by one?"

"You'll figure it out. The dog in you is strong, master!"

Miryoqub left and went to the owner of the brothel. The owner paraded eleven women in front of Miryoqub four or five times. Miryoqub looked at their faces the first time, but then their gaits caught his eye. He took a long look at the seventh.

"Send her to my room. Have her sit there until I come in. Don't show her to anyone! Wait, do you have a bath? Have her take a bath. Send the rest to the far room. Let our master have a look."

Miryoqub had another room beside the two that he had set aside for mingboshi. It shouldn't be a surprise that mingboshi's rooms didn't hold a thread to the comfort of his because Miryoqub was Miryoqub and as for mingboshi, well he was just an Akbarali. Akbarali had nothing besides his government seal and his animal lust. Miryoqub had brains and quick wits! Mingboshi might have liked to think that Miryoqub was his tail, a hanger-on. But Miryoqub knew that mingboshi was the camel whose reins he, the camel driver, held. Now the mingboshi Akbarali would release his dog on these worthless girls. Even if all of Turkestan burned, he wouldn't care: "Send it to its death!" The real man named Miryoqub was neither a mingboshi, nor a trader, nor a farmer, just a person without a profession. He set aside the best of the eleven for himself and went to noyib to'ra to report on local business— that is, to do mingboshi's work.

The ten girls, who weren't to Miryoqub's liking, would enter and surround mingboshi. Because mingboshi was a dog in a man's body, he would throw himself at each of them in attempt to catch them in his grasp. Unable to satisfy his lust because of his clumsiness, like a lion made fat in captivity, he would fantasize about tearing them apart. ... Finally, intoxicated and weak, he would blindly grab at the most complaisant of them, dirtying her with his disgusting paws as they both sank into a bottomless swamp of filth. Can you really pick a woman without a full command of your senses? To the drunk, a cat is an elephant and an elephant a cat. Drink is nothing but an enchanted mirror that shows an old woman as the most beautiful of young girls.

Miryoqub was no dog, he was a man! He picked his girl as if he were picking out a new shirt from a tailor. The seventh was a good one: the beauty in her face struck him from his first glance. It was not for nothing that Miryoqub had the owner turn off the lights so that he could bring her over to the window. Everyone could understand that except for those who wore a silver belt around their waists!

The owner of the establishment knew Miryoqub well. He knew him as a well-to-do client, a fastidious buyer, and a connoisseur with fine taste. When he saw Miryoqub pick the seventh girl, he slapped him on the back, "Well done, Miryoqub! The son of a sart is a Frenchman!" He knew that Maria Ostrova,[27] the seventh girl, was fairly young. Not long ago she was the favorite daughter of an affluent family. According to the owner, a betrayal of some kind led her here. The owner kept a close eye on her. He showed her to Miryoqub, but not to anyone else. And the girl herself was discriminating. Not in men, but in money! She needed just 1,500 rubles. As soon as she got that, she would leave for some far away country and make a life for herself there. She would have time to lament her sins there. Now she had just over half of what she needed. She managed to get 800 rubles after just three "meetings" with men. Just another ten days and she would have everything she needed for her new life!

"Hey, your friend is going to the bath!" said the owner from the porch, showing the girl to Miryoqub.

---

27 The 1988 serial publication of the novel has Maria's surname as Astrova; all subsequent publications spell her name as Ostrova. Astrov/a is a surname that could only be given to a student of a seminary (i.e., a male in Maria's recent genealogy) in place of an unacceptable surname (many peasant surnames were derived from offensive nicknames), while Ostrov/a would be a surname derived from a nickname. Both are equally rare, and the character's background does not suggest one or the other, so I have used the variant employed in most publications.

"Have a good maidservant wash her."

"Don't worry, Miryoqub, she has her own servant."

"I'm disappointed in you."

"You're joking!"

"Disappointed ..."

"Really, Miryoqub?"

"Really."

"Why?"

"You know why. For such a girl money is no object."

"I know."

"If you know, then why did you show her together with the other girls? You even put her in the middle."

The owner burst out laughing.

"I wanted to test your eye! I knew that you'd pick her!"

Miryoqub laughed, pleased with the compliment.

"You say she's earned eight hundred rubles so far?

"Eight hundred!"

"And how much did you make?"

"A bit more than that. ..."

Miryoqub suddenly had a thought. He paused for a moment and then made his decision.

"Not bad. By the time she makes 1,500, you'll have 2,000. Have a heart and be fair!"

"Of course, but such opportunities are rare. Our profession is such that if you let this kind of chance pass, you're doing yourself a disservice, so ..."

"How much do you want from me?"

"Just one hundred fifty, no more!"

"And how much of that will you give to her? Fifty?"

"No! You give her what you think is fair."

Miryoqub stood up. His friend slapped him on the back again.

"You're a devil, friend, a real devil! Hellfire awaits you!" said Miryoqub, quickening his pace as he left the establishment.

....

Noyib to'ra apologized to Miryoqub:

"The governor called me. I have to leave now. It would be better if you came a little later."

"Of course. I don't have much to do. I was only going to take the paper-work I thought you had. Besides that, I found something for you."

He took out an object, which had been wrapped in newspaper.

"Excellent, very good!" said noyib to'ra. "You'll give it to me later at home. Where is Akbarali?"

Miryoqub put the object back and answered:

"Here."

"In the city?"

"Yes, in the city."

The telephone rang. Noyib to'ra picked it up.

"Yes, Aleksandr Vasil'evich,[28] it's me. All right, I'll go now. I'm leaving."

He put the telephone down.

"In the city, you say? Why?"

"It's difficult to explain."

"All right, you'll explain that later as well. Goodbye for now."

He opened the door and called his secretary.

"Ignatyuk! If there are any papers for Akbarali bring them now!"

Noyib to'ra hurried outside and sat in his phaeton. Miryoqub gathered the papers and slowly headed towards the bathhouse.

After washing up and styling his beard and mustache, he returned to the rooms at the brothel. Mingboshi was already sleeping in the back room. The table and the floors were reminiscent of a home abandoned in a hurry. Even the air in the rooms was foul.

As he left, he ran into the owner.

"Did you feed mingboshi?"

"Not yet."

"Fine. When he wakes up and asks, serve him. But you'll have to clean up the room before then. Have someone start now."

By the time he slowly opened the door to his own room, the young girl had already taken off her clothes and fallen asleep on the bed. Her head had slipped off the pillow and her hair had come unplaited.

Miryoqub stepped out and went back to the owner.

"Go wake her, friend. Have her get up, wash herself, and put her clothes on. I'm not going to just go straight to bed with her."

"What's wrong, Miryoqub?" asked the owner, smiling.

---

28 Aleksandr Vasil'evich Samsonov (1859–1914) was the governor-general of Turkestan from 1909 to 1914.

"Nothing. That's just what I always do. I don't make acquaintances in bed."

The owner left laughing. It took close to an hour to get the girl made up. Although Miryoqub sat calmly waiting, the owner, nervous, checked on him repeatedly.

Finally, Miryoqub opened his door a second time. The young woman stood in the middle of the room, washed up and dressed in fine silk. Her white cheeks shone brightly in the flickering light of the electric lamp. Miryoqub entered and greeted her. He looked at her as if they were old friends and smiled. The girl took his hand with the kind of apathy typical of women in her line of work. When her hand touched his, it had a coldness that almost said, "Yes, a new buyer for my old body." Miryoqub, who always offered a firm handshake, squeezed her little, soft, white hand with all his strength. Only, his grip had no fire, no heat to it, as if his hands could sense his estrangement, "A girl greedy for my deep pockets." The exchange of gestures, greetings, and handshakes did not break the pair's isolation from one another. Any attempt toward mutual understanding between these two "businesspeople" would be in vain. Their eyes, however, suggested a connection. The eyelids of the girl were weighed down by a palpable agony, but her eyes, blue like a summer sky, battled that pain with an unyielding youth and femininity. They seemed to ask: "You don't look like the others, who are you and what are you doing here?" In Miryoqub's round black eyes, usually able to draw any woman out of her indifference, one thought ruled: "Oh, you mute creature, what are you doing here?" Miryoqub turned off the light, went over to the girl, and under the glow of the setting sun the two looked into one another's eyes for several minutes until they found that unspoken understanding they were searching for. Miryoqub saw in her eyes confirmation of everything he had thought about when he first saw her among the eleven. The girl noticed in his sly eyes (as she described them) an Asiatic man whose mannerisms and behavior looked nothing like those of the previous "buyers." "This man too," she thought, "must have big pockets if he's taking me. Like those others, he'll pluck a flower from the garden, throw it at his feet in the dust and dirt, and then raise his cold hand to give a meaningless goodbye. He'll leave, never to come back! Like … like some traveler from Lodz.[29] She suddenly remembered a meeting with a client the previous week.

---

29 Cho'lpon here refers to a Jewish social and literary type. Lodz, a city now in Poland, was a major textile industry center of the Russian Empire from which Jewish salesmen (known as *kommivoyazhers*) travelled to other areas of the empire. The "traveler from Lodz" often figures in Eastern European Jewish literature as a social and literary type, sometimes humorous and trivial, sometimes cruel and calculating.

The owner knocked on her door around two in the morning. She had already undressed and gone to bed for the night. "Get up, Maria Stepanovna," he said, "go to room number three. Quickly now! There's a charitable man there ready to pay all the money you need. He's waiting." "Alright, let me get dressed and I'll go." "No," said the owner, "no! There's no one on the porch. Just cover yourself in a sheet. You're beautiful even without clothes!" He laughed, threw the sheet on the bed around the surprised girl's shoulders, and led her outside with both his hands on her waist. The young girl, who still wasn't used to the coarse demands of her new "profession," felt her whole body shaking. Her young, pure body, and her still resolute soul were almost screaming. "Did you catch a chill?" asked the owner, gripping her waist tighter. "No," she sputtered, lips quivering, "I feel nauseous! Such lowliness!" The owner suddenly stopped and in the light of the lamp on the porch, looked her in the eyes. "Lowliness?" he repeated. "Those looking to make easy money without working must trample their pride with their own two feet. The world revolves around money and making it isn't easy! If you don't want this easy money, then why not go labor? Over there on the street, there's a sart guard Tursunboy; he sweeps the street every day. He makes six rubles a month. Why not go do his work? He's happy enough! When you see him he's always singing. He flirts with my servant girls. Spends all his money on them and goes hungry himself."

The young girl lowered her head and bit her still quivering lips.

"Quit your useless whining! In half an hour, you'll get your check. You can kiss it (kiss the back side, otherwise the numbers will rub off)! Kiss it like a mother kisses her child; a lover, his beloved; a nightingale, its flower; a Bedouin, his camel; like a warrior, his sword! After all, you're always talking about that bank check. The bank is where the money is. And what is money if not, if I can speak openly—God! Granter of wishes!"

The owner opened the door to room three, pushed her in there, and slowly closed the door. "Those kinds of women should be sent out to the cotton fields in this heat!" he muttered to himself.

But our girl needed only one thing at that moment: to warm up! To stop her inapposite shivering on this stifling summer night. That was the first thing. The second was to attend to her "task." Here they didn't much care how the "task" was done—beautifully, tenderly, pleasantly—it didn't matter. The law was firm and those who objected weren't tolerated for long. It said, "If you've gone in, then submit!" and it was, in its own way, just!

The lamp in the small, bare, and truly vexing room had been put out; nothing was visible. "How wonderful! The one charm of night, the one good thing about the dark is blindness!" The dim light from the dim candle on the porch barely illuminated the old faded bed, the chair next to the bed, the pants on the chair, and the pair of boots on the floor. When the door opened, the naked man lying on the bed lifted his head and moved over a little bit, probably to free up the space next to him. The young woman, without as much as a thought, threw the sheet to the ground and lay down with the stranger, entering his unfamiliar embrace.

"You're so cold!" said the man in a raspy voice. "Like ice."

The woman was silent. She was still biting her lips.

When morning came and the light hit the floor of the room, the woman got up, covered herself in the sheet and turned around to look at the now uncovered man. He was round like a watermelon—his stomach distended, his two cheeks meaty and protruding. A monster with two little, insignificant eyes. He was snoring in a deep sleep! Oh, now he's woken up. Without getting up, he lifted his head. He started smiling. Oh, what an ugly smile! Two cold teeth burning like dying embers. Sparse hair like a half-harvested field.

"How did I spend a whole night with this?" said the woman to herself, biting her lips again.

"Come here!" barked the man.

The woman, biting her lips with such force that she drew blood, thoughtlessly, like a soldier fulfilling his duty, approached the bed.

"Bend over a little!"

She bent over.

"Not bad!" the man chuckled. Then he pointed to the window pane: "There's your check!" and he put his head back on the pillow.

The woman grabbed the check quickly and left without saying goodbye.

When she got to her room, she looked in the mirror. Whether she was terrified by her own face, I can't say—but she threw herself on the bed sobbing. The three-hundred-ruble check fell from her hand and fluttered under the bed.

For that reason, she knew that she couldn't look at Miryoqub the way she looked at her other "clients." "At least this one knows how to value something he's bought," she thought, "he knows how to approach a woman like the most educated Frenchman! If only all the clients were like that!" The woman was, in her own way, right, of course. Those who beat their workers might get fifteen hours of work a day from them, but those who use a kind word can get twenty.

"Sit!" said Miryoqub in sart. He lit the lamp and gestured to the far side of the table. They sat. The woman knew her "task" well, so she wasn't expecting talk. She couldn't understand this mockery. "As unique as he might be, he only wants the same thing. There can't be any other desire in this place," she thought to herself. As for Miryoqub, he was puzzled and didn't know what to say. All the locals respected him as a businessman with international connections, but he could barely express himself in Russian, particularly in the bedroom. Across from him was a soft Russian woman who had only recently become acquainted with Asia, but even if she knew Asia well, would she have stooped so low as to learn the sart tongue? There wasn't a shred of evidence in her appearance that suggested she would have! "This woman would sooner speak French with me than mumble a word of sart!" thought Miryoqub. But there was so much to say, so much to ask. Only now he realized that he couldn't look at this woman the way he had looked at women before her. There were new plans swirling about in his head.

To break the silence, he poured a glass of wine and set it in front of her. He poured half a glass of vodka for himself.

"Drink" said Miryoqub again in sart.

She hadn't noticed the intimacy implied by his address the first time, but now she viscerally reacted to it with a mix of surprise and shame. "This Asian is addressing me as an intimate,"[30] she murmured to herself. They clinked glasses. Miryoqub now attempted to say what he had long intended. In some kind of language barely recognizable as Russian, using hands and eyes more than words, he managed to get his message out. The woman could hardly contain a smile, and her cheeks turned bright red. With Miryoqub's insistence, she continued drinking and listening to the broken words that emerged from his mouth.

"When you leaving?" he asked. These were his first three words.

The woman didn't understand. She shook her head. Miryoqub repeated himself with a few movements of his hand.

"Where?" she asked.

"I don't know. You know."

This completely stupefied the woman. "What do you want to say, my favorite little Asian?" Miryoqub gave up and tried a different angle.

"Have you 1,500? Or have you still eight hundred?"

---

30 Uzbek contains two second-person pronouns, formal and informal. Maria here notices the impropriety of Miryoqub's use of the informal pronoun.

The woman began to understand but was caught off guard. "What is this strange Asian saying? How does he know that I need 1,500 rubles and have eight hundred so far? This is bad, very bad!"

Gradually the needed words were found and where they were not, the two sides came to understand each other through contextual clues, hand movements, and facial expressions. The woman's pleasant, almost ringing voice, pierced Miryoqub like little needles but at the same time brought the highest kind of bliss.

Miryoqub only became more assured of the decision that he had made earlier: he would take this young pretty thing with him to the Crimea for one or two months of relaxation. There he would give her 2,000 rubles and, if possible, take her further, to Petrograd. From there, she could take what she had left of the money and leave for Germany (an enemy country!) and meet up with her rich brother. She, through a series of gestures, relayed that these plans were close to her heart and that the revelation of these secrets would be disastrous for her.

Miryoqub took an old satirical journal from the windowpane, found a picture of a camel in it, and tried to explain to her the old sart saying about a camel.

"Have you seen camel? No!" he said to her.[31]

"Yes, I've seen a camel before," she answered, misunderstanding Miryoqub's intention. Miryoqub became excited. He continued pointing at the camel and repeating his question.

"Yes, I see it, I see it!" she said in Russian.

Miryoqub heatedly shot up from his seat, went over to the woman, and thrust the magazine at her, putting his finger in his mouth. Then, after a bit of silence, he repeated his question.

The woman, unable to understand what Miryoqub's frustrated flailing meant, came to her own understanding of the saying: "He's a tricky one, this Asian," she thought. "He means he won't tell my secret to anyone. He'll be silent as a camel." She looked up at Miryoqub from where she was sitting, batting her eyes and smiling softly.

"Yes, I understand, I understand now. Thank you!" she said.

With that Miryoqub calmed down and returned to his seat.

This woman, though young, had a strong head on her shoulders. She knew the sweet words that men said before the shaking in the bed, and as soon as they

---

31   The saying is used to signify that a conversation or information will be kept secret.

were done, they talked differently. This girl, who hadn't finished the last year of school, had managed to learn French and, though she never got a handle on geometry, she became an avid reader of romance novels. When Artsybashev[32] was all the rage, she and her friends would stay up late, reading their favorite author, and she would imagine that each man she came across in the capital's large parks was a lover and that each young lad from school was a seducer. "And this, this wild Asian … Is what he's saying, is that a promise? He'll just forget it tomorrow. Tomorrow he'll just go to his harem with his forty women! Could I even find him? I don't know his name or his address and the houses all look the same on these winding streets."

But then she thought: "If he just wanted to bed me—well, there's the bed and I'm at his service. Why is he talking? Why isn't he doing his 'business'? No, he's not like the others! He must have some other plan!"

"You've convinced me. But I need some kind of guarantee that you'll do what you said and won't just disappear tomorrow," she said.

"Guarantee? I don't. … Show it to me. I'll say 'yes' or 'no.'"

"If you are being honest, you won't touch another woman!"

"As long as you do the same!"

The woman agreed to the conditions of this "fanatical Muslim" who was like any of the tyrants out of *One Thousand and One Nights*. But she could never fulfill that condition here. They decided that she would move to the city's best hotel on Miryoqub's tab. She gave her word that she would wait for him, and he accepted it. They would leave within the week.

· ·

It was late. The lamps on the street had already been lit. Drivers were already heading home, whipping the tired horses to urge them on. The horses and the carts rolled along slowly. Miryoqub unhurriedly made his way toward noyib to'ra's home. He was thoroughly distracted by the new thoughts beating around his head.

"Miryoqub is no longer the same Miryoqub," a part of him thought. "Why is he walking so slowly? Is there any person on earth that has seen him walk so purposelessly, putting one foot in front of the other as if he is counting the steps? What has happened to him? Is he not the same lustful dog that mingboshi is?

---

32 Mikhail Petrovich Artsybashev (1878–1927) was a writer popular in Russia in the first decade of the twentieth century. He was particularly known for his scandalous novel *Sanin* (1907), which many reviled as pornography.

Has he never been an animal? Could it be that he is softer than water, whiter than milk, more harmless than an ant, and more pious than a dove?"

"No!" another part answered. "He is one of those thousands of dogs that are just like Akbarali! The only difference between the two of them is that he holds himself in higher esteem. This esteem, this pride suppresses the dog within him, hides it from him and deceives him."

"No, there is a mountain of difference between him and Akbarali! Hell, that blue-eyed beauty from Petrograd is a witness to the difference! Compared to Akbarali, Miryoqub is an angel! The Petrograd girl confirmed it! There is no dog in Miryoqub! There may have been before, but now none of it is left. That blue-eyed beauty somehow banished it from him with an imperceptible strength; she has taken it out by its very roots!"

"Did she really uproot it? Could she have really gotten every piece? No! Impossible! There is nothing that could remove those roots that have God knows how many years expanded, grown into branches, and embraced everything in sight! Its roots still have ample power in Miryoqub's body! Was it not that power that had stopped him now so suddenly? Was it not that power that had forced him to sit down on the steps of the house in front of him? The dog inside him raised its head."

"What is all this pointlessness? So he came across a member of the world's oldest profession in our most famous brothel. So what? True, she doesn't seem like the other girls. She looks different. Young, beautiful, and pure. What happened? But as charming as she might be, she's just another woman from that place. Why did he go to the brothel? He knows why he went. When he came in, she was already naked—that's what he came for. Well, what was he supposed to do with her in all honesty? It's clear enough: he should have opened the door, gone in, turned off the light, and got in the bed with her without saying a word. Hadn't she been waiting for that since morning? Isn't that why she washed herself and did her hair? Is she really Layli to his Majnun, and is he meant to moan and groan among the wild animals in the wilderness until his tragic end?[33] Where is the wilderness? He's in the city. A city that has become cultured, 'Europeanized.' From its every corner, the city coquettishly flashes

---

33 A love story that takes place in seventh-century Arabia and that was later immortalized by Nizami Ganjavi in his twelfth-century narrative poem. Other poets subsequently wrote their own versions of the Layli and Majnun story, often polemicizing with Nizami. The protagonist of the romance, Qays Ibn al-Mulawwah falls desperately in love with the heroine, Layli, leading observers to describe him as *majnun*, meaning "possessed by love." Layli's father refuses to give her in marriage to Majnun, despite their mutual affection for one another. After Layli's marriage to another, Majnun wanders the desert reciting poetry to himself, hence Miryoqub's reference.

its eyes at him. Now they don't make graves and pilgrimage sites for those who call themselves majnuns. They just say: "Well, he was crazy and he died," smile, and keep on walking, passing the corpse on the street. And if the dogs eat the corpse, the soul of the dead is only happy. Better than rotting and stinking up the place."

With these sinful, "canine" thoughts, Miryoqub was dumbfounded as to how he had somehow ended up at the steps to the brothel again. A smile expressing unsatisfied lust ran across his eyes and cheeks. He approached his room and saw the soft light from the candle that barely lit the porch through the thin curtain. His heart began to flutter and he slowed his gait. His "canine" lust began to subside. His hand stopped short of the doorknob. From inside, the pitiful song of a young woman's soft voice floated out. It was that same sweet, ringing voice, wound tight like a dutar string, that acted on him so.

"What kind of voice is that? Is there any 'dog' in it? Could that kind of voice really lure someone into bed? Not at all! No! The whole of his past was a dream ... a nightmare! He needed to hear more of that nightingale's song to awaken from his nightmare! There, she's singing! She was singing with that voice that only the two of them together knew! That voice that promised and obliged so much!"

"Hey, leave! Leave me now, you damned devil! I am not Akbarali! I have no silver belt, no tsarist seal. I am Miryoqub, Miryoqub. ..."

"Oh, Miryoqub! Sly Miryoqub! Tricky Miryoqub! Miryoqub, you fox! You devil, Miryoqub! Miryoqub, you are slave to passions, you are depraved and shameful! Have you ever bowed your proud head in your life, have you ever abandoned your dog for even a second? Is that it? If you're a dog, then don't hurry, you'll still have time to jump on your bitch. You'll have time. You have the money! That money can buy you whatever you want. You have enough to have an unending chain of pleasures to satisfy your canine urges!"

"The seventh is yours! Yours! That tender creature has nothing but you now! That woman is yours now! You can't have her like a prostitute anymore! You can't hurt her! You can't destroy her hopes! She looks at you as a man now; you're no longer a client; you've managed to get rid of that impression. Do you hear her voice? This isn't the voice of a depraved woman waiting for her next buyer. That's the sad song of a woman who curses her fate. The song is not one of lust! It is the innocent song of a woman waiting for her bridegroom! It is the song of a young creature who has finally been linked with her love! The grateful melody of a mother bird who has returned to her nest! Miryoqub! Miryoqub! Miryoqub!"

Miryoqub was now two: one fleeing, the other pursuing; this escape and pursuit between his two selves had him panting by the time he reached noyib to'ra's home and rang the bell.

....

The lady of the house wasn't home. Noyib to'ra was standing in the large hall behind the dinner table, drinking tea and reading his newspaper.

"Yes, is that you, Miryoqub? Come in!"

"It is me, to'ra. How are you? Are you well? How is your family?"[34]

"Thank you. Not bad. Sit down! Have some tea, help yourself. Take some bread. Here's the butter. Candy, rolls. Have some. My house is yours, you need no invitation."

"Thank you, to'ra," said Miryoqub, sitting, "I'll help myself. What news is there for us? You read the big newspapers."

To'ra took the gold-rimmed glasses from his eyes, put them on the table, and looked down at the newspaper on his lap.

"The big newspapers have big news. Each piece is worse than the last."

Miryoqub moved his chair closer; he poured himself some thick tea and put two candies on his plate. Then he took something wrapped in a newspaper out from underneath his robe and began to open it.

"What is that?" asked to'ra. "Is that the thing we were talking about?"

"Yes, it's a Persian quatrain. I showed it to master Shahobiddin, the learned man, who said that the calligraphy belongs to a poet called Ado, who served as a judge under Umarxon."[35]

"If that's the case, it's not all that old," said to'ra, taking the manuscript. "But if it really is Ado's handwriting, then it is sacred indeed. Thank you, Miryoqub."

To'ra put on his eyeglasses again.

"'Limuharririhu.'[36] Beautiful writing. Was Ado really a calligrapher? Because illustrations were forbidden in the East, the Islamic East, that is, calligraphy developed as a result. Good, good. Let's try to read it: 'Pink tears flowing over yellow cheeks, beautiful like rubies encrusted in gold. If you are, like an

---

34 It is typical for Uzbeks to greet one another with a flurry of questions about life and family. The usual answer to this greeting is "thank you."

35 Amir Umarxon (1787–1822) was the khan of Kokand from 1810 until his death in 1822. He was also a talented poet and historian. See note 15 on p. 88 for more on the Kokand Khanate.

36 An Arabic phrase meaning "by the editor."

almond, from your head to your legs only an eye, then you can see nothing; you only start to see when a kohl of love is applied to your contours.'"

To'ra was a scholar of the local language and literature. He knew Persian literature very well and endeavored to obtain all kinds of manuscripts related to Turkestani history. After he found out about to'ra's little passion, Miryoqub had managed to find a few such manuscripts. He even employed his good friend Shahobiddin to find him some of the more expensive things. Noyib to'ra never forgot Miryoqub's efforts. The two of them each did their fair share of little favors for one another. Miryoqub made sure that to'ra always had reason to value him, whether thanks to a gift, a rare manuscript, or money; to'ra did likewise, protecting Miryoqub from local officials. They each scratched each other's backs and everything always went well! To'ra often thought to himself: "If everyone got along like we two, this world would be paradise!" Miryoqub probably thought that too. The two of them were one soul, if not one body!

"We've never seen such a strophe from Ado. Another reason this manuscript has value."

"And what does the strophe mean, to'ra?"

"A beautiful line. Generally, Umarxon was a very intelligent ruler. A learned man and a poet. All his advisors were poets too. Rulers after him just weren't the same. How did Shahobiddin know that this was Ado's work?"

"He said you can see the judge's seal at the bottom. That seal was Ado's."

"Is there really a seal? Wait. Yes. Here it is: 'Judge Abdullatif,' 'Sayyid al-muslimin[37] Amir Umar.' This really is a piece from Umarxon's time. But it can't possibly be Ado's hand. Ado's name was Sultonxon. I've read it before, it's not Abdullatif. Shahobiddin must be mistaken. Your scholars don't know these things well."

"I didn't know, to'ra. Shahobiddin the master said so. I'll ask him again and bring anything I find."

"You've found me plenty of rare things already, Miryoqub. Your service to civilization is unmatched. Last year you gave me a history book about which I wrote an article for a Petrograd miscellany. I thanked you in the acknowledgements. They've already written about that book in England, France, and Germany. All thanks to you, Miryoqub! Your service is very much appreciated."

The two were silent. After a moment, Miryoqub spoke.

---

37 A common title given to Umarxon, often used interchangeably with *amir al-muslimin*. The latter means "ruler of Muslims" in Arabic, while *sayyid* denotes a lineage that can be traced back to the Prophet Muhammad. Umarxon attempted to create a genealogy linking him to the Prophet during his lifetime, but it was not accepted by his contemporaries. They did, however, accept and use the title *sayyid al-muslimin*. See B. M. Babadzhanov, *Kokandskoe khanstvo: Vlast', politika, religiia* (Tokio-Tashkent: Yangi nashr, 2010), 338–352.

"Tell me about what you've read in the newspapers, to'ra."

To'ra's face, which had a big smile running across it until then, suddenly turned gloomy. He furrowed his brow and his lips began to quiver. He put the manuscript on the table.

"Well, my friend, things are bad. Our army's numerical superiority no longer means anything. Every action that our commanders undertake is in vain. Our fortifications, one after another, are falling into enemy hands; the enemy has occupied cities and territories. ..."

"Where is the tsar? Doesn't he know what to do? Our beloved tsar."

"That, Miryoqub, is what we are all asking one another. None of us can find an answer. We are asking ourselves. All of us are thinking, straining ourselves to come up with something, but nothing has worked! It's impossible, Miryoqub!"

Figure 4. Left: Xudoyorxon's palace in 1872. Source: *Turkestanskii al'bom: Chast' etnograficheskaia, 1871–2*; Right: Xudoyorxon's palace in 2016. It has been restored several times. Photo by translator.

"Don't say that, to'ra. We, the sarts, trust the White tsar second only to God."

"It's good that you trust him. We, all of us, trust him like you do. Just— and don't repeat this—trust, work, and results are all different things, opposed to one another! Our Russian intellectuals, our students are up in arms. They attribute all these bad things to the tsar. ..."

"The tsar? Does any tsar desire to give his lands to the enemy?"

"Neither your khans nor our tsar cared too much about land, I think. When your Xudoyorxon[38] was told that the Russians had taken Oqmachit,[39] he

---

38 See note 15 on p. 88.

39 Noyib to'ra here refers to the Russian conquest of the fortress Oqmachit (also transliterated as Aq Masjid) in 1853. Noyib to'ra reads the conquest in an eschatological fashion, citing Xudyorxon's carelessness as to his territorial possessions as the beginning of his downfall.

asked, 'How many days is that from here?' And when they told him it would be a month's journey, he said, 'If that's the case, I have no need for such a distant land. Let them take it!' Our tsar, by God, is not too different."

Miryoqub didn't know what to say. What could he say, having never concerned himself with politics much up to this point? To not allow too long a pause, he said, "Before it took a month, but now by train, it's only three days."

"And tomorrow with an airplane it will be only three hours. Distance won't have any meaning soon enough, Miryoqub. Our superiors don't want to understand the speed of our age. Our saying 'slow but sure' will only lead us to misfortune. Why is Germany so strong?"

"You know better, to'ra."

"Of course, I know, but you need to know too. Germany wins with speed. And speed is made by machines. Germany is several times smaller than us and has only a third of the population, but they don't have even an inch of territory that is not covered by asphalt roads and iron rail. Today, let's say, they need to bring a force from Samarqand to Oqmachit, it would take them only a day. But by the time our forces got there, the war would be over. Why are the Germans conquering France only piece by piece? Because in France, like in Germany, they have speed. They have all the same machines. And we have our broken wagons and you have your steady, slow carts. Both can put a man to sleep."

"What can we do, to'ra?"

"I'm afraid to think too much about it, Miryoqub. Let's just have a drink first."

To'ra stood up and headed toward the shelf. By his gait, Miryoqub could tell that to'ra had started without him. That explained why to'ra had spoken so openly with him about these issues.

"Come, let's drink, Miryoqub! We Russians know how to drink vodka better than anyone. Your people are talented students, of course, you're already catching on."

They clinked their glasses. To'ra started to toast, but all Miryoqub heard him say was, "To the health of …," before he swallowed the rest of the words along with the vodka.

The conquest of the fortress indeed spelled the end for the Khanate, but largely because of the Russian Empire's immediate tactical concerns. Russian forces had to push further south because the nomads of the areas surrounding the fortress were still loyal to Kokand and because it was difficult to maintain a garrison in Oqmachit, which had little land amenable to agriculture. See Levi, *The Rise and Fall of the Khoqand, 1709–1876: Central Asia in the Global Age*, 178–179.

"So you're asking what we can do," to'ra said, continuing their conversation. "We nobles can't find any solution. True, if we need to repress an internal enemy or the masses, the solution is simple. We have our Cossacks, police, gendarmes, and soldiers. Just point and shoot! But when an enemy comes from the other side of the border, we have no answers, we don't know what to do. Even our allies have stopped trusting us. It's bad, it's a very bad situation, Miryoqub. Come, let's have another drink."

"You still haven't said anything, to'ra. We have our sayings: 'There's no disease without a treatment'; 'Everything but love and death can be cured.'"

"That's all nonsense, nonsense. ... Our internal enemies, the revolutionaries, they'll show us the solution. But they'll show it in their own way."

"Who are these revolutionaries?"

"They'll drive out the tsar and the nobles. Get rid of the police, kill the gendarmes, put an end to the war; they'll take land from the rich, the factories from the managers, and give it all to the people. By people, they mean the poor, the black masses, the penniless. Let them rule, they say."

Miryoqub laughed. "Those people would eat horse dung, not rule! They're uneducated, and these revolutionaries say they should rule. Take the land from the rich and give it to the poor to have them work it. No matter how much you curse the poor, they'll never work your land with any kind of eagerness. Do you think they'd do more without the owner? That they want to end the war is good. Since the war everything has become more expensive. Though those who knew how to trade and were well-off to begin with haven't had any problems. They've become even richer. But it's terrifying just to look these poor in the eyes now, to'ra."

"Yes, right! The greatest danger is from those eyes. Those terrible eyes. There's no escape from them. If we can just beat back the Germans, then the eyes would calm down. But God forbid, if we continue like this, the eyes will eat us alive."

To'ra was silent. Miryoqub stared at him. To'ra, clearly absorbed in thought, began shaking his head. Still shaking, he said, "In short, this great ship ... this great empire is stuck in a sea storm, looking on at the unknown, at oblivion. There's no course visible that can stop the storm or lead the ship to safety. Maybe there is no such course. ..."[40]

"You said something, to'ra: 'Empi.' What is that?"

"Yes, empire, empire."

"What is it, to'ra?"

---

40 The metaphor used here echoes with Cho'lpon's ode to Lenin, printed in 1934, in which Cho'lpon states that Lenin has guided the ship of the country through the turbulent storm of war and revolution. See Cho'lpon, "O'n yil Leninsiz."

To'ra thought for a little bit. He pointed to the picture of the tsar on the wall and the epaulettes on his shoulders.

"That is empire."

Miryoqub didn't understand a thing.

After a deep breath, to'ra continued. "Look at me, Miryoqub. Stop this talk!"

"Yes, of course, to'ra, let's not talk about these terrible things. 'Only an ass mourns tomorrow's losses' we say. Tomorrow, if God wills it, the tsar will …"

"You said that Akbarali is here. Why did he come to the city when he just took another wife less than a week ago? Does he have some business here?"

Miryoqub told his elder confidant everything that had happened.

"Aha, well that's how it is!"

"Yes, like that, to'ra."

"Akbarali is an idiot! A jackass!"

"Yes, to'ra. He's not the sharpest one."

"Your Sharia permits four wives. That law, really, isn't entirely wrong-headed. Every man knows it. But it was good fifty, one hundred years ago. The times allowed it. Now times have changed, Miryoqub. Now what need is there to take four wives and all their troubles along with them? One, of course, cannot satisfy a man. We know that. But do you really have to get married again and again? Why make extra fuss for yourself?"

To'ra lowered his voice: "There's really no need to get married to have a little fun. You're one of us, so I tell you this in confidence. I have a lady friend of my own: the wife of an officer who's gone off to the war. A young, pretty little thing. And there's another one: recently at a party I met the wife of a rich merchant. And I'm going to her place tonight. A very pleasant, open woman. That's all you need! Akbarali is an idiot!"

"Right, to'ra, right. I make myself 'happy' with just one. But I have my fun on the side."

"Yes, good," said to'ra. "One wife and as much enjoyment as you need." Then he pointed his finger at him judgmentally. "You're a dangerous one, Miryoqub."

At first Miryoqub blushed a little, but then he smiled and answered: "The rivers of Allah's forgiveness are wide, they say, to'ra. Believing that, we have our fun here and there, ever so rarely."

"And those mountainous sins, are they just here and there?"

Miryoqub laughed. "Those mountainous sins we'll learn from you now, to'ra, if God wills it. You, after all, are a learned man."

To'ra laughed too. He looked at the clock: quarter after eight. He got up.

"You sit. I have to get dressed. We'll leave together."

When to'ra was ready, Miryoqub got up to leave.

"Come this way. We'll go out through the garden. My wife hasn't come home yet, and her mother's sleeping. There's no one to close the door."

They went out to the porch, and to'ra suddenly stopped.

"Miryoqub, have you heard the news?"

"No, to'ra."

"In the mountains, a mob started a rebellion and set fire to a few homes of the officials. Tomorrow afternoon I'm going to take a contingent up there to sort this out. Today seventeen were arrested. They say it's a real rebellion."

"When will you return?"

"I'll be there for two to three days probably. Tell Akbarali to go home quickly."

"Yes, of course. We should leave tomorrow."

"We recently talked about giving seven more men to each mingboshi. That should be approved soon."

"That would be good."

Having heard their voices, to'ra's cook Zunnun came out of the kitchen.

"Miryoqub, are you leaving now? Come see us for a bit. I'll give you some tea. I had something to tell you."

Miryoqub looked at to'ra.

"Good! Have some tea and talk. Zunnun hasn't had anyone to talk to lately."

To'ra, tapping his silver-headed cane on the ground, left through the grated door, while Miryoqub and Zunnun went into the kitchen.

....

Zunnun's home was in between the kitchen and the grain storehouse. These one-story, narrow-windowed, mud-brick buildings only highlighted the majesty of to'ra's finished and decorated brick home. The garden was behind the little buildings. Zunnun's little window and door looked out onto the garden. The kitchen's back door also led into his house.

They sat down on a bench in the garden. Miryoqub had wanted to go see his new star and check in on mingboshi, whom he had left alone to his own devices. Mingboshi was like a child: he couldn't be left alone for long. Miryoqub didn't let the cook go inside to put the tea on.

"Zunnun, I'm in a hurry. Say what you have to say."

Miryoqub's voice was full of anxiety, and Zunnun sensed it.

"What happened to you, Miryoqub?! You seem troubled."

"Nothing's happened, I'm just in a hurry."

"Don't say that. I know you. Our to'ra is worried too. His wife is constantly asking, 'If we leave for Russia, will you come too?' Everyone who comes to call on them senses the tension. I talk with lots of Russians here. They say all kinds of things, but if you really think about it, they're all thinking the same thing: 'Something bad is going to happen.'"

Miryoqub looked up.

"The Russians are saying that? Tell me, what else do they say?"

"I told you. They talk of all kinds of things. But underneath it all, they seem to say: 'Something bad is going to happen.' What it is they're worried about, I can't guess. But something very bad."

Miryoqub didn't consider it necessary to hide the secret from someone who knew about it anyways:

"You're right. To'ra told me a number of things, each worse than the last. When I heard it, I thought to myself, 'These are the end times. Judgement day is coming.'"

"That's why I wanted to speak with you."

Zunnun sat down beside Miryoqub.

"I just turned forty and still don't share my bed with anyone. I lie down on my wide mat by myself. But I still dream of getting married and having children."

"Good. There will be a girl for you, of course."

"There already is a girl. I have an aunt in the village, and she brought me this news. She's been very persistent."

"So get married, what's the problem? Get everything ready, and we'll put together a party."

"I thought that I needed to let the master know somehow."

"Yes, he is your father now. You'll have to tell him."

"That's what I'm saying."

Zunnun smiled. He moved a little closer to Miryoqub.

"I thought that you could talk with the master about it."

"And why can't you?"

"I ... can't get up the nerve."

"Why? Tell me."

"You tell him."

"Fine, I'll tell him."

Miryoqub suddenly turned to his interlocutor.

"How are you with the lady of the house?"

"Very close. ..."

"Well, tell her then, and she'll tell her husband."

Zunnun stood up laughing. He put his hands on his temples and stepped away from Miryoqub. He then turned his back to his interlocutor, shaking his head. But after an instant, he turned around and rushed back. His face red, he bent over towards Miryoqub.

"You don't know, friend!"

"Of course, I don't know. How should I know your heart? Tell me!"

Miryoqub's words came out sounding harsh. He didn't want to play these children's games with this cook, who clearly was not his equal. Zunnun again sensed the change in Miryoqub's voice and sat down next to him.

"All my misfortunes are from the lady!"

Miryoqub's eyes bulged, and he turned to Zunnun.

"What are you saying?"

"If it weren't for the lady, I would be getting married tomorrow, friend!"

"God take you!" said Miryoqub, hopping up from his seat. He shook his head. He put both hands on Zunnun's shoulders.

"What is it? Is she in love with you?"

Zunnun started laughing again.

"Hey, madman, I said speak! What is it between you two?" an agitated Miryoqub spat.

Zunnun kept laughing.

Suddenly a woman's voice wafted in from the courtyard: "Zunnun, Zunnun!" It was the lady's voice.

Zunnun jumped up to go.

"Wait here. Go in my house! Watch from the window but don't turn on the light."

Miryoqub quickly went in and sat in front of the window. Zunnun turned off the electric lamp in the flower garden and rushed into the kitchen. The flame of the candle in the kitchen shone through a crack in the door. Outside, in the flower garden, it was pitch black. Miryoqub kept his sharp ears trained on the kitchen where he could clearly hear the whispering of two people. His heart started pounding like the blades of a waterwheel.

"Wait, Zunnun, wait! Here isn't a good place."

"You say here isn't good, but you won't come in my house."

The lady answered slowly.

"And don't expect me to! Don't even talk about that!" Then she lowered her voice: "You know well enough how to come to my house. Wait, Zunnun! You're so insolent! I said wait! Where is my husband?"

"He left somewhere. He said he'd be back later. He had something urgent to do."

"Enough, I said! Are you deaf? There's a time for everything! I'm getting upset! So you say he'll be back by morning! Oh, these husbands!"

"Yes, he said he would come back late."

"Are you that insolent? What's wrong, are you drunk? Come, let's go into the garden. You beast!"

Just then the light in the kitchen went out.

"Don't put out the light! Zunnun, light it again, my love. Light it!"

Miryoqub heard what sounded like the smack of a kiss. Then the light went back on. In the moonlit darkness, two people passed in front of the window, arm in arm. Their words were inaudible. As if to show Miryoqub his prowess as a lover, in front of the window he embraced the lady and sat her down on the windowsill. Inside, Miryoqub clutched at his heart: to'ra's wife breathed heavily as she planted her lips on the cook Zunnun's.

After a minute, the lady stood up, and the door to the kitchen opened. Again, her voice was heard from the courtyard.

"I'll tell you myself … at this time … you well know …"

The kitchen door closed. Zunnun came in a moment later and lit the lamp in his house. Miryoqub had gone completely pale.

"So this is what it is!" he said. "This is what you were talking about!"

"It's been this way for a year or two now. Let's go sit in the garden."

They went and sat down on the bench again, and Zunnun continued.

"That's the situation I'm in. Did you hear what she said? She didn't know that the master left. When he's at home, she's always asking, 'When will you come back? Are you going to come back in the middle of the night or in the morning again? Should we stay up waiting? Should we keep the samovar warm?' He'll answer her nagging with, 'I have some important business. The head of the garrison will be there. That's why I'll be back late. I won't be back before two. You just go to bed.' He asks for forgiveness from his wife, the poor thing. As soon as he leaves, she calls me to her. In front of her mother she commands me: 'Until he comes back, just sit in the hall. When you hear him at the door, walk quietly! Don't disturb our sleep!' I sit in the hall, one door of which leads to her room. Her mother and her child sleep way over on the other side of the house. She is already sleeping soundly. The son, soft and kind, in his room … I stay in the hall. The door to the lady's bedroom is always open. And then when the master rings the bell, I close her door and sleepily yawning open the door for him. The master, in most cases, comes home drunk and notices nothing. When he comes to a bit, 'That's enough, go back to your house! Go quietly, don't wake the lady. You don't know how to walk on these wood floors, you ox!' he says."

Miryoqub was astonished. He had completely forgotten that he was in a hurry. He sat, shaking his head and listening. He stopped and sank into thought, only to start shaking his head again.

"How can their empire not die?" he said. "How many thousands, how many thousands of souls are in their hands? In the hands of such villains!"

"What are you saying, Miryoqub?"

"About what? About your wedding?"

"Yes."

Miryoqub was thinking about something else entirely.

"It's good. Get married!" he said. "It's good to take a virgin."

"I know that. I was asking how to tell the master."

"Ah, that's what you mean. Good. I'll talk with him myself. Not now, but after a few months."

"It will be winter by then!"

"Winter is exactly when you need a woman. In summer, it's hot even without her."

"Good. That's what I want to hear. I'm relying on you."

"I could talk to him tomorrow. Your master is leaving for the mountains tomorrow afternoon. He'll be back in a few days he said. A week from now I'm leaving for Crimea. Don't have the wedding without me, Zunnun!"

"Yes, of course, of course! What kind of wedding would it be without you and mingboshi?"

"All right."

Zunnun chuckled again.

"So the master won't be home tomorrow?"

"That's what he said."

"Look at me, Miryoqub."

Miryoqub turned to him. Zunnun moved in closer and asked, "How do you like our lady? Does she interest you?"

Miryoqub didn't answer immediately. He was thinking.

"Tell me, brother. You can trust me."

"She's not bad. A little fat, chubby in the face, fair-skinned. She's retained her beauty and still looks young. She can't be too much older than twenty-seven or twenty-eight."

"She's twenty-seven, I think."

"I've still got it. And you're asking if I'm interested? I'm not sure what to say. You know us men. We're dogs! The devil is always on our shoulders. Always pulling the bridle to the left ... But the two of you are probably enough for the poor girl."

"Why two? It's just one."

"What do you mean?"

"Her husband is only a husband in name. He's always with other women and has plenty of mistresses."

"How do you know?"

"I know them all. His wife knows about a few of them. It's not a coincidence that she's always hanging on me. It's not two—just one, I'm the only one! Perhaps there's another ... But no, if there were, I would know. Listen, if the master isn't home tomorrow, come by later. One of his mingboshis brought over some game birds, and I've cooked three of them. I'll make a good pilaf. The lady will be here too, if you're in the mood. ..."

Miryoqub stood up without saying anything. He took out some money and handed it to Zunnun.

"Good. I'll come after dark. Use this money to get some drink. We'll see how it goes."

Although Zunnun didn't want the money, after Miryoqub persisted, he had no choice. He took it and threw it on the table. With an obsequious smile, he told Miryoqub, "Tomorrow I'll be waiting."

"Good," said Miryoqub. Still shaking his head, he left.

While returning to the room at the brothel, he continued thinking to himself.

"The empire has rotted through. It will fall apart and no one will even think twice. Why has this raised so many strange thoughts in me? I don't know what it is myself. ... No one talked about these things before. And now I want to ask someone something about it, to find out for myself. Or could I find an eshon to put me on the right path? Could I ask a lawyer and have him explain the law? Or a teacher, who could explain the matter? I'm just not sure what to do ...

"'Empire is like a ship,' he says ... no, it is a ship, a ship. ... If only I understood this! When I asked what empire was, he pointed to the tsar and his epaulettes. He had told me who the tsar was before, I know who he is now, and tomorrow it will be even clearer. ... Then there are the epaulettes. Those are just cloth, even if they are gold. Machine-sewn. We always say, 'There's a saddle for every ass.' I guess there's an epaulette for every officer. And that's why the empire is crumbling."

"What will become of us? What will happen to the poor? What will happen to all the things and money we've accumulated? Oh God, who should I ask? Wait: my new friend! I'll ask that trickster woman who has captured me without chains! She's Russian. She'll know. No, wait, what will happen to her? If such a big empire falls, will she be ok? What, for God's sake, is empire? Who do I ask? Who?!"

....

Around eleven o'clock Miryoqub arrived at the hotel and immediately went to mingboshi's room. He was sleeping, his arms wrapped around a woman on each side. As soon as he entered, Miryoqub yelled as loud as he could: "Get up, master! There's a fire!"

Mingboshi startled awake and jumped up from the bed.

"Where were you, scoundrel? You left me here all by myself?"

"Who's a scoundrel? You have two beauties at your side and you're complaining about being alone."

"I'm bored of your girls. Sick of them. Start moving, let's go!"

"I congratulate you on ridding yourself of your dog! Praise be to God, a thousand times praise, you've become a man again."

"Sit!" yelled mingboshi.

The two women were cowering. Miryoqub started laughing.

"Where were you?"

"The empire is burning. I went to put it out."

"What is burning?"

"The empire ... the empire ..."

One of the women went to Miryoqub's side.

"Did you say 'empire'? she started. "We have an 'empire' in our town. The Empire Hotel. It's on top of a mountain, below it is a river, and in front of it—a grand park that faces a ravine."

"Well, the empire has fallen into the ravine," said Miryoqub. The woman sat on his knee and began to nuzzle against him.

"What did you say? I don't understand," she said, putting her arm around Miryoqub's neck. Miryoqub gently removed her hand from his shoulder and stood up, all the while looking at mingboshi.

"I'm leaving. I have some business in the old city."

"Wait!" barked mingboshi. "I'm going with you!"

"Stay here for today. You're not hungry, correct?"

"Of course, but I'm bored. When are we leaving?"

"The day after tomorrow in the morning, if God wills it. If you get bored, I'll move you to a different hotel tomorrow. That place is good."

"If we have to wait two days, have a musician sent up to play the dutar and sing. I'm bored with these mutes."

"Very well, master. Tomorrow afternoon everything will be as you ask. We'll destroy the empire the day after tomorrow."

"What do you mean?"

"I meant we'll do away with lust ... sweet dreams, master! Goodbye, ladies!"

Miryoqub went straight out as quickly as possible. As he passed the porch, he could see the red glow of the lamp from his room. "That means she's in my room," he thought.

He opened the door slowly. The young woman was sitting on a chair, reading a book. When she saw Miryoqub, she stood up and invited him to sit at the table. Miryoqub countered, insisting that she sit in the place that she offered, and he sat across from her. He looked in her eyes: her exhaustion was plainly visible. He looked at the bed. No signs that anyone's lain there. A kind of joy filled his heart and enveloped his whole body. He looked at the woman again: she was trying to finish her book. One page was left. At that moment, Miryoqub felt as though he was looking at the wife he had been waiting for. Empire completely disappeared from his mind. He sat silently while she finished. Turning the last page, she put the book down and yawned. Having noticed Miryoqub's gaze, she suddenly became self-conscious and covered her face, though a smile peeked out from underneath her hand. She laughed softly. Red blood ran to her cheeks. Miryoqub laughed too and slowly stood up.

"Well, lie down and go to sleep; I have to go to the old city."

"Very well, go. Today the owner knocked on the door, but I told him I'm not well and didn't let him in."

"What did he say?"

"'A rich sart is here. You'll make more than five hundred. You'll have what you need. He's young, good-looking, original.' I told him: 'Good; let him come the day after tomorrow. I'm not well, I caught a chill from the bath.' He left, muttering, 'Alas, alas.'"

The woman, recalling the event without the slightest sign of distress in her voice, now said, as if pleading, "Tomorrow we're leaving, right?"

"Of course, I'll take care of everything tomorrow morning."

"How will we pack my things?"

"Do you have a lot of things?"

The woman chuckled.

"Just one suitcase."

"That's easy enough. Can you bring it here by morning?"

"If not in the morning, then by evening I'll manage somehow."

"Then don't worry about it. All you'll need is your clothes!"

Miryoqub got up to leave.

"No, wait!" the woman stopped him. "I can't stay there with my passport."

"Ah!" exclaimed Miryoqub. "There is that problem."

"What can we do?"

Miryoqub paused for a moment, thinking.

"We'll figure it out, don't worry."

Then, a smile on his face, he said quickly, "Don't worry, I'll find you a passport. Tomorrow morning you'll have it in hand."

"Thank you."

Miryoqub wasn't sure how to answer her "Thank you." But, for some reason, he was pleased with himself. "Miryoqub the sly has done it again," he thought, or maybe he was thinking about something even more pleasant. He was naturally cheery to begin with. He decided to kiss her on the forehead but suddenly stopped himself. "No, the two of us are a new flame. The further I am, the better!" he thought to himself.

"Good then. Lie down and get some rest. Lock the door from the inside!"

Miryoqub jumped up to leave again.

"Naturally," said the woman, slowly getting up from her place and walking toward the door.

Once outside, Miryoqub heard the door lock. "A door that opens for me but closes on others," he said to himself. Pleased with himself again, he felt as if his whole body was smiling as he swiftly made his way to the street.

Waking his driver who was soundly sleeping, he urged on the two horses as he set out to look for Ignatyuk, noyib to'ra's chancellery secretary.

....

A ten-ruble note, inserted into the clutches of the ghostly Ignatyuk the previous night, performed its work: Miryoqub came to Ignatyuk's office at ten in the morning and received the promised passport. This passport with no date of expiry registered to a twenty-four-year-old Yevdokiya Zaxarovna Kobylina[41] managed to relieve all the worries of Miryoqub's young woman. Dressing in summer clothing, she went straight to the new hotel and set herself up in the small, yet well-decorated room there. Not an hour had passed when the long-bearded, stout servant from the brothel brought her suitcase to her. The servant had made sure that all traces of her life in that room disappeared.

After Miryoqub moved mingboshi to another hotel and took care of the bill, he shook hands with his friend, the owner of the brothel.

"Goodbye, friend, I am off to the village."

"Goodbye, Miryoqub, come visit us again! How is the girl?"

"Don't ask. I'll be back in a couple days."

"She's worth it, that one, devil take her!" he said. He smiled, evidently satisfied with himself. Then he asked, "How much did you give her?"

"What business is it of yours?"

"Tell me. I just want to know the extent of your generosity. She didn't leave your room all last night."

"That's true, but it's because she wasn't well. ..."

"She caught a cold because of you; you made her wash up again. Yesterday a rich young man came, and she said she was sick. You lost me a lot of money. He was the son of a wagon master ... Vahob ... you know him? That was a rich one! Bags of money!"

"And if she's here, plenty of wagon masters' sons will come here. But don't worry!"

"Of course, of course! But how much did you give her? Tell me!"

"Not a lot. A thousand."

"A thousand?! Really?"

"Why would I lie? I gave her a check for 1,000. She left for the bank."

"Devil take her! She has more than 1,500. She won't stay now."

"Money is sweet. As much as you make, you just want more."

"True. I'll get her to stay another week or two somehow. Do you really think I'll let her go?"

"No, you'd never let someone like that go. I know you. Goodbye now!"

Miryoqub chuckled at his friend's stupidity and stepped outside.

"Tomorrow morning I'll go to the village," he told the woman, whom he was sure he loved. "At the most I'll be back in five days. We'll leave for Crimea when I get back."

---

41 Various versions of the text record this name as "Kabilina" or "Kobilina." "Kobylina" is the only corresponding extant Russian surname.

"I thank you, dear friend. You have truly been a sincere friend. Come, let me kiss you like a sister."

By the time Miryoqub understood what she meant, she planted her lips on his forehead. However careful and free of passion that kiss was, that the woman had come so close to Miryoqub made him shiver. The woman was calm and indifferent. After the kiss, she didn't back away from Miryoqub. She looked into his eyes but was still completely unaware of what was going on inside him. Miryoqub retreated a few steps.

"Where is your old passport?"

"I left it in the old room."[42]

"You don't need it?"

"No, no, no! Everything is fine. I've rid myself of that dark past forever. All thanks to you. After this I am not Maria Stepanovna Ostrova; I am Yevdokiya Zaxarovna Kobylina. An ugly name, I don't like it. But there will never be another name as valuable! Wait, no, forgive me, the name of the man who gave it to me. That is far more valuable! Thank you again, dear friend."

She approached again and with both hands took Miryoqub's hand and shook it. "What warm and tender hands!" he thought.

"Thank you, dear friend!"

This naïve "Asian" did not know how to answer her gratefulness. His entire body began to quiver. He took another two steps back and reached the door. The woman, sensing this, invited him in.

"No, I must go. Lock the door behind you and don't go outside," said Miryoqub. He stepped out towards the hall and heard the door lock behind him. "A door that locks for others but opens for me!" Miryoqub thought again. Unable to contain himself, he ran down the steps.

Inside the room, the eyes of the young woman, who was now imprisoned of her own volition, became wet with tears of joy.

....

"Come in, Miryoqub. You're late."

"We're leaving for the village tomorrow. I had to finish a few things."

They entered Zunnun's house from the kitchen. Zunnun's house was very well kept. A big new rug on the floor, paintings on the walls, a large table in the

---

42 This is something of an error on Cho'lpon's part. Cho'lpon's narrator earlier states "the servant had made sure that everything of her life in that room disappeared."

middle, a white tablecloth. The table was covered with food and drink. There were pretty tulle curtains on the windows. Around the table were several chairs.

"Your house is unrecognizable, Zunnun."

Zunnun laughed with that same laugh of the previous night.

"It's all the work of the lady."

"What are you going to do when you get married?"

"I want children, I want a family."

"Only those that don't have children want them. But there's no more kidding with kids," Miryoqub punned.

"No, Miryoqub, I love children!"

"Ok, when I get back from Crimea, we'll have your wedding."

"Hurry back."

"So there's no one here?"

"She's coming. The lady is coming."

"And others?"

"There are no others. The master left. I invited him, but he apologized that he couldn't. I told him, 'We're having a little party for the holiday, master; Miryoqub is coming.' But he said, 'My wife will come in my stead, have a cup of tea with you, and talk with Miryoqub.' He cuckolded himself right in front of me. And she even acted the part, playing capricious. She grabbed her forehead and pretended to be tired, 'My head hurts,' she said. 'If your head hurts, take a pyramidone and sleep until evening. Don't offend Zunnun!' the master said. Of course, we had already discussed this with the lady."

"Wait," said Miryoqub, "she loves you. She's yours. What am I supposed to do?"

"You are a strange one, Miryoqub. Do you think she really loves me like a husband? Or that I would spend my whole life with her? This is just for fun … a little game. … Hey now, she's coming. Let her have a little drink and then you can cozy right up to her. Tonight, I'm not here! Alright?" said Zunnun.

He ran out. The lady entered, followed by her mother with child in arms. Miryoqub heard the doors and windows of the little house closing.

All of them gave well wishes to Zunnun, and after taking their seats around the table, raised their glasses to his health. They all took a moment to remark on to'ra's absence. "Such noble and compassionate men are really rare now," they noted. The lady almost every other word spoke of the kindness of her family members.

She kept her passionate and desirous eyes on Zunnun.

"All of us love Zunnun," she said. "He is the most respected member of our family. He must have been twelve or thirteen when he first started working for us. Now look at what an adult he has become. Soon we'll marry him off. Right, Zunnun, my dear?"

Zunnun blushed.

"Valya, don't embarrass Zunnun," said her mother.

Zunnun kept pouring and encouraging them to drink.

The lady picked up one of the prettier bottles from the table and showed it to Miryoqub.

"This is my favorite liquor," she said. "I drink it to intoxication. A very fine thing."

"I got it just for you!" exclaimed Zunnun.

"Zunnun knows my passions well."

The lady, as if she were revealing an enormous secret, suddenly began telling them about the incident in the mountains.

"You know, we are sitting here drinking. Making merry. We've gathered with all our close friends. What kind of situation is poor Fedya in? You know he left with one hundred fifty soldiers and some cannons. Those mountaineers are good shots. My Fedya, you have no idea, is such a brave-hearted character. He always runs out in front of his men with his sword drawn! I'm afraid that some sart or Kyrgyz will shoot him. Though the sarts all seem to like him. ... You know yourself, he loves the sart language. He reads sart books. Writes in sart. The sarts call him "Parpi to'ra."[43] You know, he loves sarts. He says they're a tender people, like sheep. As much as they have suffered, as many hardships as they have seen, they still always give thanks to God for their lot. He loves sarts for their devotion and faith."

Zunnun raised his glass to the master's health. The sound of glasses clinking created a veritable symphony together.

"God guide him. Let him return safely. ... Oh God. My heart is breaking. ... You know, the sarts have become corrupted. They're always drinking now. Always drunk. Always fighting and stabbing each other in the brothels of the new city. When drunk, a sart can be a wild animal. ... Well, raise your glass, Miryoqub, to the health of the sarts."

They drank. The lady began to ramble.

After an hour, the mother of the lady stood up.

"The child has fallen asleep; it's time for me to go. Be well!" she said.

The lady got up too.

"I should be going too. I've been running around all day. Forgive me, Zunnun!"

---

43 See note 16 on p. 93.

Zunnun waved his hand dismissively.

"No, my lady! You are a representative of the master. Stay a little longer. We still have a lot to talk about. You can sleep tomorrow!"

"Yes, tomorrow!" echoed Miryoqub.

The old woman turned to her daughter.

"You stay, Valya, talk a little bit. It's still early. You won't be able to sleep at home anyways after all this excitement."

"Fine, very well," said the lady, "Allow me five minutes, Zunnun. I'll lock the doors and then come back."

They left.

"Is she really such a talker?" asked Miryoqub. "She's a gramophone!"

"See? She's a very open person. Once she's had a few, that is."

Zunnun edged closer to Miryoqub.

"She said she'd lock up the house and come back—that's all you needed! Now you just need to play your part!"

Miryoqub had begun to turn red from the strength of the vodka.

When the lady returned and put her key on the shelf, the two men applauded her.

The drinking began again and so did the drunken revelry. The lady talked incessantly. Miryoqub heard that familiar word "empire" another several times. But he was in no condition to understand what it meant any better than he had earlier. He began straining and squinting his eyes to keep himself awake. The lady too was having trouble. But the sly Zunnun, who had been pushing drink on the other two while refusing it himself, had no problem.

"Stand up, Miryoqub, friend!" he said. "Go sit with the lady. Don't let her get bored."

Miryoqub, encouraged, went over to her.

"May I, my lady?"

The lady indicated the seat beside her with her eyes.

"Feel free."

As he sat down, he placed his hand on her shoulder. The lady turned her now heavy head and set her drunken eyes on the door. Zunnun had left. Then she turned back to Miryoqub and put her hand on his shoulder. They drank again. The lady continued talking. Her words slowed, dripping out one by one, like medicine from an eyedropper. Her drunken eyes continued to flit over to the door, awaiting Zunnun's reentrance. But Zunnun didn't come. They drank again. And again.

When Miryoqub awoke from a noise in the room, he opened his eyes to see the lady in front of the mirror, combing her hair. Miryoqub lifted his head from the pillow, attempting to get up. The lady turned around and when she saw him. She turned bright red and giggled.

"Don't rush, Miryoqub, my dear," she said. "Let me leave and then you can get up. Don't look at me."

Then she slowly came over and sat on the bed.

"I'll go home now. We had a lot to drink and my head hurts," she said and kissed Miryoqub.

"Let's do this again some time," said Miryoqub.

The lady giggled again.

"With pleasure," she said, exiting.

By the time Miryoqub dressed himself and stepped outside, the sun had already peaked over the horizon. Zunnun's uneven snoring, the drawn-out crowing of roosters from far off, and the slight sound of the door to the court-yard creaking open could be heard.

Everyone was still asleep.

....

Miryoqub stepped out onto the street. He headed toward the far corner of the district courthouse where there were always a few carts standing. This time there were more than ten. He climbed up on one, but the driver quickly turned around.

"Get off. We're all busy," he said.

The Russian police officer, having spotted Miryoqub, yelled, "Who is that? Get off the cart!"

Miryoqub got down. Surprised, he looked over the convoy of carts again. The police officer approached and looked closely at Miryoqub's face through the light of his dull lantern. He must have recognized Miryoqub because he quickly changed his tone.

"You can't be here, friend. These drivers are busy. They are bringing wounded soldiers to the hospital."

Miryoqub shook his head. He started to make his way to the old city by foot. His head felt heavy and his senses were dulled. His eyelids were hard as stone. His knees bent and buckled of their own accord. The two Miryoqubs appeared once again in his mind: one was an interrogator; the other, his prisoner.

The distance between the old and new cities was great. Dragging his numb, weak, and seemingly hollow legs, he made his way to the closest bathhouse as the sun continued to rise and the street began to fill with people. But as broken and tired as he was, Miryoqub didn't sense the distance he had traversed. His mind was far away in a dark room in which a cruel interrogator was ramping up his investigation.

"Well, Miryoqub, how are you feeling today?"

"Fine. Everything is fine."

"Don't lie, Miryoqub! You are here to tell the truth! We have read everything that is written in your soul. Just like you make copies of every promissory note, of every deed of ownership, so we have taken a copy of your soul. It's to your benefit to tell the truth here. You can't convince us with lies. Now, tell me: how are you?"

"Not so well."

"Yes, good, speak, speak!"

"I feel nauseous and sick, as if I am disgusted by something. ..."

"By what? Or by whom?"

"I don't know."

"Think harder. Who could it be that disgusts you?"

"Someone, but I don't know who."

"If you don't know, let's help you. Look at me, by whom are you disgusted? Is it not Miryoqub? Why are you silent? Am I right? Is it Miryoqub?"

"You're right. I'm disgusted by Miryoqub."

"And you should be! As high as that Miryoqub might soar, he'll never rise above himself. Because he is a dog! A vile, low, and pitiful dog! Sure, sometimes he paints himself as a lion or a snow leopard or even a man. But like a raven that flies with pigeons gives itself away with its first caw, so the lustful dog in you barks in a crowd. Everyone sees right through your human features. Miryoqub despises Akbarali mingboshi, he curses him, he mocks his mongrel lust. Miryoqub feels no shame, he doesn't bury his head in the ground from embarrassment. But the ground refuses, disdains to take his head in its mahram breast!"

"I only prepared myself to answer questions here. Now I see that the interrogator wants to accuse me of crimes! What is it that I did?! Whom did I tell what?"

"Silence, Miryoqub! We will ask the questions as we see fit and accuse you where needed. You just wait, Miryoqub! You'll have a chance to defend yourself. You'll have your word. Be patient! Be patient! Just wait your turn! Everything in its time!"

"I have the right to refuse answers to such an interrogator!"

"What did you say, valiant Miryoqub?! Do you have objections, reservations about the interrogator? For what reason?"

"Many can't tell a horse from a mule. So what? After all, they look similar to one another."

"Well, well? Speak then!"

"But those that can't tell a mule from a horse have no business conducting interrogations and leveling accusations. They have no right!"

"Well, Miryoqub, speak! We like this kind of talk. What do you want to say?"

"I strongly object to your equation of me, in whatever form you might put it, with Akbarali mingboshi. This is an insult, not a question!"

"Calm yourself, my friend. We believe there is as much difference between Miryoqub and Akbarali mingboshi as between earth and sky, of course! Akbarali is one person, and Miryoqub is another."

"Then I am satisfied with your answer. Continue with the next question!"

"Whether you are satisfied, that's your business. But we are not yet satisfied."

"Meaning?"

"We consider Akbarali mingboshi more of a man than Miryoqub."

"What, what?!" Miryoqub's words caught in his throat.

"Unfortunate, but it is so."

"Why is that? Why?" Miryoqub roared like a lion.

"Miryoqub! In whose bosom did you spend last night?"

Miryoqub was startled. He turned red. He wanted to run away.

He wanted to run away from himself. No, a person cannot escape himself!

"Speak, Miryoqub! We have that copy of your soul right in front of us. … Speak, confess now and it will be good for you."

"I spent last night in noyib to'ra's home. His cook Zunnun invited me to a party."

"Is that it? Nothing else?"

"That's it. When I left in the morning, I was told there were wounded soldiers coming in from the mountains."

"Thank you, Miryoqub! We hadn't heard about that. Thank you, but tell us now: in whose bosom did you spend last night?"

"I'm not sure what happened. At dawn, I opened my eyes. I was in bed, and standing nearby was noyib to'ra's wife. We drank a lot the previous night, I don't know what happened."

"You wanted to say that this was not a willful act; that you didn't want it. Is that correct?"

"Yes!"

"So policemen, swords drawn, surrounded you and forced you into her arms? You poor thing, Miryoqub! You've suffered so much. You were in a dungeon, a prisoner of others' desires! Is that right?"

"No! I came to her myself, on my own feet. I consciously threw myself into her embrace!"

"And did you pay for the alcohol?"

"I did!"

"And who told the woman that you would continue to see each other? Do you not know?"

"It was me."

"And who was overjoyed when she responded, 'with pleasure'?"

"Me."

"Miryoqub! Any just person would call what you did adultery: you violated another man's wife! Has Akbarali mingboshi ever done such a thing in his whole life? Do you not know?"

"He probably hasn't. I don't know."

"Very good! Who is Akbarali mingboshi to you?"

"A father. My patron."

"And you accumulated a lot of wealth behind his back? We have a copy of your soul in our hands, speak!"

"I did."

"Good. Have you heard of Poshshaxon?"

"I don't know. No!"

"Think harder. You know her well!"

"Yes, I know her!"

"Who is she?"

"Akbarali mingboshi's, if I'm not mistaken, second wife."

"Correct. Now tell us: she was another man's wife; her husband, by your own admission, is your father, your patron. Why did you corrupt her?"

"You're slandering me! I didn't corrupt her!"

"No need to get excited. We're listening. Why did you corrupt her? Do you deny having an affair with her?"

"I don't deny it. If anything, it was she who corrupted me."

"Why?"

"If you'll allow it, I'll tell you what happened."

"We need to know the truth. Tell us!"

Miryoqub cleared his throat and began his story.

Just like mingboshi's other wives, she kept good relations with my family. As we sarts tend to, we visited each other and had dinner together frequently.

About, maybe, four or five months ago, it must have been spring, my wife tells me, "mingboshi's second wife Poshshaxon is such a nice woman! She is so kind to us, there are simply no words. She's always bringing food and keeping me company. Sometimes we'll even talk deep into the night and she'll stay over."

"Mingboshi," I tell her, "really tortures the poor woman. She's a young thing, and she comes to us, never telling her husband, because she gets bored and cramped in that house." My wife could only agree.

One day, around evening, she came to us. I looked in from the tashqari and recognized her from her paranji and her gait. She went into the ichkari before I could meet her outside, so I followed her in. There was no one there, and she was looking around.

"Voy, there's nobody here! Where did they all leave to?" she said to herself.

"Their mother took all the children to her mother's house," I said.

"Voy, woe is me! Is that you? I didn't know. I came to talk. Oh well … "

She started to leave the house. I turned to follow, but then ran out in front of her and stopped in front of the porch. She paused close to the courtyard wall.

"Oh well. … I came to talk," she repeated. "I'm bored in that house. … By the way, when are they coming back? You don't think they'll be back soon?"

"If they come back early, it will be sometime tomorrow evening. Not before."

"When did they leave?"

"Last night."

"Shame on me! I didn't know. … Dammit! I have to go back to that stuffy house. Dammit!"

Her eyes, underneath the dark veil, began flitting here and there again.

"Oh, God take me now! It's dark already. How am I supposed to get home now? I'm scared to death to go alone."

"I can't take you?"

"Oh! What would they say if they saw us together?"

At that moment, I began to doubt whether she had come to my house just to talk. That doubt made me bold. "I'll start the talking now," I thought, but she suddenly asked:

"You're all alone?"

"Yes, nothing to be done."

"Poor thing. Damn loneliness! I've endured my fair share of loneliness, you know."

"What do you have there with you?"

"I brought a few dumplings."

That convinced me that this woman had an ulterior motive. And me, I'm just like everyone else. The dog in me started to hunger.

"You always were a good cook, especially your dumplings. Damned that we can't enjoy them now," I said.

"Why can't we? Take them, go inside and eat them. Bon appetit! I made them just for you, after all."

I moved a little closer to take them, when she stopped me.

"Oh, woe is me!" she said. "Your gate is wide open here! People on the street could be watching and listening. Can't you close it?"

But she was covered by one leaf of the gate; anyone passing on the street could only see me. And there was no one on the street. I saw clearly.

After all these hints and gestures, if I didn't answer in kind, then I'd be an angel ... or crazy! I closed and locked the gate. She laughed a laugh that not even the devil could manage.

"Oh, God shame me, I am imprisoned!" she said, feigning shame.

I took the dumplings from her.

"Come," I said, "you're tired. Relax a bit. We'll have dinner together. Then we'll think of what to do."

She took a few steps and then stopped.

"Hey, wait. Are you alone?"

"Yes, I'm alone."

"Really?"

"God strike me down!"

"Don't curse! It brings bad luck. If you're alone, I have something I need to tell you ... about your master. ... I have a complaint. ... "

She lost her previous caution and followed me. It was dark inside. When she crossed the threshold, she stopped.

I set the food she brought on the shelf.

"Well, sit!" I said.

"Oh, God take me! Your door, your windows are wide open. Can I really sit here?"

I got up and shut the window. I locked the door of the room as well.

When I lit the lamp, she suddenly yelled:

"What kind of a woman is your wife?! How can you have a window without a curtain? You can see everything in here. ... "

I hung a curtain on the window.

"Fine, now sit!"

"Fine now ... now ... now ...," She repeated the word, drawing it out more each time.

"You're like a brother to me!" she said. "Do I really need to avoid your eyes?" With that she took off her paranji.

The next day towards noon, she took her dumplings and left my guest room.

"That was my first tryst with Poshshaxon. I've said what I had to say."

"You haven't lied. We believe you. We ..."

Since the beginning of the interrogation that word "we" had been used many times. When Miryoqub heard it this time, he began to feel that he was on trial in a courtroom. His mind was working incessantly, releasing billows of smoke like the smokestack of a train. Miryoqub, now having recognized that the court consisted of men like himself, rich and wealthy, became emboldened. He stopped evading the questions and began to give honest answers. How could a court for the wealthy have it in for him? The rich, as much money as they had, could not look on the prospect of more with indifference. Money was something that Miryoqub did not lack. And who could say that the interrogator did not love money?

"We don't fault you for what happened in the first meeting with Posh-shaxon. You bear no guilt there! But we don't want to accuse Poshshaxon either. She had no choice in the matter. The young thing couldn't free herself from her confines in any other way. If she hadn't come to you, she would have gone to someone else. It was easier for her to come to you. The fault here lies mostly with mingboshi. That being said, we cannot absolve you of all blame."

"What? Why?!"

"Calm down, Miryoqub! Even if you didn't betray mingboshi with his lawful wife, you must admit that you betrayed your own wife."

"And is there a man in this ephemeral world of ours who hasn't betrayed his wife? Among us sarts is there a man who doesn't have in addition to his wife—or even his two or three wives—a lover on the side? My betrayal of my wife wasn't the first time, it was the thousandth! Read that copy of my soul!"

"Very well, we won't forget what you've said. None of us are innocent of adultery, of course. But you could have stopped Poshshaxon from corrupting herself; you could have arranged a divorce and then helped her find a man worthy of her. You did not do that! You ..."

"Wait, sir, wait! Why was I capable of that?"

"If you answer our questions quickly and truthfully, then the matter will clarify itself. If there is one person in the world who can influence mingboshi, it is you. Correct?"

"Correct!"

"Poshshaxon sent a friend of her father's to beg mingboshi for a divorce: 'give her to another, marry her to another. She's still young, she still has desires and dreams. Don't let the rest of her life go to waste!' You were present during the conversation. Are we lying?"

"No, you are right!"

"And what did mingboshi say?"

"I don't remember."

"Then listen to what we have written here. Mingboshi, for your information, answered curtly: 'If I give my wife to another man, how could I expect to show my face among the people? She married me, so her fate is mine to decide. I will not give her a divorce! Let her just try to leave without my permission!' And then he drove the petitioner off. Are we lying?"

"No!"

"Did you say even a single thing at that point? If you had, might mingboshi have acted otherwise?"

"I said nothing. Perhaps I could have changed his mind."

"Why did you say nothing?"

"Can I speak openly?"

"Of course!"

"After I first met Poshshaxon, I convinced her not to leave mingboshi."

"Of course, you saw each other at least once a week. She was happy to have you. But why did you convince her to stay with mingboshi? For what reason?"

"I well knew that my master isn't long for this world. He has a sickness in his heart. ... Lately he has had trouble breathing. ..."

"We know, we know! To the point!"

"When he dies, I had planned to marry Poshshaxon, so that mingboshi's inheritance wouldn't go to waste."

"Good, very good. Of course, all of us want to inherit a fortune. That is a lawful desire. But mingboshi has five heirs already. Would Poshshaxon's share really satisfy you? You are, after all, already a rich man!"

"I have no profession, I'm not a trader, I have no stocks and bonds. Can I really become rich with the land and water that I have?"

"You cannot deceive us, Miryoqub! We respect you immensely. We're even ready to ask your forgiveness for the inconvenience of this interrogation. You're one of the most esteemed among us. The Russians praise those like you in their books. You're an artist, able to make money out of anything. You're a man who keeps the cogs of the factory turning. But you don't pay a kopeck in taxes to anyone. Someone like you does not enter into any business without thinking it over thoroughly. So tell us what your plan is with Poshshaxon!"

"How can I tell you? I'm not sure. After mingboshi's death either no other heir would be left, or we would make sure his will indicates that everything would go to her."

"We know that this is certainly within your power! We therefore cannot fault you in the matter with Poshshaxon. Such daring plans should not be condemned but encouraged!"

"Thank you! So I may leave now?"

"No! Wait now! We still accuse you in the matter of noyib to'ra's wife! We ..."

"No, sir! The court that has acquitted me of the matter with Poshshaxon cannot condemn me for the matter with noyib to'ra's wife. You must proceed logically."

"Then speak!"

"My betrayal in the matter of Poshshaxon was great: I betrayed mingboshi and his four heiresses. And don't forget that the girl, Fazilat, whom Xadichaxon raised, is another victim of my betrayal. My treachery is great! Have you cleared me of them too?"

"We have cleared you!"

"Then you must clear me of this second matter not once, but a thousand times! Empire, they say, is the tsar, noyib to'ra, and his epaulettes. The fates of the poor, yours and mine as well, are in the hands of noyib to'ras, the owners of the epaulettes; but the wills of the noyib to'ras all belong to their wives. Poshshaxon was a weapon to obtain a large inheritance; inheritance, the money, is a key to power. Empire is the epaulettes, they say; epaulettes continuously demand money. And many give their money without receiving anything in return. But those who know their business, give their money and with the help of an epaulette, get that money back five times over. I am a master at such deals. Last night the drunken kiss that I put on noyib to'ra's wife's drunken lips had one meaning: money! Sirs, I did not bed noyib to'ra's wife out of lust. Strike me down now if I lie! That was just our first meeting. There, as we might say, negotiations were opened for our future business collaborations together!"

With those words, the interrogator and his followers, it seemed, simply disappeared. The hall of the courthouse emptied. Miryoqub opened his eyes.

The high dome in the central part of the bathhouse. The snapping of a towel. Under his head a coiled towel hard as a fist. A tea pot with green tea. In his head remained the court, noyib to'ra's wife, and the blue-eyed girl still waiting for him in the room.

Somewhere a somber voice sang, its melancholic sounds echoing against the walls of the bathhouse: *The affairs of Muslims have fallen into the hands of an infidel, woe, friends, woe.*[44]

11

At dusk "father" and "son" entered the city through the large gates. Hakimjon, lying on the porch, started reporting to Miryoqub, ignoring mingboshi.

"Everything is still calm in the country. Nothing particularly bad has happened. There are a lot of little complaints, of course. I took care of most of them. There are five bigger ones that I couldn't handle myself.

"In the ichkari, things have quieted down. The father of the new wife spent the last two nights in the house and then left in the morning. The girl has finally calmed down, it seems; the co-wives made quite an effort. Every day mullahs come and read blessings to ward off evil. Since the master left, the girl's seizures have stopped. I'm not sure that they won't start again now that he has returned. She spends the days happy, playing the dutar and singing.

"By the way, the master's third wife, Sultonxon, has returned from her father's house. Everyone was saying that she was at fault for the whole ordeal with Zebi. Then, according to the rumors, Sultonxon was suffocating and didn't know what to do with herself. And now it's like she's become a different person. Everyone is surprised. The senior co-wives say they can't think of a reason for her sudden change of character. They say as soon as she got home, she went straight to our new family member and embraced her as a girl does a dear friend. And they have, I guess, become the closest of friends. Surprising for Sultonxon, who just the other night was cursing the air and threatening to kill her. Now our new bride is always asking, "Where is my auntie Sultonxon?" You would think that the arrival of a new wife would hardly be good for Sultonxon. Why has she changed so much? I'm surprised, Miryoqub, I can't explain it!"

"Don't be," said Miryoqub. "No one knows a woman's heart but God. If she's changed like that, she's hiding something. We'll need to keep an eye on her."

---

44 This sentence was excised from the 1988 serial publication.

"That's what I mean," Hakimjon retorted.

"I'm surprised at another thing," said Miryoqub. "I'm surprised that Hakimjon, with all his interest in women's affairs, hasn't become mingboshi's fifth wife."

"Damn your tongue, Miryoqub! What the hell do you mean?!"

"How did you find out about all these intrigues, these bits and details? Those are the things that women deal in."

"Hey, Miryoqub! You and the master are going from city to city and village to village, enjoying yourselves! I haven't moved an inch. It's as if I'm nailed to the ground here. I'm here when I have work and even when I don't. I have a lot of free time. I get bored. I talk with all the women, with the girls since there's no one else. I have one friend in particular, Umrinisabibi. You remember, Bahri's mother. I heard most of this from her."

"Enough. Let's talk about tonight. Tonight we have to put an end to this and bring the bride and groom together. Otherwise, he'll go up in smoke without any fire. It wouldn't be good. And people would start to talk."

"Of course. The rumors are flying already. They're saying that the new girl is no longer what she used to be. Talk with Xadichaxon."

Miryoqub went to the gate and called Xadichaxon. She retold Miryoqub word for word everything that he had already heard from Hakimjon. Miryoqub smiled. Miryoqub began thinking that if he told the girl that mingboshi had agreed to listen only to her dutar playing and her singing, to control the dog within himself, to bridle his lust with a pure love, then she wouldn't say no. If he could just get her past the first night without another seizure, then the rest would be easy. He suggested just that to Xadichaxon, who, without a moment's thought, answered affirmatively.

"If that's what he'll do, then it'll be easy," she said. "I'll go in and talk with her now. By evening, hopefully, I'll bring you good news. You go to the groom on the porch. There's some food there, and I'll have more brought out."

She got up and looked askance at Miryoqub.

"The hardest task is yours, Miryoqub!" she whispered. "Mingboshi is a child, and you're his mother now. If you're not there now, he'll die of hunger."

After dinner, they drank two pots of tea. Hakimjon brought over two petitions and tried to ask mingboshi for advice.

"Have you lost it, Hakimjon?!" exclaimed mingboshi. "Can I listen to complaints now?! My ears are on the ichkari! Let it stand until morning. If they're a few days late, it's no tragedy! If you're really in a hurry, ask impious here!"

Miryoqub, who had just returned from checking on Xadichaxon, slapped mingboshi on the shoulder. Mingboshi's eyes didn't move from him.

"A suyunchi for me, master! Today you'll hear a song."

"Oh, praise be! Praise be to God," the groom couldn't contain himself. "Your mouth is sugar!"

"Know this, master," Miryoqub took on a stern look, "you made me a promise! Only dutar and singing! You leave your dog at the door."

Then he lowered his voice and said softly, "I am telling you this for your own good, master. Do not scare her. She is a young thing."

Miryoqub went home. To pass the "few years" of time, mingboshi went to his guest room to sleep.

⋯⋯⋯

Miryoqub went straight home, and after telling his wife that he had to leave for two months on an urgent business matter, he handed his wife a wad of money. Then he gave her a few instructions. He went out to the market and charged the grocer there to take care of his family. Afterwards, he went here and there, taking care of a few things. By evening he had made his way back to mingboshi to check on him. In the house, they told him that mingboshi was in the ichkari and that the first night passed without any seizures, but they still hadn't heard any singing or dutar playing. Nevertheless, Miryoqub was relieved. He assigned Hakimjon a few tasks and told him he would be leaving for the city tomorrow morning. Then he left.

His wife was crying in the ichkari. The children were sleeping. A heap of pilaf lay on a plate in the kitchen. Rice had been scattered everywhere. The children must have eaten the pilaf. And their mother hadn't touched it.

"Why are you crying?" Miryoqub asked.

"You just came back from the city, and now you say you're leaving for two months. It would be fine if the children were older."

"I left enough money for the children. I found a grocer who will take care of everything. Whatever you say you need, he'll bring it. Is two months such a long time? It will go by in the blink of an eye. If it wasn't for work, I wouldn't go, but I have no choice. Just tell me not to work and earn for us, that you'll do everything, and I'll stay home, fine."

His wife was silent. She barely held back her tears.

"Give me a match. I'll light the lantern in the tashqari."

"I made up a place for you on the platform. If you're leaving tomorrow then at least spend some time with your children tonight."

"You know that I can't sleep in the ichkari. If I lie down there, I'll never get a wink of sleep. Give me a match, and I'll go sleep on the porch of the tashqari. I need some sleep to set off at dawn tomorrow."

His wife handed him a match.

"Get up and lock the door behind me," Miryoqub said.

His wife stood up without a word of protest, dried her tears with her sleeve, and saw her husband outside.

"When should I wake you? What should I pack for your trip?" she asked, restraining the quivering of her voice.

"You don't need to do anything. I'll wake up on my own."

The door closed softly. The chain scraped quietly as it trembled in his wife's hands. As he reached the porch to lie down, he again heard muffled crying from inside the house.

When he opened the door to the tashqari and struck the match, Posh-shaxon was standing in front of him!

Still thinking of his golden-haired beauty waiting for him at the hotel and that dreadful interrogation, Miryoqub met Poshshaxon coldly. He asked her to return home. He tried every argument.

But nothing came of his efforts. This still young woman, who had no one to console her in life except her husband outside of marriage, threw her arms around his neck. She gripped him so tightly and passionately that Miryoqub could only submit.

In this ephemeral world can anyone maintain the path of righteousness? Miryoqub asked himself.

12

When Miryoqub opened his eyes the next morning, the train was pulling away from some station, clacking briskly along the rails. It was still early, and not a sound could be heard from the soft-carpeted corridor of the first-class car. All the passengers, it seemed, were still sleeping. A few minutes later, he heard a step, but the quiet sound quickly merged with the depths of the long corridor and disappeared.

As soon as the train left the city, it entered a sea of blooming cotton fields. A bellowing cow passed by the window. A man on a donkey was making his way to the station. The little legs of the short donkey moved along quickly, one after another, like spokes on a rolling wheel. Farther on, men on horses rode, kicking up clouds of dust. As the train picked up speed, carts, pedestrians, another donkey, and more horses appeared and disappeared in pursuit of one another.

The cool morning breeze gently blew in through the compartment window, carrying dust and dirt.

Miryoqub closed his eyes for a moment. The train made a sharp turn to the left, abandoning on the right a village street buried in dust. The mountains took shape in the distance, taking on an indigo color. The light of the morning sun shone over the tips of the tall trees on the mountains. Columns of smoke showing that people indeed lived in these nameless villages rose over the tops of the thick forests. After the train completed its turn, the cold breeze brought in cool mountain air, which softly caressed the faces of the compartment's occupants.

Miryoqub glanced down involuntarily.

The blue-eyed beauty, who had entrusted her fate to a strange Asian man, and had been overjoyed to take the fake name he had given her, was quietly sleeping. Had she been happy the previous night? Was she swimming in enchantingly sweet dreams? She had a soft smile floating across her face in her sleep. Someone like Miryoqub could never understand the beauty of such sleep!

The woman must have slept the whole night through peacefully and untroubled. One leg hung from the knee over the bed, while the other had seemingly chased after the first, stopping only at the edge of the berth. Her long robe covered almost her entire body down to her toes. Only her forearm was left uncovered by the rolled-up sleeve. She beautifully slept with her snow-white arms and hands at her side, as if nuzzling at a mother's breast. Miryoqub couldn't take his eyes from her. Looking at her from the upper bunk, he took in her whole being. "She's mine. This beautiful creature is mine, all of her is mine," he thought to himself, overcome with joy. But the interrogator had not gone away, still whispering in his ear.

"Miryoqub! What are you doing looking at this girl?! Do you have any right to stare at her with such satisfaction? Since she met you, this young girl has forgotten everything she knew. She no longer remembers that brother in Berlin. You know she sees you in her sleep, in her dreams, you villain! You treacherous friend! You're a master salesman; we know, we respect you for it! Money is your plaything, your mistress! You are sly! But you shouldn't have played with this poor creature's heart! The hearts of such girls are like beautiful teacups; coarse men like you cannot appreciate their fineness, the light ringing they make as tea flows into them—and you break them. And nothing of that beauty remains in those broken shards!"

"Your accusations are in vain. I rescued her from a terrible and unclean place. Now no haram hand, no nomahram hand can touch her. Now she is as pure and chaste as a virgin bride."

"And you? You! What about the new sins you've committed?"

"I haven't committed any new sins! It's just the old sins that are still chasing me. I'm running away to save myself from them. I'm running away. Enough with these reproaches."

"Whatever you're going to say, you may say it, but two days ago you held in your arms noyib to'ra's wife and yesterday you held mingboshi's. And today or tomorrow you're going to put your paws on this sweet creature? How do you live with yourself?"

"I'm not going to touch her, I would never. You know, since meeting this woman I don't recognize myself."

These words of Miryoqub's were true. He quite sincerely fought off the intense desire to touch her while he was seated next to her in the narrow compartment. No, they would come together of their own accord in some yet undetermined place, at some undetermined time, under undetermined conditions. She understood this too and slept soundly as if she was in her mother's arms. Miryoqub kept his distance.

What a shame that they didn't record their thoughts then and there. After all, they had nothing to do but think as the train sped north because they couldn't understand one another. If they had kept a mutual diary, it would have been quite the travelogue. It would have looked something like this:

JAKOB.[45] (the name the woman gave Miryoqub.) *I don't know where this train is taking me. I started out for the Crimea, but the tickets are to Moscow. What do I have waiting for me there? And what will happen before we get there? I don't know. Why did I even set out on this trip? When I was leaving for the village, I thought I would spend four or five days there, but I only spent the night. I got up in the morning, threw off the snake that had settled around my neck and went into the ichkari. My wife was sweeping there. I looked her in the eyes and could tell that she hadn't slept the whole night. I hadn't been able to fall asleep either. A snake had made its bed in my embrace! I was going to kiss my children goodbye that morning, but the snake, nuzzling up, had made my lips haram. I kissed the edge of my mat. She must have thought that I was leaving them for good since I didn't even kiss the children. She started crying again. The poor woman didn't know that I didn't kiss them because I love them.*

MARYAM. (the name Miryoqub gave Maria, though wasn't Yevdokiya her name?)

---

45 The 1988 serial publication consistently has "Jakov" instead of "Jakob." The difference might have resulted from editors' difficulties reading the 1930s-era Uzbek Latin script.

Oh God! Oh my God! What is this? Am I dreaming or am I awake? Where am I? What am I doing? What was yesterday? What is today? What will tomorrow be?

Jakob opened the door to my room, let me in, and left. I locked the door behind him. I sentenced myself, believing his word alone, to five days in that prison. I expected to go out only five times during those five days and only when everyone was asleep. The rest of the time I would spend in that little, sweet, safe room. Anything could happen during those five days! I had my doubts: 'What if he doesn't come? What if he gets sick of me? Maybe after a month, a year? Maybe he'll come back soon, but will he have changed towards me and be just another ordinary client? Maybe then he'll come for just an hour or half an hour … What will I do then? Will I go back to that disgusting place? No! No! It would be better to die. So much better.

Why did I trust him? Why? Why did I trade all my hopes and desires for the word of some stranger? What kind of stupid woman am I? Have I ascended a mountain just to fall painfully into that same swamp? When you live in the swamp you get used to the air. But once you're out, breathing that fresh mountain air, can you really dive back in? I must be crazy! Crazy! He's a rich merchant, I knew that. Why didn't I tell him, 'Give me a check for 1,000 rubles, then I'll believe you'? He would've given it to me. Then it would be his problem: he could come or he could not come. I would have been on my way. … Towards my goal. … And if he didn't give me the check, I would have known that he didn't love me and I wouldn't have trusted him. … I would have saved myself the worry. I'm stupid!

I didn't notice that two days had passed. The thoughts and doubts gave me no peace. I thought and I thought; I didn't know whether to laugh or to sob! I started to hear careful steps behind the door. It must be some scoundrels who have heard that a young beautiful girl is all alone in her room, I thought. Even the servant who brought the food asked why I didn't go outside. "Did someone ask about me?" I said. "No," he answered, "should someone have?" "My husband," I replied. He was silent. After that I didn't hear any steps outside the door.

Am I dreaming or am I awake? I remember hearing a soft knocking on the door. Only two nights had passed since we'd parted. He said he'd be back on the fifth day. The knocking sounded like the servant's. It must be the servant, I thought, opening the door without checking. And he came in! Oh, that Asian! We didn't greet each other, he didn't extend his hand to me, and I didn't offer mine either. He didn't say a word. Like a mute, he came in and just showed me the tickets in his hand. He called in the servant, and we paid the check. Then we left for the train station.

And now the two of us are in one compartment. Our hearts are one. Our bodies—separate. The train keeps on moving. I close my eyes. … Am I dreaming or awake?

JAKOB. *It looks like we passed Tashkent last night. Now we're headed into the miserable, boring steppe. A man with his hair cut short in a new Tashkent skullcap and a European suit appeared in our car. He has a short, well-preened mustache. Pale complexion. Not bad looking. A foppish gait. He looks like a Tashkenter. Maybe a merchant. Or a lawyer. Or a bureaucrat. In any event, he reads Russian, I see Russian newspapers in his hand. He's passed by our compartment a few times now and looked around the car. Was he looking at me and Maryam? Were his eyes on Maryam?! Those Tashkent merchants are dandies. They like European girls. They're no strangers to corrupting young women. I started to worry and closed the door. It's stuffy in the compartment. Maryam is starting to worry. I'll have to open the door again.*

MARYAM. *Jakob must love me. If he wasn't in love, he wouldn't behave like this. Oh, let it be true!*

A good-looking sart keeps looking in on us. Is he looking at Jakob or me? I don't know. He must be looking at me. Because why would a man be looking at another man? Although they say that sarts do have a custom of men loving other men. Fun!

My little Jakob, my beloved Jakob is starting to worry. He closed the door. Then I let out a sigh and he opened it. Oh, us women! Let that sart man say something and I'll really test my Jakob! If I could just test his love, then I could calm down.

I went out into the corridor. In the open window the endless steppe, the naked desert ran backwards. What complete loneliness! If I was alone, if Jakob wasn't by my side, I would die of loneliness. Jakob suddenly came out behind me.

"What a cool breeze, right?" he managed.

"It's not bad," I said, laughing the laugh of a child carelessly playing with fire.

The sart man was at the window too. Jakob walked over and stopped by him. After the train stopped at a station, the sart passed by us, but stopped at the window on the other side the of car, on my side. Jakob slowly followed him over there.

Why hasn't the sart said something to me, flirted with me? Will there be a fight? Let it happen! Let them fight and get it out of their systems. Then one of them will answer my heart's desires. That's all I need. The sart and he are both Asian! They don't know a woman's heart.

I became annoyed, went into the compartment, and shut the door behind me.

Wait! Wait! What is this? The two of them have started talking. This doesn't look like a fight.

I became annoyed again. Ughhh!

JAKOB. *Thank God, he was looking at me, not at her. He told me he wanted to introduce himself. He did. A Tashkent merchant. Going to Finland apparently. What country is that?*

MARYAM. *Jakob is getting close with that sart. Now he sits in our compartment all the time. I'm off to the side. At my side is Jakob ... my little Jakob. And at his side—the sart. He knows Russian quite well, this sart. He embarrassed Jakob. He must have said, "Why don't you introduce your wife?" Jakob looked at me. "Do you know this person?" he signed. How would I know him? Strange! I gave him my hand. "Sharafuddin Xo'jaev" he said. What a difficult name! Jakob, my little Jakob ... This one is different. A pretty one though.*

JAKOB. *I think I found someone who can answer my questions. This man is one of the big jadids. Now I can ask about empire. He talks of such things, my eyes become like teacups. It's as if I've been asleep all this time. As if all of us have been crushed by ignorance. There is this thing called the "nation"; it's what we call "the masses." The way the man said "nation" sounded sweet as it rolled off his tongue.*

But it was bad that he asked, "Who is this person next to you?" I wasn't sure what to answer. I still haven't been able to find an answer. He helped: "is she your wife?" "Yes, my wife." I was safe. Later he came into the room and asked, "won't you introduce your wife?" Before I could ask whether she was acquainted with him, Maryam was already shaking his hand. The daughter of an infidel, how could she know?[46]

Well, fine, I trust this man. He doesn't seem to be interested in women. He's too busy with his "nation."

If he oversteps his bounds, then we ordinary people can have it out like men!

MARYAM. *What a disaster this sart is. Jakob talks with him from dawn to dusk. I don't understand a thing. They read the newspaper in their language. The man translates it from Russian for Jakob. I guess it's not all bad; Jakob is becoming a little more enlightened. He's becoming a person. Becoming cultured.*

It's just that. I guess I can love him like that too. I'm starting to get bored. What should I do? If only there was a book around.

Across Jakob's lips a playful smile appeared. I looked closer: it looked like a passionate flame had been kindled inside him. Is that not his love for me? But ... if it is, then why aren't his laughing eyes and sweet smile directed at me? Why is he looking over there? Is that not the fire of another love? Oh, my God! My God!

JAKOB. *This man is not who I thought he was at first. Is this the teacher I've been looking for? Why have I been going around and cursing these jadids? If this is who a jadid is, why am I not a jadid, why is mingboshi not a jadid, why is everyone not a jadid? But noyib to'ra spoke of those who wanted to take land from the rich, take the factories from their owners. ... No, I should ask this one carefully. He'll probably tell me.*

---

46 In pre-Soviet Central Asian society, it was improper for women and men to touch one another in public, much less shake hands.

I told him about my connections with noyib to'ra, about how noyib to'ra knows our language and literature, what noyib to'ra said about empire. He started talking ... and talking ... and talking ... strange and fantastic things flowed from his mouth. It was as if his every word lifted a curtain in front of me.

And I opened up. For the first time in my life I told a new acquaintance the secrets closest to my heart. When he heard in detail what happened with Maryam, he said:

"Don't let this woman out of your sight! She's a girl from that world that brings us all our misery. We hate those people. They are our enemies! They are our enemies in every sense! It's not so often that we find a friend from among them. But those that we do find are good. Very good friends. But when we embrace them, we're always ready to escape their clutches!

"You saved her from the most unclean depths. You redefined her fate and now she belongs to you completely. I can see from the way she looks at you that her heart is yours! You are truly happy. She will bring you into a new world now just as you rescued her from that old one. You will see in her the paragon of all mothers. If the children of the nation aren't raised by truly cultured mothers, then our outlook is poor. You can learn a lot from her. If you give your sisters and daughters to the care of someone like her, then you will have done your duty as a father! In the words of our elders: 'Let you be united forever!' I say. Your union is for the happiness of our nation and the mothers of our nation!

"As concerns your nobleman friend who knows our language ... the Russian government looks at our country as a 'colony,' like a child country. That's why they don't send good officials here. They only come here by mistake. Not one of them is a friend to us. Our friend is us ourselves! Our friend is the nation! They are enemies of the nation. We are their enemies. Don't forget that!

"Why give all those valuable writings on our country's history, on literature to a Russian official? To me that's a betrayal of the nation! You gather them, and we'll make a national library. That's the right way to do it!

"Nations several times smaller than ours have independent states positioned right in the heart, right in the navel of cultured Europe. They're the ones riding the trams around Tashkent. Our misfortune is precisely in our stupidity. If the nation awakens, opens its eyes, studies, gains knowledge, enters into the group of cultured nations, then it can build its own state and find its own happiness.

"It is the task of the awakened to rouse the nation. Look at you. You look like an intelligent, conscientious, astute man. You know what you're doing. You have wealth. But your fault is in that you aren't aware of the situation around you. You don't read newspapers. Do you know what a sin that is? What great newspapers we have. In Orenburg, in Kazan, in Ufa, in Astrakhan, and especially in Moscow. Once the war ends, subscribe and read! If you send five rubles to Bakhchysarai,[47] they'll send you *Tarjimon* for a year. Do you know what 'Tarjimon' means?'"

Here I interrupted him because the time had come.

"Does it mean take all the land and water from the rich, take the factories from their owners? Tell me that."

"You're talking about the socialists," he said, "There are no socialists among us. We are far from the socialists. What does 'Tarjimon' mean? *Translator* is the father of the jadids, grandfather Ismail's newspaper.[48] It's an older newspaper. It says, 'In language, thought, and deed we must be united!' meaning us Muslims, us Turkic peoples should be of one thought and work together. What good comes of that you ask? We have no interest in the lands of the rich and the factories of the factory owners. That's their business. None of the newspapers we read say anything like that. On the contrary, they say, 'Be rich! Build a factory! Open a workshop! Hire 5,000, 10,000 workers! Develop the national industry!' Who is the owner of *Time*?[49] Rameev.[50] Do you know who that is? He's a millionaire. He owns gold mines. Don't be afraid of jadids. Know the nation, serve it. That will make you a jadid too. Your name will be written on the pages of history books. Who told you that we don't want to make money? Take me, for example: I have stores in Finland and Petersburg; every year I go to their markets. I go to Lyons in France and Hamburg in Germany. I trade leather, furs, and some of our local crafts. I make a world of money on them. My son won't be one of those who plays *uloq* on horseback; he won't be a gambler; he

---

47 A city in the Crimea.

48 Isma'il Gaspirali (1851–1914) was the creator of *usul-i jadid*, the new pedagogical method for the teaching of the Arabic alphabet to children for which jadids received their name. Gaspirali was active in all the Turkic communities of the Russian Empire through his newspaper and his work in political organizing. He founded the newspaper *Tarjimon* in 1883, and it ran until 1917.

49 A newspaper printed in Orenburg from 1908 to 1918. It published the pieces of several authors from the Turkic communities of the Russian Empire, including Cho'lpon's early works.

50 Zakir Rameev (1859–1921) was a Tatar entrepreneur and capitalist as well as a poet and public figure.

won't be giving my money to some dancing boy[51] or a prostitute. He'll study and become a real man, find a cultured profession. One of my brothers studies in a gymnasium in Helsinki in Finland. Another in the famous Oliya *madrasa* in Ufa.[52] My brother's son is enrolled in Tashkent's realschule.[53] My son is still little; he's in Finland. I left him with a special tutor."[54]

---

51 Central Asia, Afghanistan, and Iran were long known for the tradition of so-called dancing boys. Male children danced erotically for older men in opium dens and often engaged in sexual activity with those men.

52 The Oliya *madrasa* was one among several madrasas in Ufa that played a large role in disseminating jadid ideas.

53 A German-style school that was established in 1894 in Tashkent. Instead of teaching the classics as other Russian schools did, this school's curriculum focused on the natural sciences and mathematics.

54 The 1988 serial publication replaces the nine paragraphs preceding this note with the three below.

> 'Don't let this woman out of your sight. You saved her from the most unclean depths. You redefined her fate and now she belongs to you completely. I can see from the way she looks at you that her heart is yours! You are truly happy. She will bring you into a new world now just as you brought her into one. You will see in her the paragon of all mothers. In the words of our elders: 'Let you be united forever!' I say. As concerns your nobleman friend who knows our language. The imperial government looks at our country as a 'colony,' like a child country. That's why they don't send good officials here. They only come here by mistake.
>
> 'Why give all those valuable writings on our country's history, on literature to a Russian official? You gather them, and we'll make a national library. That's the right way to do it!
>
> 'Look at you. You look like an intelligent, conscientious, astute man. You know what you're doing. You have wealth. But your fault is in that you aren't aware of the situation around you. You don't read newspapers. Do you know what a sin that is? What great newspapers there are. In Orenburg, in Kazan, in Ufa, in Astrakhan, and especially in Moscow. Once the war ends, subscribe and read! If you send five rubles to Bakhchysarai, they'll send you *Tarjimon* for a year. *Translator* is the father of the jadids, grandfather Ismail's newspaper. Now it's an older newspaper. It says, 'in language, thought, and deed we must be united!' We have no interest in the lands of the rich and the factories of the factory owners. That's their business. None of the newspapers we read say anything like that. On the contrary, they say, 'Be rich! Build a factory! Open a workshop! Hire 5,000, 10,000! Develop the national industry!' Who is the owner of *Time*? Rameev. Do you know who that is? He's a millionaire. He owns gold mines. Who told you that we don't want to make money? Take me, for example: I have stores in Finland and Petersburg; every year I go to their markets. I go to Lyons in France and Hamburg in Germany. I trade leather, furs, and some of our local crafts. I make a world of money on them. My son won't be one of those who plays uloq on horseback; he won't be a gambler; he won't be giving my money to some dancing boy or a prostitute.

I don't want this jadid to stop talking.

MARYAM. *Jakob has forgotten me. He's fallen under the spell of that sart. What should I do? Fine, all right, I'll endure it. A cultured Jakob is naturally better than a wild Asian Jakob who doesn't know Russian. He pulled me out of that swamp; now if he becomes a cultured person because of me, all the better!*

Only I'm bored. I found a book. And a magazine. And I read … read … but no relief. It's a long journey. You look out the window and it's all the same. I'm suffocating of boredom. … I just want to hang on Jakob's neck and strangle him!

I finally found another Russian woman on this train. Her husband is a lawyer in Tashkent. She's going to see her mother in Moscow. At least now I have someone to talk to. The only thing we talk about is love!

JAKOB. *Strange, who would have thought a word could possess such power? Just yesterday when I heard the word "jadid," it made me furious. All the respectable, powerful, and esteemed people in our country hate jadids. Shahobiddin always told me that a jadid is the worst kind of infidel. He drove a boy out of the madrasa just for reading a newspaper. The wealthiest in our city can't say jadid without adding the words 'mischief-maker' and 'bastard.'*

Well now I'm seeing a jadid. I listen to him day and night; I can't take my ear away. I haven't seen anything bad from him. It doesn't seem that they want to take away our property. He's a rich man himself. He knows how to make money the right way. … Is that bad? If that's what a jadid is, then I am also a jadid.[55]

Finally finding an appropriate time, I asked, "What does 'empire' mean?"

"Why are you asking?"

"My friend who is an official told me that the empire is waning; he was very unhappy about that."

"When he says empire, he means the lands that are under the dominion of the tsar. There are all kinds of nations in it, including our poor nation. If the war ends unsuccessfully (*I couldn't understand that last word*), they are afraid that all the lands will splinter and break up. They want Russia, that great, immense country held together by the sword and the Cossacks spears, to stay in its current state until the end of days. Who doesn't want a milch cow? It has the whitest, sweetest milk."

"Whose milk?" *I asked.*

He'll study and become a real man, find a cultured profession. One of my brothers studies in a gymnasium in Helsinki in Finland. Another in the famous Oliya madrasa in Ufa. My brother's son is enrolled in Tashkent's realschule. My son is still little; he's in Finland. I left him with a special tutor.'

55 The 1988 serial publication omits this sentence.

He laughed.

"We're the milch cows, and it's our milk. Russians and other foreigners are sucking us dry. We're not the only ones. Look: India, Eastern Turkestan, Tunisia, Algeria, Morocco … Egypt has fallen to the British. Now they're planning on dividing up Turkey. The whole Islamic world is falling into the hands of foreigners. Look at Iran: our Ivans have taken her by the head and 'tricky Albion'—by the haunches."[56]

He talks and talks. I'm surprised. How does he know all these names? How does it all stay in his memory? Has he seen it all himself? Is he just fooling me and making things up? He said the name of some city in Finland. You'd break your tongue on a word like that … In any event, I'm fine even if this woman gives me nothing. She has lifted the curtain from my eyes.[57]

But … Maryam made friends with some woman and is having the same kind of conversations that we are. I'll go have a look and make sure there are no men messing around there.

"I'm going to go check on my wife quickly," *I said and left.*

When I glanced in, Maryam was reading a book aloud, and the other woman was listening. There was a man sleeping on the top bunk. Fine, so she's not bored, poor Maryam.

I went back to the jadid. Suddenly he asked, "Do you have a Muslim wife too?"

"Yes. … No, I'm sorry: I had one …"

"But you've lived with a Muslim wife?"

"Yes … of course."

"Well, now you know, thanks to your experience, the importance of culture and education. Just try to compare an uncultured, stupid Muslim woman with the cultured one you have now. It's like night and day! You know it immediately."

"I was thinking about sending my son to a Russian school."

"No, that would be a mistake. You can't start him off in a Russian school; you have to send him to a national school first. After he knows his own language, then give him over to a Russian school where he can learn a craft and prepare for a career. (*There were a number of words I couldn't understand in his*

---

56 The 1988 serial publication omits the preceding four paragraphs, replacing them with: 'When he says empire, he means the lands that are under the dominion of the tsar. There are all kinds of nations in it, including ours.'

57 The 1988 serial publication omits the last sentence.

speech, but somehow, he spoke quickly without stumbling. I was too embarrassed to stop and ask him every time. I got the gist of what he was saying. I'll get it when I start reading the newspapers.) After that send him to Germany, France, England or even the other side of the world in America."

"The Russians have plenty of learned people. Why send him so far?"

"Yes, the Russians have education too. They are a very developed nation. But they take everything they know from Europe and America anyways."

"Is that so?"

"It is.[58] Once this war ends, come to Finland. We'll go to Germany together, see France and England too. Then you'll see what jadids want."

"I'm still in awe of everything you've said."

"If you're enraptured, then serve the nation; awaken the people left in ignorance; open new schools! Teach your children in the new method."

"Of course, of course. That's exactly what I'll do. My eyes are open. I am enlightened. Now I'll endeavor to make humans of our nation."[59]

"Very good! Do you know Abdusamat mingboshi?"

"Our Abdusamat the bald? I know him. His village isn't far from ours."

"Aha, well there's a real official of the nation for you! If all our mingboshis and other officials were like him, then the nation would be enlightened in no time."

"I heard he educates girls in the new method."

"To educate girls he invited a special teacher from Ufa. He's going to set up a new-method school for girls in his home. He recently got permission for just such a jadid school.

"We recently sent a teacher from Tashkent to him. He is the father of the nation! The father of all of us! If you see him, say hello. Every jadid dreams of meeting him!"

Maryam called me over. I wasn't sure what was the matter. I had to cut this fascinating conversation short.

MARYAM. *Even fortune cards have gotten boring. Jakob has given me up completely. I hate that cultured sart! Devil take him!*

I've been reading my fortune and "unhappiness" keeps coming up. Not promising. He's going to take my Jakob away! Is there anything worse than this culture? That cultured sart does nothing but talk from morning to evening.

I couldn't stand it anymore. I called Jakob over. We'll have a good talk and decide this. Oh, he's coming. Jakob!

---

58 The 1988 serial publication omits the short interchange here beginning with, 'The Russians have plenty of learned people,' up to the footnote.

59 The 1988 serial publication removes this sentence.

JAKOB. *When I came in, she screamed, "Jakob!" and threw her arms around my neck. The door was open and everyone saw! Then she started to moan and cry!*

This won't end well. All my thoughts are in other places, far away places. Maryam can't know that. I tried to calm her however I could. I told her I would come back and spend the whole night talking to her. She smiled.

No, I can't go against that smile!

MARYAM. *I couldn't say a thing; my tongue seized up. I hung on him and cried. He soothed me and promised he would be back.*

JAKOB. *We'll stop in Moscow for one or two days. There we'll decide this whole matter with Maryam. I'll just have to keep her calm before then.*

The matter is a small one. It should be decided easily. But where are all these new thoughts taking me? I'm not sure.

MARYAM. *My little Jakob's demeanor has changed towards me. How happy I am! Only … who or what is he to me? Do I love him? These questions give me no peace. I should know the answer to that second question. Or at least it's time to determine that answer. Enough with these games! I have to come up with an answer before Moscow!*

JAKOB. *We left Orenburg and the sweet-mouthed jadid showed me the city through the window. I looked but the city was already well behind us.*

"There's a madrasa called Husayniya here. It's a three-floored building in the European style. There they study the new disciplines: math, the sciences. Do you know who funded its construction? One of the fathers of the jadids, Ahmadboy Husaynov.[60] A very wealthy man. He gave a lot of money to jadid schools. His services before the nation are countless.[61] If only we had such generous men! In Andijan, maybe you've heard of him, Mir Komilboy[62] hasn't given a thing to develop the nation. Ignoramus."

"He's an idiot, a jackass," *I said.* "No education. He doesn't read newspapers."

We crossed over an iron bridge and entered a forest. The trees were already starting to yellow.

"Listen," *I began,* "don't the jadids want to take the land from the rich too? Someone told me that, convinced me of that!"

"No, no! Never! I told you before: the jadids are not socialists. Never! Never! But I was just telling you about Ahmadboy Husaynov. He is considered one of the fathers of all jadids."

"That's good," *I agreed.*

---

60 Ahmadbay Husaynov (1837–1906) was one of Orenburg's wealthier merchants and philanthropists.

61 The 1988 serial publication removes this sentence.

62 Mirkomil Mirmo'minboev (1861–1918) was a wealthy merchant of Andijan opposed to the jadids and their reforms.

"Although," *said the jadid,* "there used to be some socialists among us jadids. For example, Ayoz Ishoqiy.[63] He raised hell against the rich just a few years ago. Now he prints a newspaper in Moscow with their help. He's serving the nation now. When you go to Moscow, you can find his newspaper, *The Word*. A great newspaper!"

I felt relieved. Now I could trust the jadids. There are no liars among them. They are good people!

I made a promise to Maryam. When they started turning the lights on in the car, I left for our compartment.

MARYAM. *Jakob spent the night with me. He spoke in spurts, unable to finish sentences, but I understood him. He spoke sincerely and I understood. We understood each other. Oh, how happy I am! There's no doubt that Jakob has incomparable eyes: black, playful, lively! No! I could never leave those eyes!*

What is this? Am I confessing my love? Do I love him?

Do I love him?

No?

...

I love him!

But ... what if he doesn't love me?

What if he just takes everything that he wants and puts a check in my hand?!

I'm afraid to think about it!

But ...

I'm right to love him!

I love him!

And I don't want to know anything else!

JAKOB. *The jadid started talking about Maryam again. He spoke a lot.*

"You need to let this woman teach all your children. Let them all become people."

"But they haven't studied in a national school yet!" *I exclaimed.*

"You have money, hire a tutor for them. It will be quick. If you're going to the Crimea, go to Bakhchysarai. Find the newspaper *Translator*. Talk with the teachers there. Maybe they'll help you find a teacher, they'll show the way."

He wrote the name of the newspaper on my hand. His handwriting is bad. I'll have to figure out how I stand with Maryam in Moscow. Our original plans are shot. ... Should I abandon her in Moscow and return home now? This jadid's words

---

63 Ayaz İshaki (1878–1954) was a Tatar litterateur, publisher, and public figure interested in socialist ideas in the early 1900s. After the October Revolution, he became the target of Bolshevik campaigns against bourgeois nationalists, which forced him to emigrate in 1920.

have inspired me: I want to pass on the same words to others, to affect them the way he affected me. I want to open people's eyes.

No. I can't. I can't abandon Maryam. Wait, the jadid said a bunch of things about her! "Let's learn from foreign mothers in order to train the mothers of our nation!" he said. Maryam would be a great example for others. No, I can't abandon her.

We'll go to Moscow. "Only an ass mourns tomorrow's losses," they say. The Moscow dachas are already zipping past.

MARYAM. *We're getting close to Moscow. Ah, there are the dachas. Tall buildings. a big city.*

But a doubt, an ominous feeling is gripping me. Some uncertain worry, trouble.

What is it?

A parting?

No, I won't part with him!

JAKOB. *We stopped in a clean little hotel. Each of us in our own room. An offended look flits in Maryam's eyes. The poor thing.*

The jadid left. I said goodbye to him on the train. And I haven't seen him since. Now that his sweet voice has departed from my ear, the hurried flow of his powerful words has broken. I'm weighing them to see if they add up.

Was what he said true? It wasn't a lie? For a Muslim to abandon the path of his faith and his forefathers, is that not exactly the trap that an infidel would lay? That man doesn't pray. There's not a sign of his Muslim background in the way he looks. Is it true what the mullahs have said? Why didn't I argue with him?

No, I couldn't have. It was hard to find the right words to answer him. No one can answer those words of his.

Well now, let's see, what to do now? I can't not go to the Crimea. At least for Maryam I have to go there. He said the big jadids are there. I'll find them and talk with them. If the jadids didn't have good foundations, then the Ottoman Caliph wouldn't support them, right?[64] *He says that everything is in order. The new method came from the Ottoman lands, they say … those new clothes too … all the new customs are from the Ottomans.*

These are strange circumstances I'm in. I just hope I don't lose my head. It was easy to make money and just mind my business at home. We just did what all our ancestors did. Now someone comes along and says that everything our parents have

---

64 Most Central Asian jadids were influenced by progressive Turks from the Ottoman Empire. Here Miryoqub says *khalifayi Rum*, meaning the Ottoman Caliph. The word is a slight anachronism and not a term often used by jadids, which shows Miryoqub's difficulty in grasping his jadid interlocutor's language.

done is wrong, and this new way is the right one. And he said it so convincingly you'd be a fool not to believe.

I have to pick one of these two paths. I can't walk both.

I'll have to keep speaking with jadids. I have to read newspapers. Every day only the newest newspapers. He said Moscow has good newspapers so I'll find some here. And I'll try to read some of those new books as well.

Well, let my eyes be opened. Let me learn new things. I'll learn a lot of new things. "Knowing is better than not knowing," said the jadid. Truer words were never spoken!

MARYAM. *Jakob was with me all the way to Moscow. Everything about him has changed. Did those stupid cards lie? Or did I make a mistake? Or maybe the cards say the opposite of what will happen?*

But why did we take separate rooms? That means Jakob wants to leave me. If only he loved me—we spent three nights together in the city and six nights in the train—then he would have tried to get closer.

Am I against his becoming intimate? Or is he afraid that he has to give me money? I'm not even thinking about money now. If he needs it, I'll give him my money. Just so long as he doesn't leave me!

My head is spinning. I don't know what to do. This Jakob is such a closed person, you can't understand him. They say the Japanese are like that. Is it not because he's Asian? All is woe!

Fine. Let's say we were in the same room, let's even say that he kissed me … and embraced me. If that happened, I wouldn't be able to hold back … and neither could he.

But what would happen in the end? Usually men become cold after that. If he stops talking and hands me a check. … Then it will be goodbye! No, no. To hell with the check! To hell with money! I don't want it!

What to do, what to do? I don't know.

What can I do? He bought me; he has the money, he has the power. I always look to him, to his mouth. Would it tell me to leave? Would it?!

JAKOB. *I found the addresses of two sanatoriums in the Crimea. I was going to send a telegram to ask if they had rooms for two. I almost wrote it, but no. Because a room for two or for one?*

I have to figure this out with Maryam first. I've already decided for myself, but what will she say?

Will she say, "Give me my money, I'm leaving"? Or will she want to make a life with me? What if I go ask right now? I'll ask. No! I can't ask with words. Where's my checkbook? Ah, here it is. But I don't know Russian. I'll just write the number and sign below. Good!

MARYAM. *I haven't seen Jakob all day. After lunch, he left for his room. I've waited so long and he still hasn't come. When will this end? Has he had enough of me? I'm afraid of his reticence and his pensiveness.*

What time is it? Oh-ho: almost eleven! I must have fallen asleep. Has Jakob gone to sleep? Another night of loneliness!

What if I get up, go to the washroom, bathe thoroughly, have a little something to eat, go downstairs. … I'm bored. There's no happiness for me!

It's autumn. Nature is slowly dying. My soul was resurrected so quickly. But was it meant to just die again?

…

How wonderful that cold water is! I feel revived!

What is this now? Oh God! Jakob came in when I stepped out.

A check! This is it! Woe is me!

JAKOB. *I got a handful of newspapers to read. The language is vague and unclear. My eyes get tired from it. I had wanted to sleep with Maryam tonight and give her the check, but then I thought she couldn't but understand it as the end.*

I gave her the check first. Will she understand? After a bit, I'll go to her.

MARYAM. *The more I cry, the less it helps. It looks like Crimea isn't in the cards for me. We'll be together another night or two until he tells me to get lost and then. … He'll get what little he wanted from me. I'll take my money and leave. Go back to my previous life: Petrograd, Germany, my brother. But I don't want any of it!*

What should I do? That sart ruined everything. He must have told Jakob to get rid of me and go back to his sart wife. An intellectual. Devil take him!

I've made my decision: I love him. But he's going to run me off. Fine, he'll be mine for another one or two days. I'll have to be happy that I get to spend another two fateful nights with the man I love. And then that's it!

"An omelet? Fine, bring it. And a bottle of port too!" I told the servant.

Oh, wine! It makes my heart joyous for some reason. Someone's knocking at the door. Who is it? Jakob!

JAKOB. *When I came in, she had already had dinner. And it looked like she had a bit to drink. She seems happy! I guess she understood. But I don't want to rush her. I'll still have to tell her about a few conditions. She immediately got up and threw her arms around my neck. She hung on me with drunken weight. And I didn't refuse her. … After a while, I took her hand from my neck.*

"Sit," I said.

"Don't leave me, Jakob!" she suddenly declared. "I am your guest for two nights! For these two nights, you will be in my power! I am possessed, I am flame, I am fire! Do not deny me!"

I smiled.

"I was going to ask you to marry me. Why would you be a guest? Or don't you want to live with me?"

She became pale and teared up. She lost her breath and started shivering. I went over to caress her. She came to a little bit.

"Am I dreaming, or am I awake?" *she asked herself.* "Are you telling the truth? Or joking? Those kinds of jokes are the deaths of people, Jakob!"

"You know, Maryam, I have two daughters and a son."

"That's fine."

"My oldest is twelve; the others are still babies."

"Good."

"For their sake, I'll have to be truthful with my wife. There's no other way. She won't give me the girls, but I'll take the boy and entrust his education to you. What do you say?"

She looked in my eyes as if to confirm everything I had said. I nodded.

"I am yours. Everything will be as you say!"

I sent a rush telegram to the sanatorium, asking for a two-person reservation. I threw myself in the large, soft chair by the window.

"Are you mine now, Maryam?" *I asked.*

Laughing, she approached me.

"Since the first day we saw each other," *she answered.*

Now she was very quiet and tame. She no longer had outbursts like before. None of that impatience of a hotheaded youth about to be joined with her beloved for the first time. She was calm like a woman who had been married with children for years. A warm calm.

"Press the button," *I said.*

The servant came. I told him, despite the late hour, to warm up the bath. Hotel managers will do anything for money. One three-ruble bill, and he did everything without question. I took my time in the bath, knowing that Maryam's preparations would take a while. By the time I was done, she was dressed and ready.

"What time is it?" *I asked.*

"A little past midnight."

"Let's go, then!"

Her eyes opened wide.

"Where are we going in the middle of the night?"

"Go! You're mine now, after all."

She laughed sweetly again. The sart told me that the Tatars have a mosque in Moscow. He mentioned that it was a jadid mosque: "See, being religious doesn't depend on your clothes. Our stupid Islamic learned men say that only those that wear *turbans can be Muslims. But Islam is not in your dress, it's in your heart, in your soul. There are Muslims that pray five times a day in Russian."*

In the middle of the night, we, two crazy people, as if thieves escaping from the law, rode through the streets of Moscow in a carriage.

The imam was woken.

"A wedding, hazrat," I commanded. Tatars call their learned people hazrat.

He looked at me and then at her.

"I can tell that you're a Muslim. Is the woman a Muslim?" he asked.

"Not yet."

"Then what can I do?"

He trained his sleepy eyes on me again. I handed him a ten-ruble note.

"Islam is gradualness, hazrat. I'll convert her little by little."

He took the money and, like our doctors, put it in his pocket without looking.

"Actually," began the hazrat, "the Sharia has something to say about this. …"

After a moment, he called the sufi to his side to stand as a witness for the wedding. We gave a little something to the sufi as well. And with that, my name remained the same and Maria Stepanovna became Bibi Maryam Oysha qizi.

Oysha qizi and I, now husband and wife, came back to our room at around two at night.

MARYAM. *Oh God! We're married, married! I wouldn't be surprised if I fainted from excitement. Just a few hours ago, I couldn't think about anything but death. The fog over my eyes blinded me. But I was young and I wanted to live!*

And now—marriage! My husband by marriage! Eternal salvation from that swamp of a life!

But … what kind of wedding was that? Simple like that strange faith and all its followers … and savage.

No shine and no luster! None of the festiveness, extravagance! Simple and bare like an Indian pauper. Dim and lackluster like extinguished volcanoes. Pitiful like an aging ship.

No! No! No! It must be like this for everyone. But for me, for me there can be nothing brighter, more promising, more extravagant than that wedding! Now all my suffering is behind me. All those black days in the past. Now he's mine, mine alone!

JAKOB. *Now Maryam is mine. Mine, and she won't lay even a finger on another. When I take this mischievous daughter of the enemy[65] in my arms, when I press her*

---

65 The phrase "mischievous daughter of the enemy" was removed from the 1988 serial publication. The word used for "mischievous" is fitna, the nickname Razzoq-sufi gives his wife. See the glossary.

thirsting, hot lips to mine, I have to think about the nation, about its ignorant mothers, about my poor daughter, and my sisters.

Can a person's mind really be so sharp? A mustachioed Tashkenter turned my life in a different direction after just four days! I haven't fully become a jadid. I still have my doubts about them. But my heart is urging me in that direction. I too believe the nation should become human. Now I will never say that the path of our fathers is the only one. But I can't say that the jadids are right either. Though I do understand what the jadids have to say more easily and quickly than what others say. Is it just that they talk well? Our Shahobiddin can say just three words and it's like you've caught consumption. He talks like someone who doesn't believe his own words. And that's why they have no effect!

No, our Muslims can't go any longer without reforming themselves, without setting their affairs in order.

A strange fire burns in Maryam's eyes. I could burn up in it. And I'd like to. Just ten days ago, I could have spent thousands in that brothel and what would have remained? Nothing of that fire! How much has Akbarali spent? Too much to count! I've spent money like that as well. And is there anything left from it? Not a thing! Everything's gone like the water you wash your hands with. And what do I have now? All the wealth that comes with happiness! What I have will show the nation how to be a proper mother to its children. What I have now is the start of my service to the nation!

MARYAM. *Jakob had turned out the light, but I turned it back on. This time he was surprised. I tore up the check he had given me in front of his eyes. He kissed me softly on the forehead. Then the light went out. Outside the mad wind raged. Let it howl, what's it to me?!*

13

When Sultonxon heard that Zebi was betrothed to mingboshi, she had lost all hope. That day she did not mince words.

"I'll divorce mingboshi!" she told her mother. "I'll marry another man. I don't have the stomach for a younger co-wife."

"Have a little patience, daughter."

"What is patience? How many years now has Poshshaxon rotted with her patience? And she didn't get more than five months of that ugly mug!"

"But she has remained patient, daughter."

"She may have swallowed her pride and her intelligence, but I haven't! I'm better than them. You only have one life, only so many years of youth. They threw their lives and their youth to the fire. Should I do the same? I'm young!"

"What can we do?"

"Tell Father. Have him get me the divorce."

"Won't your father be upset?"

"Just let him try not to be upset if he won't get me the divorce. I'll do such things that he won't be able to lift his head in town!"

"Don't say that, daughter. Try to think good thoughts."

"I am thinking good thoughts. I'll divorce a man that doesn't love me and marry one that does. What's bad about that? Both my sisters have good husbands. What did I do wrong? Give me Father's answer by tomorrow. If not, I'll give all of you something to be ashamed of."

Enraged, she stood up, put on her shoes, and started outside to scare her mother more.

"Don't act crazy, daughter!" her mother cried from behind her. "I'll talk with your father today. Don't pull your hair out over this!"

"I expect an answer by tomorrow!" came Sultonxon's voice from outside.

Sadriddin the lame was to blame for everything. Matchmakers had come from all around for Sultonxon. He rejected every one of them. The girl was agreed to some of them, and her mother didn't always say no. "No," Sadri the lame said, "I married the first two off to villagers, I'll give the last one to a city dweller. Someone wealthy and esteemed with a worthy house for this daughter!" When Sultonxon turned seventeen, her mother began to worry: "Why does it have to be a city-dweller? She's almost eighteen. She'll be ancient by the time you find someone!" But the stubborn cripple had plans for the family: "If we become in-laws to a city man, then we can move to the city." In the end, mother and daughter couldn't overcome his obstinacy. His daughter's beauty, her pretty face, and light skin gave his hopes strength. But mingboshi's wealth and the respect he commanded were able to break the father's foolish stubbornness. The cripple understood that if he denied mingboshi, he wouldn't have much of a life left for vain hopes. The description of the girl whetted mingboshi's appetite, but not a day passed after the wedding that he began telling everyone that Sultonxon was old. Oh how she cursed her parents and cried.

Now she was nineteen. Mingboshi completely abandoned her once he took Zebi. Such trials for the poor girl!

Sadri the lame couldn't argue with his wife, who relayed his daughter's threats, and sent his friend Abdulla the boss to negotiate on his behalf. "In good times and in bad, she served you and now you have a new servant. Might you allow her now … while she is still young … if you permit, we will find a good place for her."

Mingboshi gave the same answer to Sadri the lame's man as he gave to the man sent by Poshshaxon's father. He added an insult for good measure: "Who would take the old hag now?" The cripple had no choice but to grit his teeth and hop on his healthy leg in a rage. Could he really take on mingboshi? He could file a petition: "A lawyer will take my money and write a petition, but what good will come of it? Aren't all the bureaucrats of one mind? What have those other petitions achieved? If God hasn't stopped these tormenters, then how can I?"

His wife bursted into tears. Wiping her eyes with her sleeve, she protested: "Our daughter is distraught. She told me that if you don't get her the divorce, she'll start cavorting around with those pretty single girls. What do we do now?"

"What can you do?" said Sadri the lame, lowering his voice. "You have patience, you endure. There is no other way."

"And if she goes to those girls and takes up the dutar? She's so young. ..."

"Tell her calmly: 'Fine, do what you want, but know your limits, your limits!'"

The cripple got up to leave.

"Oh God, take me now!" said his old wife. "My cruel fate!"

Her father could do nothing, and so Sultonxon was left to her own devices. She didn't have any mahram friends, and he worried that she might have to seek confidantes in her older sisters. "But can those sisters get along? Sometimes they are friends; and other times, enemies with one another. The little one is the most belligerent!"

But that didn't happen. Instead, Sultonxon began a new life in the house in which she was born. She stopped going to mingboshi's house, and started gathering friends for games, dutar, singing, and feasts at her parents' place. Then she would go out with them to stroll around the village. But she soon became exhausted with that life and went running back to mingboshi's with tears in her eyes. Though she stayed there at night, she spent most of her time at Umrinisabibi's or Enaxon's; at other times, she went out into the fields with the twin daughters of the local grocer.

When Zebi was married to mingboshi and had her fit of seizures, the flames of competition were again kindled in Sultonxon's heart. The seizures repeated themselves day in and day out. The poor, simple-hearted Sultonxon, because of Umrinisabibi's coaxing, invested all her hopes in those seizures. "Mingboshi will get mad and drive the damn girl out!" she thought to herself. When her jealousy began to cool somewhat, she examined her plan more thoroughly: "Ok, he'll get rid of her. Good! What will happen to me after? What will I win if she's gone? He'll just find another one. And I'll be all alone again. Fine, let the damn girl stay!" But that understanding voice was soon suppressed by another: "It was Poshshaxon and Xadichaxon's doing. I won't be dragged into a fight with that girl. I have no animosity towards her. But I'll claw those two's eyes out!" It was that voice that turned her to Zebi's side and convinced her to support Zebi's seizures for a few days.

But only for a few days.

Because after just two days, she had already given up on that fight. She had heard about the two co-wives' efforts to tame Zebi's wild heart. Now neither Umrinisabibi nor her daughter were permitted into Zebi's room. The elder co-wives gave the cold shoulder to Enaxon as well. She stopped coming altogether. How long could Zebi last in there all alone?

With that Sultonxon knew that she had been beaten. What could she do now? "I'll just have to see how I feel," she told herself.

Relying on her feelings was harder than it had seemed. Because all she felt now was: "How can I, still young, satisfy all these unrealized desires?" Play and games with young, beautiful girls no longer fulfilled her. She now had something else on her mind, aspirations far more terrible and dangerous than feasts and dutar playing.

She didn't sleep for three nights, giving in fully to these dark fantasies, and only then did she come to a decision. Then she slept soundly. Her old mother, who saw her sleeping soundly until noon, was caught off guard.

"What kind of person sleeps like that? Get up, my child."

As soon as she opened her eyes, she embraced her mother.

"Mother, kiss my forehead! I've grown up overnight. I'll go to my co-wives and embrace them. I'll live blissfully with them."

"Oh, my dear child, my smart child, my youngest and dearest!" said her mother, doting upon her.

Later that day she set out for mingboshi's home.

Hakimjon had been correct when he told Miryoqub: "Sultonxon has returned a different person. She came through the gates laughing and cheerful. Everyone is surprised."

And Miryoqub rightly told him, "No one but God knows a woman's heart. We best be cautious with her!"

....

The two elder co-wives were dumbfounded at the changes in their former enemy.

"She seems to have come to her senses," said Xadichaxon.

Poshshaxon disagreed: "'Shiny on the surface, but sharp underneath,' they say. I'm afraid of that laughter of hers. You don't think there's some reason behind her sudden friendship with Zebi?"

Xadichaxon stood by her words. "What can she do? She wanted to divorce him and marry another, and he wouldn't let her. As much as her father loved her, he was more afraid of getting on mingboshi's bad side. And mingboshi paid her no heed ... What can she do? Where can she go? She's decided to just be happy in her hopelessness."

"But how can she be so close with Zebi? With her worst enemy?"

"That's also from hopelessness, my dear. She has no other choice. After all, is Zebi so bad? Who doesn't want to be friends with her? So cheerful, a delight at parties ..."

"No, dear, you're not thinking. You haven't thought it through."

"We'll see. It will all be clear enough."

"Yes, we'll see."

As for Sultonxon, she was waiting impatiently for a woman petitioner to come in. Usually the women who came with complaints had things to sell with them like cream, milk, or melons, and they would address the first of the three wives to greet them.

"My dear, my lady, give this petition to your husband. My poor son has suffered an injustice. ... My dear child, let all your hopes, your aspirations come true; God grant you children, God grant your wishes!"

Mingboshi's wives kept themselves aloof from the begging. They had no interest in the blessings of these old women.

"Give it to him yourself. We don't deal with his business. ..."

"Oh, my dear, it's no big thing to you. Just a word. ... He won't accept the petition from us."

"Grrr, woman! What a scandalous one you are. If he won't take it, give it to his secretary!"

The poor old women would leave, sobbing and cursing under their breath.

Mingboshi had been called to the city on an urgent matter. Sultonxon had expected a flood of petitioners. But there was no one. She didn't go anywhere, sitting sometimes in the house, sometimes on the porch, sometimes in the courtyard, waiting all day. No one came in. "What in the hell happened to these petitioners?" she thought to herself. "When you don't need them, they're eating your ears, but when you do, they're silent. This fickle world!"

Finally, some time in the late afternoon an old woman came in. The two co-wives were with Zebi eating.

"My dear child," began the old woman, "I've come with a petition for mingboshi. ..."

"Oh-ho, another petitioner. I'm so tired of them in my home!" rang out a voice from inside Zebi's home. It was Poshshaxon's.

"Where did you come from?" asked Sultonxon and came down from the porch.

"Let it alone," said Xadichaxon from inside. "Sultonxon is taking care of it. It looks like she's still not sick of them."

"I came from Toshloq, my dear. I walked all the way here with my old bones.

"Who are you?"

"I, my child, am Qiyomiddin *hajji*'s mother. Do you recognize me?"

"Oh auntie," said Sultonxon suddenly. "You're Qiyomiddin hajji's mother? He is my father's closest friend!"

The two "friends" embraced one another. Sultonxon spoke loudly, almost yelling, so that the co-wives inside could hear her.

"Looks like they've fallen in love!" mocked Xadichaxon from inside.

"A leper finds a leper, even in the dark!" Poshshaxon seconded.

"You mean that woman. Why say that about her? Let your tongue wither and fall off!"

That was Zebi's voice.

"Well, auntie, if Qiyomiddin hajji has a problem, I'm sure we can clear it up. Take off your paranji and relax a bit; I'll get you some tea."

"No, my dear, I can't afford to stay too long or I'll be late. I'm afraid to go home alone after dark."

"We'll send someone with you, auntie. Sit, I'll make tea."

"Oh child, I'm so fortunate."

They sat down for tea.

"Now auntie, let me see the petition."

She took the petition and looked it over. Then she put it in her right pocket.

"Have some jam, auntie. We'll get to your petition right away."

"God has sent me luck, my child."

Sultonxon gave the old woman another cup of tea and went inside. She took the "petition" from inside her left pocket and inserted it into the petition in her right pocket. Then she went back out to the old woman.

"Take some bread, have some jam!"

"I should go now, my child. Give the petition to your husband, won't you?"

"Should I send someone with you?"

"No, my dear, don't trouble yourself. There's still time, I can make it home before dark."

They stood up.

"Auntie, there's a secretary outside, Hakimjon. Give your petition to him. Tell him that Sultonxon has approved it. I'll go to him later and tell him the same. He'll take care of it."

"God grant you happiness, child."

"Auntie, I added another person's petition to yours. It's also urgent."

The old woman put on her paranji.

"Auntie," said Sultonxon, lowering her voice, "you'll have to give the secretary a little money."

The old woman started digging in her pockets.

"All I have is three coins, will that work?"

"Wait here, auntie, I'll help."

She went inside and returned with a three-ruble bill, which she handed to the old woman.

"God bless you, my child!"

Hakimjon was sitting on the platform, eating dinner.

"My child, are you Hakimjon?"

"Yes, I am."

"Here is a petition for you."

"Mingboshi isn't here. Bring it back tomorrow."

"Sultonxon, mingboshi's wife, approved it. Here, two petitions," said the old woman, handing him the money.

After putting the money in his pocket, he opened the petition. "Very well. You go now. Friday morning you'll have your answer."

The old woman left, saying prayers as she went. Hakimjon, as was his custom, read the petition from top to bottom. "This is an easy one," he told himself as he folded it and put it in his pocket. Then he opened the second one.

"Oh God! What is this?"

He brought the petition up to the light. On the back of tea paper, written with an ordinary pencil, was a quatrain:

> *O ruler of charm and commander of beauty,*
> *Are you genie, angel, or fairy?*

> *Did you exhaust the book of love with your pen,*
> *What have I done for you to condemn me to loneliness?*

Below those lines was another pair written in an illiterate and ugly hand:

> *I have suffered in all your pain,*
> *Is there a way to see you again?*

Hakimjon read the letter over and over again. This quiet and inoffensive young man's heart for the first time in his life disobeyed his will. It was as if a club had been raised and was continuously hammering again his chest. Strange, ambiguous feelings appeared in his head.

Both the "petitioner" and the recipient didn't sleep that night.

The next morning the two elder co-wives sat down for breakfast in the court-yard with Zebi. On the table were freshly picked grapes, wet with morning dew. Upon Zebi's request, the two co-wives called their hated enemy, Sultonxon, to the table.

"Agreed," said Sultonxon, "let's eat together. Let me go talk to Hakimjon about Qiyomiddin hajji's petitions first. He's a good man. Then we'll have our fun."

She led Xadichaxon back to the pool and went to the door of the tashqari. She stuck her head out the door slightly and looked around. No one was there.

"Hakimjon, hey, Hakimjon!"

Hakimjon came over from the guest room.

"Yes? Who's calling?"

"It's me, Sultonxon. I have a few things to tell you."

She spoke from behind the door. Hakimjon was bright red, glowing like an ember. He stopped at the door. His two eyes were fixed on the gate to the street.

There were no signs of fear or hesitation in Sultonxon's voice; she talked loudly and unhaltingly. Each of her words were clear and crisp. "It must have been someone else who wrote the letter," thought Hakimjon. "Such sensitive things cannot be said without fear."

"Where are the guards?" asked Sultonxon, lowering her voice; she remained covered by the door's shadow.

"Two of them are in the city, I sent another for the ellikboshi."

"You did well."

Now she spoke with her full voice.

"Yesterday an old woman gave you a petition, I think. I instructed her to."

"Yes, she did."

"The petitioner is a friend of my father's. If mingboshi won't touch it, then take care of it yourself. He's a good person. Qiyomiddin hajji from Toshloq."

"It's a simple matter. I'll take care of it."

"Do that, secretary."

She lowered her voice again.

"Has your guard not come back yet?"

"He'll be a while. It all depends on where the ellikboshi is."

She stuck her head out from behind the door and Hakimjon saw her for a moment. He blushed and stepped back.

"What are you afraid of? Come closer." said Sultonxon quietly. "Is someone going to eat you?"

"No …," barely managed Hakimjon.

"Did you read the letter?"

"Yes … I read it. …"

"Did it upset you?"

"Why, no, why … I was glad. …"

"You were glad? Really?"

At that moment, the cackling of the co-wives carried over from the pool.

"My head … touched the sky from excitement."

"How old are you?" asked Sultonxon suddenly, showing herself again. Hakimjon was taken aback by the unexpected question.

"Twenty-four."

"Twenty-four? You're still young. Do you flee from everyone? What are you scared of? Just come a little closer."

Hakimjon took two steps forward, but he stopped and didn't lift his eyes from the ground. Sultonxon stuck her head out and stared at Hakimjon. Her coquettish eyes burned. She let out a little sigh. "Cheeks of red hot coals," she thought to herself.

"Are you that bashful?"

"I'm not bashful."

"Liar! Why are your cheeks so red?"

"I don't know. …"

"You weren't upset by the letter?" Sultonxon asked again.

"No … Why? I was glad. …"

"You're not bored spending all day and night in your little cell?"

Hakimjon understood.

"If I get bored, what can I do? God will grant me some delight."

"It's not bad to air such wishes candidly. Yes, now go, I've kept you too long."

Hakimjon couldn't move from the spot. The cackling could again be heard from the pool. Sultonxon threw a few last thirsty glances at the blushing young man before slowly backing away.

Because Sultonxon not long ago had been mingboshi's youngest and favorite wife, the largest and best home in the ichkari had been given to her. This house, standing on the space in front of the pool, was twice as big as all the others. Was that not the cause of Poshshaxon and Xadichaxon's pain? It's not strange, of course; the best house goes to the favorite wife!

When just a few days were left before Zebi's wedding, the two co-wives took advantage of Sultonxon's absence and emptied her house; they moved all of Sultonxon's few household items and clothes into the little, wooden-roof house with simple decorations. So that Sultonxon wouldn't be too offended, Xadichaxon arranged her things neatly in the new house. In any event, Sultonxon's things, which had looked as though orphaned in the big house, now seemed just right in the small one. Her pretty Kashgar rug that had suffered in a corner of the big house now brilliantly fit the small floor of the new house. And just like that, the forced move made Sultonxon the owner of a comfortable little home.

Inside the house, parallel to Xadichaxon's entryway, was a storeroom that housed fruit and melons in the winter; a couple of large squashes were rotting there too. On the right side of the room, there was an abandoned hearth, some firewood that had been lying there for years. On the wall hung two hollowed out squashes. And nothing more! On the left side, there was a narrow little door about the height of half a person. Since the little house had been built, the little door had been opened maybe three times. If you went through that door, which had long been forgotten by everyone in the ichkari, you arrived in a large and unmanaged garden. Five steps to the left of the little door, an old adobe wall separated the garden in the ichkari from that in the tashqari. And in that wall was an old forgotten door that locked from the ichkari. Behind the door was a part of the tashqari garden onto which only the window and door of the secretary's office looked out. In front of the window stood Hakimjon's desk. His office opened into the entryway of the main house where another door led to Hakimjon's room. There wasn't another window or door in the ichkari that looked out onto that part of the garden because that garden was the street and the street was nomahram. And it's every good Muslim's duty to keep his chaste wife from nomahram glances!

Sultonxon, who had returned to her husband's home with all kind of plans, was now beyond glad about the forced move. She secretly applauded the vindictive decision of her co-wives.

After the four women had finished their happy breakfast, Sultonxon gathered up the mat on which she had been sleeping outside and began to carry it into her new home.

"Oh, there's still so much time until winter. You're already going to start sleeping in that house?" asked Xadichaxon.

"She's already cold without a husband, the poor thing," Poshshaxon said from afar, barely concealing her mockery.

"I've stopped relying on him now!" retorted Sultonxon loudly. Then she looked at Zebi, who was following her, and commented, "The day before yesterday, I found a huge scorpion under this mat. Then I killed a June bug, crushed it like a walnut. Now I can't sleep at night. I dream of them and startle myself awake. It will be nice inside the house, dear friend."

"The frosts come at night now. You're right, my friend! No need to sleep outside," said Zebi. Zebi's "my friend" sounded so sweet to Sultonxon's ear. So sincere, the words rang like fine china or the dulcet twanging of the dutar. Sultonxon hugged her co-wife tightly and kissed her on the cheeks.

Towards evening mingboshi brought news from the city. They heard him talking, so the four wives went to the door to the tashqari to listen.

"Don't tell me that impious Miryoqub went off to fool around at such a sensitive time," screamed mingboshi, looking Hakimjon in the eyes. "They say he left for Sevastopol with a Russian woman." Mingboshi burst out laughing. In the ichkari, Poshshaxon dug her nails into her chest. "That son of a bitch! They say he found himself a pretty one, and he'll play with her, take her around for two months. The nobles here are angry like a storm. Best to avoid them now. There's talk that the governor is going to give each mingboshi ten more armed men: every *amin*, two; and every ellikboshi, one. Half the money for it comes from the treasury and the other half from us! We have to find some men now. The governor-general told all the mingboshis: 'Be ready, all of you! We won't let what happened in the mountains happen again!'"

"By the way, what happened in the mountains?"

"The people revolted. They killed a mingboshi. Two amins fled for their lives. The ellikboshis joined the mob to save themselves. They set fire to the chancelleries, beat a few rich moneylenders. That's something to tell Yodgor the old. Maybe that will serve as a warning to him!"

"Fine, fine, but what happened after, master?!"

"Our noyib to'ra went out there with 150 soldiers and suppressed the revolt. He leveled two villages. Almost 400 people were slaughtered. The soldiers took 137 to the city to lock them up. There will be a big trial of them all soon. Noyib to'ra said they'll rush the trial. They'll all be sentenced at once! Four or five soldiers died. Maybe twenty wounded. From what they say, it sounds like the soldiers had their way with a few of the Muslim women in the villages. Not good."

"What will we do, master?"

"What do you mean 'What will we do'? We'll find another seven men. And we'll be vigilant." Mingboshi paused to think for a moment. "Hey, our lands are peaceful, all our people are obedient like sheep. And I am their shepherd. I'm not strict with them, I'm not cruel. Why do they revolt? Sleep peacefully, I say to them! You can sleep in your garden, knowing that I'm keeping you safe!"

Clearly pleased with himself, he moved in the direction of the ichkari, still laughing. The women retreated from the door. He stopped after a few steps.

"By the way, Abdusamat really embarrassed himself!"

"What's this?" responded Hakimjon, perplexed.

"The governor-general berated him in front of all the other mingboshis. He hired a Tatar woman and opened a new-method school; he even sent an invitation to Tashkent for a teacher so he could open a new-method school for boys. That's what the governor scolded him for. 'Why are you doing all this?' asked the governor. 'Don't follow those Young Sarts,' he said. 'They learned from the Young Turks,'[66] he said. Whatever that means. Who are these Young Sarts, these Young Turks? What are they teaching? I don't know. If Miryoqub was here, he'd figure it out, that impious one! Fine, you can relax now! Go sleep!"

A little later Zebi's sweet voice and her dutar could be heard. The co-wives went to lie down on the courtyard platform. Sultonxon was awake for some reason; she didn't go to her home but stayed on the edge of the porch. Finally, everyone fell asleep. Zebi's song went silent and the dutar playing stopped. It stopped as if angry, as if someone had thrown the instrument to the ground. With that, the entire house went silent.

---

66 A group of Ottoman exiles, students, servants, and army officers interested in political reform in the Ottoman Empire. In 1908, they succeeded in forcing Sultan Abdul Hamid II to recognize a limitation of his powers, which opened what has been called the Second Constitutional Era. Many Central Asian jadids studied in Istanbul in the early twentieth century and had contacts with Young Turks. The governor general's reproach of Abdusamat is generated not only by the very real threat of democratic thinkers and jadid reform, but also by a paranoia that the Ottoman Empire was attempting to overthrow Russian rule in the Turkic parts of the Romanov Empire via covert agents.

The few autumn leaves that had fallen to the ground rustled in the cold evening breeze. Except for the rustling of the leaves and the dogs barking, there wasn't another sound.

After that Sultonxon slowly went into the house. She drank a cup of cold tea to keep her heart from fluttering. She left the window open, shut the door from the inside, and disappeared in the darkness.

Hakimjon, who still hadn't fallen asleep, suddenly heard a soft knocking at his office window. There was no one else in the tashqari. The guards were sleeping in the gatehouse and the stables. His heart was thumping, but he knew he was alone, so he quickly went to the office, and, so as not to make a sound, opened not the door but the window.

He shut the window, and with the untimely guest behind him, he silently returned to his room. He still couldn't lift his bashful eyes from the ground. But the young, impatient girl couldn't contain herself. An involuntarily powerful voice shot from her throat like a cork popping out of a bottle.

"You heartless … !" she screeched.

And she threw herself into his embrace.

14

Having returned from the city, mingboshi set to work on the governor's orders. He called all the amins and ellikboshis under his command to his home. After impatiently waiting an entire day, he finally sat down with tea and called his "council" to order. He chaotically and inarticulately talked about "the current situation," the events in the mountains and their results, before getting to the matter at hand.

"That's it, my good friends," he said, "another seven men will be added to my three. The amins will get two more men, and the ellikboshis—one. All the men will get new rifles. Do you think we'll find some good shots among them?"

No one answered. Everyone was silent.

"Why don't you speak? Have you all stuffed your mouths with cotton? Speak, Matxoliq!"

"Well, if the leaders are giving an order, then they must know what they're doing," said Matxoliq amin.

"Yes, of course they know," said an ellikboshi.

"What can we say? It's a good order," said another. Then he looked at the others next to him and asked: "Isn't that right, my good men?"

"Yes, right, right!" resounded from each of them.

"It would be right even without your approval," said mingboshi, raising his voice. "I know that. I'm asking if we'll find shooters. Answer me that!"

"There are a lot of them. We'll find some," said Matxoliq amin.

"If they don't know how to shoot, they'll learn," said Hakimjon from the corner. "No reason to stop looking for men. We'll find people here and call someone in from the city to teach them."

"Right," said mingboshi. He laughed. "All of you are no smarter than this little one. Shame on you."

The officials were silent.

Mingboshi continued.

"Well then, the order is this: every amin is to find two more men for himself within two days and inform me."

"Each of you will submit a list," added Hakimjon.

"Yes, submit the list," repeated mingboshi. "And each amin is to find me one man. I'll get the rest from this village. After that the amins will go from village to village telling the people."

Mingboshi stopped. He went to put out the candle and started to pour more tea. Those seated began to look at one another: "What should we be telling them?" they whispered. Mingboshi still hadn't finished speaking.

Hakimjon asked, "What should they tell the people?"

"Yes, by the way," said mingboshi, "I forgot: tell them about the men. And then about the money."

The officials shuddered.

"What money, sir?" inquired Matxoliq amin.

Everyone's eyes were on his mouth, and then they all quickly shifted to mingboshi to hang on his lips. The officials listened, mouths agape.

Mingboshi laughed.

"What other money could it be? Half the money for the men comes from the treasury, and the other half from the people."

From the mouths of all those seated there came a single voice. As if they were groaning in unison, perhaps even howling. And again, the house became silent like a grave. Hakimjon let out a barely audible sigh, stood up from his place, and moved closer to the group. He stepped lightly, as if any sound would disturb those seated.

They all looked at the ground, silently playing with the long tassels of the mats on which they were seated.

"Why are you all suddenly mute?" screamed mingboshi in a booming, authoritative voice.

"How much is half, sir?" asked Matxoliq again. "The people are going to pay for five of the seven men you're getting?"

"Yes, you think I'm paying?" coarsely retorted mingboshi.

They were silent again. Mingboshi continued.

"You'll inform the people within three days and tell me what happens."

"Yes, sir!" said Matxoliq.

The others were still silent. Mingboshi screamed now.

"Why are the rest of you silent? You're all sons of bitches! I never should have made you all amins!"

"You could dismiss us, sir," said one amin. Everyone turned to look at him.

"I'll have you thrown in the stables and flogged before I do that. Just try me!"

"Sir, sir!" their voices rose from all around.

"What's done is done, my good men," said Matxoliq, addressing the group. "We'll call all the leaders from the people and tell them the order. That's our task. And if the people say no, then those leaders will think of something."

"Just let them say no!" barked mingboshi. "It's the order of the tsar! Just let them say no!"

"They've never refused before, they won't now," said Hakimjon.

"You are correct, secretary." Mingboshi smiled. He elongated the words to emphasize them. "You won't find a single person who will refuse."

"You are right, sir," said Matxoliq. "They shouldn't say no. But because I'm one of the tsar's humblest servants, I have to tell you what I know."

"Tell me. Who's told you to be silent?"

Everyone stared intently at Matxoliq.

"The mood of the people is poor, sir. They don't want to hear any more orders. And reason no longer works with them. They're like opium addicts during Ramadan, sir. That's the majority of people. We have to be careful."

Everyone suddenly confirmed his words.

"It's true, sir, it's true!"

"Fine, it's true, none of you are lying. But who rules: the people or the tsar? What do you say to that? Well?"

No one opened their mouths. Matxoliq spoke again.

"We say the tsar, of course, sir!"

"Then enough. Amen, God is great! Go and do your duty."

The ellikboshis stood up and moved about. Mingboshi called Matxoliq over. He pulled him in close and whispered in his ear.

"If I can get rid of Abdusamat, I'll make you mingboshi. You're a smart one, you son of a bitch!"

Matxoliq smiled.

"I'm grateful, sir, to be in your service. Thank you."

Mingboshi again pulled him closer.

"I have no melons, no watermelons in this cold winter. Put together a few wagonfuls; I'll make sure you're compensated."

"Of course, master, with pleasure."

Matxoliq started off, but mingboshi called him over again.

"By the way, I forgot. Tell everyone to have the people come out and pray more. It's an order!"

Matxoliq called those assembled together and loudly proclaimed the new order. Then they all departed.

....

After conducting his "council meeting," mingboshi set to work gathering his men. Thirty candidates from his village alone came forward for the seven places.

Hakimjon reported the situation to mingboshi.

"Things are good, sir. We told them seven and look how many showed up."

A conspicuous falseness sounded clearly in Hakimjon's words, but mingboshi didn't sense it.

"There are a lot of loafers in the village!" exclaimed mingboshi.

"No, master, I talked with them. All of them are laborers. 'We're tired. Our children are hungry,' they say."

Mingboshi suddenly burst with coarse laughter. Hakimjon was puzzled at this sudden mirth. Mingboshi explained himself.

"If they're exhausted, that's good!" he said. "The exhausted fight well. If the tsar finds himself in need from this war, I'll send him all the soldiers I can! There's lots to do, secretary."

He kept laughing and left for the ichkari.

Darkness had come but dinner was still not ready when a guest arrived. Hakimjon received him cheerfully. A little later mingboshi came in from the ichkari and courteously greeted the man. But the falseness of that courtesy was immediately visible, and the guest's eyes signaled his knowledge of it to

Hakimjon. Hakimjon asked forgiveness with his brow. The guest seemed to be asking, "What is this, what kind of reception is this?" but only smiled.

After eating their fill of pilaf and drinking green tea, the three of them began to converse. The guest was a young Tatar man by the of name Hasanov who was an inspector of village cooperative credit organizations.[67]

"Tell us about the war! What's happening with the war?"

"You know the war better than me, mingboshi. Let's hear from you," said Hasanov.

"How would I know about it? I can't read the newspapers!"

"But you're the head of the district."

"Eh, it means nothing! If you need my position, take it!"

Mingboshi was serious when he said that, but the guest only laughed.

"Are you tired of the work, sir? True, in these times power can be quite a burden."

Hakimjon intuited that his master's mood was souring, and he therefore stepped in.

"True, Hasanov," he said, "being an official is very difficult lately. You don't know, but I, for example, am always at my master's side. I know. It's very hard."

"Oh, I know, I know very well," said Hasanov. "Of course, it's not easy."

Mingboshi was still silent. He played with the empty teacup in his hand. Hakimjon continued.

"If it wasn't a difficult time, would the mingboshis be increasing their troops?"

"Is that what they're saying now?" asked Hasanov.

"It's not a rumor, it's an order. We called everyone in the village. We're adding seven men to our three."

Here mingboshi inserted himself into the conversation.

"We'll give them all rifles. We'll train them. What do you say to that?"

"Excellent!" said Hasanov. He drew on his cigarette and began thinking.

"What's excellent?" asked mingboshi crudely.

"It's very good, mingboshi sir. But … I don't have confidence in …"

---

67 The tsarist government had Turkestani state banks form local cooperative credit organizations to lend money to local farmers in order to meet harvest goals. These organizations were intended to combat the problem of usurious local money lenders, like those depicted in the novel, who charged high interest rates and often took the land of poor farmers when they could not pay.

Figure 5. A mingboshi with his soldiers. Source: M. V. Lavrov. *Turkestan: Geografiia i istoriia*. Moskva, Petrograd, 1916.

"What don't you have confidence in?" mingboshi spat with that same coarseness.

"Do you really think the government will give our Muslim men rifles? The government has some sense."

Mingboshi was astonished. Such a thought was something that he never would have even dreamed of. He looked at the guest, his eyes bulging. In that look were both surprise and fear.

"Why shouldn't the tsar arm them? He ordered it, didn't he?"

"Some idiot must have thought up the order, sir. A smart person wouldn't allow this."

Mingboshi said nothing. Hakimjon, listening attentively, trained his eyes on the guest. The guest continued.

"The government won't let weapons into Muslim hands. We—Muslims, Turks—we won't get weapons unless we take them ourselves, and our enemy won't give them to us."

"Who's our enemy?" asked mingboshi. The question held a bit of a threat in it. The guest unhurriedly answered.

"I'm not talking about your enemies, sir. I'm talking about the enemies of Turks and Muslims.

"You mean the Germans?"

Hakimjon barely managed to stop himself from laughing.

"That's it, sir! I'm talking about the Germans. They would never give weapons to Turks! The Germans are the mortal enemy of Turks!"

"Well, we'll gather everyone in the village, give them all rifles, and send them off to fight the Germans. What do you think of that?"

Mingboshi said these words with pride.

"What can I say? If you did that, I'd call you a ghazi, a holy warrior. The Muslim nation would never forget your service."

"I'm not interested in your nation. I don't know your Turks either. This secretary was just saying that everyone in these villages is sick of their miserable conditions. If I send them all to the war to fight against the Germans, the tsar will have his victory and these villages will be rid of the misfortune of their naked, rebellious poor!"

"Hear! Hear!" said the guest. "If only others were so noble! You're doing a great service, sir! Such a great service!"

Hakimjon suddenly began to see mingboshi differently. He now felt something other than devotion and respect. After mingboshi went in for the night, Hakimjon expressed his new view to the guest. That confession lit fires of excitement in the guest's eyes.

"All of our woes," the guest began excitedly, "are because we can't tell friend from foe. Did you hear what he said? Germany and its ally Turkey—Turkey which is our fellow in nation and faith—are somehow enemies to us."

The guest stopped for a moment. He took a long puff of his cigarette, shaking his head.

"They are all walking tragedies born of ignorance, Hakimjon! The products of stupidity. Those empty-headed animals in their greasy turbans sell off the finest treasures of our noble Bukhara and poison the minds of our people, bringing us to our sorry state. Ehhh!"[68]

The guest, who spoke so freely and passionately, stopped talking only when Hakimjon started falling asleep.

The two made their beds on the porch, but their sleep was interrupted by the early crowing of roosters. They started talking again, complaining about mingboshi, about all officials in general, about the government and its chancelleries. The guest even told Hakimjon the same things that noyib to'ra had told Miryoqub but in more detail. Hakimjon, who knew so little about his own

---

68 The 1988 serial publication omits Hasanov's speech here, beginning with "that confession" three paragraphs previous.

mingboshi's affairs, much less about the affairs of other mingboshis, began to reexamine himself, to organize his raw, confused thoughts. As they were organized, they tore down curtain after curtain in his mind. He could sense himself changing: "From this day forward, his views on everything would be different! Mingboshi was no longer the same mingboshi, that one was far away. The new one was a bloodthirsty murderer. And Miryoqub with his deftness, his skill. 'If he could find the right way then he would be a rare person indeed!' And every turbaned man of learning now seemed like a doctor feeding poison to the infirm. Every eshon who lowered his head in reverence was reaching his hands into the pockets of the poor. And when he thought of Abdusamat mingboshi, he became animated: 'If I could just see him, look at him, I would kiss his hands, and do whatever he asks!'"

Hasanov's opinions, particularly those about the new armed men, exacted an influence on mingboshi too. Mingboshi feared Hasanov somewhat and for that reason thought of him coldly, but he couldn't help but agree with his thoughts on arming Turkestanis. When he went into the ichkari for the night, he lay down to think.

"Forget what that son of a bitch said! For whatever reason, when you hear his words, you get scared: as if … as if he were cursing the tsar! As if someone who overheard their conversation would denounce mingboshi to Yodgor the old or Umarali the noseless! And they would denounce him to the governor immediately! They would say that mingboshi was only delighted when Hasanov cursed the tsar! And then the governor would call him and unleash his rage! He would strip him of his title and shame him in front of everyone! Abdusamat, Yodgor the old, and Umarali the noseless would all denounce him with trumpets."

"But that son of a bitch infidel isn't speaking from ignorance. Whatever you might think, he's read his law books, he's spent time among the Russians, speaks their language as freely as water flows in a creek. Our bosses are Russians, after all! There's no Russian that would help a Muslim. That's true! Hasanov was right in that! Would they ever give guns to Muslims? No! If I were a Russian (God forbid!), I would never give a weapon to a Muslim! Never! Hasanov was right."[69]

With those thoughts, mingboshi just barely managed to fall asleep.

When he woke up, he started thinking about the men again. Whether it was three or ten was all the same to him. "There will be as many problems as there are men," he thought. "But. … But …"

---

69 The 1988 serial publication omits this entire paragraph with the exception of the first sentence.

"If I can just find ten men and with my own money give them good horses, good clothes and weapons and ride through my district, hell, even through Abdusamat's village. That would be enough! After that, I won't need more men!"

With that he decided to start the conscription tomorrow. After three days, he had seven recruits. He asked around, had others ask, and, in some cases, got physical to ensure that each of his seven had a horse, a hunting rifle, and ammunition. Then he put on his gold-brocade robe, his gold belt, hung his long sword at his side, mounted his dun mare, and set off.

15

Two days earlier, mingboshi had come to Qumariq village with seven armed men. His arrival was quite strange. Without stopping to talk to anyone, he went straight to the mosque and talked with the imam. Those amins and ellikboshis who had found out about mingboshi's arrival by other means were in shock: "Why didn't he call us?" they asked one another.

One of the ellikboshis ran and told the imam that the mingboshi had arrived. Because the imam had not long ago been but an unmarried student, when he heard that the mingboshi was summoning him, he began to panic. He put on his turban and robe and headed for the mosque, thinking, "Why in the world would he come here?"

There was no obvious reason why mingboshi should be looking for him, so the imam naturally found himself engrossed in his imagination.

"The day before last when I went to the city, I had a little fun with the madrasa director's son. ... But he brought it on himself: he put on a silk turban to attract my eyes. That little bitch couldn't have complained about me, could he?"

"Or maybe this is because I spent the income from those *waqf* lands on myself. Did someone raise a fuss about that?"

"Or maybe because last week, when picking melons, I came across one of those Tatar teachers of a new-method school and cursed him. Abdusamat mingboshi apparently opened the school, but I hadn't heard that. ... Did Abdusamat complain about me to our mingboshi? But wait, later when I found out that the school belonged to Abdusamat, I went back and made up with the Tatar teacher. It's too bad I didn't know from the start ... oh well! It must be all that ellikboshi Abdurahmon's fault, son of a bitch! Dog! He was there and overheard everything. If it weren't for him, I'd be fine. But I did go apologize to the teacher, I made up with the damn jadid, though. I told him, 'Of course, Tatars are Muslims, Sunnis, Tashkenters are Muslims, Sunnis. We're all the same. The natural sciences are permitted by Sharia too, and our prophet said that even in China their science is valuable. A very apt hadith!' The jadid teacher was glad. He said, 'If all of our 'ulama were like you, the nation would make great progress.' It was that 'nation' word that set us off again. Abdurahmon ellik-boshi asked the Tatar teacher what his nation was. At first, he said Islam, then he said Islamic and Turkic, adding Turkic for some reason. I couldn't stand it anymore. 'No,' I told him, 'if you ask a Muslim what his nation is, it is incumbent upon him to say the nation of Ibrahim. Over in O'zgan there is a people called Turks, they are from Eilat. There aren't as many of them as sarts, and you certainly couldn't call them a nation!' Then, to support my point about the prophet Ibrahim, I cited from Sufi Olloyor:

> They built a great fire to burn Ibrahim,
> But before he could step in, the fire turned to green pastures.[70]

"The jadid teacher responded that 'Ibrahim was the prophet of the Jews and didn't have even one of the four books.'[71] 'Repent, you ass!' I screamed. I became heated. I was out of sorts. Now it's no use. Oh, woe is me! Woe is me!"

Not long after the imam came, mingboshi exited the mosque. He mounted his horse and spoke a few words to one of the ellikboshis. He then looked at the rest of them reservedly and started off on his way. The people in the market were astounded and looked at one another. "What was he doing here if he could come and leave so quickly?" they asked each other in vain.

"Why did he have them bring the imam instead of the amin?"

"Why did he leave as soon as the imam came?"

"Why does he have so many men with him for the journey?"

"Why did he go towards the river and not back to the village?"

"Why did he pass us and not say anything?"

---

70 These lines are from the opening of Sufi Olloyor's *Firmness of the Weak*, a book that was commonly used as a textbook in madrasas in Central Asia from the eighteenth century until Soviet times. Here Sufi Olloyor refers to Allah's miracles as relayed through Islamic tradition. According to tradition, Ibrahim was condemned to death by burning for his non-belief in the Babylonian gods, but Allah saved him by extinguishing the fire before he set foot in it. The imam cites the lines here to condemn the jadid teacher for his interest in a false knowledge.

71 Islam recognizes four holy books: the Qur'an, the Torah (Tawrat), the Zabur (usually understood to be the Book of Psalms), and the Gospel (Injil).

"Why? Why? Why?"

Rumors began circulating. From every side different voices were heard, and not one managed to gain the agreement of others. It was all a din. The imam came out of the mosque, and everyone looked at him.

"Hey baldy, did you see? When he went in, the imam had such a frown on, and now he looks happy. Everything must be ok."

"Let's ask, knucklehead," said baldy.

"You ask, shinyhead. He'll tell you."

"Let's ask, pumpkinhead. What's there to be afraid of?"

The imam slowly but confidently walked over to the crowd. Greetings came from both sides.

"Sir, there's tea!" said baldy. "Let's get you a cup."

"I'd be happy to!" said the imam, stopping. "But I should be going home."

"We know, sir, that we can't keep a newlywed for long! We wanted to ask what mingboshi told you."

The imam smiled.

"It's not because I'm a newlywed, Hasan," he started. "When you're not scratching your heads, you're wagging your tongues, eh?"

Everyone laughed.

"Well, we wanted you to scratch our itch, sir!" said Hasan the bald.

They all laughed again. The imam turned bright red.

"Mingboshi just asked if everything was in order here. He didn't say anything else. Can I go now?"

He stepped in the direction of his house. But the crowd wasn't satisfied. Hasan the bald spoke up again.

"When an ordinary person like one of us lies, then let he who doesn't believe cough with skepticism. But when an official or an imam lies, we should all pick up our shoes and walk home barefoot."

The crowd laughed again.

The imam went around them, but ran into Umarali the rich at the head of the bridge.

"Ah, imam, what did Akbarali say?"

"Mingboshi didn't say a thing. He just asked if everyone was attending the prayers. I said that they weren't really. He told me he'd have the ellikboshi 'convince' more of the faithful to attend. That was it."

Umarali laughed loudly and coarsely.

"Did you ask him if he had ever once put his forehead to a prayer rug?"

"He's an important person. What could I say to him?"

"Good bye, imam!" said Umarali and went on his way. Then he turned back, laughed and added, "This really is the end of days, sir. An impious leader demanding piety of the rest of us!"

Three days later on Friday, a massive crowd gathered for the prayer. Even those who had never attended before found places for their foreheads to touch the rugs. They bowed and lifted their heads too early, before the imam. As the imam said, "God is great" and bent in prayer, they sat up. Subdued laughter and whispering began. Impatient coughing sounded out among the "faithful" who were ready to leave, when the thin voice of an angry Sufi rose, sounding like the creak of unoiled wheels.

"People! Come closer and hear the imam's sermon!"

The amins and ellikboshis seated among the people knew they had to support the Sufi.

"Yes, people! You must listen to the imam!"

The imam stepped outside the mosque, stopping by the grated door, and began to speak to the large crowd.

Several days earlier mingboshi had gone around to all the mosques and told the imams there that they should emphasize the need to maintain peace and not listen to the evil temptations that lead to discord and eventually to hell. The imam started with considerable difficulty, unable to find the right words, but he eventually came into his own. Though his audience was largely illiterate, he made sure to season his speech with the perfection of Arabic and the elegance of Persian. And he added his favorite lines from his eshon wherever he could. In the process, he praised the governor and mayors, the great learned mullah Akbarali mingboshi, and the equally erudite Abdusamat mingboshi: "These perspicacious, conscientious, wise, generous, and munificent men." "Just let that jadid teacher hear me now," he thought as he began to praise new-method schools, where they learn the Qur'an alongside the natural sciences, where young students know the teachings of the faith better than adults, where students sing from the Qur'an so well that a passerby cannot but break down and cry, where even ... even the teacher can say to his pupils that the world is round like a walnut or a watermelon and his teaching is not against the Sharia of the Prophet because great thinkers like Sufi Olloyor, Emir Navoiy, Mavlono Fuzuli, and Eshon Hazaniy all spoke of the revolutions of the heavens.[72] Just as a pot boils over a fire, so the imam became heated and began to bubble over, words flowing out of his mouth one

---

72 Mavlono (also Mawlana) Fuzuli (1494–1556) was the penname of Muhammad bin Suley-
    man, a poet and thinker, best known for his contributions to Turkic-language poetry and the

after another in a meaningless babble. He started to talk about how the people weren't going to Friday prayers, how the rich weren't giving alms, how people in the village had given themselves over to vodka. Now it would be tough to stop this spiritual gramophone. He found a reproach for everyone. Only the ellik-boshis and amins remained safe from his tongue.

When the imam had finally finished and people got up to leave, the raspy voice of Umarali rang out from the porch of the mosque.

"The imam spoke so well! Well done, imam!" he said. "We all pay for the impious among us!"

"Because of you polygamists?" asked someone from below.

"Let Umarali speak of his own sins! Go on!" another person yelled.

Umarali became angry. He stepped to the edge of the mosque's porch.

"Who cursed me? Who is the infidel that dared curse me?!" he screamed, though shuddering himself.

There was no answer.

"Give the imam his stick and have him beat the impious!" said Yodgor, coming out from inside.

"Yes, listen to the usurer! He's one to judge!" said another voice from below.

"The money is mine! That means it's my business what percentages I take. My business! What's it to you, thief?" spat Yodgor.

"Oh, now the thief is calling others thieves!"

"What, what?"

"Shut up already!"

"You know, sir," interjected Umarali, "everything is the fault of these officials. That Akbarali, he's never once prayed, his wives are all promiscuous, he's an amoral drunk! Why are we cursing others?"

"Hey, Umarali, don't say that," said the imam, "don't slander our great Akbarali. The people know no misery thanks to him. And if he has his fun now and then ... well, that's what's allowed for rulers."

"I have nothing against Abdusamat," added Umarali.

"Everyone is satisfied with Abdusamat," seconded Yodgor.

"There's no official like Abdusamat!" continued Umarali. "But is Akbarali even a man? Is he really an official? If I were him, I would close all these indecent

---

divan tradition. He resided in present-day Iraq and served in the courts of both the Safavids and Ottomans.

Eshon Hazaniy is most likely a fictional character, the imam's Sufi master. The imam adds him to this list to inflate his master's credentials.

The "revolution of the heavens" is a common phrase in Arabo-Persian poetry.

teahouses. Then everyone would be praying. In the summer, I'd beat everyone that didn't pray, and in winter, stick them in ice."

"And that's why God hasn't given you power," said someone in the crowd.

"Give wings to a camel, and he'll shit on everyone!" yelled Hasan the bald.

Everyone laughed.

Umarali continued.

"If I were mingboshi, I'd send a few loiterers to Siberia!"

"Yes, excellent!" Yodgor cheered.

"We'd all go to Siberia, and one of you would infect half the women while the other would impregnate the rest!"

"But the country would run well!"

"You'd both stand over the river so that not one drop of Qumariq's water went beyond your fields. Thank God you're not in charge!"

"I will be!"

"We'll see!"

"We'll see!"

Umarali was red in the face and spitting.

"You'll see! I'll show all you bastards!"

The crowd began yelling indignantly.

"Who's a bastard?!"

Groups of people ran towards the mosque with their fists raised. Cries and screams abounded. The blows of heavy fists sounded as everyone began fighting. An amin fired his pistol into the air, but no one paid any heed. One young man landed a punch on the amin's arm, knocking the pistol loose. Another man picked it up, smiling proudly at those around him. The two ellikboshis who saw this made a break for the village gates. The old, rotting grate on the mosque door, behind which the imam and the rest of the officials were hiding, cracked loudly under the force of the crowd.

And just like that, the entire village was in revolt.

....

During his visits to the villages, mingboshi reminded the amins and ellikboshis about finding more soldiers. He continuously badgered Hakimjon for updates. He wanted the matter taken care of quickly in order to show the governor the degree of his loyalty. But the worries that that crazy Hasanov had put in his head had not left him. His trip to the villages was in part to alleviate those fears.

"I proved myself! I proved myself well! Even though I couldn't send a rider through Abdusamat's village, the survey trip was not in vain. Abdusamat must have heard about it. Would his people not tell him? Let the son of bitch's heart burst out of his chest!"

But his amins and ellikboshis decided on a different course of action. When they got home, they locked themselves inside. They didn't know how to tell the people about the new taxes. A week passed. Not one amin or ellikboshi spoke a word about the soldiers or the taxes.

Mingboshi was starting to get nervous.

"Have those damn jackals of yours forgotten?! Or have they lost all their dignity in their silence? Write an order and send it out to them!"

"Yes, sir!"

The messengers mounted up and set off.

Everything in his ichkari had finally settled just as mingboshi wanted. The nightingale of the city, his dutar-playing Zebi, had now landed in his hand. The same night that Sultonxon made her way into the tashqari, Zebi, though not without conspicuous disgust, submitted herself to mingboshi's will.

What could she have done otherwise? Was there another way? And what would it be? Is she not one of the thousands, tens of thousands, no, hundreds of thousands such pitiful young slaves with which our country is populated? A concubine at our crowded slave markets has no means of saving herself. Therefore, all of our women have already prepared themselves to submit their bodies to harm, even to death. Are the girls that are sold by their parents to old men few? Has one of them ever managed to escape? Has a single one been able to free herself by guile or force? There's not one folktale about that kind of thing. Our folk tales only tell of girls who submit to their fate. They tell of the wild who are inevitably tamed, of the proud who are humbled, of the insane who are healed, of the fires which are extinguished, and of the screams which are muffled. We regale only to induce a tear or a shake of the head.

Zebi knew of her father's vicious character. Her father came from the city after hearing about the seizures. Tears flowed from his eyes onto his white beard. "Daughter," he started, "if you're going to shame me like that, then God tear your head from your neck. You'll never escape him." For a girl who had been told she was a powerless slave all her life, who had been told to fear her parents because they were second only to God, how could the curses of her father not have had an effect?

Zebi loved her mother more than anything in the world; she knew that her mother had endured so much from her hard-hearted father. The old woman still couldn't bring herself to return to the city. Had their house not been ruined by now? Her poor mother cried every day: "my dear girl, have mercy on me at least," she said. "I raised you with all my motherly kindness; I have no other sins. If you've been given to someone you don't love, it was your father's doing, not mine. Could I have done something? How? You know yourself. Your father is a mean one, as they say, 'He puts his coat on backwards.' He told me, 'If she's going to embarrass me before mingboshi, then I don't need a daughter, and I don't need you!' My dear, my child, I'm afraid of your father. I can't return, and I can't stay here. Have mercy, my child. My dear child, the apple of my eye!" These words, which her mother repeated daily in various forms, finally had their desired effect. After all, Zebi was a soft-hearted girl.

She began thinking to herself: "Can I continue resisting this all by myself? Can I continue if he's a monster, and I am just a little thing? Can I continue if my mother can't go back home and just sits at my side every night and cries? The two co-wives comfort me day and night. They're so polite and always soothing, always telling me, 'Don't do this, my dear!' Sultonxon, who tried to keep mingboshi away from me with all her might, is now repeating the other two's words in my ear every night. I don't know! They won't let Umrinisabibi in nor her daughter. Enaxon rarely comes now. And when she does, she only repeats what the wives say. If I'm all alone, then I cannot resist. I have to accept my fate. Oh God, to whom can I complain when You've left me too?"

Just like that, the young girl recognized the inevitable. She drank deep the cup of powerlessness, filling herself with the intoxication of an unwanted and long-feared pleasure.

That fateful evening, Zebi gritted her teeth and stomped on the ground in fury. She poured all her anger into the strings of the dutar and her song. To not torture herself further, she didn't light the lamp in the room. She continued playing in the dim light that came from outside, not turning to face mingboshi as he entered. From the very hour of the wedding, in the middle of Zebi's room a magnificent wedding bed made up of ten mats awaited the consummation. Like every day, mingboshi came in silently, stripped down, and lay on the bed. He pulled the sheet up over himself and listened to Zebi's song. Having promised not to indulge his dog, he restrained himself as best he could. What shame was holding him back, I'm not sure. "Tonight, I will fall asleep to that beautiful melody," he thought to himself. But Zebi stopped singing. After everyone outside had fallen asleep, she threw the dutar on the ground. Mingboshi raised his head to see what the matter was, and he saw Zebi coming. She climbed under the sheet into his embrace without protest like a slave. The next day she fought herself even less. As time went on, nature did its work. Zebi's body, having bloomed from the country's hot sun, took her resigned soul in its warm embrace.

The next morning Xadichaxon and Poshshaxon laughed and applauded their new co-wife. With their laughter, they hoped to choke out any remaining optimism in Sultonxon. Little did they know that she had spent the last few nights with the secretary, choked with happiness. She heard the laughter and understood it. To their dismay, Sultonxon ran to Zebi, embracing the girl tightly. She grabbed her with the same passion that she had grabbed the secretary the previous night and kissed her. With every kiss, she thought to herself: "As happy as you are, I'm ten times happier! You embrace your pain and misery, but I have a living person to hug every night! Who's the fool? Who's the fool?!"

Sultonxon, the poor thing, thought her co-wives idiots. But the inhabitants of these crowded quarters, this chained, imprisoned society, this country forbidden to outsiders are always deceiving one another, always endeavoring to demonstrate their competitors' idiocy. Those who cannot win by strength survive by guile. What else is there? A woman in such a denigrating environment becomes a master of deception. The merchant that puts handcuffs on his wife and locks the door behind him never understands that he is the biggest fool.

16

After he sent the messengers with his order to the amins, mingboshi entered the ichkari. Because he now felt a little relieved, he went to visit his wives, flirting with each of them. Then he entered Zebi's house. Zebi was in the tashqari. Xadichaxon ran into the courtyard to warn Zebi to go home to receive mingboshi. Zebi smiled as did Xadichaxon. Only a co-wife can understand what that smile means. Before Zebi came in, mingboshi started plucking at her dutar. But nothing melodious came out! "Can hands accustomed to swords learn the dutar?" he assured himself.

Zebi entered and picked up the dutar. She started playing and soon added her voice to the song. Suddenly someone called mingboshi from the tashqari. It was the first news of the revolt in Qumariq.

Not half an hour went by before mingboshi and six of his men had readied their horses and set off.

The person who told mingboshi about the events at the mosque and the situation with the pistol was one of the two ellikboshis, Qosim the stork. He explained what happened as they rode toward Qumariq, exaggerating the details as best he could. He warned that half the village would be butchered by the time mingboshi arrived. Qosim the stork really was in a rush to "open the eyes" of his master, but hardly from fear. No, Qosim hurried to mingboshi because the matter involved Umarali and Yodgor, whom he didn't like. They paid the tsarist taxes later than everyone else and never paid the local taxes. It wasn't just Qosim the stork who didn't like them, but also the other ellikboshis and amins and those higher up still. After all, officials need their share too.

Qosim the stork had to exploit such a serendipitous occasion!

"Mingboshi sir, let's give the horses a break; the poor creatures' mouths are frothing! I have to tell you a few things."

Mingboshi slowed his ambler. The men were still far behind the two conversants, but they too slowed their pace.

"How can you ride that jade without shame, like a woman, stork?!" barked mingboshi.

"My ambler was at home, sir. I couldn't get home when I left the mosque. There wasn't time. The only horse in the market was this one; I got on it and came running."

"Good, stork, good! If you serve the tsar like that, then you'll climb the ranks quickly."

"Thank you, sir."

"Well, speak now."

"I have to tell you about Umarali and Yodgor. They caused the whole matter. They're always paying their tsarist taxes late and not paying the other ones. And if you ask them, they only curse you. They know how to threaten. Today too, after the imam's sermon, one of them started cursing those who don't come to the prayers. As if they frequent the mosque. The people really hate those two; they own a fourth of all the land in the village but drink up all the water from the two canals. Everyone is scared of them. We've tried talking to them, but all they do is go above our heads and complain."

Qosim the stork coughed a little and looked back. Then he continued.

"They insulted you in front of everyone."

Mingboshi stopped his horse again.

"What, what? They insulted me? What did those bastards say?"

Qosim the stork told mingboshi everything that had happened, never neglecting to embellish the egregiousness of Umarali and Yodgor's actions here and there. He even passed along what Umarali had said to the imam on the bridge the day mingboshi was there. He must have had long ears; how he could have heard what no one else did, I don't know, but he spoke with confidence. He told mingboshi such things that when Akbarali arrived in Qumariq, he had already decided the entire matter.

As they approached the village, the sun was already setting. Mingboshi's ambler stopped in the market. Someone came up and grabbed the horse's reins. Mingboshi dismounted. Everyone seated hopped to their feet immediately. Not a soul was seen in the mosque; the "faithful" all gathered in the village center. Only the two landowners, Umarali and Yodgor, were absent. Those gathered were the "bastards," the farmers, laborers, and servants.

Mingboshi went to one of the cleaner teahouses, ignored the mattress that had been laid out for him especially, sat down on the edge of a rug, and ordered a *chilim*. After taking a few long puffs, he released the yellow smoke from his mouth and screamed at those seated.

"What the hell did you do, you sons of bitches?!"

Everyone was silent. Here and there were some coughs.

"Tell me now! What the hell did you do?!"

No one broke the ominous silence. Mingboshi addressed himself to Qosim the stork.

"Well, stork, you speak then!"

"I am a tsarist official, sir. What can I say? Let the people talk. The truth will come out."

Qosim the stork had already told mingboshi everything on the way there. He had no desire to do that again in front of the people, who might dispute his story and blame him.

"Then all of you speak! Why are you silent?! I came to find out the truth."

Finally, one of those that had raised his fist against Umarali and Yodgor stood up. Though there was rage sparking in his eyes, he spoke calmly and measuredly.

"If they hadn't called us bastards, then we wouldn't have touched them."

"They called all of us bastards, sir."

"They're bastards themselves!" excitedly interrupted mingboshi.

The unexpected agreement from mingboshi breathed some life into the crowd. They all started yelling.

"One at a time! One at a time! If you're all speaking, how can I understand you? Speak one at a time."

One man came forward.

"They said we don't pray, sir. They said we were impious, sir. Who are they to say that? A leader or an imam? If it's true, then the imam should deal with it."

Another person came up.

"Better to say *they* don't pray, sir. They only come to the mosque when they want to. True, they were there for the holiday prayers, but that's it."

"And one of them is a terrible womanizer. Our wives and sisters are afraid to go out on the streets. He flirts with all of them, saying shameful things."

"The other is a usurer. Others just lend you things, one to one, but he wants five, ten times back what he's given. All of us are destitute because of him, sir!"

"And they're forcibly taking everyone's land. We have no land now and we're forced to work on theirs as laborers. We work and we work and they give us nothing. And for every ruble we take in debt, they demand ten back."

"There's a ledger they have that they write in, but they also erase. We don't know what they do with it, sir. They just tell us 'you have this much debt, so we'll take this from your pay and leave you only this.' How are we supposed to know what's fair?"

"We never get out of debt."

"And now the White tsar wants to draft us, we hear. Just draft us already and we'll all go. We're sick of this, sir."

Those behind the speakers were all nodding in agreement and began to speak up themselves.

"That's right, sir. We're sick of this life!"

"All of us have children. A few of them are still babies. We're used to the poverty and misery, but our children don't understand. They cry for bread and water."

"What kind of time is this when you work day and night and you still can't fill your stomach?"

Mingboshi put a stop to the complaints.

"Are all of you done now?!" he screamed.

"We're not guilty, sir," said one.

"It's not our fault!" cried the crowd.

Just then the amin Umar ran up panting.

"Umar, where were you?" asked mingboshi, clearly annoyed.

"Greetings, sir! Welcome. I was busy with the consequences of this revolt. I had lost my pistol, you know, but we found it."

"And where are the two landowners, Umarali and Yodgor?"

"One of them is at home unconscious. His arm is broken, it seems, and he has a shiner on his head. The other is hiding somewhere. We haven't heard from him."

"If those two stay in the village, then we'll all leave!" said someone in the crowd.

"Yes, we'll leave!" the crowd yelled.

Mingboshi didn't know what to do or say. Finally, he announced a decision.

"Everyone go home. Look to your families. We'll find those responsible and punish them ourselves."

The amin repeated the decision loudly so everyone could hear.

"Investigate this right. The people aren't guilty!"

"Umarali started cursing us when we hadn't said anything."

"He cursed all of us."

"He cursed the mingboshi, the damned bastard!"

The amin shot over to the last speaker and threatened him: "Be silent, idiot! Don't say such things!"

The crowd, still grumbling among themselves, slowly began to disperse. Mingboshi went to the mosque to inspect the site of the revolt. They found the imam for him, who retold the events in detail. Either because he was afraid or because he had some other plan in mind, the imam told the story without embellishment, without blaming anyone or offering approval. After that, the imam was permitted to leave. Now mingboshi, the amin, and two ellikboshis went out onto the porch of the mosque where Yodgor was waiting. Before mingboshi's eyes even fell on him, Yodgor was already screaming.

"Mingboshi is loitering around now that he has four wives! No one here has a day free from these poor, these murderers and thieves! What kind of time are we living in?"

Mingboshi stopped at the edge of the porch.

"Stop it with the screaming, Yodgor. I have ears."

"There's no one in our district left who has your ear! Now we have to sell all our lands and water and move somewhere else."

"What happened, Yodgor? Calm down," the amin insisted.

"Don't speak, you bastard! I'm not afraid of your superior, much less you!"

"What's this now?" mingboshi barked angrily. "You've gone mad, Yodgor! You don't even know how to talk to people. The people did right, it sounds like."

"Justice!" screamed Yodgor. "This is Akbarali's justice! At the head of all these thieves, murderers, and poor is Akbarali! At night, his men rob people! All his men are bandits! Thieves!"

"Get this son of a bitch out of my sight! Lock him up!" cried mingboshi, his hands now shaking from rage.

No one moved.

"Just try to lock me up, just try! I'll show you! Thief! Bandit!"

"Hey, boys, I'm talking to you!" screamed mingboshi. "Take this bandit and throw him in a cell!"

Three of the men in front of the gate grabbed Yodgor. Yodgor didn't address the three, he just kept screaming curses. More men had to seize him to stop his thrashing and carry him to the Sufi's cell where they locked him inside. People began to gather in front of the mosque again, having heard the commotion. Mingboshi put one man in front of the door to the mosque and assigned another two to help him. He whispered some instructions into the ear of the man at the door and then mounted his horse. He had a few words left for the amin still holding his horse's reins.

"The people have calmed down, the landowners too. After this, they won't be acting up again. Speak with the people; don't let them take matters into their own hands again. Tell them to complain to us. We'll take care of it—we'll punish the guilty parties."

He turned the horse's head, and his men followed him back to his village.

Darkness set in. The dried-up cotton plants and bare lands on both sides of the road awaited the first snowfall. The horses, which had been driven quickly the whole way, slowed their pace from exhaustion. Only the legs of mingboshi's ambler still moved quickly and untiringly to the rhythm of his whip, but he too slowed his pace. The whips of the men had no influence on their horses anyway. Knowing their master was impatient, the men struck up a song. On this dark night, in the cold weather the melody was for some reason to mingboshi's liking.

"Well, men, a little louder!"

The men drew out their song, and the horses were comforted, slowing their gait to the tempo of the song.

Mingboshi himself suddenly saw the pointlessness of his haste.

"Today, an entire village revolted," he thought to himself. "They almost killed a man, broke the grate in front of the mosque. Another man escaped to save himself. Otherwise, they would have killed him or at least crippled him. It was a real riot. No joke. The village's two ellikboshis and one amin, unable to do anything, came right to me. Getting dressed however I could, I came with my seven men. But what was the result? Did I change anything? What did I do? I heard the poor's complaints (mingboshi avoided the words "the people" for some reason), locked up Yodgor. Let him calm down a bit. Although I'm not sure whether he'll come to or not. He thinks they'll let him out tomorrow regardless. And when he gets out, he'll attack me. He'll take the matter all the way to the governor-general. He won't just let it go. What good are my weapons, my money, my rank, if I can't shut up one man?! True, I don't know what he'll do. Even being a mingboshi, I don't know. I can't hold him there very long. Either I send him to the city tomorrow with a convoy or let him go. There are no other options. Which is better? Which one will fix the situation? I don't know. I'm surprised at myself. If only Miryoqub the sly was here. He'd tell me in one word what to do. I could keep my sheep and feed the wolf. If it weren't for his weakness for women, that impious! He found himself an infidel and left for a few months!"

Mingboshi trotted on with these worries under the peaks and troughs of the somber song. For the first time in his life, mingboshi discovered that he couldn't do anything without Miryoqub. As much as he thought, he couldn't come up with the proper course of action for Yodgor. His mind began to tire. His eyes closed from the pain in his head. "Fine, forget it," he told himself, "Let's go home. I can ask Hakimjon if I need to."

He turned back to the men.

"Sing something a little livelier! It's like a funeral out here."

The men laughed. When they exited the small village along the way, they started a new song. The cold and bitter winter wind picked up; its needles pricked and pierced the travelers' faces and ears. Snowflakes fell on their cheeks. Seeing that mingboshi's ambler was still moving quickly, the men whipped their horses and made it to their villages just as the inhabitants were falling asleep. Not much time passed before two of the men mounted new horses and set off again for Qumariq: the order to release Yodgor had been given. A sleepy Hakimjon left Sultonxon in his room to see the two men off with mingboshi.

"You made a mistake, master!" he told mingboshi. "What will come of releasing him?"

"Let it be," said mingboshi. "They might take my position, but they won't take my life, right? I've served loyally for too long."

"Service doesn't mean a thing in this fickle time, master."

Mingboshi became angry.

"You're still asleep, secretary!" he said. "Go lie down! We'll talk tomorrow. Sinner!"

Mingboshi headed toward the ichkari. The secretary was relieved that mingboshi had cut him off short and left. He returned to his room where mingboshi's third wife was clutching her chest in fear.

"Don't be afraid," said Hakimjon, covering her with his coat, "you're in your home."

As little as Hakimjon slept, mingboshi slept even less. In the middle of the night, he woke Xadichaxon and had her fry him some meat. He ate the meat and went through a bottle and a half of vodka before falling asleep, howling like a wolf.

17

The previous night, a hand's length of snow fell on the ground. The frost decorated the windows with the strangest patterns. A cold breeze came in through the door of the house, whistling with the thin voice of an abandoned baby swallow as it settled in the rafters. As if the wind itself was trying to hide from the cold and play inside!

Like the mischievous wind, Hakimjon's words had played on mingboshi's mind. Those words combined with the one and a half bottles of vodka were a weight on his head. The morning light snuck in under his eyelids and woke him. As he opened his eyes, it felt as if his head were bursting like cotton run through a press. He turned over with difficulty. His lovely nightingale, her hair let down, was still relaxing in a sweet sleep. "What should I do? Should I wake her up? Or let her be?" he thought to himself. But an evil spirit took an ax and came down on some firewood in his head: he had no choice but to scream.

"Get up, hey! Get up, I said!" This was the first time mingboshi addressed his love informally. "Are you deaf, you bitch?!" he prodded Zebi. "Get up, I say, get up!"

Zebi opened her eyes and immediately looked over at the door.

"Who is it, who's calling?"

"It's me. Me. Get up now!" said mingboshi behind her shoulder. "Get up and bring yesterday's vodka!"

"What happened to you?"

"Later. Go, bring the vodka now!"

He poured the vodka into a teacup and drank it in one swig.

"Oh, thank God!" he said. "Now you can sleep. It's still early."

He stood up with difficulty and went out to the tashqari. There wasn't a sign of life there; everyone was sleeping. The newly fallen snow crackled like new boots. The gate was open. The men must have gone to pray with O'lmas the elder. He went to sit on the platform, but all the mats were buried in snow. The round pillow, with its top covered in snow and dry bottom, looked strange, like a half-painted egg. He sat on the rug on the porch and shook his head. The pain had disappeared, and he felt at ease. But he still couldn't gather his vague and ill-defined thoughts, which were like clouds mounting clouds. He lay down on the rug and put his hands under his head. He wanted to fall asleep right there in the cold morning of the untimely winter. But no, sleep didn't come to him. Even when the curtains of his eyes lowered, he couldn't bring those in his mind down. A vein bulged from his meaty forehead, throbbing. "What happened to me?" he tried to think, but couldn't put even these words together. The four words fled to the four corners of his mind and sounded out separately: "What … happened … to … me. …" He dipped his handkerchief into the water of the little canal, wrung it out, and pressed it to his head. As if ill, he lay down and fell asleep.

It was approaching eleven when Hakimjon came and woke him. Still lying down, he drank half a bowl of hot soup with three or four chili peppers. Hakimjon threw a big mat over him. Mingboshi lay and sweated. A little later his mind fell into place and he sat up.

"There's a letter from Miryoqub," said Hakimjon.

"Who brought it?"

"They sent it from the city with some other papers."

"What does it say?"

"Let me read it."

Hakimjon began to read. First, as usual, long greetings and well wishes to mingboshi; then he addressed everyone else, name after name.

"Skip that," said mingboshi.

"After that he talks about his travels."

"Skip it."

"After that a description of the mountains in Crimea and the sea. A few pages …"

"Skip it! Enough with the blabber! Did he say when he's coming back?"

"No," Hakimjon replied. He began reading it to himself silently.

"Nothing about his whore?"

"No. In one place he said, 'I'm very happy. I don't lack for pleasure.'"

"I've got no time for his pleasure. Everything is burning around us! Skip it!"

"Here's something: 'If some sensitive matter comes up and noyib to'ra demands to know where I am, have Zunnun speak with the lady. Let Allah see to it that these difficult matters are settled.'"

"Yes, that, that. Read that again! And did he say where he is now?"

"Yes, there's an address here."

"Good, send him a telegram now. Tell him he has to come quickly. Understood?"

"Very well, master. Listen to me, sir. There's something strange at the beginning of the letter. We passed it."

"Well, well? What is it?"

"Here, listen: 'To our most respected father, our pillar of faith, father of the nation and bearer of progress, the learned Akbarali mingboshi many greetings. Let it be known that …'"

"What kind of nonsense is that? Has he gone mad? A bunch of meaningless words."

"You know, master, those are the words that jadids use. I saw the letter of one jadid *mufti* from Samarqand to Abdusamat mingboshi. He called him 'father of the nation, bearer of progress' too."

"What does that mean?"

Hakimjon avoided the meaningless question with the laconic answer: "I don't know."

"Well, that means he's equating me with Abdusamat. I guess this is what I can expect from Miryoqub now."

A childish frown rippled over mingboshi's face. Hakimjon saw this and smiled subtly. Quickly suppressing any sign of bemusement in his face, he gave mingboshi some "advice."

"No, master, don't say that. Miryoqub has no one else but you. He would never consider even the smallest of evils against you."

"And I would?" replied mingboshi nonsensically.

An alarming thought came to his mind: "Do I have anyone besides Miryoqub?" Mingboshi changed the subject to avoid the thought.

"Well, have the men returned yet?"

"No, master."

"What now? They still haven't come back? How long is the road from Qumariq? We sent them just after dark."

"I don't know, master."

Just then one of the men galloped in with his horse foaming at the mouth. He hopped off the horse before they could even open the gates, and, still panting from exhaustion, ran up to mingboshi.

"What happened? What has you all worked up?"

"It's bad, master. Very bad."

The young man couldn't speak.

"Sit, catch your breath! Speak slowly!"

Mingboshi pricked up his ears. The man was given a cup of tea. After he managed to catch his breath, he began recounting the events.

Before mingboshi's two men could leave their village, another riot broke out. This time Yodgor's two sons and one of Umarali's sons, To'xtasin, started it. The latter had a gun, a Smith & Wesson. First, they freed Yodgor from the prison and then they went to shoot Mamaturdi, the alleged leader of the mob that beat up Umarali. Mamaturdi had worked twenty years as a servant of Umarali.

That night, after mingboshi had left, To'xtasin headed to the middle of the village, his gun glinting in the sparse light of the dark streets, and began to yell.

"What kind of person raises his fist in anger at his master, at the person who fed and clothed him?" he asked. "You can't leave that kind of person alive. If we leave him then others will follow his example!"

Yodgor's two sons cheered on To'xtasin as they all made their way to the mosque. The boys seated by the fire in the middle of the town square rushed off to tell Mamturdi what they had heard. After digging his little finger in his ear, Mamaturdi put on his robe and left. About ten people gathered in front of the bridge on the grocer's porch. A vanguard of snow descended and formed ranks, while the wind took up the tambourine and began beating a march.

"I didn't want to hurt anyone," announced Mamaturdi. "Who started the whole mess at the mosque? They did! If they hadn't called us bastards, then we wouldn't have started fighting."

"Yes, of course," the young men there agreed.

"And we won't fight anyone now. But if they attack us, then we'll fight as long as there's still life in us."

Only the squab To'xtash wasn't convinced.

"If we start fighting only after them, then we'll be late, brothers!" he protested. "We have to find them and attack them first!"

Erali the fat's son, To'xtamish,[73] supported him.

"Better to do the beating than be beaten!"

"No, you don't understand," said Mamaturdi, "'Even if he's a hunchback, he's still the son of a landowner,' they say. Who has power? Those with money! The tsar, the officials, the governor—everyone listens to those with money."

"'Whoever has the money has the right,'" another man said.

"Yes, so if we do anything first, they won't hesitate to have the whole village shot. We'll wait and see what they do, and then we'll react accordingly."

---

73 The repetition of similar names—To'xtasin, To'xtash, To'xtamish—adds a Gogolian ridiculousness to the scene. The root of all three names, *to'xta*, means "stop" or "cease" in Uzbek.

"Yes, yes, that's right," said the men assembled.

After a little thinking, Mamaturdi raised his head.

"Listen here, boys! He wants vengeance against me. Let me fight him. Don't interfere. He has nothing against you."

All the young men responded in one voice.

"No!" they yelled. "We won't let him touch you!"

At the same time, the three heirs were trying with all their might to free the "poor" old Yodgor from his cell, but it was to no avail. Mingboshi's two guards stood fast, holding their rifles at the ready.

"If you come any closer, I'll shoot you! No one touches him until mingboshi's order comes," the first barked.

To'xtasin, hiding his pistol under his shirt, cursed the two guards vehemently, but the three ultimately left as quickly as they had come. They went down the narrow street on the left side of the mosque straight to Mamaturdi's house. When they discovered Mamaturdi wasn't there, they began searching his house, thinking he must be hiding. Mamaturdi's frightened wife yelled that he had left, but they ignored her. When she saw the white handle of the pistol tucked into To'xtasin's shirt, she ran outside and started screaming.

Mamaturdi heard her screams and instantly realized what had happened. Mamaturdi's supporters ran back to his house. As To'xtasin exited the house, he saw Mamaturdi and fired a bullet that landed in his left shoulder. The squab To'xtash picked up a large stick and broke it over To'xtasin's hand, flinging the pistol onto the ground. Yodgor's two sons started throwing rocks at the crowd. The young men immediately rushed into a fist fight. In the end, one of Yodgor's two sons had been killed while the other managed to escape, badly beaten. Without his pistol, To'xtasin ran off and hid. Mamaturdi, who was losing blood rapidly, collapsed on the ground. His wife lost consciousness at the sight.

At the same time in the mosque, Yodgor broke down the door and was attempting to leave, but the two guards weren't having it. They fought with him for a long time before finally managing to bind his arms and legs and throw him back in the cell. Mingboshi's two messengers came at precisely that time. They untied Yodgor, who then reviled them vehemently with unprintable words. "If I don't have you all shot, then I'll change my name!" The four men just stood without a word, though they couldn't help but crack a smile. One of the messengers even started laughing for which Yodgor slapped him. In answer, despite the orders of the senior guard, the messengers beat Yodgor viciously.

And while all this was going on, neither the amin nor the two ellikboshis made an appearance. As soon as mingboshi had left, they all locked themselves in their homes.

....

Mingboshi was completely numb. He didn't know what to do. He had no idea whom to ask for advice. "If I ask that rascal Hakimjon, what kind of ideas will he get?" The Qumariq matter had really thrown him between two fires: on the one side were the people who were clearly in the right, but on the other were the two landowners, who had money and esteem. Mingboshi wasn't afraid of the people; whatever he said, they would do it. But as for the landowners, they respected neither the people (he could tolerate that) nor him (that was intolerable!). They openly cursed him and threatened him in front of the people. If it were up to him, he would send the two of them to Siberia. But he could never do that. As right as the people were, the Russians would always take the side of those with money; they wouldn't let them suffer. And now Yodgor and Umarali wouldn't keep silent: they would take all their complaints to a lawyer and write up thousands of petitions; they would go to noyib to'ra, the district manager, and the governor himself. They wouldn't stop until they had his head. If only Miryoqub were here! He would do something. He wouldn't let this stand.

"Alas," mingboshi said to himself, "the villagers haven't helped. If only they had killed Yodgor and Umarali the other day. It wouldn't have been my fault because I wasn't there. It would've fixed everything. Alas, alas."

Not knowing what to do, he passed through the ichkari and the tashqari into the courtyard, and then paced on the street thinking. He came in late and went straight to Zebi where, together with his dinner, he drank another bottle of vodka. Then he lay down on the mattress and with his ugly and coarse voice began to sing.

The three co-wives stood in front of Zebi's door, listening to his singing, unable to contain their laughter. But in Poshshaxon's eyes there was a seriousness that reflected the agony inside her. If her co-wives had looked her in the eyes just then, they almost certainly would have jumped. But her co-wives were unaware, caught up in their rivalry-induced worries. "Didn't she win, didn't she get exactly what she wanted? Why should she be sad?" they must have thought.

But in fact …

In fact, the smartest and most lively of mingboshi's wives was dissatisfied with how the battle against Sultonxon had resolved itself. She was now dreaming up even more plans than she had before Zebi's marriage. Her ambitions were like rivers, flowing ever farther. Could she even catch up with them now?

"What happened? We brought Zebi here, and after days and weeks of hardship, we broke her will, turned her into a sweet, little lamb and gave her to mingboshi. Mingboshi is happy now. Zebi is too, at least as far as I can tell.

"And why should she be upset? Mingboshi may be old but everything down there works; if he finds pleasure in a woman, then surely she can find it in him. And after all, 'A young woman only gives more life to an old man,' they say. That's what old men must be thinking when they marry young girls. Would Zebi have been happy if she hadn't married mingboshi? There's no way of knowing. Who can say whether there would be a young man in place of the old one? Is Zebi's father someone who would have considered his daughter's caprices? No, of course not! How could Zebi not have known that? One day Zebi even told the co-wives: 'Who cares about what the girl wants?! Can a girl really marry whom she wants? I curse my father for giving me to this old man, but if he hadn't, whom would he have given me to? Would it have been someone I love? No, he would have just gotten mad and married me off to his eshon. And he's five times uglier than mingboshi!' Is mingboshi, as people say, ugly? Yes, uglier than most. … And so disgusting. … But there are people uglier and more disgusting than him in the world, surely! Who can say that she or I wouldn't have ended up with one of them? Nobody!"

Poshshaxon's thoughts, like a spider's web, spread across her mind, and she, like the fly, became stuck in them. She had no peace from those thoughts!

"Zebi has now taken Sultonxon's place. Mingboshi has built a nest in her home. From the house are sometimes heard the laughter of the young bride and sometimes the howls of an old man. Sometimes a sweet young voice accompanied by dutar playing, and sometimes the sounds of the gramophone that mingboshi had recently bought. That's life! That's marriage! Were Poshshaxon and Sultonxon ever newlyweds in that way? Didn't mingboshi say when he first sent matchmakers to Zebi's home that he would give everything to her if she would be his? That if she could just give him a child, then she would be his sole heir and none of his other wives would get anything? He even told Hakimjon more recently: 'I have found happiness. Everything of mine is hers. Give the others each a few acres of land, but everything else to her.' Didn't Miryoqub, with his black eyes, take Poshshaxon in his arms and tell her that everything of mingboshi's would be hers? Didn't he promise that? How else could she have found someone like Miryoqub, with such pretty eyes, a beautiful body, who knew how to talk to a woman before indulging himself? If she had that inheritance, then Miryoqub would almost certainly return to her! He went off somewhere with a Russian woman, they say. Men are all a bunch of dogs. They find a bitch in heat and follow her. Fine, let him have his fun. He can't leave that inheritance."

Poshshaxon's thoughts howled as they flew, and she struggled to catch up.

"But the wealth that Miryoqub promised will go to Zebi soon. Mingboshi, after all, is older than all his wives. And lately he's really taken to vodka. If he keeps that up, then he'll burn his heart out completely. He'll die soon! The country is in chaos. The people don't respect mingboshi anymore, and they don't respect his superiors either. The riots in Qumariq are like poison to mingboshi; he can't decide what to do. Even if he doesn't die, he might lose everything anyways. Or he might fly into a rage and leave for the war. What will happen with his wealth? To hell with it! It will destroy all of us, that wealth. Before, it was going to be split between four people; now it's five. Before, we had hoped that everyone would get their share, but now each of the wives will get a handful of land and Zebi will get the rest. Are there idiots in the world that would chop off their own legs while they're standing on them?"

Poshshaxon looked at herself in the mirror: "There's that very idiot," she told herself. She laughed a laugh that sounded little different from a sob.

Yet another enraging thought fell into Poshshaxon's mind: Sultonxon's insouciance. That insouciance, her constant cheery laughter made Poshshaxon sick—sick!

"What happened to that girl?! Now she's happily playing, talking, singing, laughing, joking with her co-wives. Since the snows began, she's had snowball fights with half the women and girls of the village. She even played snow letters with three of the women.[74] What in the world happened to her? She comes home late after the last prayer and locks herself in her house. She disappears until dawn. Zebi should be her worst enemy, but instead she's become her closest friend. The two are confidantes, mahram."

Those sleepless nights that had tortured Sultonxon not long ago now kept Poshshaxon's eyes open. Every day from dusk till dawn she tossed and turned on her back thinking. From all that thinking, she finally came to a decision: "I'll kill two little birds now with one shot!"

....

---

74 During the first snow, girls throw into the air so-called "snow letters," little pieces of paper with their desires written on them, and whichever of them catches one is obligated to organize a party and invite the others over.

As terrifying as Poshshaxon's decision was, the execution of it would be fairly easy and quick. Stoking the little pot all day, she boiled some women's bane that she had secretly bought from the grocer. She planned to pour the water from it into a teapot and place it in Zebi's house the next morning. During that time, the other three wives would be at the wedding of Dadaboy the grocer's daughter. As for mingboshi, he had been called to the city on urgent business. Unable to hide his fear of his Russian bosses, he left early in the morning. The other wives didn't insist on Poshshaxon's presence at the wedding because she had a relative over. As they were leaving, Xadichaxon told her to come just as soon as the guest left.

Poshshaxon, all alone, entered Zebi's house without any trouble. On Zebi's shelf was a little teapot of holy water; Razzoq-sufi had his eshon bless the water. Zebi was supposed to drink it in order to become pregnant and give birth safely. Poshshaxon poured out the holy water and in its place filled the teapot with her decoction. That was it! "Zebi will come back tonight, drink this water, and die! Everyone will accuse Sultonxon, of course. Could the murderer of the fourth wife be anyone but the third? Even a child knows that."

When she was done, she left home and headed straight for the wedding. She talked with her co-wives and friends, laughed, joked. She even hugged and kissed the girl she was going to poison. Though Zebi's kisses were passionate and hot, Poshshaxon nevertheless felt she was kissing a cold corpse, and she shuddered like blades of spring grass in the breeze. Even when she was laughing and enjoying herself, she sensed her hand involuntarily grasping her breast as if a sharp piece of ice lay within, piercing her innards. She coughed repeatedly to free herself of that ice, but the coughing seemed to emerge not from her mouth, but from somewhere, someone else.

"What's wrong, my dear? You haven't caught a cold?" asked Zebi.

In Zebi's simple, kind, even childish words there was nothing other than sincerity, but Poshshaxon heard only mockery: "What do you expect to gain by murdering me? Do you really think you'll get away with it?"

That sharp piece of ice in her chest began to chop. It was as if a witch's freezing cold hands had run up and down every part of her body. She went pale.

Her co-wives surrounded her.

"What's wrong, Poshshaxon?"

"Maybe I've caught a cold."

"Go home, lie down."

She went home without touching the food. She couldn't even lift her head until the next morning.

18

"Akbarali, what you've done…," started noyib to'ra. "I can't defend you anymore."

Mingboshi didn't know what to say; he stared at the ground in silence.

Noyib to'ra continued.

"Yodgor and Umarali found a lawyer and filed two handfuls of petitions with the governor. The governor reprimanded me over the telephone. Today he forwarded me the complaints and demanded information about them. I looked at the petitions. They don't look good. I'm afraid no one can defend you now."

Mingboshi involuntarily lifted his head and looked in noyib to'ra's eyes; then he looked down again and kept his eyes fixed on to'ra's lacquered boots.

Noyib to'ra continued.

"I sent someone to Qumariq just before you came here. The police chief is already there. He'll imprison everyone who threatened the two landowners. There's no other option. I ordered that an official sign of our gratitude be extended to the imam. He spoke well that day, they say."

Mingboshi couldn't take it any longer.

"Noyib to'ra, sir, I'm confused: those who we've imprisoned have done nothing wrong. How does that work? If you were there, you would have shot Yodgor and Umarali."

"I know," said noyib to'ra, "I know very well. I respect a single word from you more than a thousand of their petitions. They really did commit a crime, I looked into it. But they've already been punished for that."

Mingboshi worked up the courage to defend himself.

"If that's true, then why do we allow injustice in our just kingdom?"

Noyib to'ra laughed.

"You're so naïve, Akbarali! The tsar defends the country's most respected people. And respect comes from wealth, you know that. If we let these villagers act however they feel best, we'll soon have to let loose the whole territory. You're not much for politics."

"I'm a simple man," agreed mingboshi, "I don't know your politics. I've served the tsar as best I could. He won't take into account my long service?"

"I've been thinking about that. Akbarali, go home for now. I will try my best to defend you before the governor. If I can't, then we'll put another person in your place. You're wealthy, though; you won't starve. You've gotten old anyways. Service isn't for you anymore."

"Very well, sir," said mingboshi, somewhat relieved, "if you remove me, that's fine. I don't have the energy to go through these trials in my old age."

"If it were left to me, I wouldn't touch you, Akbarali. But the governor is in charge. It's hard to change his mind, and I'm afraid to say anything. Because it looks very bad. Alright, go now. If I can, I'll talk things out with those two mongrels. Maybe they'll ask to close the matter. If Miryoqub were here, this would be so much easier for you."

"Without question! My head is spinning from all this."

Mingboshi, his spirit broken, left the office. He wasn't so upset at the prospect of losing his position—he would get used to it somehow—but the news of his removal could be devastating. Yodgor, Umarali, and Abdusamat would take that news everywhere. The news would fly on pigeons' wings, in the arms of the wind, in drops of rain, and in the breast of the sky. Every time a crow spreads its wings, it would caw about mingboshi's failure. Just like that, the news would circle the world and arrive at holy Mecca within two days. There mingboshi's old friend, Nasriddin the loud would decry him in Arabic from atop the holy Kaaba. Wouldn't it be better just to die?

He sat down next to Zunnun on the low bench in front of noyib to'ra's house.

"I heard too, old friend. It's all very ugly," said Zunnun.

"Yes, very bad. That's why I came to you. I recently got a letter from Miryoqub that said to speak about some sensitive matters with Zunnun and he'll tell noyib to'ra's wife. That's why I came."

"With pleasure, old friend! Even if Miryoqub hadn't said anything, I would have helped. What do you need?"

"Everything is in the hands of the governor, they say. I'm not sure what to do. Talk with the lady of the house, ask her what she thinks."

"Go to the old city until later tonight. I'll talk with her, and tell you when you return. Then do whatever she says."

Mingboshi waited impatiently for evening to come. The dusk prayer had still not been read when he returned to Zunnun.

"You'll need a lot of money," Zunnun said abruptly.

Mingboshi, as if a mountain had been lifted from his chest, began to breathe easily.

"If I can solve this with money, then good. Money I have."

Seeing mingboshi finally at ease, Zunnun was relieved too.

"Our lady said she'd try to speak with the governor's wife. It's a delicate matter, and she can't say ahead of time if anything will come of her trying.

Whatever happens, you'll need a 1,000 to 1,500, she said. 'Akbarali,' she said, 'is a dear person to me. If I can do this for him, then he'll know how to thank me, but the matter is very delicate, I just don't know. Just have him bring the money. And he shouldn't just rely on me; don't let him loiter, he has to act,' she added."

"Thank you, Zunnun, I'm very grateful. It seems this isn't something that will just go away. Fine then, I'll bring the money tomorrow or the next day. We have to try. If it works, it works, and if not, to hell with it."

"Let's go inside, friend. I'll put on some tea."

"No, Zunnun, I have such a lump in my throat that I can't swallow a thing."

Mingboshi stood up and left without saying goodbye. Leaving noyib to'ra's, he went straight to a tavern. After a bottle of vodka and some kebab, his head swelled like dough in water, and he swayed back and forth on his horse as he returned to the village.

His wives had already lain down to sleep. His head spinning, barely on his feet, mingboshi stumbled into Zebi's house. He could hardly think: he now planned on gathering 3,000 rubles by the day after tomorrow. Nothing could stop him from doing that.

"Get up now!" he roared at Zebi.

Zebi rolled off her mat and lifted her lamp.

"Set the table! What do we have to eat?"

"There's some pilaf."

"Bring it here."

Even though she knew he was drunk, Zebi was surprised at his uncharacteristic rudeness on this night. She looked at him, pondering: "Is this the same man or a different one?"

"Why are you looking at me? Are you drunk, idiot?" shouted mingboshi.

Zebi silently set the table.

"Open this!" Mingboshi handed Zebi a bottle of vodka.

"I don't know how," said Zebi; tears had come to her eyes.

"My wife doesn't know how to open vodka?" shrieked mingboshi through laughter. "Then learn! Watch!" He hit the bottom of the bottle with his thick palm twice. The cork popped out, hit the ceiling, and then fell into the copper dish on the shelf with a ring.

"Haha!" cried mingboshi, "I rang your bells last night and again today, you fool!"

He drank cup after cup, wiping his mouth with his sleeve. Then he poured a cup and handed it to Zebi.

"Here, drink! Be a man!"

"Oh, better to die! How could I drink vodka?! Stop, enough!"

"Be a man, I said! Take it! Take *it*!"

Zebi retreated and started to cry.

"Stop it now. Fine, you don't have to drink," said mingboshi. "I'll drink myself!"

He finished the bottle and dipped his unwashed hand into the pilaf. Half the pilaf fell between his fingers onto the tablecloth, the sleeping mats, his pants and shirt. Zebi leaned her back against the wall and watched her husband in terror.

Mingboshi, his mouth full of pilaf, sang, "I remembered my dear girl. ..." The song cut off as the words fought with the food in his oily throat. Mingboshi started to choke and quickly spit out the rice into the bowl from which he was eating. Forgetting the incident quickly, he dipped his hand into the bowl again. Zebi felt nauseated. She slowly retreated to the door and then ran out. In the entryway, she drank a cup of cold water, but her nausea didn't pass and there was no more water. Through the open door, she saw mingboshi open another bottle of vodka and begin pouring it. Zebi went outside. She washed her hands in the fresh snow, threw it on her face and ate a little. When she could no longer endure the cold, she went back in to find mingboshi lying on his back. Stepping over him, she quietly cleared the table. Then she covered herself with another mat, extinguished the lamp, and fell asleep. How much she slept, she didn't know, but she woke up to the furious screaming of her husband.

"Water! Water!" he cried.

Zebi, still sleepy, lit the lamp. Mingboshi's frightening voice only continued to increase in volume.

"You idiot girl, water I said! Water! I'm so sick. I'm burning inside! Water! Water!"

Zebi moved hurriedly. She quickly took the holy water in the teapot from the shelf and without a moment of thought gave it to mingboshi.

Mingboshi downed the water in the teapot in one gulp. Zebi began waiting for him to calm down and fall asleep. She put two soft pillows at his side and laid a mat over him. After that, he seemed to calm down.

When Zebi's eyelashes finally touched one another again, mingboshi let out a terrifying scream. He shot up and began to strip himself quickly of his belt and his robe. Zebi, watching from her corner, thought that this was just another drunken outburst. She picked up his robe and belt and hung them on hooks. Then she made a bed of mats for the two of them and rolled her husband over to it.

Mingboshi's eyes were bursting out of their sockets. He began grasping at his shirt, tearing it off, and clutching at his throat. He breathed heavily and with difficulty. In a hoarse voice, he managed, "Don't choke me!"

He took two steps towards the wall and leaned on the wardrobe there. After a moment, it seemed his breathing had slowed, but then he began to grab at his throat again. He beat his chest. He raised his hand and put it on his head. In his eyes, large tears began to form. He cast a strange, pitiful look at Zebi. Suddenly his arms fell limp and his head slumped over. His backside slowly lowered to the floor as if he was sitting down, and then his body fell to one side. He stopped moving.

Did Zebi, holding her breath and with her back to the wall, understand what had happened or not? In either case, she ran outside, adorned in only her night shirt, and involuntarily screamed for help.

All the co-wives woke up, and just as the call to morning prayer sounded, it became mixed with the cries of mourning women.

Among them was Poshshaxon, whose arrow had missed its mark. Who knows whether she was crying for mingboshi or because of Miryoqub's treachery or maybe because her women's bane had been the bane of another.

19

This crime of womanly jealousy, in a time of revolt, was like fat thrown on the fire. The small-minded officials of the small district's capital suddenly raised this worthless victim of an accident to a hero of their time. These officials endeavored to boast of their accomplishments before their superiors by lionizing a success of tsarist policy: a tamed and submissive servant, whom they had drawn from the ranks of a "wild" people. If they let their leaders be poisoned (by a woman and her bane no less!), then how could they command authority among the people? Especially among these "wild" people. What would the ineffectiveness of their power say to those "wildlings"? There could be no political wavering in a colony on the doorstep of British India. No, the result would be very bad! Terrifying!

Dispatches full of panic and fear flew to Tashkent, and just three days after the event, a delegation of the colony's military court arrived in the village. The investigation was already concluded by the time the court arrived. The investigation was so quick, in fact, that the court's translator quipped: "Why is the speed here and not at the front?!"

The translator wasn't one of those old foxes who prowled around the courts, but, for some reason, one of the new officials summoned from other territories, though he was a Turkestani Muslim. The officials in the city and locals didn't know him well. After all, he was just a lowly postal worker.

But the lawyer whom the court assigned to be Zebi's defender ... oh, the lawyer was from another world altogether! This man, no, this magnificent individual was from one of the faraway places in Turkestan (maybe just north of Iran?). He had, they said, embezzled quite a bit from the government treasury as a military official. If the tsar really respected the laws, he would have had this man shot or exiled somewhere. But just as he always covered his head with an umbrella in this hot, practically uninhabitable country, he had friends in high places to cover his indiscretions. They would never let one of their own burn. With their help, he lost only his military rank and then exiled himself from colony to colony, finally settling into a career as a lawyer. Of course, he did! Because is it really difficult for a man who deceived and stole from an entire state to steal from ordinary people? Experience is its own wealth! But among that experience and wealth, his most valuable assets were his connections! No self-respecting lawyer could take on the suspect cases that he did and win most of them. It was easy for this reborn Plevako[75] to take these ignorant locals for all they were worth.

When the local investigator handed the military prosecutor's official indictment with the examination record to the lawyer, our lawyer friend was already talking about another case with another person like himself. Who was this "person like himself"? A local whom everyone, wherever he happened to be, knew and feared. The local Muslims called him "Obrezqora"—black washbasin. He was of average height, swarthy complexion, and rather thin. If our lawyer was a Russian lawyer, then Obrezqora was a Muslim lawyer. If some court needed

---

75 Fyodor Nikiforovich Plevako (1842–1908) was a famous lawyer in tsarist Russia who worked only in Moscow. Like many lawyers in late nineteenth-century Russia, he achieved celebrity status for his passionate speeches in court, which newspapers often relayed for an avid readership. Though Cho'lpon invokes his name here to signal corruption, his ire is more directed at the profession itself rather than at Plevako as an individual. Plevako was not noted as corrupt or wicked in contemporary pre-revolutionary accounts. See L. Liakhovetskii, "Plevako, Fedor Nikiforovich," *Entsiklopedicheskii slovar' Brokgauza i Efrona* (Sankt-Peterburg: Koshbukh-Prusik, 1906). Cho'lpon's hatred of lawyers for their corruption is a Soviet-influenced attitude. Before the revolution, most jadids esteemed work in the law as a worthy profession, whereas the Bolsheviks always distrusted the institution of law as an impediment to the exercise of proletarian power.

false testimony, then Obrezqora was ready. Everyone knew of his deception. Judges, landowners, and other respected leaders all fought with him, and they always lost! "Obrezqora won't stop with his banditry," they would tell each other.

With Obrezqora's case in front of him, one from which he could work the client for no less than 5,000, spending time on a military case defending a local seemed rather trivial to our lawyer. He quickly ran his eyes over the indictment and the investigation notes and tossed them aside. Like Sufis in a trance ignore the world around them, the lawyer put the case out of his mind until the very day of the trial. Why could the little Plevako of a little town not spare the time to look over two pages? Across the street from the town's train station, there was an opium den in which he and Obrezqora spent all day gambling. It wasn't a matter of time, but interest.

On the day of the trial, he found the two orphaned pages and read them cursorily over breakfast. He read them so quickly and carelessly that his tea on the table didn't have time to cool. The content of the two pages seemed to him like childish banter, and he smiled while reading them as a grandfather does at the mischief of his children.

But we cannot fault the defender's indifference as the only factor contributing to the travesty of our impending trial. The investigator's secretary didn't have a type writer, so he painstakingly wrote the record by hand. The names of local Muslims he wrote like any barely literate child, in place of Akbarali sometimes recording Umarali, sometimes Amir o'g'li, and sometimes Qambar vali. And really what's the difference? How can you write what no one can pronounce? If it's Akbar or Qambar, they're both the same, right? They're sart names!

To be fair, in its final form the examination record was very neatly written. The paper was flat like train tracks. And just look at the d's and b's! You'll be amazed! The tails on the b's curved up and to the left, and those on the d's—down and to the right. Both their little tails, like coiled snakes, turned around and around! It wasn't a record but a spectacle! And what a spectacle!

The record described the crime, the victim, the victim's many years of service to the Russian state, and the ingenuity and mastery he had demonstrated in state matters. The murderer woman's identity was passed over with a few words. The witnesses (mingboshi's other three wives) all unanimously confirmed that they hadn't aided the crime: "No one other than Zebi participated," they said. The neighbors, however, said: "Mingboshi's other wives were accustomed to neglect and subservience. Zebi, on the other hand, had long resisted her husband and faked illness. Later, she seemed to have acquiesced to him, and they lived happily together a few days. Her recent softness, we think, was a ploy to throw us off. She must have planned this all along." Mingboshi's second wife, Poshshaxon, a day before the murder, had fallen ill and was lying in convalescence. She was questioned in that prone position.

The questions to and answers of the accused were given the least space in this magnificent record. So little, in fact, that the secretary didn't even have to dip his pen in ink a second time. What a pity for all the poor investigator's copious efforts with Zebi!

He asked her all of two questions to which Zebi gave all of two answers. The questions were short, and the answers shorter still:

"Who gave mingboshi the water?"

"I did."

"So you killed mingboshi?"

"No."

The official indictment was pithier than the examination record! It contained the conclusion of the record and a few words about mingboshi's great service. A laconic demand followed: "Let such and such be punished by such and such according to such and such an article."

The lawyer arrived half an hour before the trial. He spoke with the accused in the improvised courthouse's little garden. Their conservation was quick as well, though the number of questions increased from two to four.

"Who gave the water to mingboshi?"

"I did."

"The water was from a teapot. Whose teapot was it?"

"Mine."

"Did you know what kind of water was inside?"

"I knew."

"The water in the teapot was poisoned. So you gave your husband poison, correct?"

"I didn't know there was poison in the teapot. I didn't kill my husband."

The lawyer shrugged and left.

A few days had passed since the murder. They still hadn't heard about it in the city, and even if a few people had heard about it, Zebi's parents were probably completely unaware. They had even prepared more holy water for Zebi to ensure her pregnancy. Razzoq-sufi was going to visit her on Friday. Even if they had known earlier, neither the old man nor his wife knew how to get a lawyer nor where to file a petition. Instead, Razzoq-sufi would have exhausted his patience, run to his eshon, beating his chest and sobbing. That's all![76]

---

76 The 1988 serial publication omits "That's all!"

As for Zebi, since the poisoning, she had largely kept silent. Her mind was paralyzed. She looked on the entirety of the investigation, the police escort, the trial, and the lawyers with a strange indifference, as if not mingboshi but she had died. She didn't think about what they were saying or how to defend herself. In some faraway corner of her mind, there was a vague, unformed thought. That thought was so remote that she could not quite understand it. When she focused closely on it, it took this form: "I didn't kill him. ... That much is clear. ... Someone has framed me. ... Will I be able to go back? What's the use? My mother? I'll go back to her. 'My husband has died,' I'll tell her. I'll cry."

The winter winds whipped through the big hall of the court. The rows of Vienna chairs for the observers and participants seemed as if they still hadn't woken up from their week-long slumber. In the front row the governor, noyib to'ra, the garrison commander, the head of police, and the priest were seated. In the third row on the far side was an old Muslim in a snow-white, tall turban; he was the mosque's thin-voiced imam. On one side of the court was the lawyer; and on the other, the translator. No one else was permitted in.

Zebi came into the courtroom in between her two escorts with their unsheathed swords. She went to the front of the court, covered from head to toe in a velvet paranji, black face veil, and black leather boots without galoshes. Her dark countenance was far more terrifying than the glinting swords or the court's imminent judgment. She looked like one of those black-clad cardinals of the Spanish Inquisition. The priest looked at her and shook his head. The imam looked and stroked his beard as he said "Allah forbid" in Arabic.

The judge addressed the translator.

"Tell the accused to uncover her face."

The translator explained the demand to Zebi.

"Oh, no! God take me! I have to show my face to all these nomahram people? It would be better to die!"

When the translator relayed her words, those seated below, almost to a man, and even a few of the court delegation cracked smiles. The fat-torsoed garrison commander surpassed them, crowing like a rooster. Everyone turned to him. He quickly shut his mouth and started to wipe his face with a handkerchief. Then the imam, in his thin, whistle-like voice, involuntarily let out a "Allah has willed it." And when everyone turned to him, he blushed bright red and lowered his head in embarrassment.

"Explain to the woman that it is unacceptable to give testimony with a covered face. This is the rule of the court. We are obliged to compel her to uncover her face in order to ensure that another person has not taken her place. Tell her there is no point in resisting!"

Like a child upset with her playmate's cheating in a game, Zebi turned away from the court.

"Explain," the judge started again, "that I cannot begin the trial unless she uncovers her face."

"Fine, then, don't begin," said Zebi to the translator. "Let him do what he knows best!"

The translator laughed, then turned red from his breach of decorum. He translated what she said.

The judge raised his voice.

"Is she mocking the court? Tell her to remove the veil voluntarily or it will be done forcibly!"

"Oh, dear God! With all these men seated here?!" she protested, "It would be a thousand times better to die!" Then she lowered her voice. "There is a respected man of faith here like my father's eshon. How can I look at him with a bare face?"

The judge responded calmly this time.

"Tell her: 'Address the court and turn your back to the imam.'"

Zebi again didn't speak. The imam stood up.

"There is nothing to fear, my child!" he said, "I will not look!"

"What about the others?" asked Zebi, indicating the members of the court.

The imam moved closer to the front of the court and addressed himself to the translator.

"Honored sir! If you'll allow it, I have some advice for the woman."

"Please!"

The imam went to Zebi's side and began to whisper to her. Zebi, though her resolve had weakened, argued with him. The imam soon turned to a disputed matter of the faith, but as the words began to emerge from his mouth, he immediately regretted them. He stopped mid-sentence and tried other arguments. When those didn't work, so as not to test the court's patience, he was forced to return to that disputed matter. Forced! For that reason, he spoke quietly.

"There is no difference between an infidel and a dog. Would you cover your face in front of a dog? You wouldn't, so you wouldn't cover in front of an infidel either. It's permitted to uncover in front of them."[77]

---

77 The 1988 serial publication has the imam voice a different argument, presumably because referring to Russians as dogs was too offensive, even if done by an unsympathetic character.

Zebi was convinced.

"So you'll sit far away?"

"Yes, my daughter, yes," he said. He went back five rows and sat.

While everyone's eyes followed the imam, Zebi removed the veil and turned towards the judge, shielding her face with one hand.

"Now, on with the questioning!"

Some in the court averted their eyes to not embarrass "this simple Muslim girl," while others kept their eyes trained on her, following the quick movements of her lips.

Once they established the accused's identity, the court secretary stood up and read the indictment. Then began a trading of short questions and answers. The number of questions and answers this time increased quite a bit.

"Did you hear the indictment?"

"Yes."

"Did mingboshi ask for the water?"

"Yes, he asked for it."

"Was he drunk?"

"He had drunk a lot of vodka."

"Who gave him the water?"

"I did."

"The water in the teapot?"

"Yes."

"This teapot?"

"Yes."

"Whose teapot was it?"

"Mine."

"Yours?"

"Yes, mine."

"Did you know what kind of water was inside?"

"I knew."

"What kind of water?"

"Holy water."

"For whom was the water blessed?"

"For me."

"Why did they bless the water for you?"

The 1988 publication's imam says the following: "These men are infidels. There is no need to hide your face from them. It is permitted to uncover in front of them!"

"So that I would get pregnant."

Everyone other than the imam laughed.

"Why did you give this water to mingboshi?"

"He was very thirsty and it was close by on the shelf."

"Did you know that there was poison in the teapot?"

Zebi laughed.

"You're a strange one. (Zebi addressed the Russian informally; you cannot address a Russian with respect).[78] How would I have known?"

"So you killed your husband?"

Zebi answered seriously, elongating her words for emphasis.

"Noooo! I would die if I killed him."

In that last answer was the innocent sincerity of any girl speaking to a mahram friend. The tone of "God take me! How could you say such a thing?"

But how could Zebi know that the judge was not a child? How could she know that these men would never understand something that was as clear as the moon? "There are Muslims along with Russians here; they all know that I couldn't have killed mingboshi," thought Zebi. "They already know and yet it's strange that they keep asking. Or are they playing the fool?"

When the judge stood up to speak, Zebi thought, "Well, the questioning must be over. I guess now I'll have to find my way home when they release me."

"Sit," the judge told Zebi.

She slowly and carefully sat down. The judge began speaking.

"The case is so clear that, in my opinion, there is no need to continue the trial. The accused has herself admitted to the crime with her very answers. After closing statements, we will adjourn to deliberate the sentence."

The questions and answers to Zebi were repeated and the examination record was read aloud in translation. The rest of the deliberation was conducted in Russian. Zebi, who didn't know the language, simply watched the officials talking with one another.

The judge turned to the prosecutor.

"What do you say, sir?"

The prosecutor got up, put both hands on the table in front of him, and bent over.

---

78 The 1988 serial publication omits this parenthetical. The parenthetical explains that one cannot call a Russian *siz*, the formal second person in Uzbek, and therefore Zebi uses *sen*, the informal.

"I am not against your proposal. Of course, I have my own thoughts on the matter. In a time of war, I cannot look at this murder as any ordinary crime. The victim was a man recognized for his outstanding service to the Russian state and the tsar. Those Young Sarts, those secret agents sent by our enemy Turkey to undermine the state, hated him. I am not sure that this 'simple' and 'innocent' sart woman was not a toy in the hands of these agents. We are too used to looking at the sarts with indifference: we tell ourselves that they are innocent like lambs. Of course, this view of ours is true to an extent, given our easy conquest of the region. But we must rid ourselves of these illusions. The 1908 Young Turk Revolution, the mass revolt we had across the empire in 1905, the constitutional movements in Iran. The sarts are not blind to these. Those jadids, who dress like Europeans and are outwardly Russified, those Young Sarts, most of whom are seemingly friendly merchants and landowners, do not lag behind the Turks in their hostility to our empire. True, most of the sarts are loyal to our dear state, to our beloved tsar. The merchants and landowners, and especially the ʿulama battle valiantly against those Young Sarts, combatting their influence; we know this. But if we do not increase our caution and vigilance in this territory, the people will soon rise up under the banner of the Young Sarts. You know yourself that the Decembrists in their revolt against the state and the tsar in 1825 in Peter's city rocked the whole country from just one city square.[79] In 1905, those city squares multiplied beyond measure.[80] Here we are not that far

---

79 The Decembrists were groups of Russian intellectuals and aristocrats in the early nineteenth century who were enthused by the ideas of democracy and freedom popularized by the French revolution and radical French and German thought. They participated in secret societies within and outside government with the hope of advancing these ideals. They received the name "Decembrists" for their organization and execution of a revolt against the Russian state on December 26, 1825. After the death of Alexander I on December 1 of that year, many in the Russian army swore allegiance to Constantine, Alexander's elder son; but he, acting based on a secret agreement with his father, subsequently renounced the throne in favor of his brother Nicholas. Members of the secret societies began organizing to support Constantine, whom they thought (correctly) more liberal than his brother. On the day of Nicholas's assumption of the throne, Russian army officers led 3,000 soldiers to Senate Square in St. Petersburg to assert their support of Constantine. Nicholas crushed the revolt with those soldiers that had sworn allegiance to him, killing over 3,000 soldiers and civilians in the process. The thirty years of his reign, beginning on this poor note, were characterized by obscurantism and repression at the hands of a tsar ever fearful of liberal sentiments in his subjects.

80 The prosecutor is referencing the Russian Revolution of 1905. After a strike at the Putilov plant (a railway and arms manufacturer) in late 1904, hundreds of thousands of workers rose in sympathy strikes across the Russian Empire. The strikes reached an apex when on January 22, 1905, the priest Georgy Gapon led workers to the Winter Palace in

removed from the eshon's revolt.[81] Our respected ally England had a joke with us then, but we won't let our enemies, Germany and its puppet, Turkey have any laugh at our expense. The oh-so-recent events in Qumariq should not be far from our minds, sirs![82]

St. Petersburg to deliver a petition. Government troops opened fire on them, killing as many as 1,000 in a massacre that became known as Bloody Sunday. The strikes then grew in number and support, spreading to other areas of the empire. Alongside the strikes, soldiers began to mutiny in ever greater numbers, while minority nationalist groups used the occasion to demand additional rights and privileges. Russian chauvinists also began a series of pogroms against the Jewish population in the eastern lands of the empire. On October 30, 1905, Nicholas II acquiesced to liberal demands by signing the October Manifesto, which granted basic civil rights, expanded the electoral franchise, and established the Duma as the country's elected legislative body. Many of the strikes ended, while others were repressed with force. Though the provisions of the manifesto nominally went into effect, the tsar quickly undermined them the following year, transforming his State Council into a second legislative assembly to compete with the Duma and asserting his power to universally appoint and dismiss ministers without Duma consultation, which led most Duma members to tender their resignations a few weeks after the first elections in early 1906.

81 The prosecutor is referring to the 1898 revolt in Andijan, the city around which the action of the novel most likely takes place. The uprising was led by the Naqshbandi Sufi Duxchi eshon (also known as Muhammad 'Ali Sabyr). Approximately 2,000 men under his leadership attacked a Russian garrison in the city. They killed twenty soldiers and wounded twenty more, but the rebellion was suppressed easily. As Alexander Morrison notes, the rebellion did not constitute much of a threat to Russian rule in the area, but the fact of the uprising contributed greatly to Russian fears and policy as seen in Cho'lpon's prosecutor. See Alexander Morrison, "The Andijan Uprising of 1898 and Its Leader Dukchi Ishan as Described by Contemporary Poets by Aftandil S. Erkinov (Review)," *Ab Imperio*, no. 1 (2013): 388–393.

82 The Qumariq rebellion depicted in the novel is part of a larger 1916 revolt against Russian colonial rule. In the urban and agrarian areas of Turkestan, those inhabited by sarts, revolts took place in the Ferghana valley, around Jizzax and Tashkent, and in the Kyrgyz areas with Russian settlement. In sart areas, which had little Russian settlement, urban Central Asians attacked native colonial officials, while the Kyrgyz, who for years had been subjected to infringements upon their land rights by Russian colonists, attacked Russian peasant settlers themselves. In Soviet historiography of the 1920s and 1930s, the revolt was treated as anti-colonial and progressive, consistent with Cho'lpon's presentation. In the 1930s, Uzbek and Tajik authors also read class exploitation into the causes of the urban revolts as we again see in the present novel. There is little comprehensive scholarship on the revolt in English, but Jörn Happel has written an excellent book on the subject in German: *Nomadische Lebenswelten und Zarische Politik: der Aufstand in Zentralasien 1916* (Stuttgart: Franz Steiner Verlag, 2010). Aminat Chokbaeva, Cloé Drieu, and Alexander Morrison plan to release an edited volume on the revolt this year. See *The 1916 Central Asian Revolt: Rethinking the History of a Collapsing Empire in the Age of War and Revolution* (Manchester: Manchester University Press, 2019).

"With these facts in mind, I demand that this so-called 'simple,' 'harmless,' and 'innocent' sart girl receive the highest punishment. The matter is clear, and the girl admitted to the crime herself. There is no need to discuss this any longer. I have given my opinion to the court and ask that it be addressed."

The lawyer, without waiting for the judge to ask him his opinion, stood up:

"I decline to make a closing statement," he said and sat back down.

The members of the court adjourned to another room.

"Now," thought Zebi, "it's ending. Everything is clear. They'll release me. Will I be able to find the way home?"

After fifteen minutes, they returned and read the sentence. The document stated that the case had a sufficient political character, though the crime was not necessarily a political one. The political nature of the crime would be determined as needed by separate courts. As concerned the murder, the identity of the culprit was obvious and the court was not obligated to call forth any other witnesses because the accused had herself admitted to the crime.

After that, the sentence read as follows: "Because the nature of the crime is grievous and because it was committed in a time of war against a figure of the state, the convicted will be punished under such and such articles. The travelling delegation of the territory's military court has duly considered the fact that the convicted is a member of an inferior, uncultured people, is young and inexperienced, and has freely confessed to the crimes. Therefore, according to such and such articles, she will be sentenced to seven years of exile. This sentence is subject to appeal in the appropriate fora."

The translator relayed the sentence laconically.

"The convicted Zebi, daughter of Razzoq-sufi, according to the decision of the military court, has been sentenced to seven years of exile in Siberia. If you are dissatisfied, the sentence may be appealed."

As soon as the sentence was read, the audience got up to leave. The judge signaled to the two escorts with their unsheathed swords to see Zebi out. Then the members of the court exited. Only the translator, the lawyer, and the imam remained. The imam still didn't know why he had been called in the first place, though he had proven useful.

The translator approached the imam.

"Sir! Wait here a moment. I will return shortly and we will speak."

The imam, heart thumping in his chest, turned pale from fear, and his lips began to quiver. The lawyer and the translator went over to Zebi. Zebi, having donned the veil again, was sobbing deeply.

"What do you want to do? Should I prepare an appeal?" the lawyer asked through the translator.

Zebi was barely able to catch her breath through her heaving sobs and answered haltingly.

"To who?"

"The higher court."

"And what will happen ... there?"

"What usually happens: they'll question you again, examine the case again."

"Who will examine it? Those same people?"

"A different court."

"It's all the same ... they don't understand ... something that is so clear! Would others understand?"

"Should I not appeal?"

"Leave it ... don't bother ... for me. ..."

The lawyer smiled at the translator and slapped him on the back. He started off in the direction of the door to leave.

"Hey, wait, managed Zebi. "In the city ... the city ... my parents are there. ... Can I see them?"

"They'll let you see them after you have been processed."

The lawyer again moved to leave. The translator said goodbye to him and returned to the imam.

"My good sir," began the imam, still startled, "Why did they call me?"

The translator smiled.

"You, sir, were called by the judge in case we needed to have her take an oath according to the Sharia."

"But she didn't take an oath."

"There was no need, sir. The woman confessed herself."

The imam didn't understand and repeated the answer as a question.

"She confessed?!"

The translator smiled again.

"Yes, she confessed. Didn't you hear?"

"She didn't confess. Didn't she deny it?"

"Don't worry yourself over it, sir. It was a complicated matter."

"Yes, of course, of course."

"Now, sir, the judge has a request for you: you heard yourself that this woman, a certain Razzoq-sufi's daughter, poisoned her husband. Her husband served as a mingboshi. During our deliberations, the prosecutor demanded that she be executed, but she was given seven years in Siberia instead. Tomorrow, after the Friday prayers, the court would like you to say a few words about the matter."

"About what, sir?"

"Something like: 'Those who raise their hand against the tsar's servants will receive punishment like this.'"

"Very well, good sir, very well. Of course, I will say something, of course. May I leave now?"

In the imam's final question sounded the undisguised worry of a person who knew he had done wrong. As if he had asked, "They won't lock me up?" The translator probably sensed this and answered coldly.

"Go now."

The imam, like a child dismissed from class, rushed to the door and disappeared. "That's the piety of the pious for you," the translator said to himself and chuckled. He slowly made his way to the door and turned around when he reached it. The large room was empty. All the chairs, before in neat rows, were left in disorder like horses at an oasis guest house. On the green upholstered desk, one of the members of the court had left his spectacle case. The little stove in the middle of the room was still burning.

The translator shook his head and said quietly in Russian: "What a mess, what a mess!"

20

After the Friday prayer, the impatient faithful inside all stood up at once and began to leave. Those on the porch outside joined them. Here and there a few waited with their heads down for the blessings. Once they had left, the imam started his speech. He had never liked speaking to the masses. He sustained only the minimum of interaction required by his position, saying nothing other than greetings during the time he was outside of his home, like a new bride.[83] He cleared his throat a few times and in his thin, raspy voice said enough to fulfill his official obligation to the court. Then he went back inside and sat down. After those in the lodge left, he coughed a bit, got up, and headed towards the door. The inside of the lodge was dark. From the darkness came a voice.

"Sir, I have a request."

The speaker, covered by darkness in order not to be seen, startled the naturally fearful imam.

---

83 After a wedding, an urban Central Asian newlywed is expected to show her humility and obedience by serving her husband's family and following her mother-in-law's commands in silence.

"Allah forbid!" said the imam hurriedly in Arabic and retreated slightly with his hand on his chest.

The speaker came into the light and continued.

"Excuse me, sir. Which one of Akbarali mingboshi's wives murdered him?"

"What kind of person are you? Couldn't you have warned me you were here by coughing or something? You're some kind of animal!"

"I'm sorry, sir, I didn't know."

"'I didn't know!' How long will it take you to learn?!"

"I'm sorry, sir, I am at fault. Akbarali mingboshi had four wives. One of them was my daughter. That's why I'm asking, sir."

The imam stopped his retreat and stepped towards the person, giving him a look that said, "get lost!"

"I forgot her name. ... She was in a black paranji. ... Allah remind me ... something-sufi. ... Yes, Razzoq-sufi ... the daughter of Razzoq-sufi."

He repeated the name a few times and then exited. Razzoq-sufi, who was left standing in the room, had lost all color in his face and was shaking. He grabbed the door to prop himself up.

Finally, he regained his senses and left the mosque. Without bothering to inform his wife, he gave half a ruble to a cart driver and headed to the village. There was no one in mingboshi's home other than Hakimjon. Hakimjon explained what happened and how Zebi had been questioned and then taken to the city. Hakimjon didn't know what the court had decided.

"What should I do now?" asked Razzoq.

His voice quivered with pain and a feeling of powerlessness. A deathly pitiful quiver. Hakimjon stared at Razzoq-sufi. There was not a trace of the proud, conceited Razzoq who had stood in front of him a week ago. He looked like the candles in a mosque, yellowed and sickly. But Hakimjon maintained his composure and answered coldly.

"What can you do? Try petitioning in various places. In our turbulent times, I'm not sure if much will come of a petition. I don't know. A higher court can change the decision of a lower one. It's a difficult time ... a difficult time."

Razzoq-sufi's next words suprised Hakimjon.

"It must be tough for the Russians as well,"[84] said the old man, "they'll have to get a capable official from China because they won't find any here."

---

84 The 1988 serial publication replaces "It must be tough for the Russians as well" with "I don't know."

Hakimjon grabbed the gate out of shock and used it to stabilize himself: "Was this the same man talking as before or someone else?" he thought as he stared at Razzoq-sufi. In place of Razzoq, it seemed there was just a shadow or a ghost. Hakimjon began to pity him, but didn't break from his official tone.

"Someone has been appointed as the new mingboshi. He'll be here in two days."

"So there's no shortage of people for the Russians,"[85] Razzoq-sufi responded despondently. Hakimjon only then understood that Razzoq didn't comprehend what he himself was saying. Razzoq-sufi continued.

"Who is it?"

The question again caught Hakimjon off guard. "Is he serious or is he trying to make a fool of me?" thought the secretary. He answered angrily.

"You don't know him! His name is Zunnun! He was someone who served noyib to'ra for many years."

"He must be an enterprising one then," said Razzoq-sufi.

Hakimjon now felt a kind of open disgust. Razzoq continued to stare at him, wearing a smile that seemed like it was crying. The young man could no longer stand it. He marched inside.

"Fazilat!" he yelled, "set the table for our guest!"

When there was no answer, Hakimjon, stomping his feet and barely keeping himself from cursing, went back out to the street.

When Fazilat finished her bread with raisins, she stepped outside, but neither Hakimjon nor Razzoq-sufi were there.

....

Razzoq-sufi first went to his eshon for support. He left Hakimjon immediately, not staying for the meal that was offered. He took the same cart back to the city and then walked straight to the mosque, but his eshon wasn't there. They told Razzoq that he had left for a wedding. Razzoq-sufi sat down to wait and began thinking.

"What can our eshon do? Does he know the law to file a petition or a complaint? Does he know Russian to talk to officials and the court? But if I went to a lawyer, an official, or someone at the court, I would need money. A lot of money. I thought that Zebi would help me with money when I needed it. But now when I need it, she can't help.

---

85 The 1988 serial publication omits "for the Russians."

"Our eshon won't give a thing. He'll say he'll give me whatever he has, but he'll never part with a kopeck. He has enough to sate the appetite of any lawyer. But what can you do with a man who never learned to give, only to take? The addicted always indulge, they say. Our eshon could never unlearn his greed. If a beggar came to the lodge, the eshon would look at his empty hand and ask, 'what happened to your offering?'

"I have to tell the girl's poor mother what happened! I am stone, I can take it, but her love for that girl is so strong that she can break stones! No, I can't go home tonight. Tonight, I'll stay here. I'll talk with the eshon, ask his advice. He'll know what to do. But I haven't been home in two days. When I left, I said that I was only going to the Friday prayer. What will the old woman think? And if she hears this horrible piece of news from someone else, she might turn to stone herself! No, I should go and support her. … No! Whatever happens, wait for the eshon. But what will he say?"

Finally, the eshon came. His spirits were high and there was a playfulness in his voice. "He must have been drinking fermented horse milk at the wedding," thought Razzoq-sufi. "They say if you drink a lot, it can ruin you. Where did he get fermented horse milk in winter? Fine, he knows best."

The eshon had heard the news already but didn't know that it concerned his murid Razzoq-sufi. As Razzoq retold the events as he knew them, big pearls of tears appeared in his eyes. His master smiled as he listened (smiled!). That cheerful smile, along with his high spirits, did not recede. Even when Razzoq-sufi arrived at the most terrifying part, the eshon's face didn't change. "It's like I'm talking to a stone," thought Razzoq. He immediately repented of his thought. When he finished, Razzoq stared at the eshon's mouth, hoping for some words of wisdom. But the eshon only became more elated.

Humming a cheerful melody, the eshon began swaying his head to and fro. He opened his mouth to sing:

> This ephemeral world is ours for five days, only five days, ho-ov,
> Break your Sufi oath, break it quickly now, ho-ov!
> Let our crystal glasses overflow with wine, wine bearer hey,
> Otherwise, our lodge will be dark as night, as night, ho-ov.

Razzoq-sufi's eyes bulged in disbelief. This was the first time he had bulged his eyes at his master.

"Sir, if you could just give … some advice. …"

"Advice?" asked the eshon, guffawing. "What advice can there be for the father of a murderer, Razzoq? Why didn't they sentence the father along with the child, idiots! Do those infidels know what justice is?!"[86]

It was as if Razzoq-sufi's body had suddenly caught fire. He felt as if his whole being was burning. His hands raised involuntarily over his head and balled into fists. He wanted to bring his fist down on the eshon's head. But who was in front of him? His master! His eshon! The great elder eshon! No, he couldn't raise his fist against him! After a moment, Razzoq-sufi melted like snow and his shame drove him quietly out the door.

He went home and lay down without uttering a word. He didn't answer his wife's questions. "Again, his mood has soured!" she thought. The poor thing still hadn't heard about Zebi.

The next morning over breakfast, he carefully told her everything that had happened. The fist that he was about to bring down on the eshon's head the previous night now came down on his own head. And that fist was so powerful that Razzoq-sufi only had time to think: "Oh, if only yesterday I had …"

By the time he went out on the street, having left his tea untouched, Razzoq-sufi no longer recognized himself. He moved swiftly and unconsciously as if carried by the quick legs of Muslims in a funeral procession. He closed and opened his fists. In a powerful wave, a scream forced its way to his throat, but it got stuck there. Those who passed him on the street went without greetings, questions went without answers from him. Women cursed him as they passed. "Is he crazy? What's wrong?" they said, but Razzoq-sufi only heard "who is crazy? The Russians or us?"[87] The cart-drivers' "Get, get!" sounded like "Die already!" He stared at the snout of a horse that stopped near his shoulder and said, as if to everyone and no one, "die yourselves, just die!" The cartdrivers then just went around him. At the bazaar, a baker offered him a basket of bread. Razzoq-sufi involuntary reached out and took two loaves, but quickly put them back and chuckled at the baker: "I take and I give," he said, "but that man knows only how to take." And he went on his way.

He slowed his gait as he began to think.

"God, even God, gives and takes. First, he gives life and then he takes it. Land too. Land gives its fruits and accepts bodies. It takes what it gives! What are you, master, you? Are you better than God? Better than the land? You take, but you don't give. You take, but you don't give!"

---

86 The 1988 serial publication omits this sentence.

87 The 1988 serial publication omits this sentence.

Razzoq-sufi's mad screaming broke the "meditative silence," that is, the sleep of the eshon. He was startled awake. He opened his eyes, but before he could look around, Razzoq came running in shrieking. Foaming at the mouth, he shook his head and yelled:

"God! God gives life and only then does he take it away. Who are you? Are you better than God?!"

"My God! May your tongue fall off, you wretched thing! Infidel!"

Razzoq-sufi continued to talk that way, bringing his face in to meet the eshon's.

"First the land gives and then it takes. Are you better than the land?!"

"What's wrong with you, Razzoq? Have you gone mad?"

"You're mad yourself, sir, yourself! Your ass is mad, your dog is mad!"

"Oh, who are you now?! Children, come now!" cried the eshon as he stood up and backed away.

"Don't run, sir! Open your hands! I may be a beggar, but my pockets are full. I can feed people like you for years."

"Children!" the eshon continued to yell. He backed his way into a corner of the room.

"Sir, don't scare your poor murid. What have I done to you?"

Razzoq-sufi suddenly began to cry. The murids came in from outside.

"Where were you? I went hoarse calling you! Get rid of this madman! Throw him in the water!"

The murids all seized Razzoq-sufi.

"Don't touch me!" Razzoq snapped. "I escaped the Russian court.[88] Do you think I'll leave your eshon alive?!"

The murids begged God's forgiveness and cursed Razzoq-sufi.

"Let your tongue wither and fall off!"

"Infidel!"

"Apostate!"

"Damn you!"

Outside they made a hole in the ice. After they stripped Razzoq-sufi naked, they lifted him and threw him in. His body burned like the stones in the mountains of Arabia in summer. Razzoq's body almost deceived his mind that he had finally made the pilgrimage. But instead of delight, he howled in pain in the water. The murids looked on laughing.

"Enough!" the eshon cried from inside. "Now lash him a little!"

---

88 The 1988 serial publication removes the word "Russian" from this sentence.

They dragged Razzoq out of the water and whipped him with thin quince branches. The branches contacted his naked, wet skin with a loud cracking noise. After several blows, he let out a long scream and then lost consciousness, falling into the murids' arms.

He lay immobile for twenty-four hours. Towards evening, he started running a fever. When the murids brought him a bowl of hot soup, he threw it in their faces, for which they thanked him with another beating. But the fever prevented him from suffering; the blows felt like a massage. In the morning, he came to, his fever having dissipated. He opened his tired eyes and began to feel the burning in his whipped body. They burned some reeds, put the ash on his wounds, and bandaged them. He finally had some relief, though it was largely from exhaustion. He fell asleep.

After two days, he was soft and compliant like a dove. He began walking around and smiling at the murids. But he didn't respond to them. His thoughts were in a different place, and he only shook his head. He looked at the murids with his smiling eyes. The murids asked their eshon, "Should we kick him out now?"

"Let him walk around. He'll figure it out eventually and just leave," the eshon said, chuckling.

After another three days, on Friday morning the murids went into the mosque to pray only to find their eshon dead. His pointy beard had chunks torn out, and there was bruising on his neck from strangulation. The eshon's cabinet in the corner of the room had been opened, and his books strewn across the floor with pages ripped out. There they found several ripped-up three- and five-ruble notes.

"Son of a bitch! He destroyed the eshon's life and his things!" said one murid. The others could only nod in agreement.

Razzoq-sufi had disappeared without a trace.

....

When Qurvonbibi arrived at the eshon's, without her paranji and in torn clothes, she was already raving mad, but the murids had barely any will left to restrain her. The eshon's eldest wife eventually asked the murids to "Take mercy on her." They grabbed the mad woman and tied her to a willow in the courtyard. For a time, she talked to herself there unceasingly. When someone approached, Qurvonbibi would praise her Zebi, her dutar playing, her singing, her sewing.

She told them about the beauty of her gait, eyes, and eyebrows. She would ask them, "Where, where is my Zebi?" and would burst into tears after.

Towards the end of winter, her relatives came and took her to their village. They gave money to the elderly, to teachers, medicine men, healers, and bards so that they would read prayers for her, free her of the madness somehow. But it was of no use. She continued to tell passersby, as she did at the eshon's, about her daughter; and through tears she sang a song of her own invention:

> Zebi, Zebi, my Zebi
> I am the fool on your path.
> Your father sold you,
> Let me be your grave!
>
> They poisoned your food,
> My master ate your head!
> Zebi, Zebi, my Zebi!
> Where are you now, my baby?!

Glossary

This glossary explains terms, ranks, and titles specific to early twentieth-century sedentary Central Asia and the Ferghana valley in particular. Because of the ad-hoc nature of Russian conquest and rule in colonial Turkestan, the ranks in the colonial administration described here should not be treated as transferable beyond the Ferghana valley, nor should they be thought of as particularly well defined in their duties and functions. For example, the rank of *mingboshi* in the Ferghana valley was equivalent to that of *amin* in the Zarafshon valley around Samarqand. Often the duties of these figures overlapped (an *ellikboshi* might also be an *amin*) and were defined by circumstance.

Similarly, the Islamic titles here should not be thought of as possessing overly strict definitions. While Muslim Central Asia had educational institutions and a system of governance (the Bukharan and Khivan khanates continued to exist as Russian vassals down to the Soviet period), there was no universal accreditation nor a system of Islamic ranks that designated authority or deference to other ranks. The extent of religious authority and the ability to claim a title were often locally decided on a daily basis in contested interactions.

Amin—In the Ferghana valley of Russian colonial Turkestan, an *amin* was a local Muslim administrative post. An *amin* was elected from the same franchise as the *oqsoqols* to supervise their work and conduct policing duties. See also *oqsoqol*.

(As)salom alaykum—Literally "peace be upon you," this is the everyday greeting in most of the Muslim world and in sedentary Central Asia. The addressee of the greeting answers *Vaalaykum assalom*, meaning "and peace be upon you."

Chilim—An opium pipe.

Chorak—A measure of weight equal to about 5–7 pounds.

Dutar—A two-stringed instrument popular in Central Asia.

Ellikboshi—This minor local official was chosen from among approximately fifty households of the sedentary Muslim population in Central Asia to serve their interests as an elector of the *mingboshi* and other officials such as judges (*qozis*). They had some policing duties. See also *mingboshi*, *amin*, and *noyib to'ra*.

Eshon—The third-person plural pronoun in Persian, which a speaker often assigns to an individual as a sign of respect. In Central Asia, this title was given to Sufi masters, who took on students known as *murids*.

Fitna—An Arabic word, the meaning of which is "test" or "trial." The word is often used to indicate a kind of God-sent temptation or test of a believer's faith. The word has also come to indicate a "rebellion," "revolt," or "civil war" that creates a schism in the community of faith. Razzoq-sufi's nickname for his wife thus characterizes her as a test of his faith. The name is also a literary allusion to the sharp-tongued slave girl Fitna of Nizami Ganjavi's epic poem *The Seven Beauties* (1197).

Hajj—The pilgrimage to Mecca, which every Muslim is obliged to make at least once in their lifetime if they have the means. Russian colonialism provided new routes for *hajj* pilgrimages from Central Asia.

Hajji—A title applied to someone who has completed the *hajj*.

Halal—An adjective, often substantivized, referring to what is permissible and lawful according to Islamic law.

Haram—An adjective, often substantivized, describing things and deeds forbidden or proscribed by Islamic law.

Hafiz—a singer of verses from the Qur'an.

Ichkari and *Tashqari*—Literally "inside" and "outside." In pre-Soviet sedentary Central Asia, houses were divided into male and female spaces. Only women, children, the master of the house, and certain male relatives were allowed in the *ichkari*. There, women could safely unveil in front of others who were *mahram* to them. If male guests came, they remained in the *tashqari*. Such a division of space existed in most households, but it was most actively observed in the homes of the wealthy who had *nomahram* male servants and guards. For wealthy men, the *ichkari* was similar to harems in other contexts of the Muslim world. The mother of the master of the house or his eldest wife, if the mother had died, controlled the workings of the *ichkari*, delegating household chores and regulating when and with whom the master would sleep.

Imam—The title of a prayer leader in Sunni mosques. The *imam* reads Friday prayers to the worshippers assembled.

Jadid—Jadids were Muslim reformers in turn-of-the-century Central Asian society. They were so named because of their support of *usul-i jadid*, a pedagogic method for the phonetic teaching of the Arabic alphabet; but they had interests in a wide range of causes, including the advancement and development of the nation, women's liberation, secularism, and democratic reform.

Madrasa—A traditional Muslim secondary school, which trains students as Islamic scholars through study of the Qur'an, hadiths (sayings of the Prophet), and other Islamic texts.

Mahram—Mahram normally refers to those family members, who, according to Islamic custom, are considered close relatives with whom sexual intercourse/ marriage would be *haram*. Males who are *mahram* to a woman can escort her in public and see her unveiled. In this novel, *mahram* also refers to homosocial relationships between women. Women are all *mahram* to one another in that, in private, they may look upon one another without the veil. They may also participate in customs and rituals of friendship that are only possible between women. Cho'lpon often uses the word to denote homosocial confidantes.

Maktab—A traditional Muslim primary school in which all the boys of a community, regardless of age, learned the Arabic alphabet and several principal texts by rote memorization.

Mingboshi—According to the legal system established in 1886 by the Russian state for the Muslim population of the Ferghana valley, a *mingboshi* (literally "head of one thousand households") was a *volost'* head drawn from the local population. A *mingboshi* was formally elected by the district's *ellikboshis* (heads of fifty households) with the approval of a Russian colonial official, locally called a *noyib to'ra*, the executive authority of an *uezd*. While *mingboshis* were nominally elected, they all had to preserve their relationships with Russian colonial power and the *noyib to'ra* in particular, for Russian administrators could remove them at any time for any reason. Their candidacy for these positions was thus often secured via bribes and favors to Russian officials and to the local factions that elected them. Their duties included tax collection, census management, and execution of court decisions.

Mirob—An official charged with managing the distribution of water via the canal system in a given locale.

Mufti—A clerk or scribe who typically worked for an Islamic judge (*qozi*). *Mufti* was also the title given to the head of the Orenburg Spiritual Assembly, the state-recognized head of all Islamic communities, excluding Turkestan because of its later incorporation and status as a military colony within the Russian Empire.

Mullah—A title and sign of respect extended to an Islamic educated man (occasionally to a woman at this time).

Murid—Student of a Sufi master, who was known as an *eshon*.

Nomahram—The opposite of *mahram*. The word is used by women to speak of men with whom intimate interaction outside of marriage would be *haram*.

Noyib to'ra—A military authority drawn from the European population of the Russian Empire, called an *uezdnyi upravitel'* in Russian. This official served as the executive authority over an *uezd* in Turkestan. He supervised the local Muslim authorities in his jurisdiction and often appointed them to their posts, despite those posts being nominally electoral. See also *mingboshi, ellikboshi*.

Oqsoqol—literally meaning "white beard," this post was originally a designation for a village elder who carried out police and other duties for the village. The Russian Empire adopted the position and made it an electoral one. See also *amin*.

Paranji—The covering worn by urban Central Asian Muslim women outside the home. Its use increased in urban settings with the beginning of Russian colonization.

Sart—an ethnonym for the sedentary Muslims of Central Asia, who would later, under Soviet rule, call themselves Uzbek or Tajik. *Sart* was likewise a designation for the language used by the local population, which was a mix of Persian and Turkic (the contemporary two distinct languages were not thought to be distinct by many speakers at this time). The ethnonyms *sart*, Uzbek, and Tajik existed alongside one another throughout the period of Russian rule and perhaps earlier. Russian Imperial ethnographers spent considerable effort trying to differentiate the three from one another, but the meanings of the terms were often fluid and thus elusive. In the 1910s, *jadids* rejected the name *sart* for the nation they claimed to represent because they believed it was an outsider ethnonym that Russians and others used to demean their nation. Like Russian ethnographers who sought an essential, immutable meaning of the term from classical sources, *jadids* relied on their readings of Islamic texts to identify *sart* as a derogatory name. However, it is unclear whether local Muslims called themselves *sarts* prior to Russian rule or did so entirely as a result of the use of the term by imperial officials. In contemporary Uzbekistan, the term *sart* is viewed as *jadids* saw it—that is, as an ethnic slur.

Sochpopuk—Decorations, including silk threads, beads, cotton-paper, which sedentary Central Asian Muslim women plait into their braids.

Sufi—Sufi has two meanings in this text which are not mutually exclusive. As a sobriquet or title, as in Razzoq-sufi or the Sufi that appears in Qumariq, it indicates that the person performs the call to prayer. This is a nomenclature unique to Central Asia. Elsewhere, the person that performs the call to prayer is called a muezzin. Sufi also indicates an adherent of a Sufi order, either a *murid* student or an *eshon* teacher. For the second definition, see Sufism, *murid*, and *eshon*.

Sufism—Sufism (*tasavvuf*), a form of mysticism peculiar to Islam, was widely practiced across the Islamic world and had many orders (*tariqat*). Most Central Asians adhered to the Naqshbandiya order, introduced by the Sunni Muslim Muhammad Bahauddin Naqshbandi al-Bukhari in the fourteenth century. See also *murid* and *eshon*.

Suyunchi—A gift given in honor of good news, such as a wedding or a birth.

Tanob—A measure of area that varied from 0.15 hectares to 0.5 hectares depending on the location in Turkestan.

Uezd—A territorial administrative unit of 250,000 inhabitants or more. An *uezd* was composed of several *volost's*.

'Ulama—The Arabic plural of scholar (*'alim*). These men (occasionally women) were the collective of religious educated intelligentsia of a Muslim community. In early twentieth-century Central Asia, they were the conservative rhetorical opponents of the *jadids*, though *jadids* often had the same educational background and could themselves be considered members of the *'ulama*.

Uloq—One of the Turkic names for the game more commonly known in English as *buzkashi* in which mounted players attempt to place a goat or calf carcass in a goal.

Volost'—A territorial administrative unit of around 2,000 households.

Waqf—An endowment for mosques or shrines created by earmarking taxes on certain lands and holdings.

Zikr—A chant performed by Sufi mystics to abandon their earthly senses and commune with God.